# SMOOTH CRIMINALS

## STEALING TIME

LUSTGARTEN • SMITH • RIDDEL • PEER

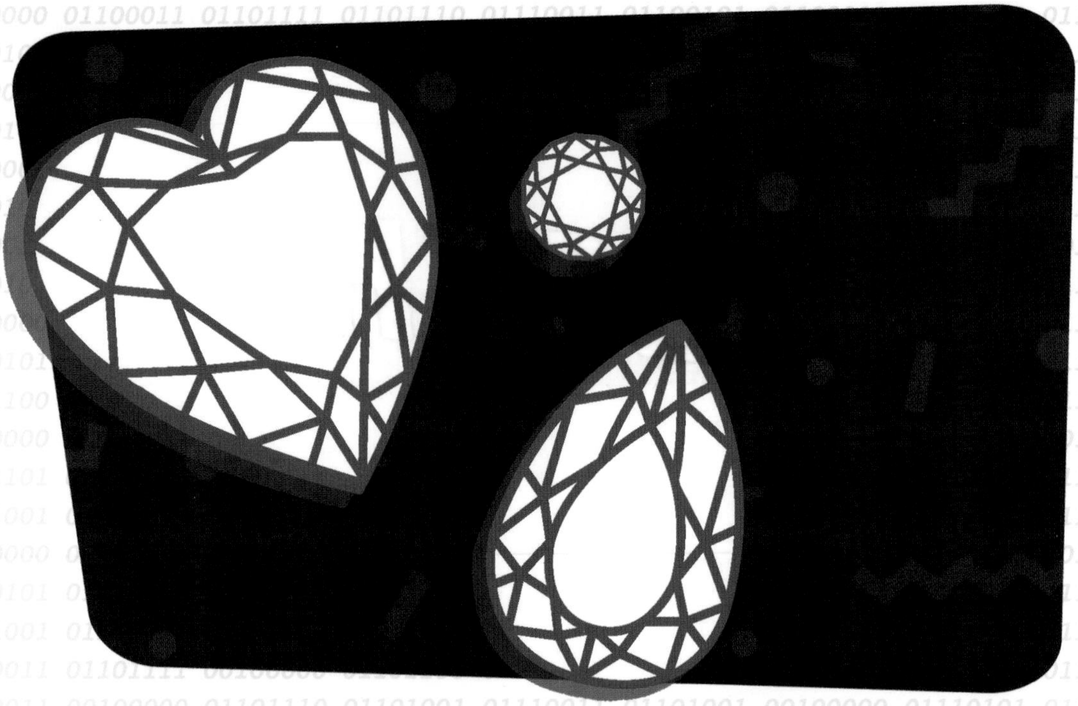

MIA & BRENDA CHARACTER DESIGNS BY
**CHYNNA CLUGSTON FLORES**

SERIES DESIGNER
**MARIE KRUPINA**

COLLECTION DESIGNER
**KARA LEOPARD**

ASSOCIATE EDITOR
**SOPHIE PHILIPS-ROBERTS**

EDITOR
**SHANNON WATTERS**






BOOM! Studios, 5670 Wilshire Boulevard, Suite 400, Los Angeles, CA 90036-5679. Printed in China. First Printing.

ISBN: 978-1-68415-385-5, eISBN: 978-1-64144-368-5

# SMOOTH CRIMINALS™

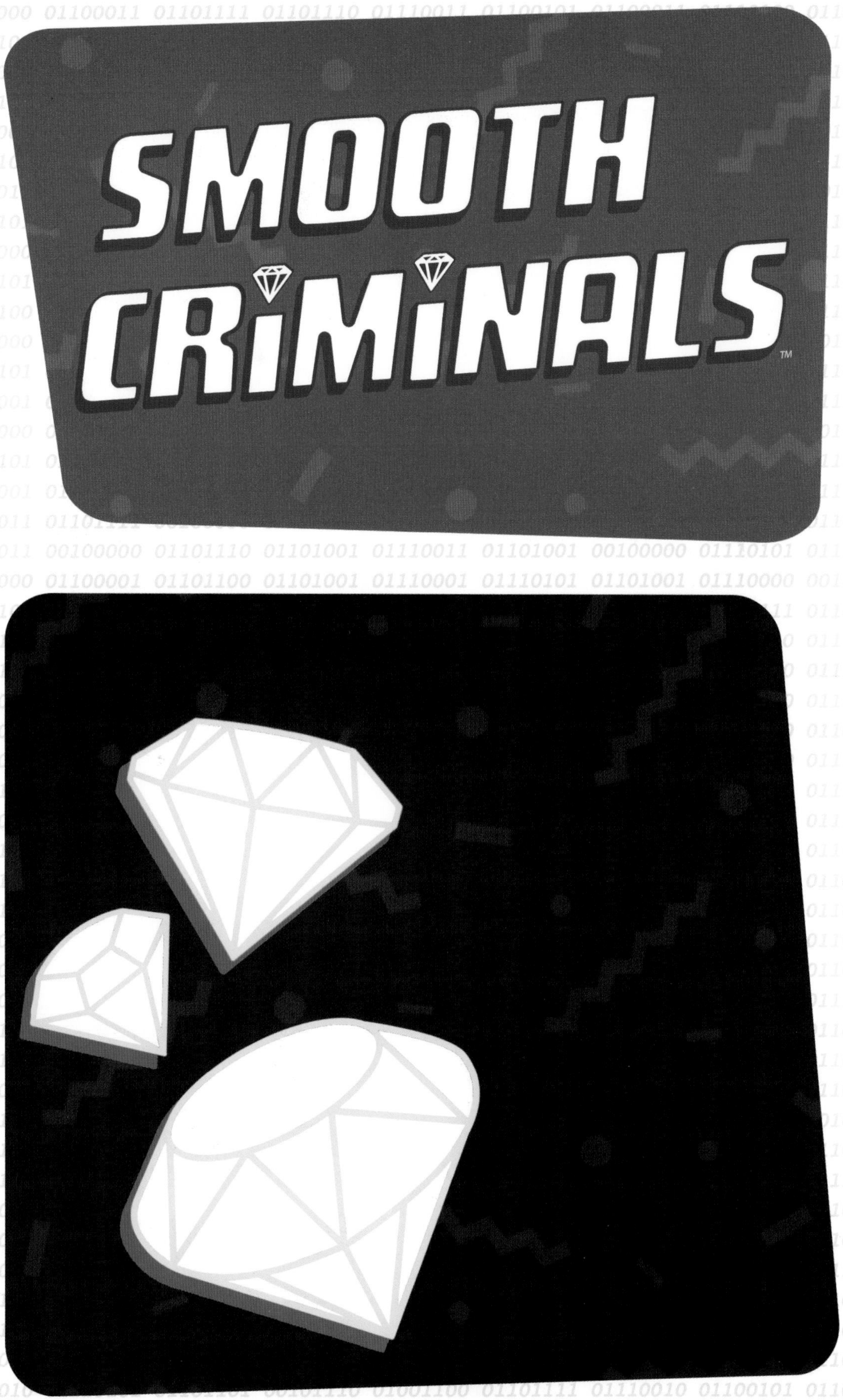

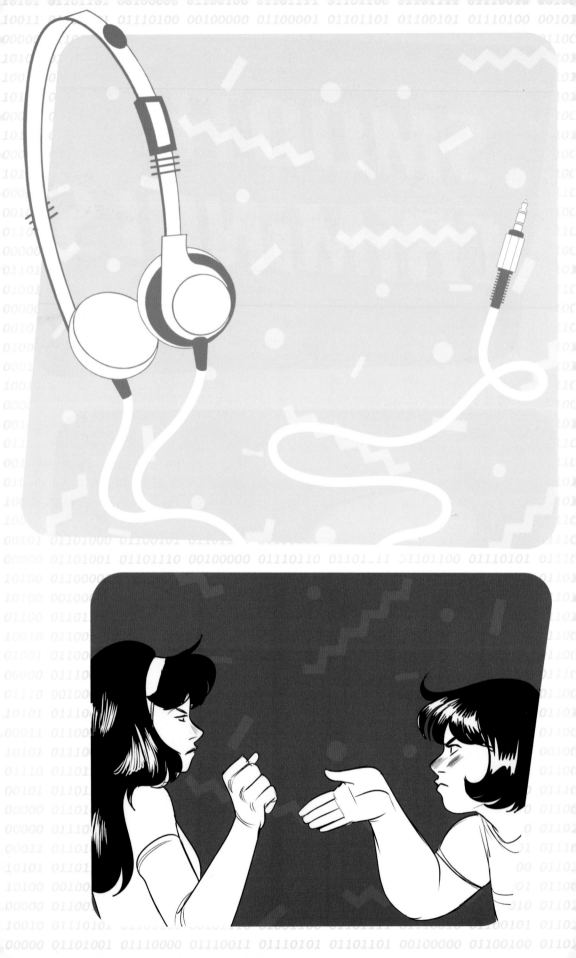

CREATED & WRITTEN BY

**KURT LUSTGARTEN & KIRSTEN 'KIWI' SMITH**

ILLUSTRATED BY

**LEISHA RIDDEL**

COLORED BY

**BRITTANY PEER**

**WITH JOANA LAFUENTE ON CHAPTER 2**

LETTERED BY

**ED DUKESHIRE**

I code
DO NOT TOUCH!
WHATEVER

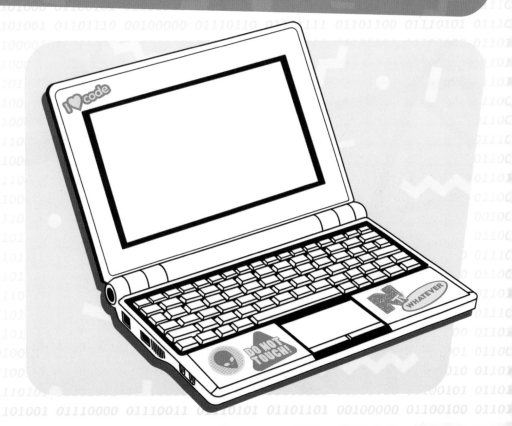

# CHAPTER ONE

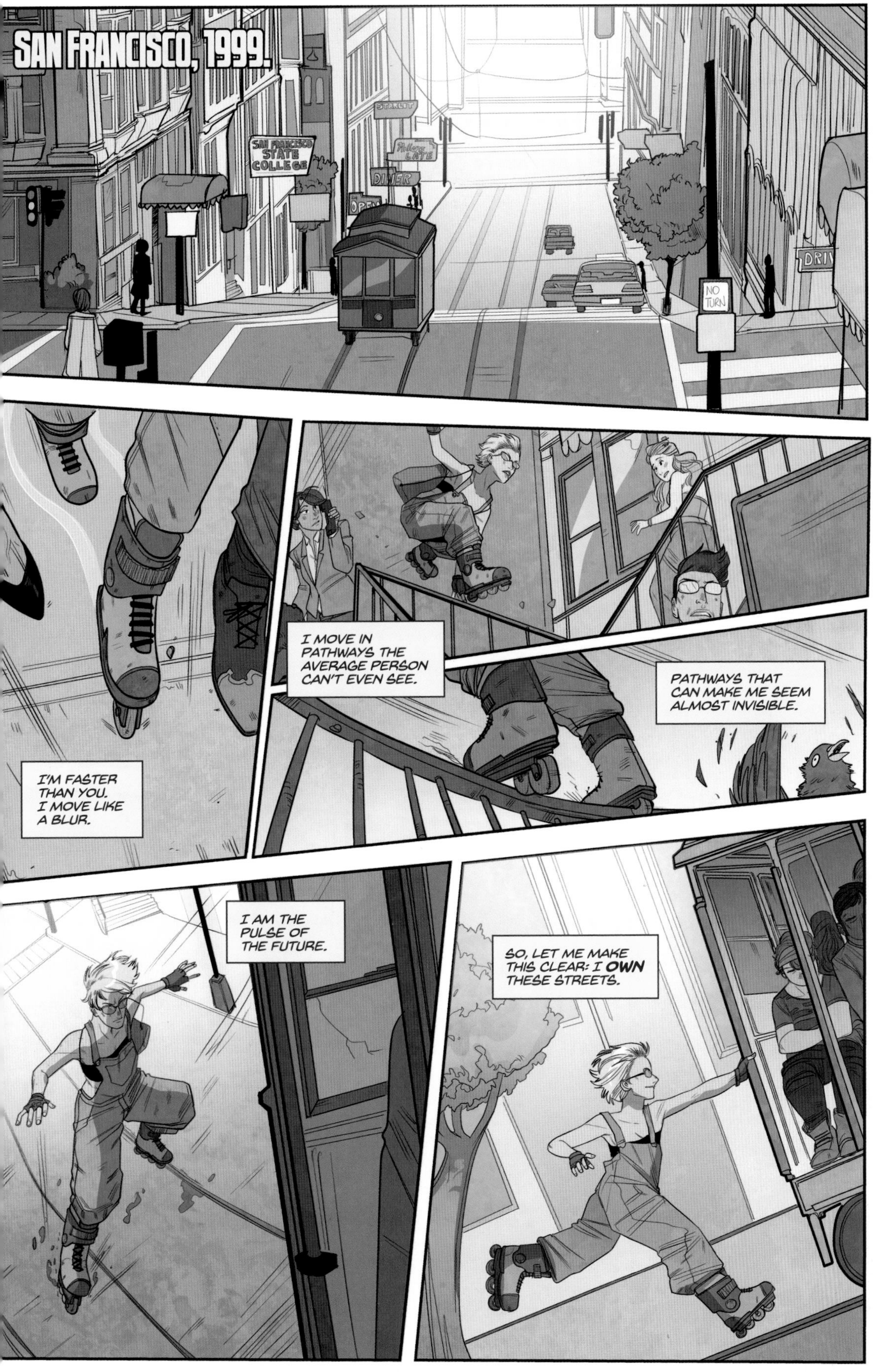
SAN FRANCISCO, 1999.
SAN FRANCISCO STATE COLLEGE
DINER
NO TURN
I'M FASTER THAN YOU. I MOVE LIKE A BLUR.
I MOVE IN PATHWAYS THE AVERAGE PERSON CAN'T EVEN SEE.
PATHWAYS THAT CAN MAKE ME SEEM ALMOST INVISIBLE.
I AM THE PULSE OF THE FUTURE.
SO, LET ME MAKE THIS CLEAR: I **OWN** THESE STREETS.

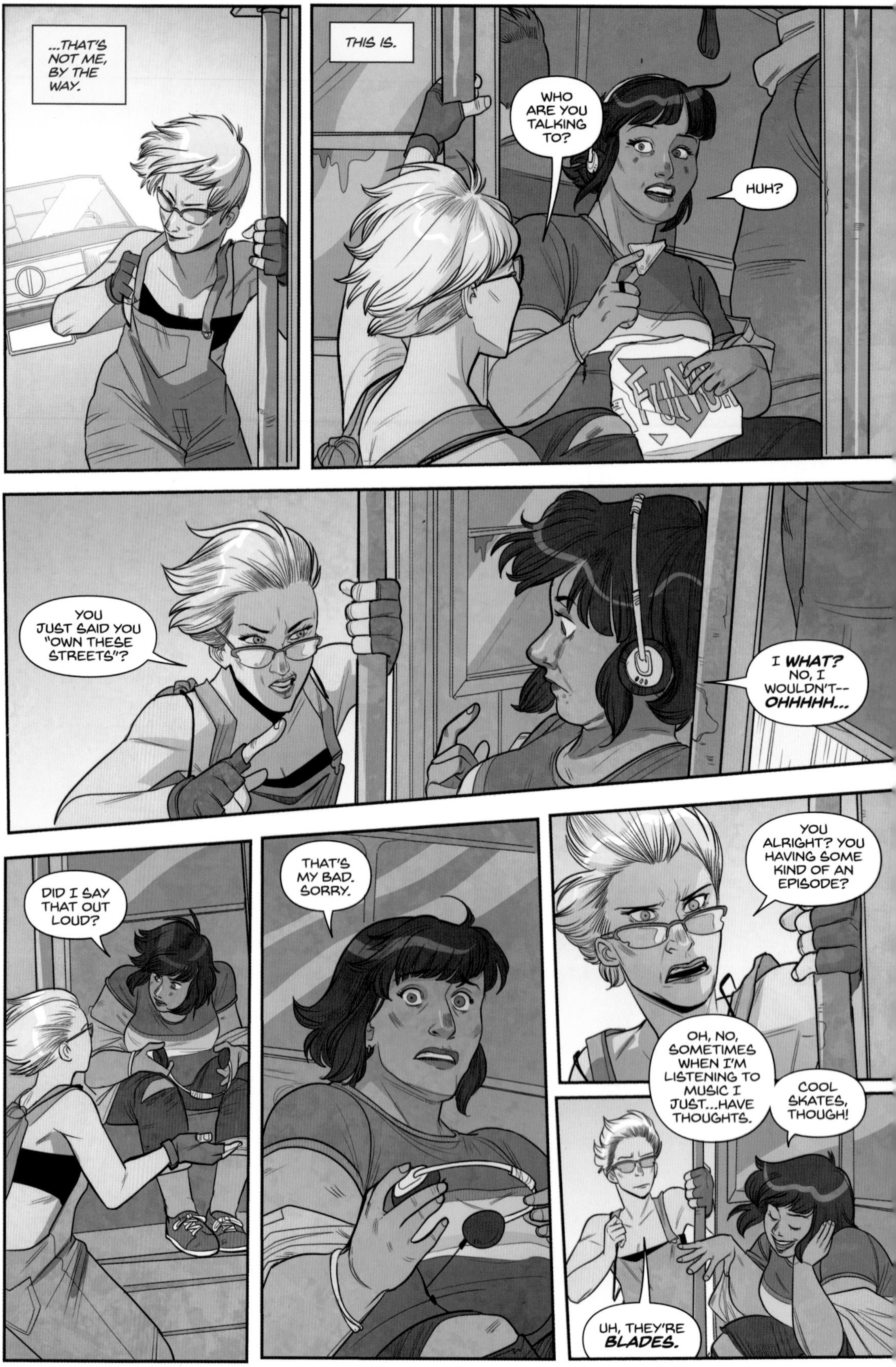
...THAT'S NOT ME, BY THE WAY.
THIS IS.
WHO ARE YOU TALKING TO?
HUH?
YOU JUST SAID YOU "OWN THESE STREETS"?
I *WHAT?* NO, I WOULDN'T-- *OHHHHH...*
DID I SAY THAT OUT LOUD?
THAT'S MY BAD. SORRY.
YOU ALRIGHT? YOU HAVING SOME KIND OF AN EPISODE?
OH, NO, SOMETIMES WHEN I'M LISTENING TO MUSIC I JUST...HAVE THOUGHTS.
COOL SKATES, THOUGH!
UH, THEY'RE *BLADES.*

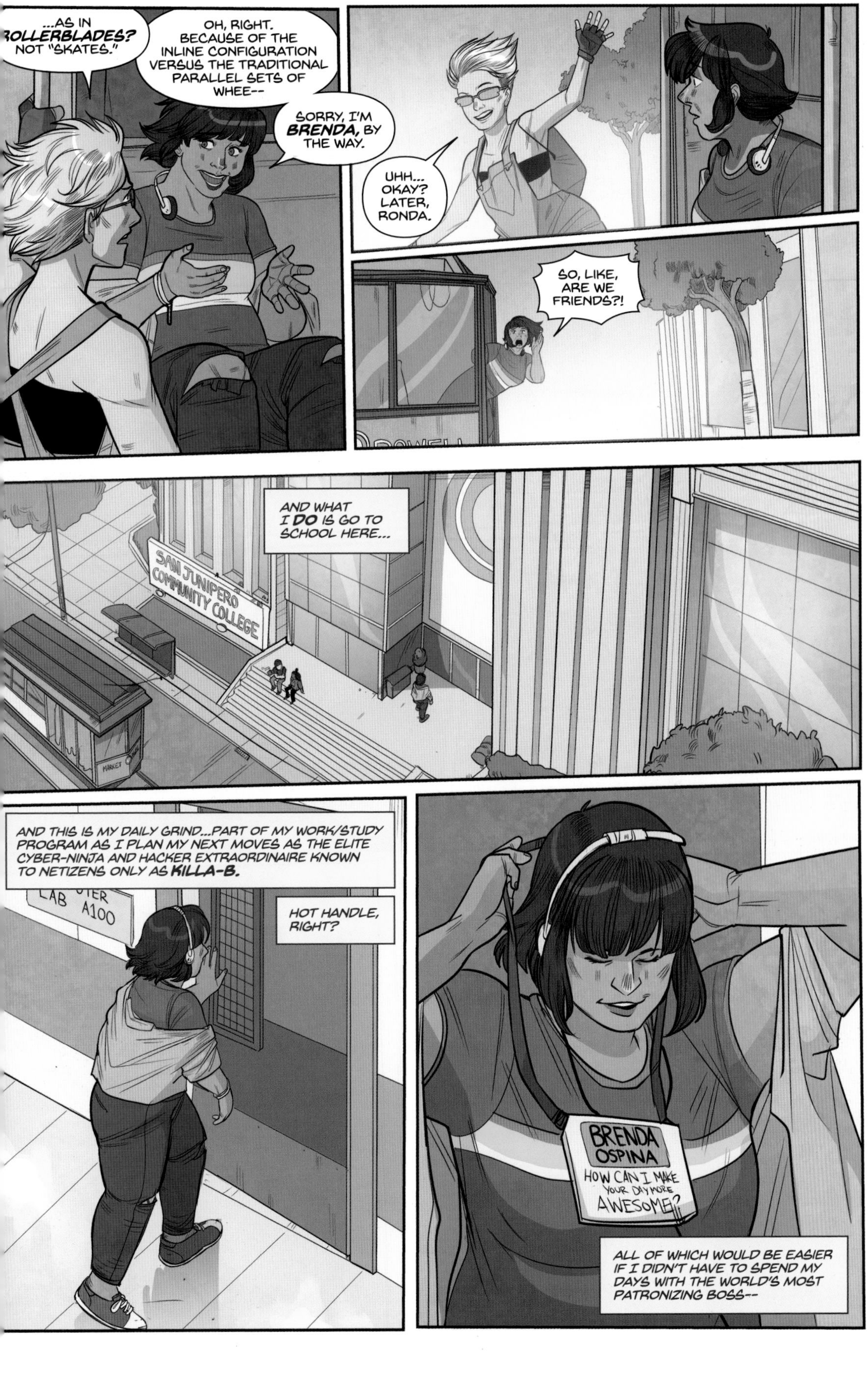
...AS IN ROLLERBLADES? NOT "SKATES."
OH, RIGHT. BECAUSE OF THE INLINE CONFIGURATION VERSUS THE TRADITIONAL PARALLEL SETS OF WHEE--
SORRY, I'M BRENDA, BY THE WAY.
UHH... OKAY? LATER, RONDA.
SO, LIKE, ARE WE FRIENDS?!
AND WHAT I DO IS GO TO SCHOOL HERE...
SAN JUNIPERO COMMUNITY COLLEGE
AND THIS IS MY DAILY GRIND...PART OF MY WORK/STUDY PROGRAM AS I PLAN MY NEXT MOVES AS THE ELITE CYBER-NINJA AND HACKER EXTRAORDINAIRE KNOWN TO NETIZENS ONLY AS KILLA-B.
LAB A100
HOT HANDLE, RIGHT?
BRENDA OSPINA
HOW CAN I MAKE YOUR DAY MORE AWESOME?
ALL OF WHICH WOULD BE EASIER IF I DIDN'T HAVE TO SPEND MY DAYS WITH THE WORLD'S MOST PATRONIZING BOSS--

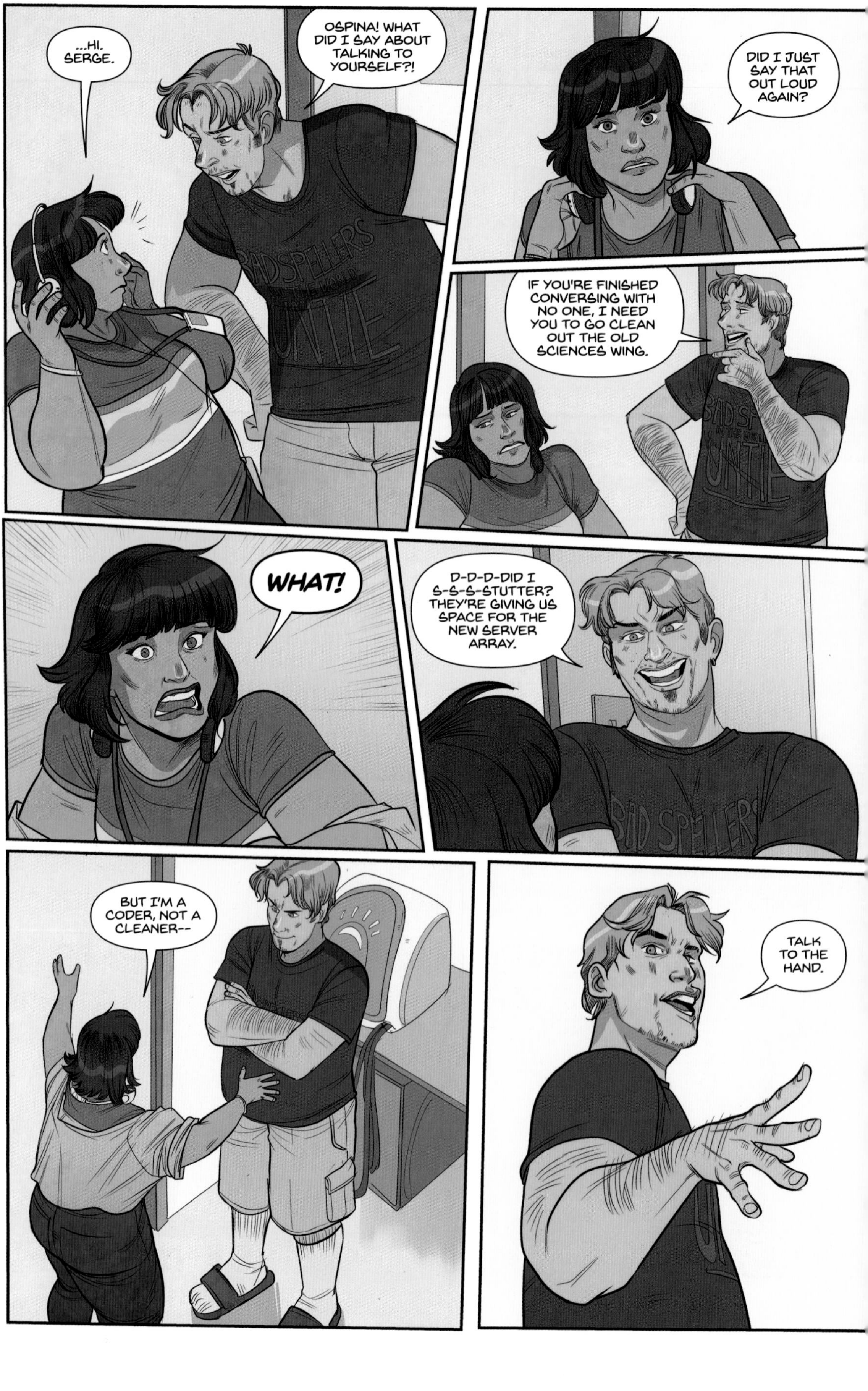

...HI, SERGE.
OSPINA! WHAT DID I SAY ABOUT TALKING TO YOURSELF?!
DID I JUST SAY THAT OUT LOUD AGAIN?
IF YOU'RE FINISHED CONVERSING WITH NO ONE, I NEED YOU TO GO CLEAN OUT THE OLD SCIENCES WING.
WHAT!
D-D-D-DID I S-S-S-STUTTER? THEY'RE GIVING US SPACE FOR THE NEW SERVER ARRAY.
BUT I'M A CODER, NOT A CLEANER--
TALK TO THE HAND.

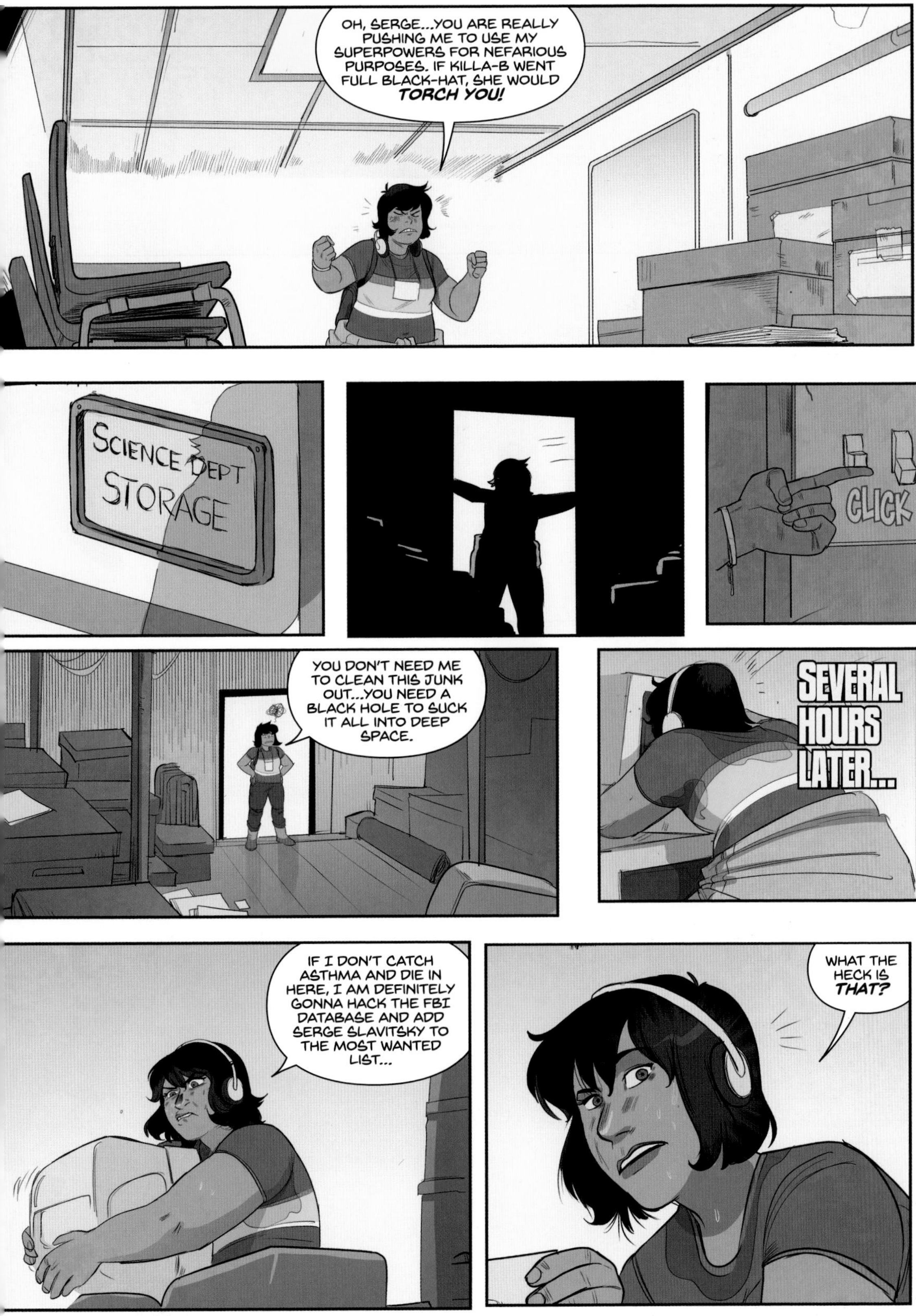
OH, SERGE...YOU ARE REALLY PUSHING ME TO USE MY SUPERPOWERS FOR NEFARIOUS PURPOSES. IF KILLA-B WENT FULL BLACK-HAT, SHE WOULD *TORCH YOU!*
SCIENCE DEPT STORAGE
CLICK
YOU DON'T NEED ME TO CLEAN THIS JUNK OUT...YOU NEED A BLACK HOLE TO SUCK IT ALL INTO DEEP SPACE.
SEVERAL HOURS LATER...
IF I DON'T CATCH ASTHMA AND DIE IN HERE, I AM DEFINITELY GONNA HACK THE FBI DATABASE AND ADD SERGE SLAVITSKY TO THE MOST WANTED LIST...
WHAT THE HECK IS *THAT?*

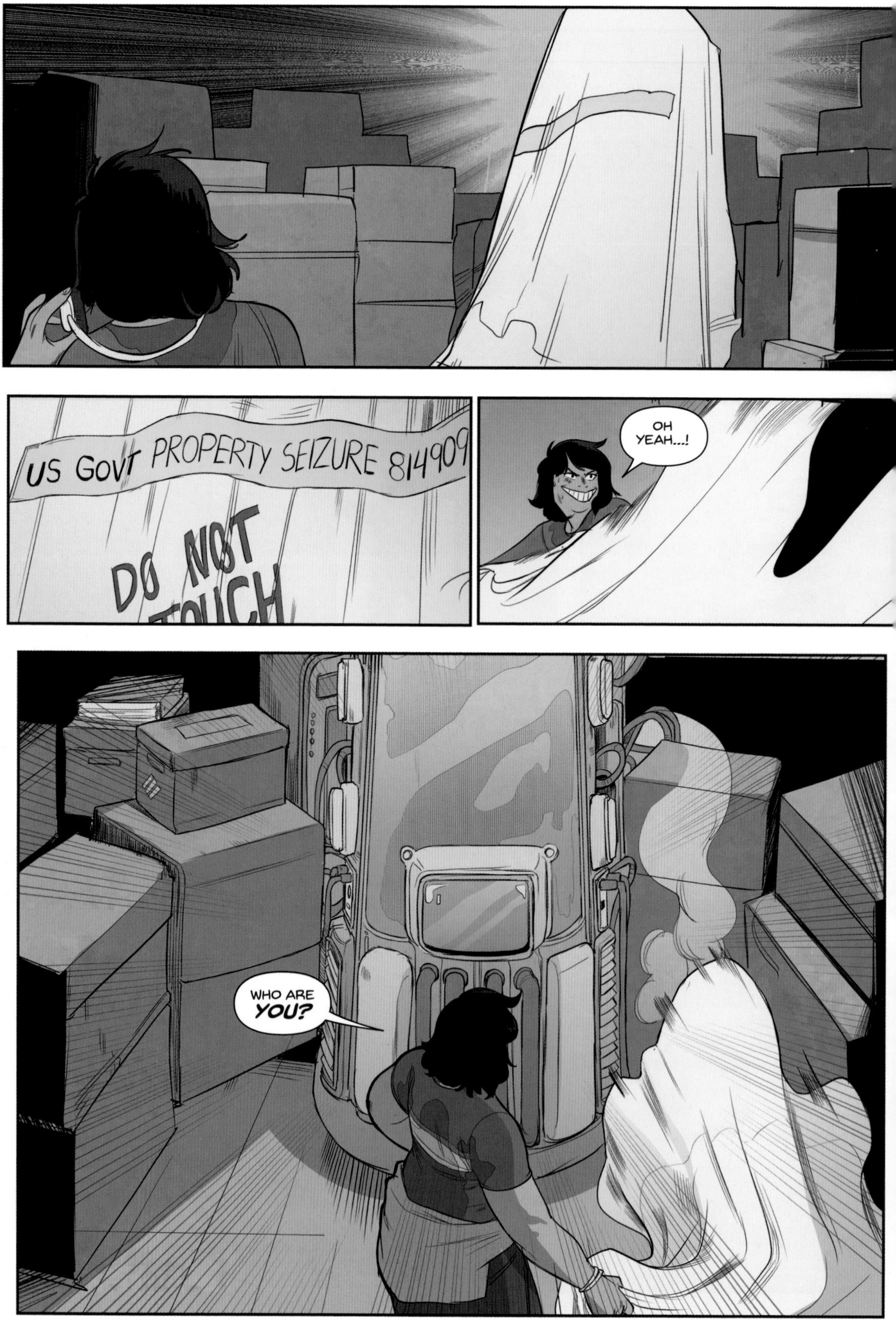
US GOVT PROPERTY SEIZURE 814909
DO NOT TOUCH
OH YEAH...!
WHO ARE *YOU?*

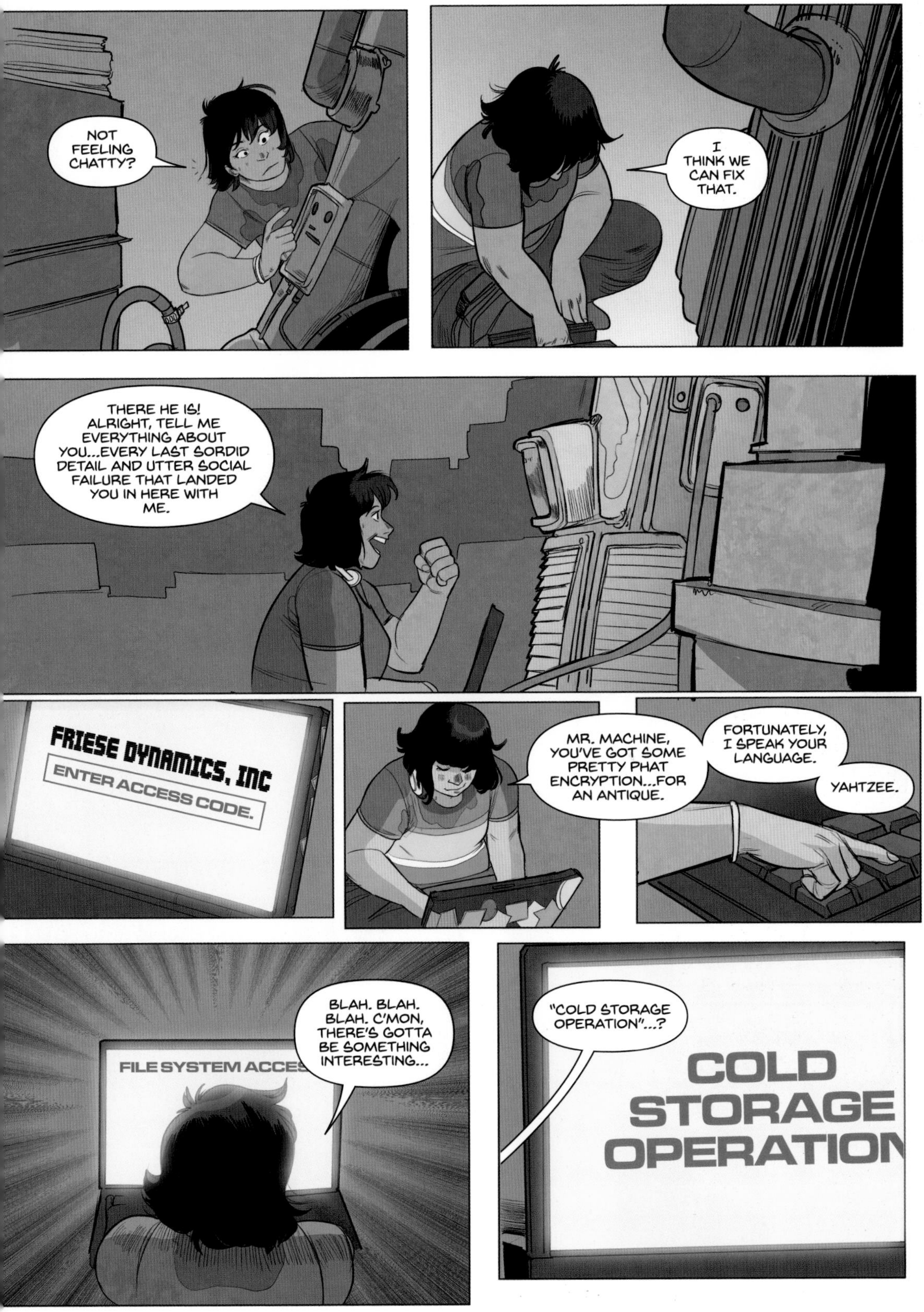
NOT FEELING CHATTY?
I THINK WE CAN FIX THAT.
THERE HE IS! ALRIGHT, TELL ME EVERYTHING ABOUT YOU...EVERY LAST SORDID DETAIL AND UTTER SOCIAL FAILURE THAT LANDED YOU IN HERE WITH ME.
FRIESE DYNAMICS, INC
ENTER ACCESS CODE.
MR. MACHINE, YOU'VE GOT SOME PRETTY PHAT ENCRYPTION...FOR AN ANTIQUE.
FORTUNATELY, I SPEAK YOUR LANGUAGE.
YAHTZEE.
FILE SYSTEM ACCES
BLAH. BLAH. BLAH. C'MON, THERE'S GOTTA BE SOMETHING INTERESTING...
"COLD STORAGE OPERATION"...?
COLD STORAGE OPERATION

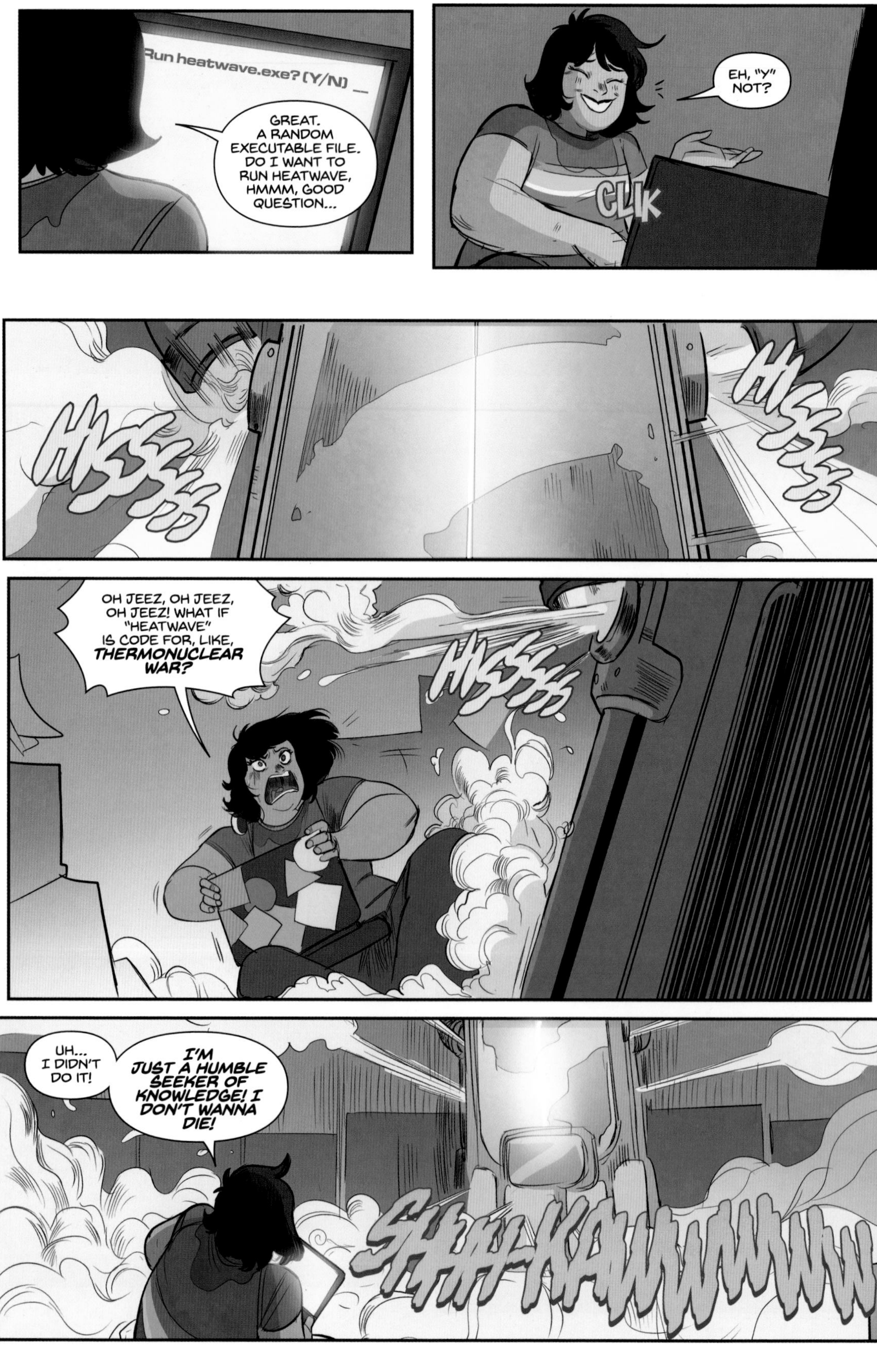
Run heatwave.exe? (Y/N) _
GREAT. A RANDOM EXECUTABLE FILE. DO I WANT TO RUN HEATWAVE, HMMM, GOOD QUESTION...
EH, "Y" NOT?
CLIK
HISSSSS
HISSSSS
OH JEEZ, OH JEEZ, OH JEEZ! WHAT IF "HEATWAVE" IS CODE FOR, LIKE, THERMONUCLEAR WAR?
HISSSSS
UH... I DIDN'T DO IT!
I'M JUST A HUMBLE SEEKER OF KNOWLEDGE! I DON'T WANNA DIE!
SHH-KAWWWWW

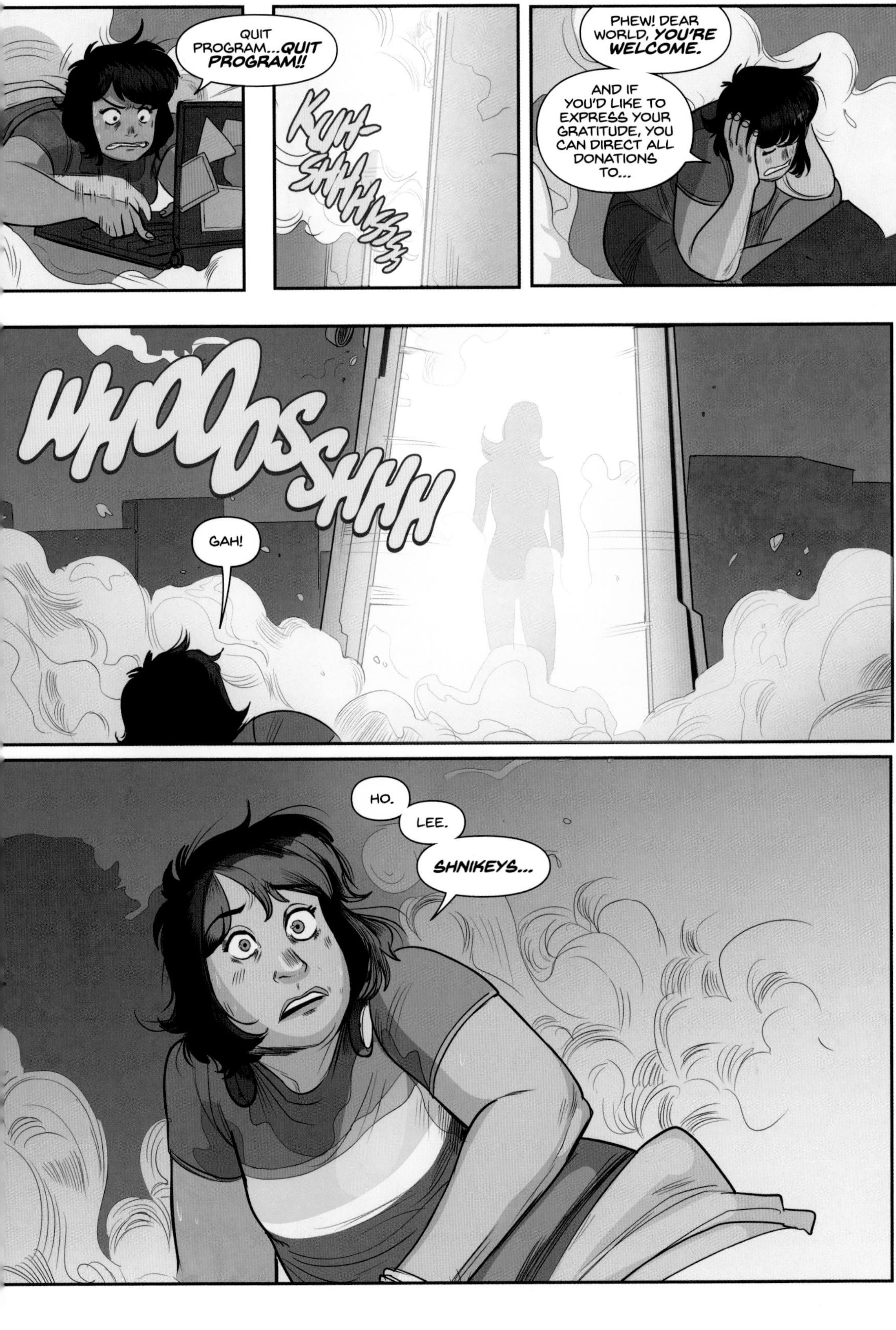
QUIT PROGRAM...QUIT PROGRAM!!
KUH-SHHHSSSS
PHEW! DEAR WORLD, YOU'RE WELCOME.
AND IF YOU'D LIKE TO EXPRESS YOUR GRATITUDE, YOU CAN DIRECT ALL DONATIONS TO...
WHOOOSHHH
GAH!
HO.
LEE.
SHNIKEYS...

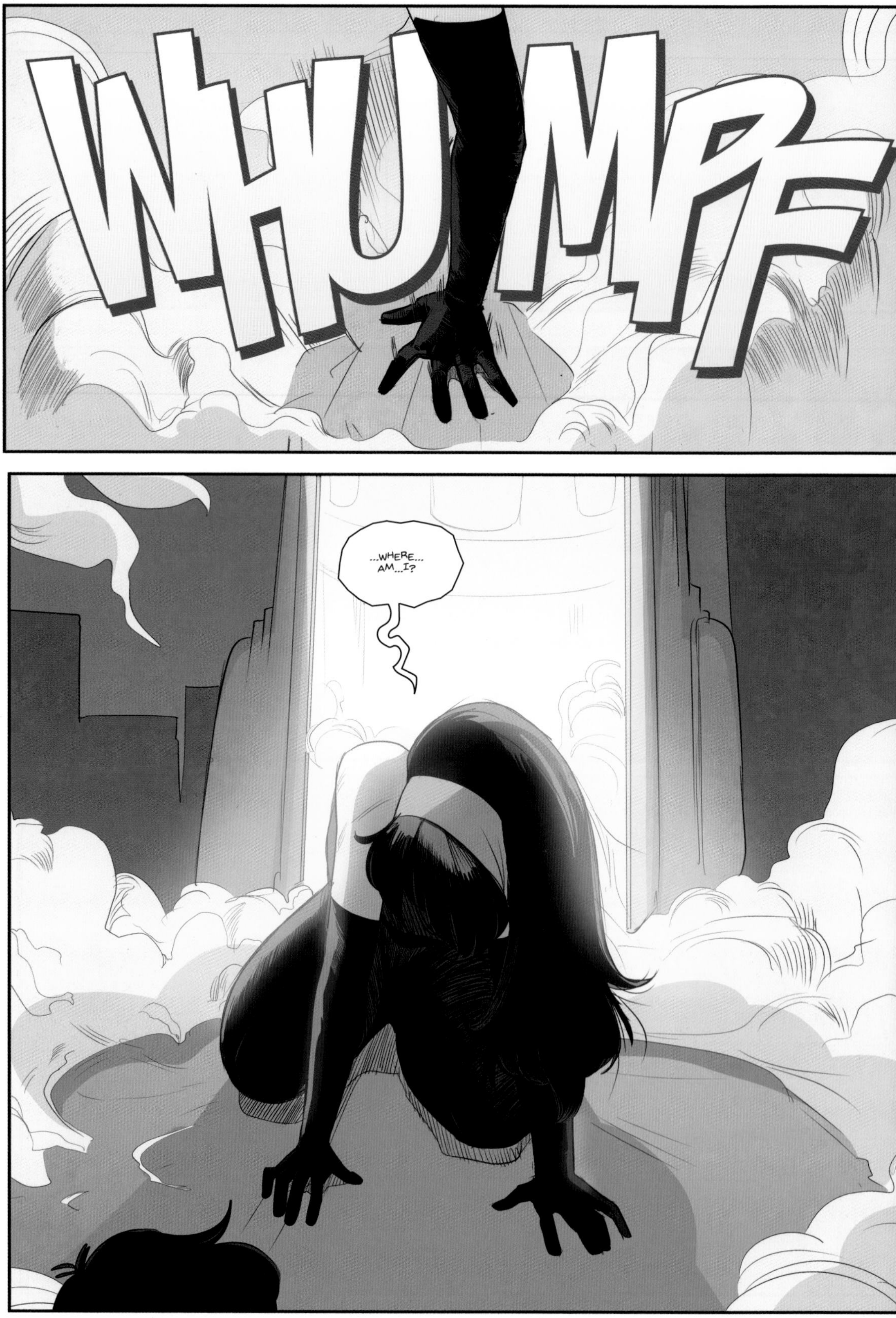
WHUMPF
...WHERE... AM... I?

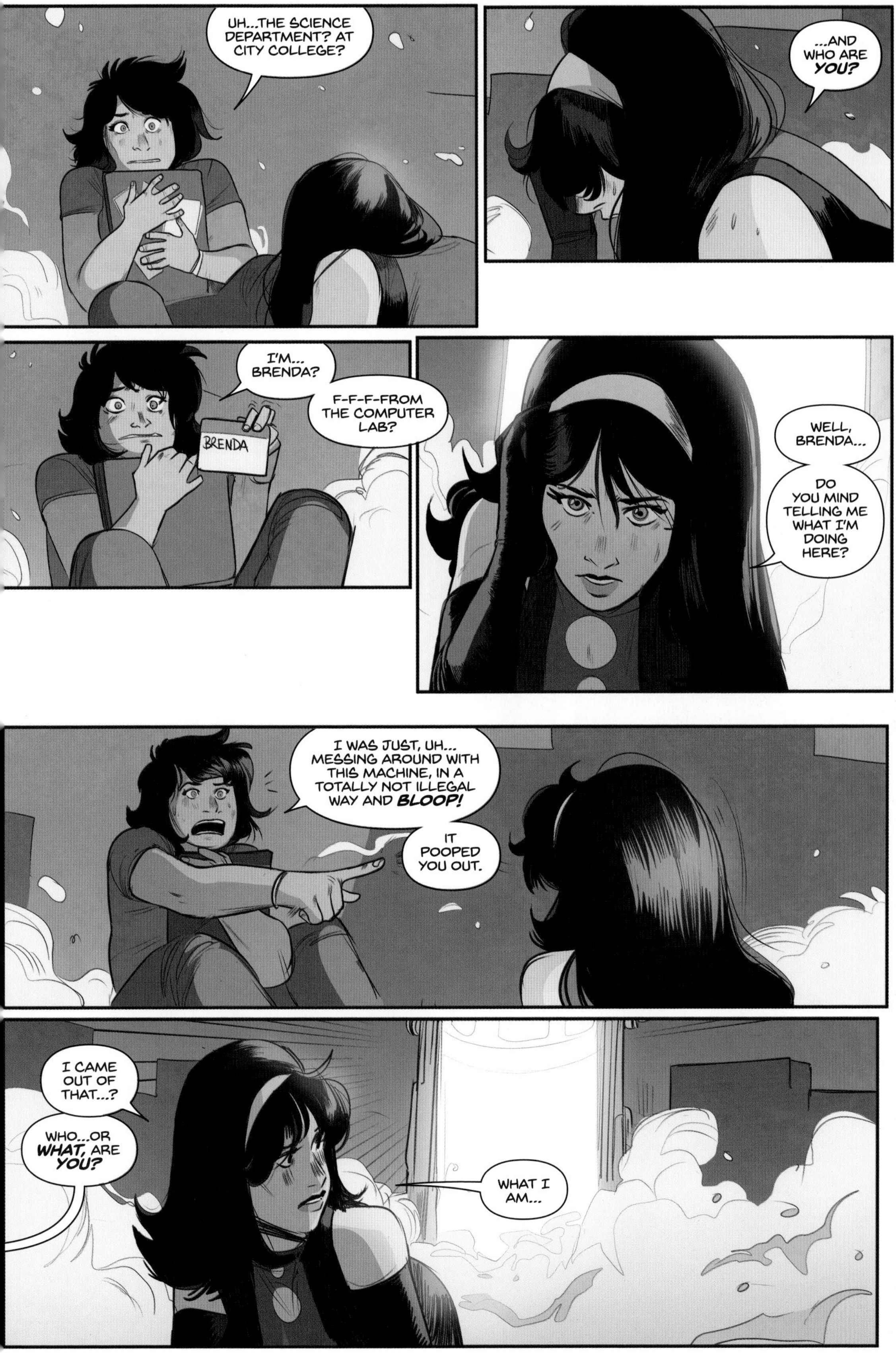
UH...THE SCIENCE DEPARTMENT? AT CITY COLLEGE?
...AND WHO ARE YOU?
I'M... BRENDA?
BRENDA
F-F-F-FROM THE COMPUTER LAB?
WELL, BRENDA...
DO YOU MIND TELLING ME WHAT I'M DOING HERE?
I WAS JUST, UH... MESSING AROUND WITH THIS MACHINE, IN A TOTALLY NOT ILLEGAL WAY AND BLOOP!
IT POOPED YOU OUT.
I CAME OUT OF THAT...?
WHO...OR WHAT, ARE YOU?
WHAT I AM...

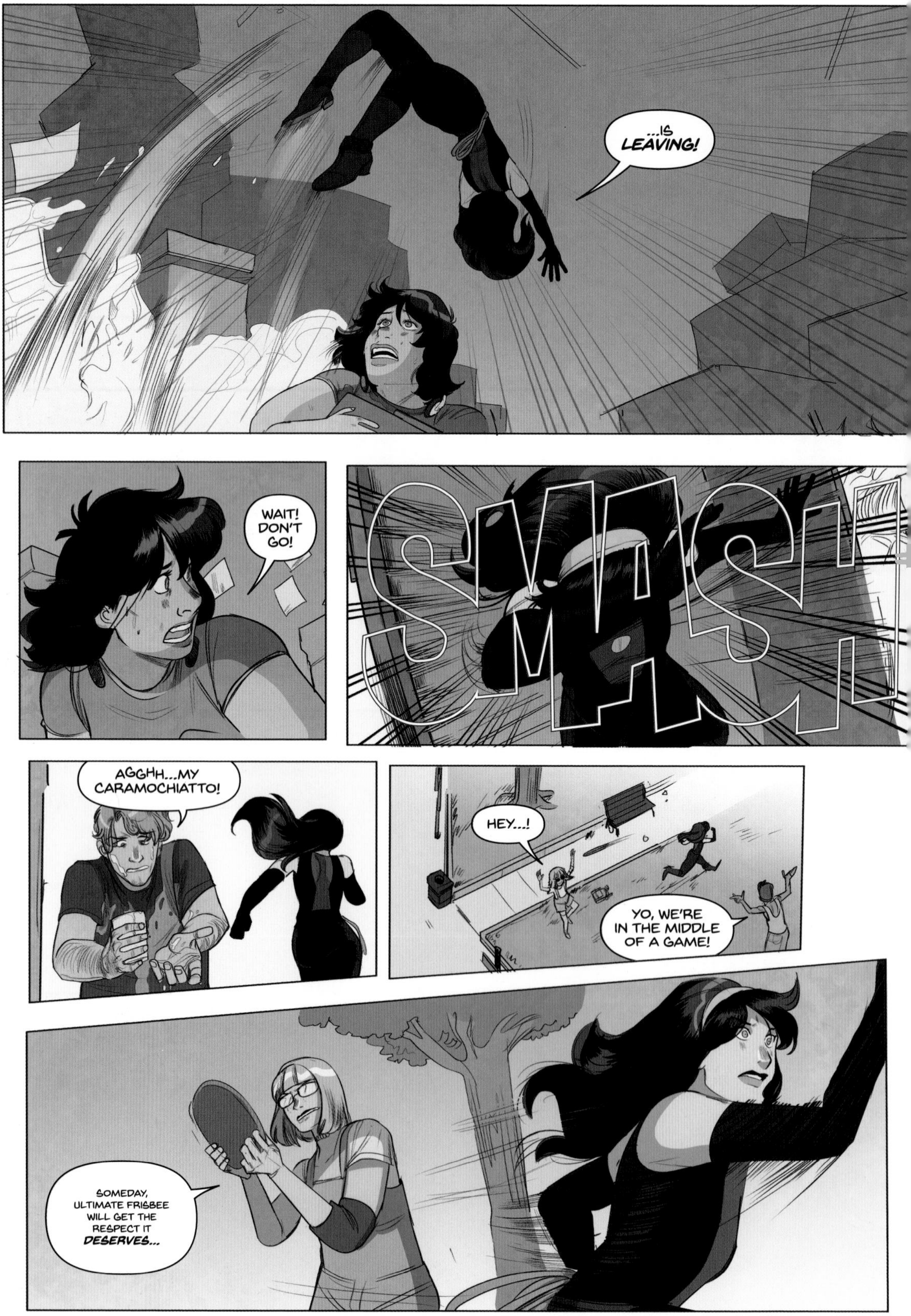
...IS LEAVING!
WAIT! DON'T GO!
SMASH
AGGHH...MY CARAMOCHIATTO!
HEY...!
YO, WE'RE IN THE MIDDLE OF A GAME!
SOMEDAY, ULTIMATE FRISBEE WILL GET THE RESPECT IT DESERVES...

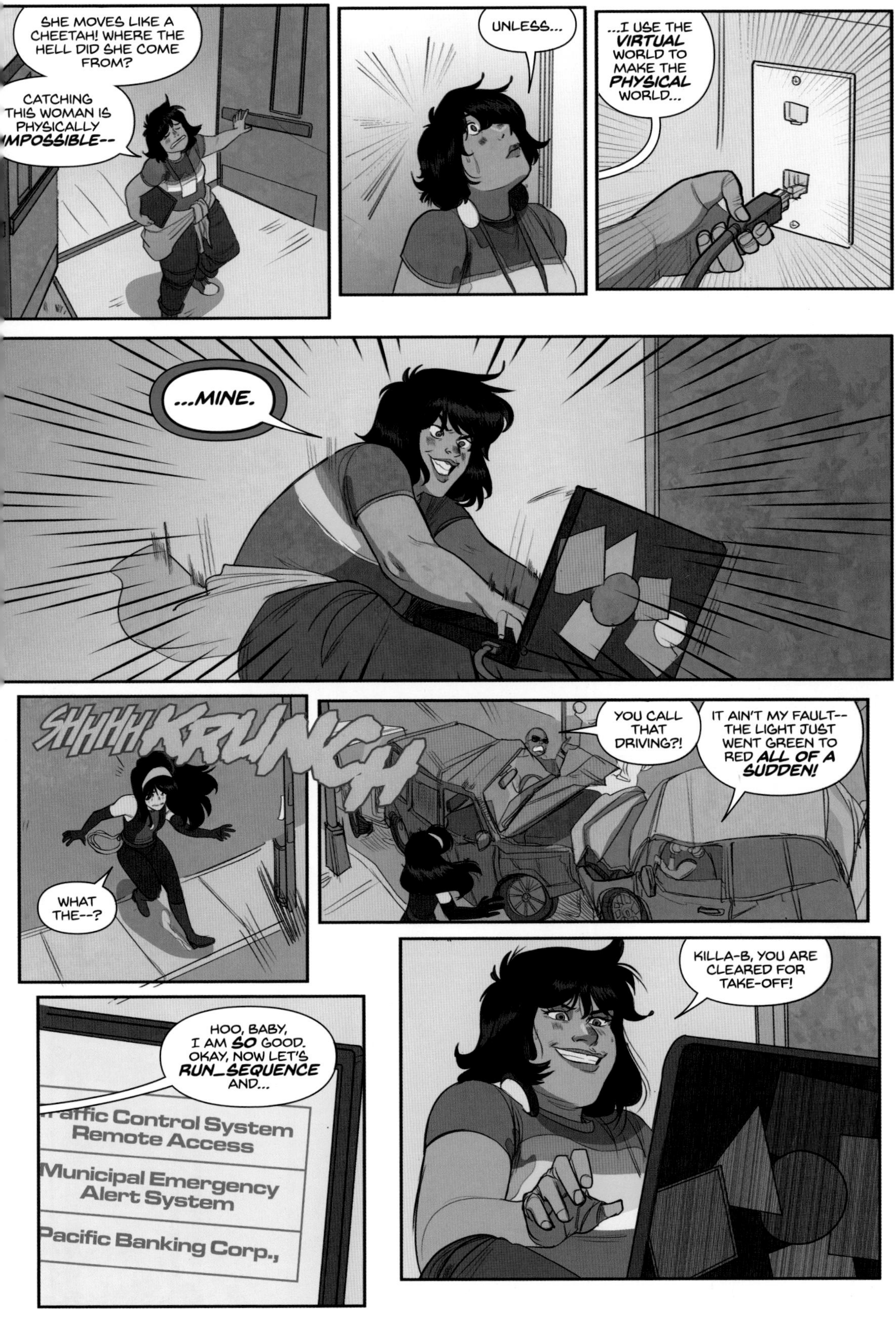
SHE MOVES LIKE A CHEETAH! WHERE THE HELL DID SHE COME FROM?
CATCHING THIS WOMAN IS PHYSICALLY IMPOSSIBLE--
UNLESS...
...I USE THE VIRTUAL WORLD TO MAKE THE PHYSICAL WORLD...
...MINE.
SHHHHKRUNCH
WHAT THE--?
YOU CALL THAT DRIVING?!
IT AIN'T MY FAULT-- THE LIGHT JUST WENT GREEN TO RED ALL OF A SUDDEN!
HOO, BABY, I AM SO GOOD. OKAY, NOW LET'S RUN_SEQUENCE AND...
Traffic Control System Remote Access
Municipal Emergency Alert System
Pacific Banking Corp.,
KILLA-B, YOU ARE CLEARED FOR TAKE-OFF!

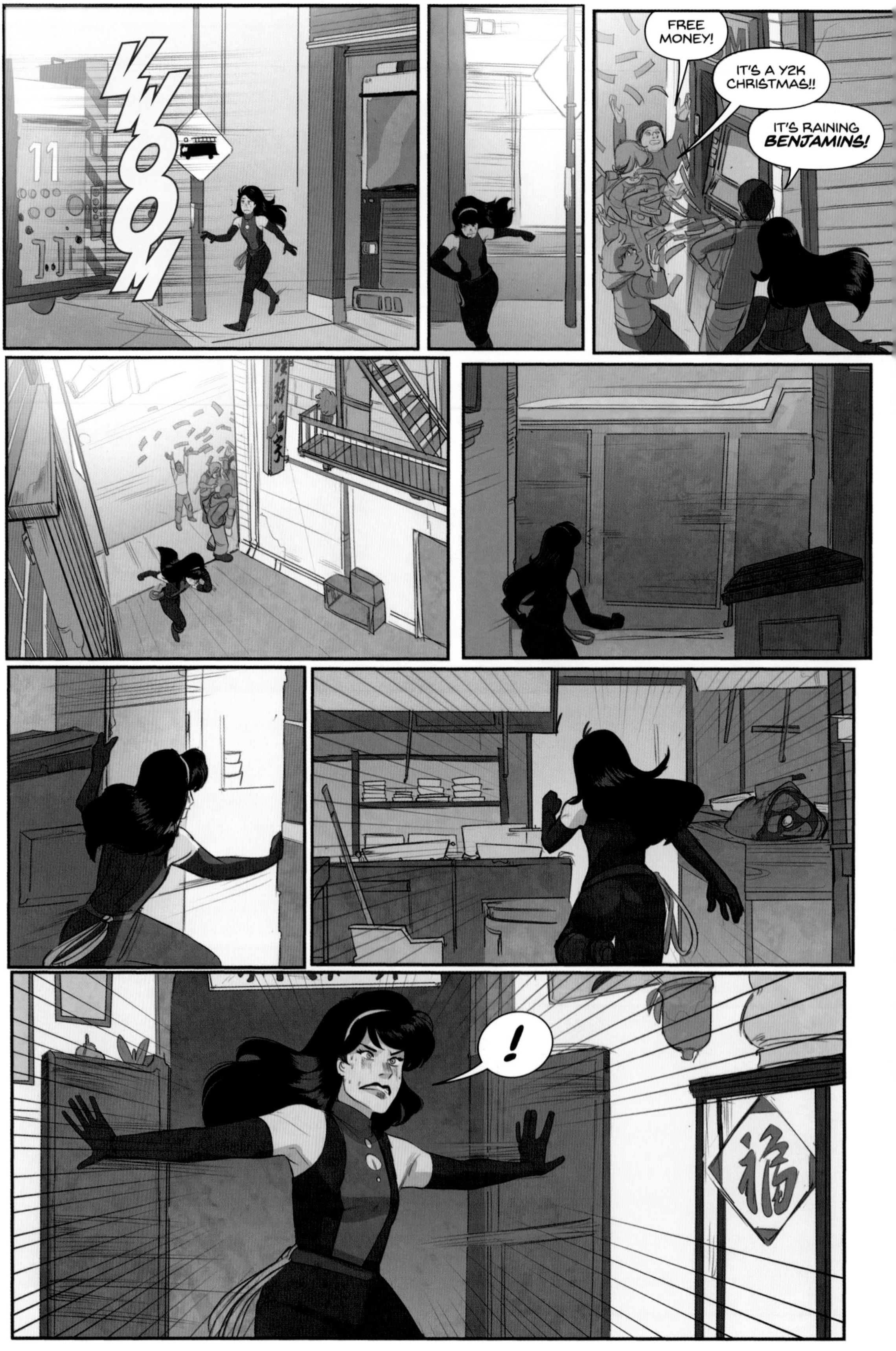
VWOOM
FREE MONEY!
IT'S A Y2K CHRISTMAS!!
IT'S RAINING **BENJAMINS!**
!

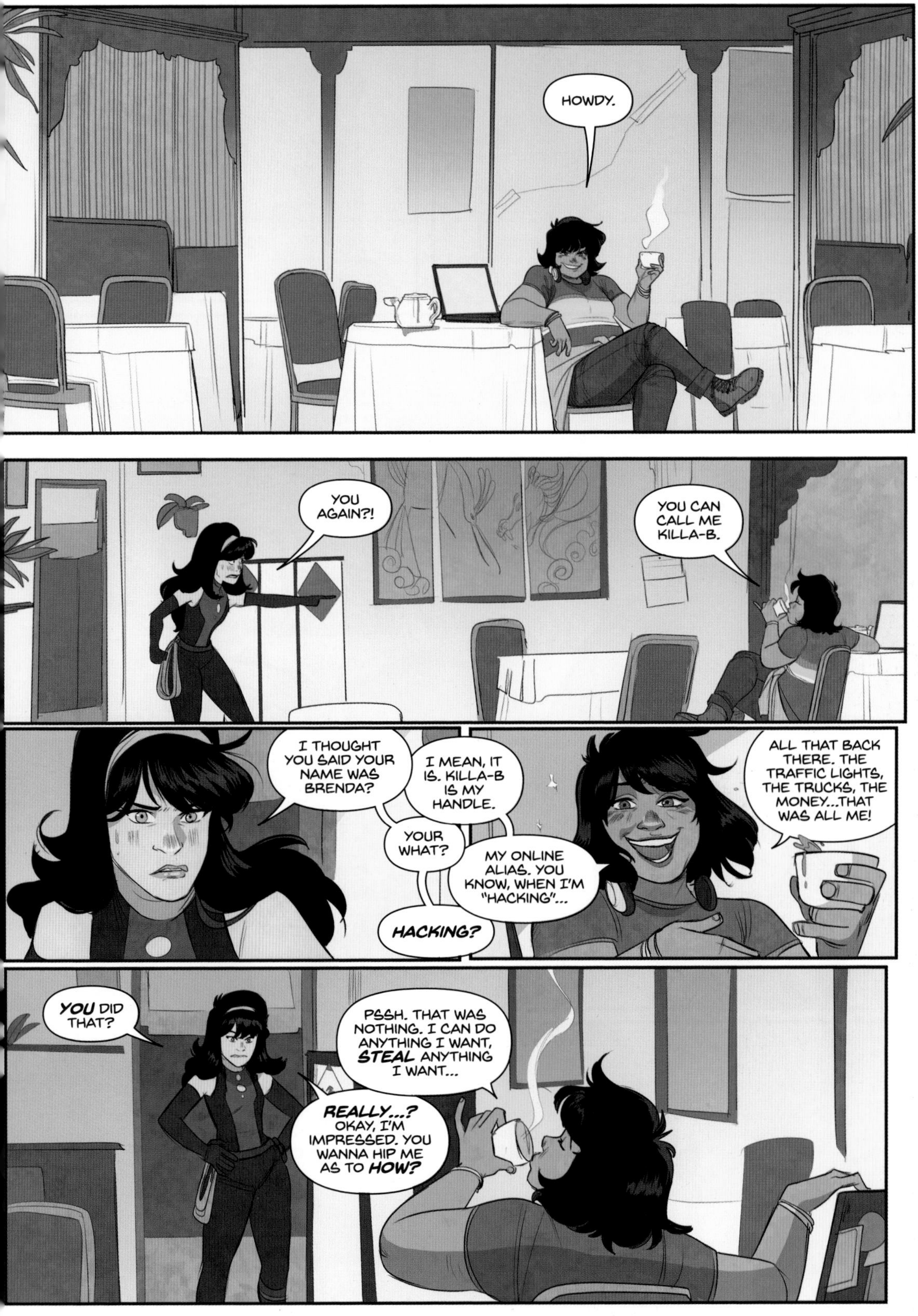
HOWDY.
YOU AGAIN?!
YOU CAN CALL ME KILLA-B.
I THOUGHT YOU SAID YOUR NAME WAS BRENDA?
I MEAN, IT IS. KILLA-B IS MY HANDLE.
YOUR WHAT?
MY ONLINE ALIAS. YOU KNOW, WHEN I'M "HACKING"...
HACKING?
ALL THAT BACK THERE. THE TRAFFIC LIGHTS, THE TRUCKS, THE MONEY...THAT WAS ALL ME!
YOU DID THAT?
PSSH. THAT WAS NOTHING. I CAN DO ANYTHING I WANT, STEAL ANYTHING I WANT...
REALLY...? OKAY, I'M IMPRESSED. YOU WANNA HIP ME AS TO HOW?

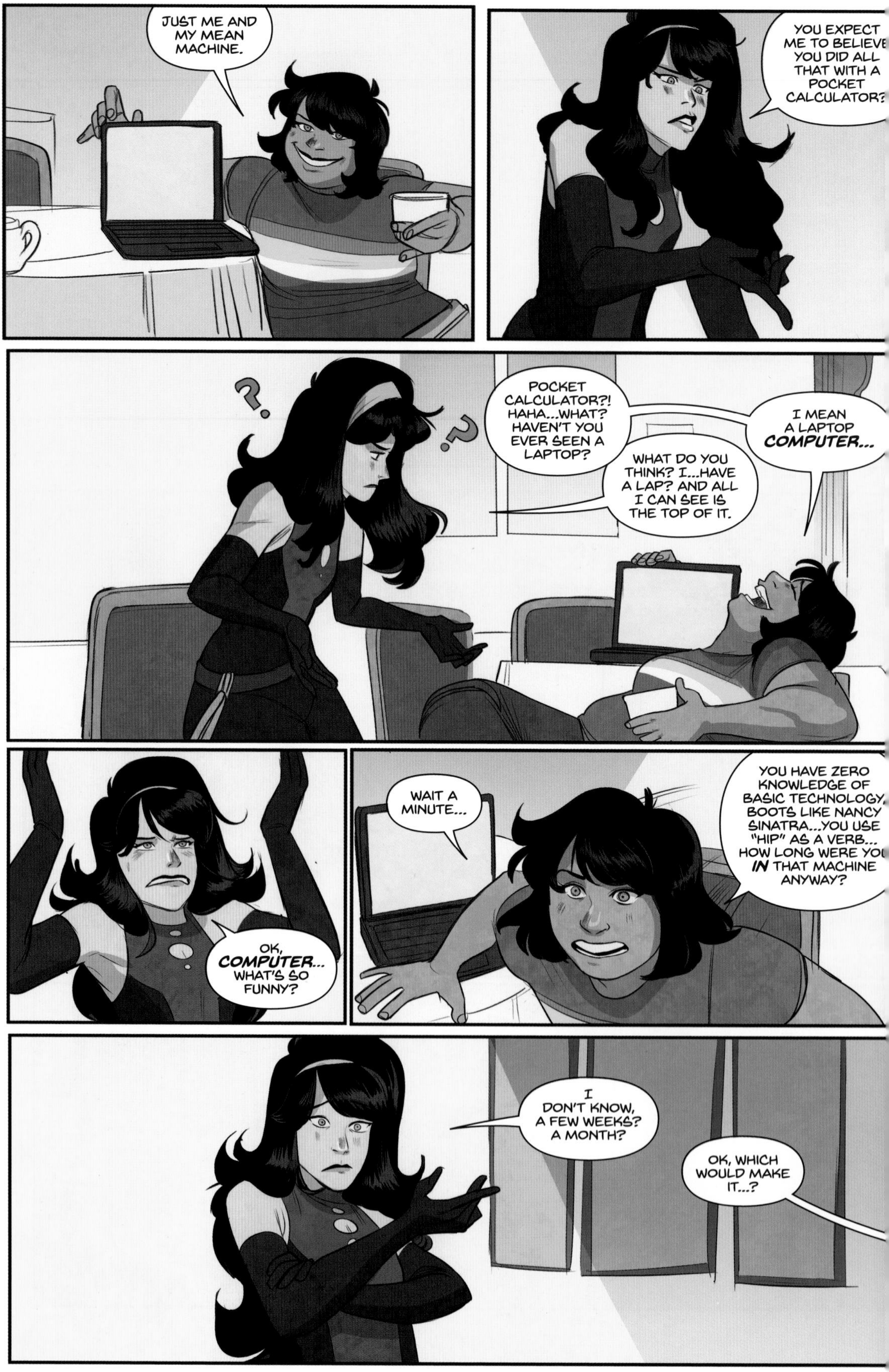
JUST ME AND MY MEAN MACHINE.
YOU EXPECT ME TO BELIEVE YOU DID ALL THAT WITH A POCKET CALCULATOR?
POCKET CALCULATOR?! HAHA...WHAT? HAVEN'T YOU EVER SEEN A LAPTOP?
WHAT DO YOU THINK? I...HAVE A LAP? AND ALL I CAN SEE IS THE TOP OF IT.
I MEAN A LAPTOP COMPUTER...
OK, COMPUTER... WHAT'S SO FUNNY?
WAIT A MINUTE...
YOU HAVE ZERO KNOWLEDGE OF BASIC TECHNOLOGY. BOOTS LIKE NANCY SINATRA...YOU USE "HIP" AS A VERB... HOW LONG WERE YOU IN THAT MACHINE ANYWAY?
I DON'T KNOW, A FEW WEEKS? A MONTH?
OK, WHICH WOULD MAKE IT...?

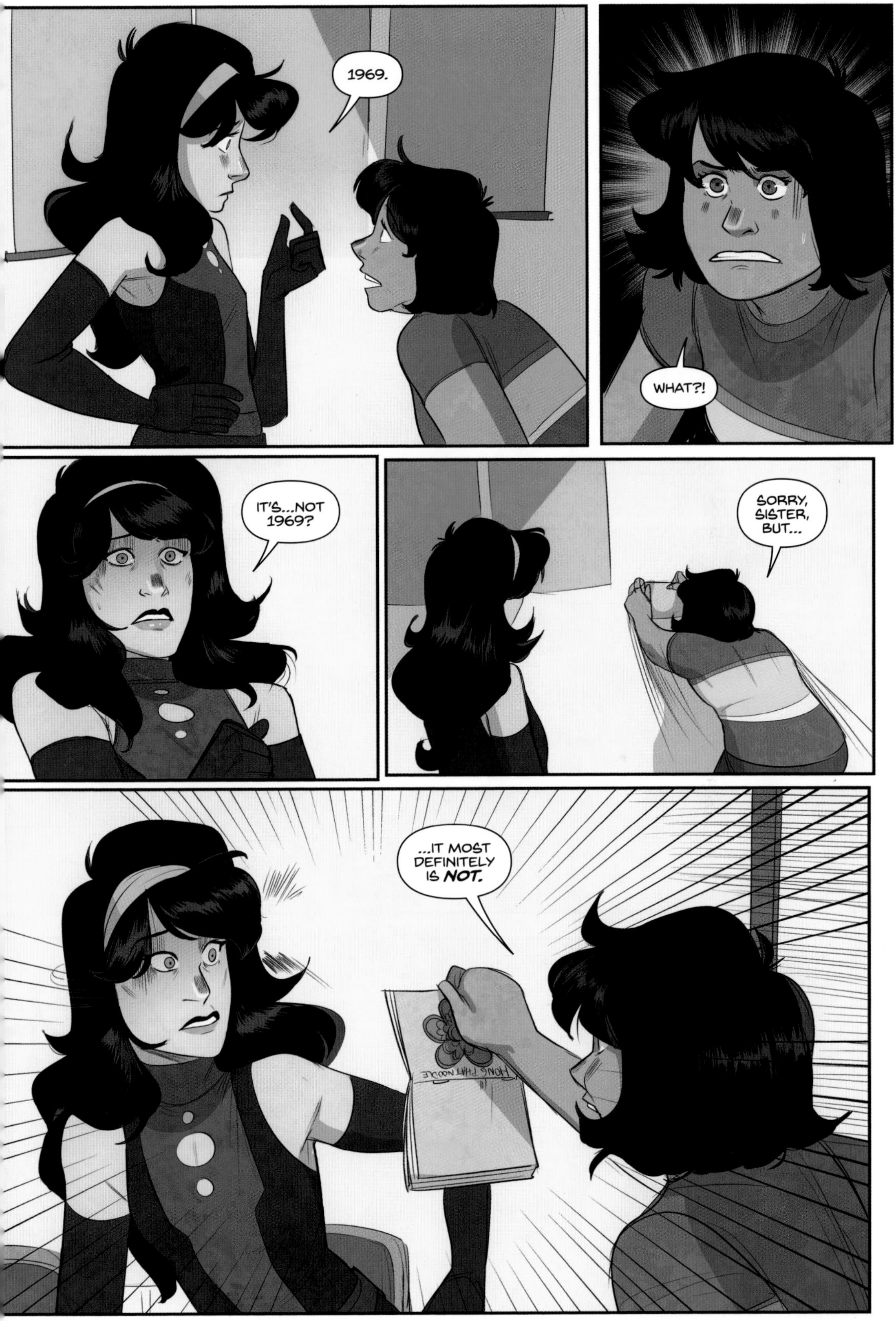
1969.
WHAT?!
IT'S...NOT 1969?
SORRY, SISTER, BUT...
...IT MOST DEFINITELY IS ***NOT.***
HONG PHAT NOODLE

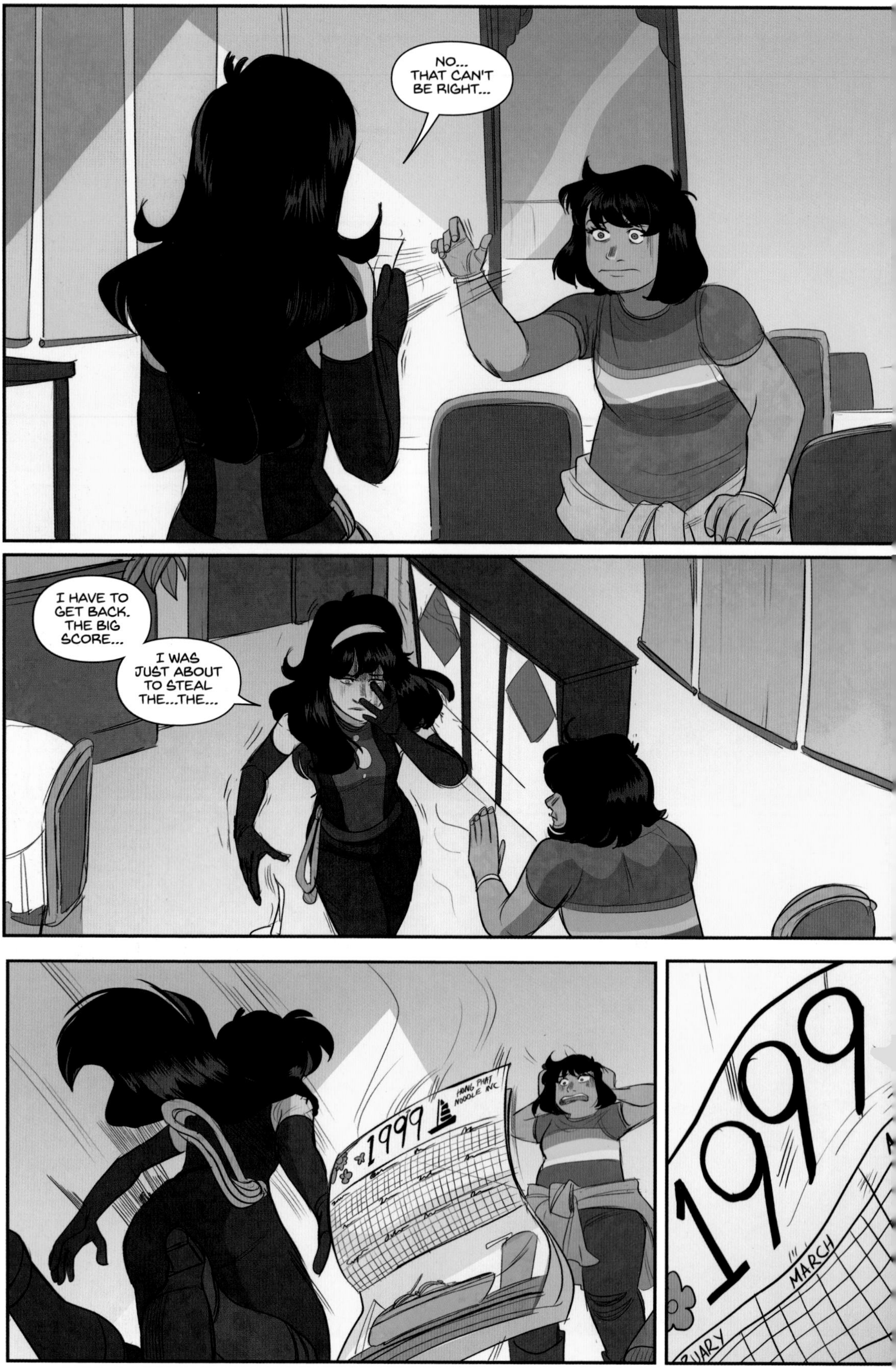
NO... THAT CAN'T BE RIGHT...
I HAVE TO GET BACK. THE BIG SCORE...
I WAS JUST ABOUT TO STEAL THE...THE...
1999
HONG PHAT NOODLE INC
1999
MARCH

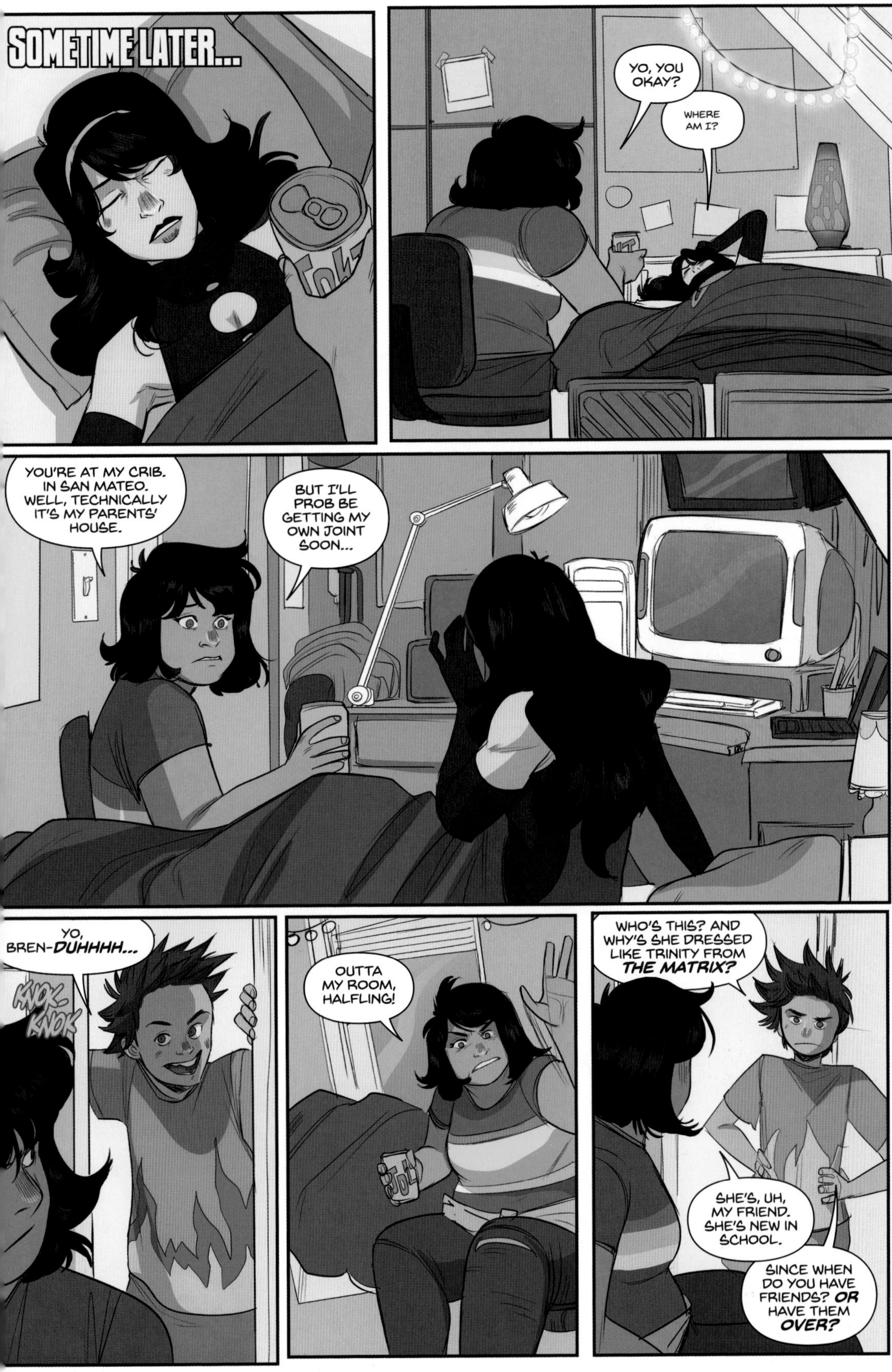
SOMETIME LATER...
YO, YOU OKAY?
WHERE AM I?
YOU'RE AT MY CRIB. IN SAN MATEO. WELL, TECHNICALLY IT'S MY PARENTS' HOUSE.
BUT I'LL PROB BE GETTING MY OWN JOINT SOON...
YO, BREN-DUHHHH...
KNOK KNOK
OUTTA MY ROOM, HALFLING!
WHO'S THIS? AND WHY'S SHE DRESSED LIKE TRINITY FROM THE MATRIX?
SHE'S, UH, MY FRIEND. SHE'S NEW IN SCHOOL.
SINCE WHEN DO YOU HAVE FRIENDS? OR HAVE THEM OVER?

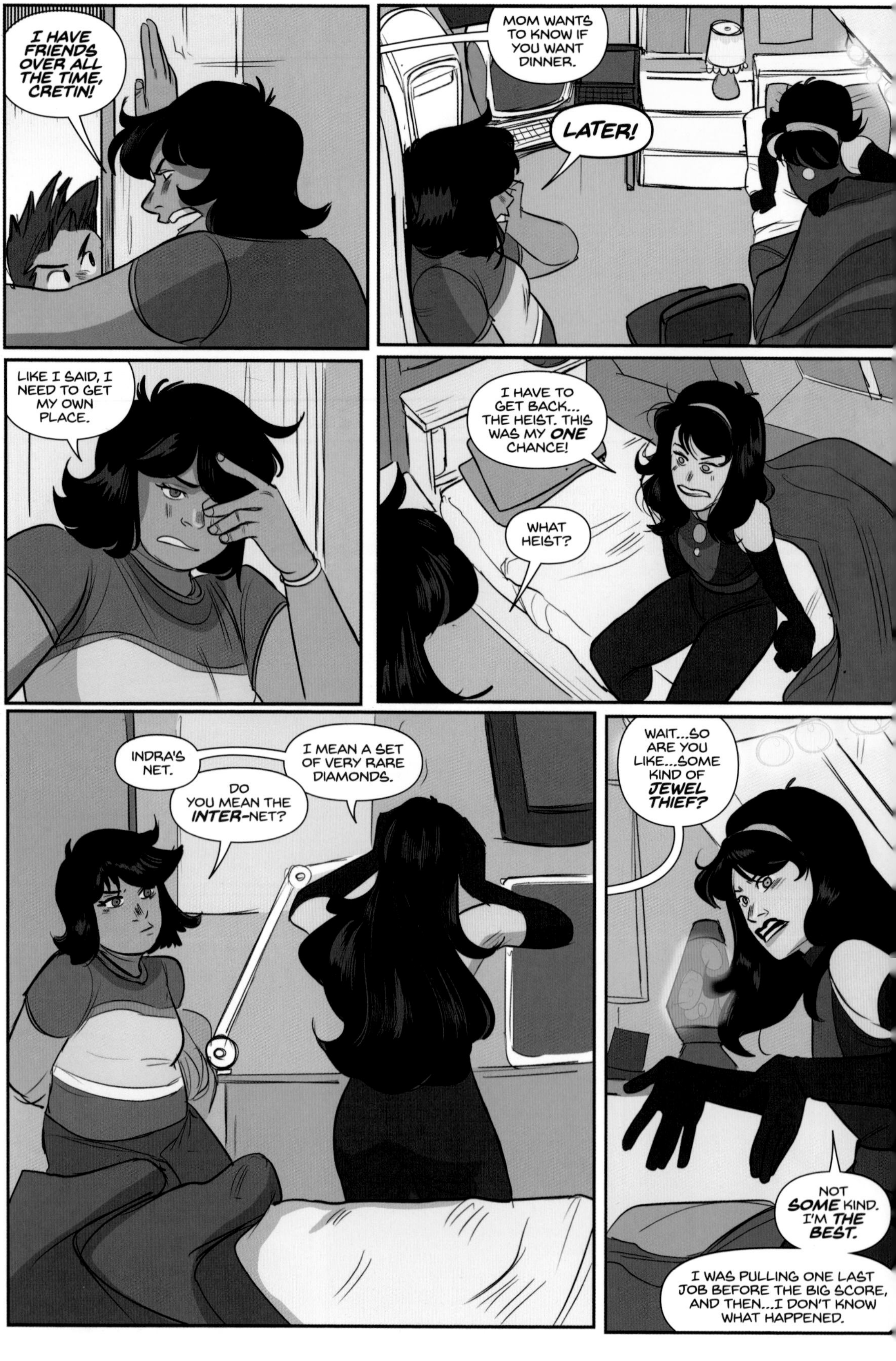
I HAVE FRIENDS OVER ALL THE TIME, CRETIN!
MOM WANTS TO KNOW IF YOU WANT DINNER.
LATER!
LIKE I SAID, I NEED TO GET MY OWN PLACE.
I HAVE TO GET BACK... THE HEIST. THIS WAS MY ONE CHANCE!
WHAT HEIST?
INDRA'S NET.
DO YOU MEAN THE INTER-NET?
I MEAN A SET OF VERY RARE DIAMONDS.
WAIT...SO ARE YOU LIKE...SOME KIND OF JEWEL THIEF?
NOT SOME KIND. I'M THE BEST.
I WAS PULLING ONE LAST JOB BEFORE THE BIG SCORE, AND THEN...I DON'T KNOW WHAT HAPPENED.

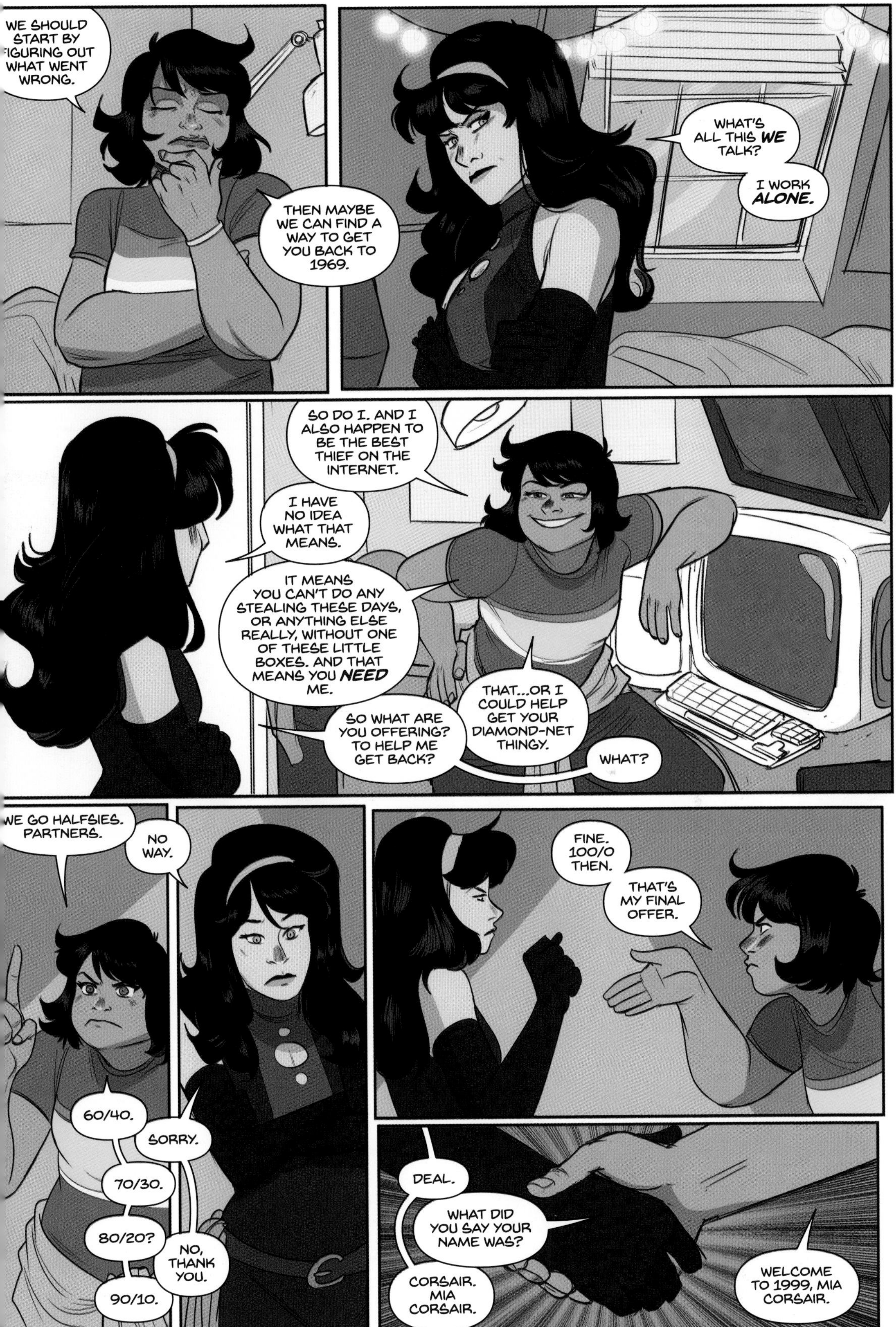
WE SHOULD START BY FIGURING OUT WHAT WENT WRONG.
THEN MAYBE WE CAN FIND A WAY TO GET YOU BACK TO 1969.
WHAT'S ALL THIS **WE** TALK?
I WORK **ALONE.**
SO DO I. AND I ALSO HAPPEN TO BE THE BEST THIEF ON THE INTERNET.
I HAVE NO IDEA WHAT THAT MEANS.
IT MEANS YOU CAN'T DO ANY STEALING THESE DAYS, OR ANYTHING ELSE REALLY, WITHOUT ONE OF THESE LITTLE BOXES. AND THAT MEANS YOU **NEED** ME.
SO WHAT ARE YOU OFFERING? TO HELP ME GET BACK?
THAT...OR I COULD HELP GET YOUR DIAMOND-NET THINGY.
WHAT?
WE GO HALFSIES. PARTNERS.
NO WAY.
60/40.
SORRY.
70/30.
80/20?
NO, THANK YOU.
90/10.
FINE. 100/0 THEN.
THAT'S MY FINAL OFFER.
DEAL.
WHAT DID YOU SAY YOUR NAME WAS?
CORSAIR. MIA CORSAIR.
WELCOME TO 1999, MIA CORSAIR.

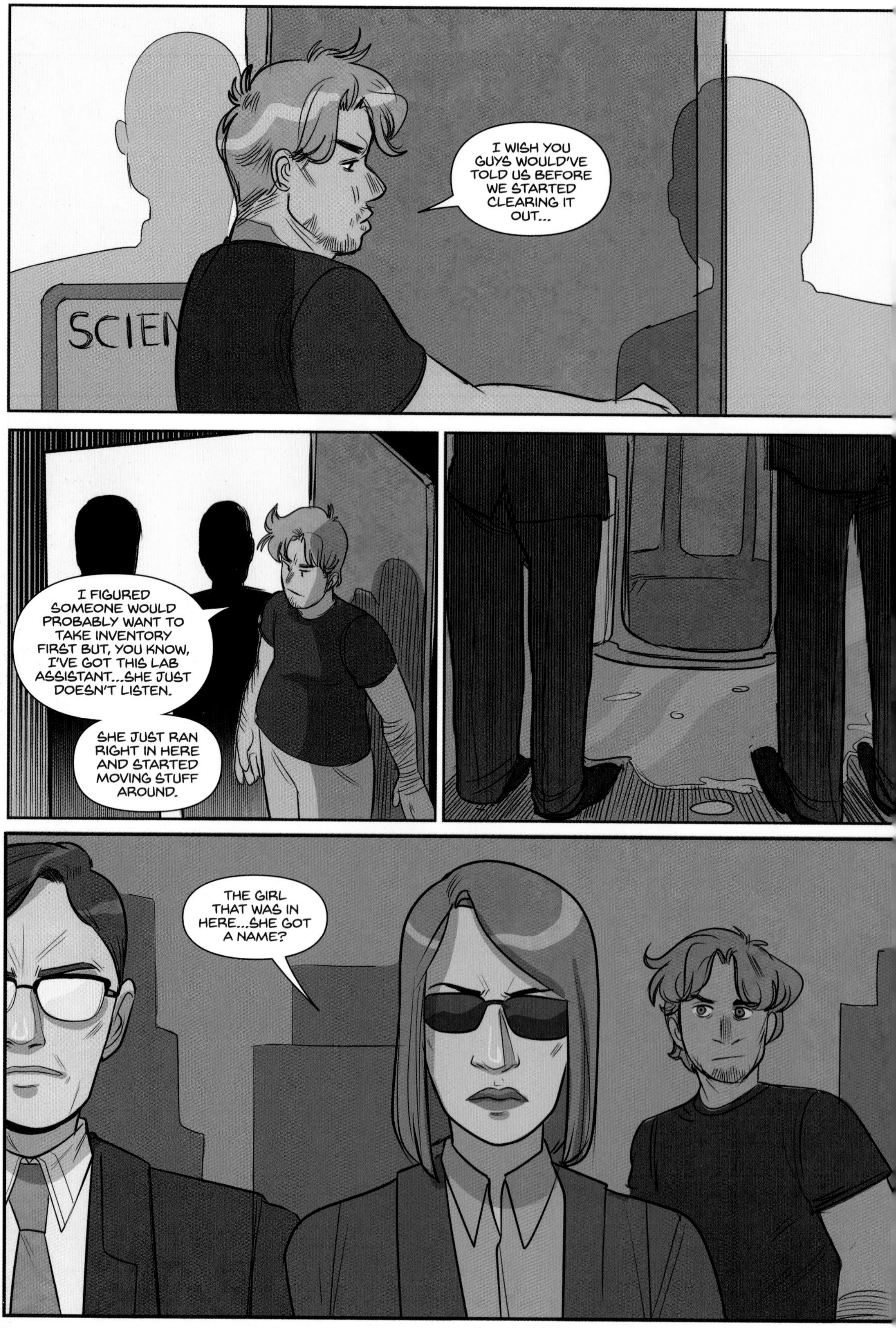
SCIEN
I WISH YOU GUYS WOULD'VE TOLD US BEFORE WE STARTED CLEARING IT OUT...
I FIGURED SOMEONE WOULD PROBABLY WANT TO TAKE INVENTORY FIRST BUT, YOU KNOW, I'VE GOT THIS LAB ASSISTANT...SHE JUST DOESN'T LISTEN.
SHE JUST RAN RIGHT IN HERE AND STARTED MOVING STUFF AROUND.
THE GIRL THAT WAS IN HERE...SHE GOT A NAME?

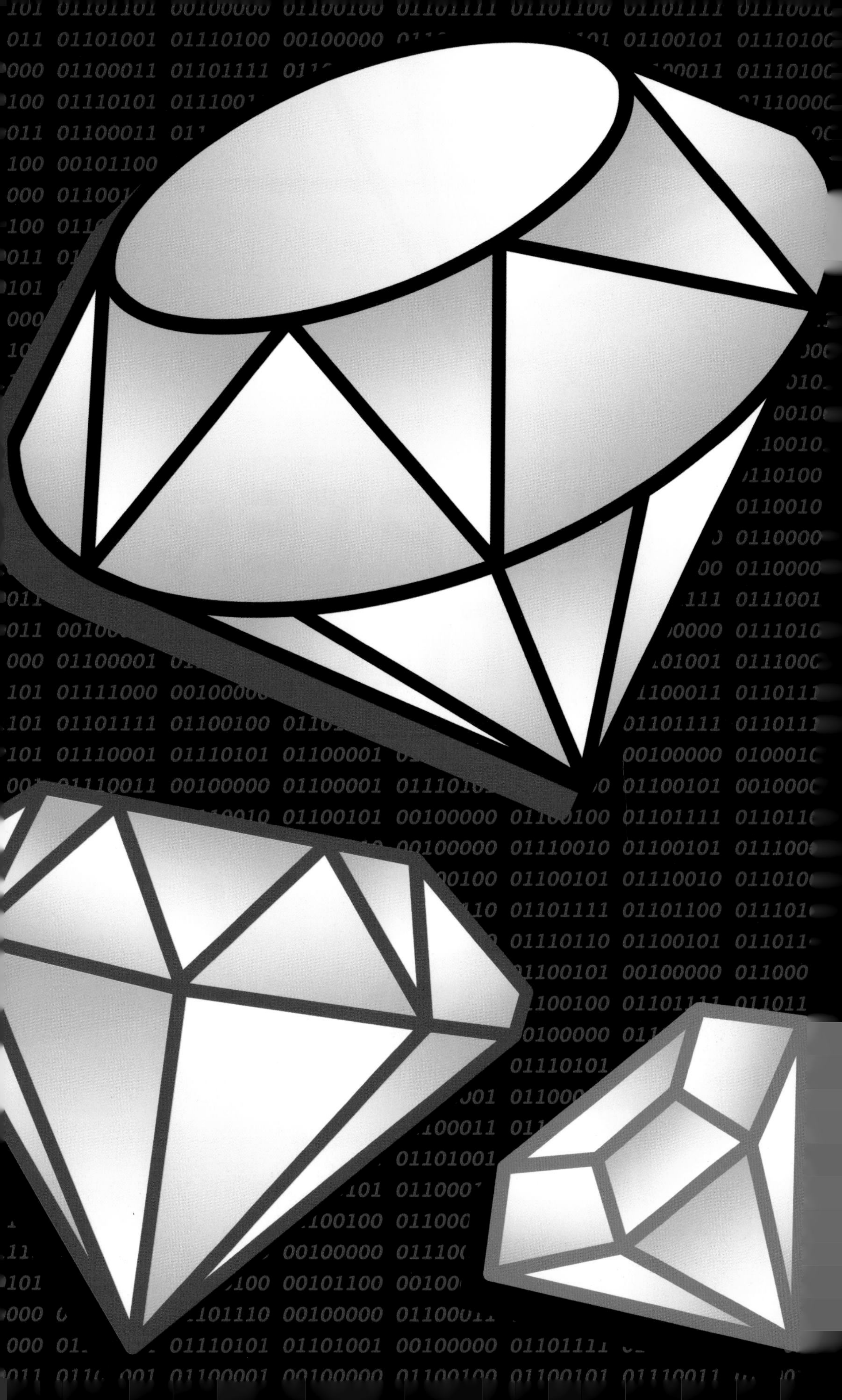

# CHAPTER TWO

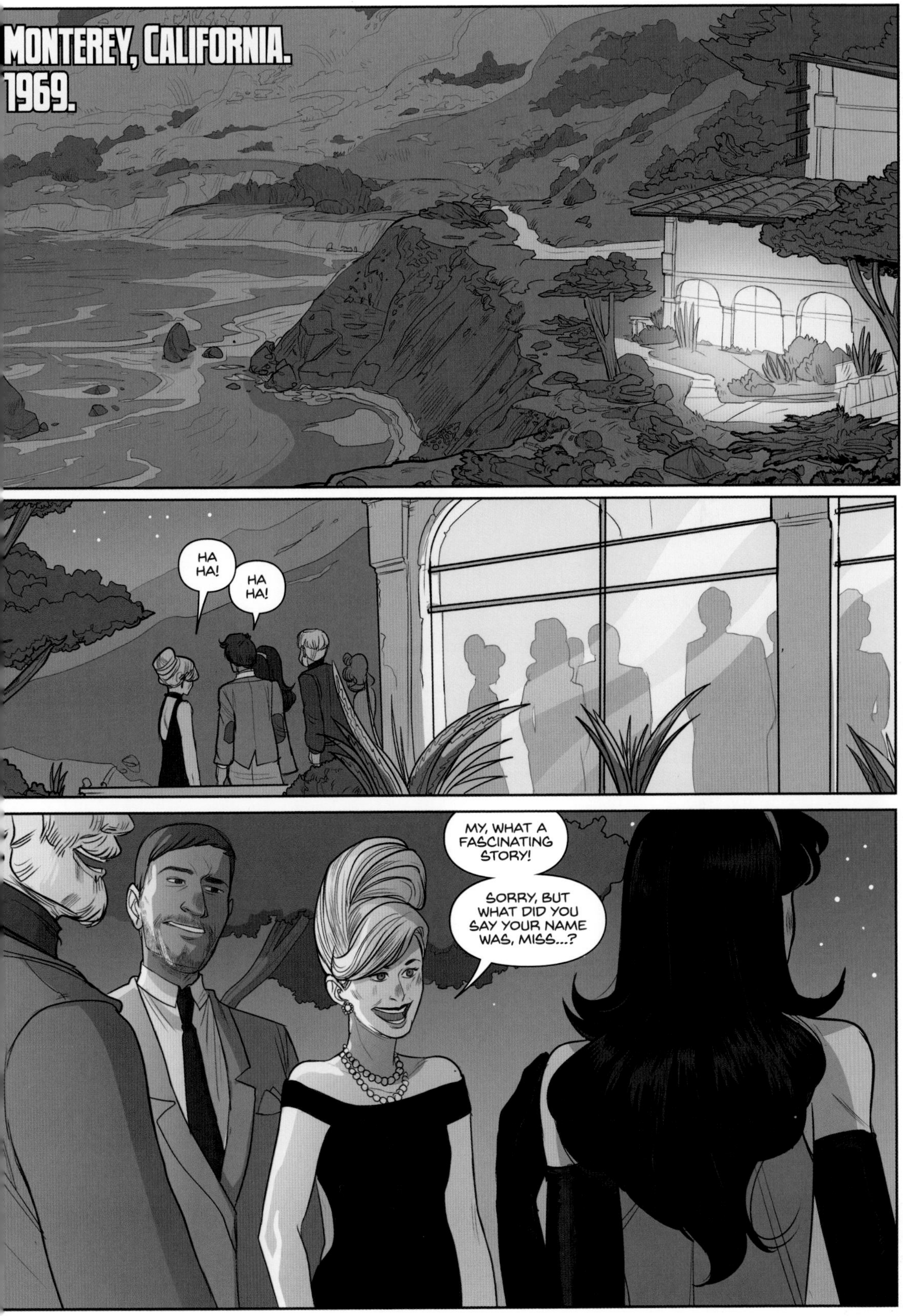
MONTEREY, CALIFORNIA.
1969.
HA HA!
HA HA!
MY, WHAT A FASCINATING STORY!
SORRY, BUT WHAT DID YOU SAY YOUR NAME WAS, MISS...?

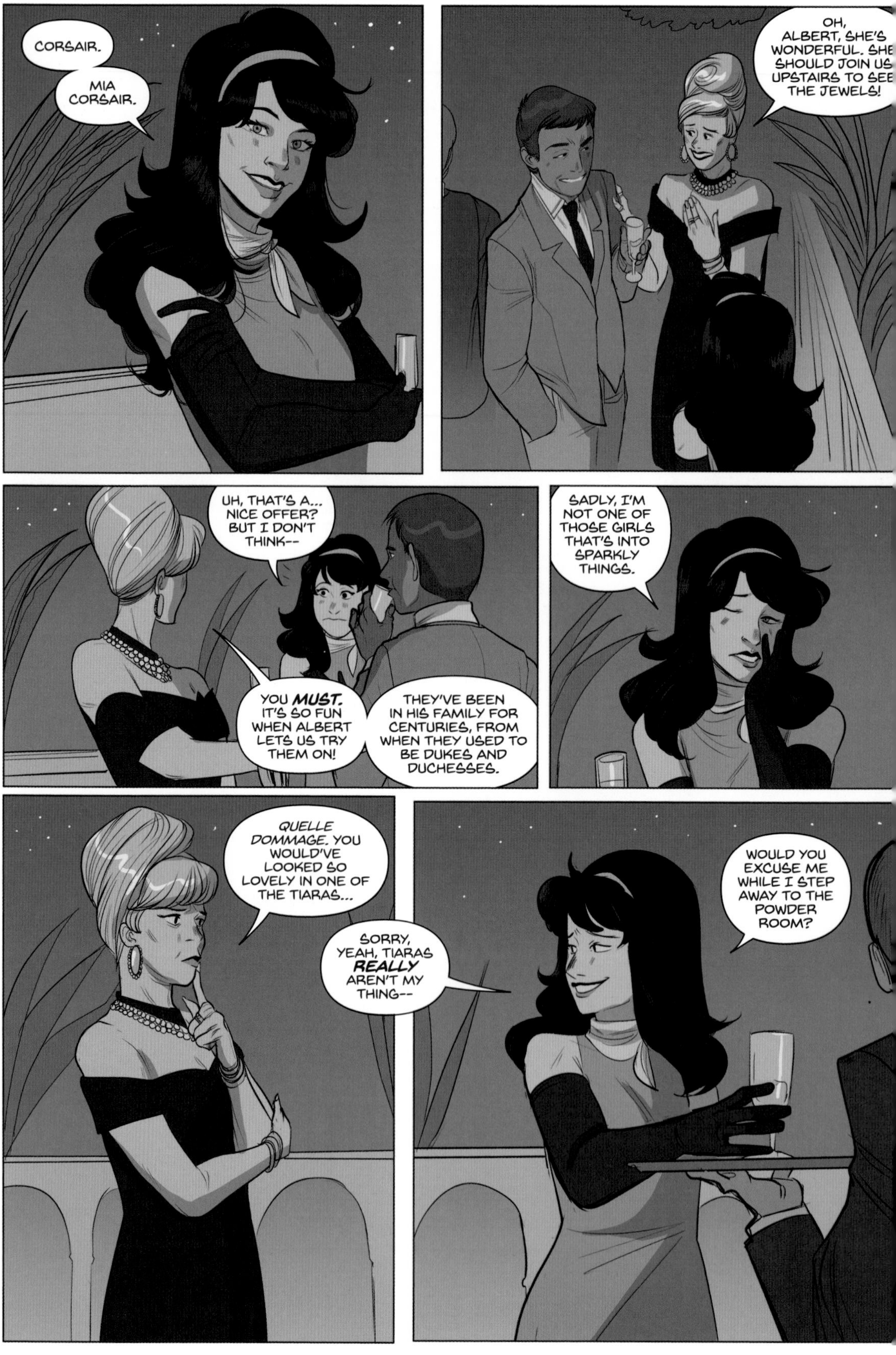
CORSAIR.
MIA CORSAIR.
OH, ALBERT, SHE'S WONDERFUL. SHE SHOULD JOIN US UPSTAIRS TO SEE THE JEWELS!
UH, THAT'S A... NICE OFFER? BUT I DON'T THINK--
YOU *MUST.* IT'S SO FUN WHEN ALBERT LETS US TRY THEM ON!
THEY'VE BEEN IN HIS FAMILY FOR CENTURIES, FROM WHEN THEY USED TO BE DUKES AND DUCHESSES.
SADLY, I'M NOT ONE OF THOSE GIRLS THAT'S INTO SPARKLY THINGS.
*QUELLE DOMMAGE.* YOU WOULD'VE LOOKED SO LOVELY IN ONE OF THE TIARAS...
SORRY, YEAH, TIARAS ***REALLY*** AREN'T MY THING--
WOULD YOU EXCUSE ME WHILE I STEP AWAY TO THE POWDER ROOM?

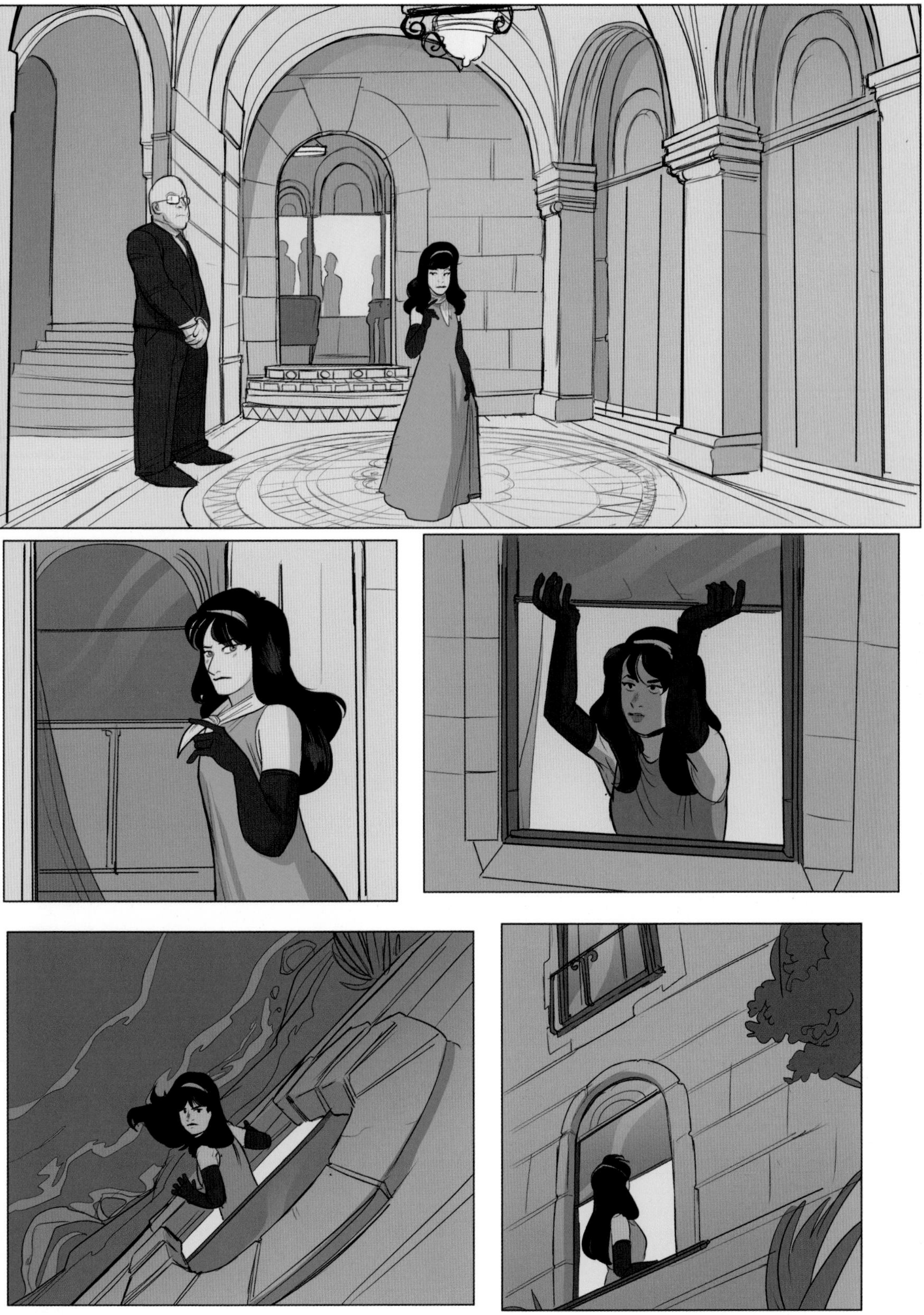

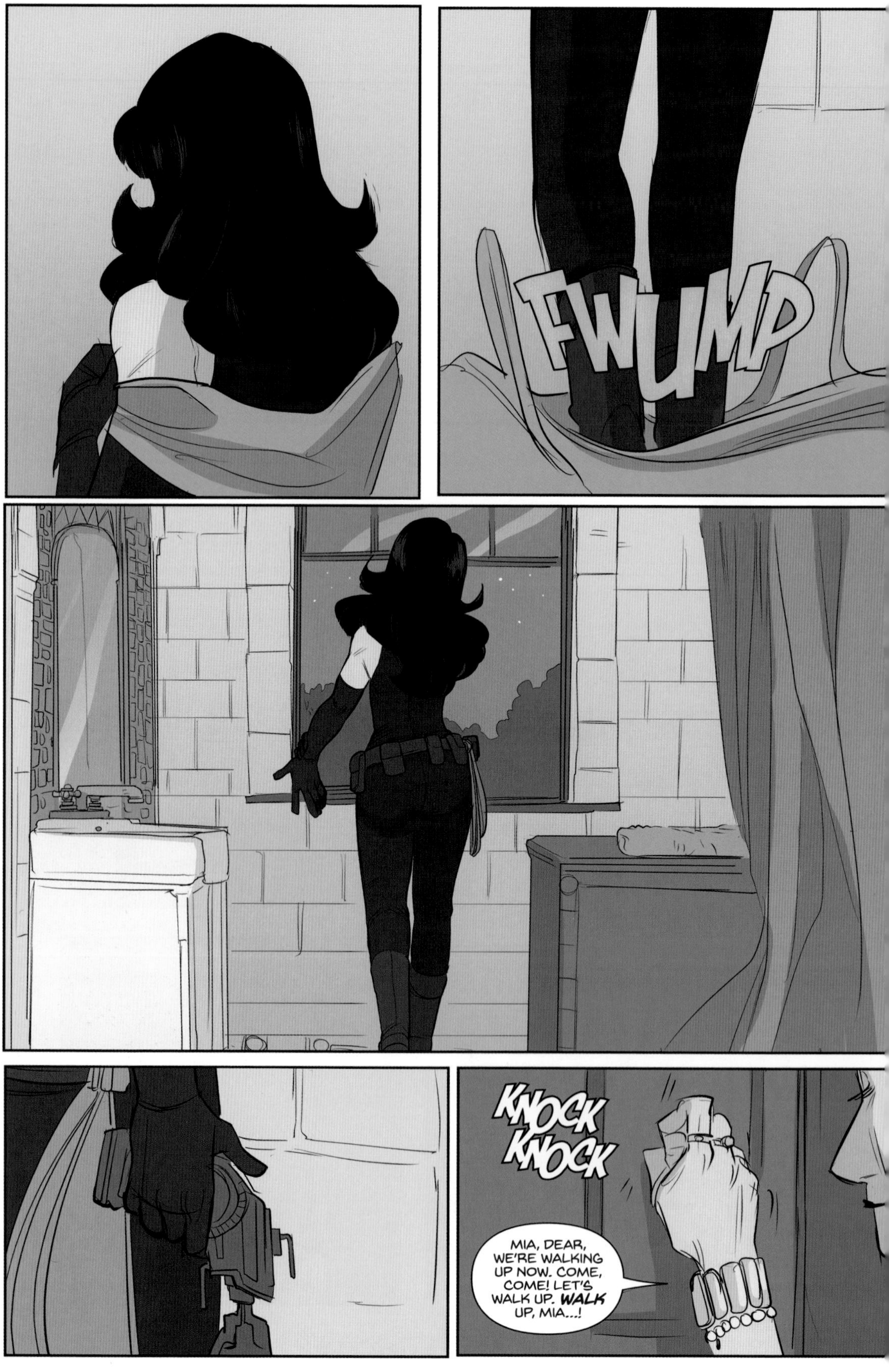
FWUMP
KNOCK KNOCK
MIA, DEAR, WE'RE WALKING UP NOW. COME, COME! LET'S WALK UP. WALK UP, MIA...!

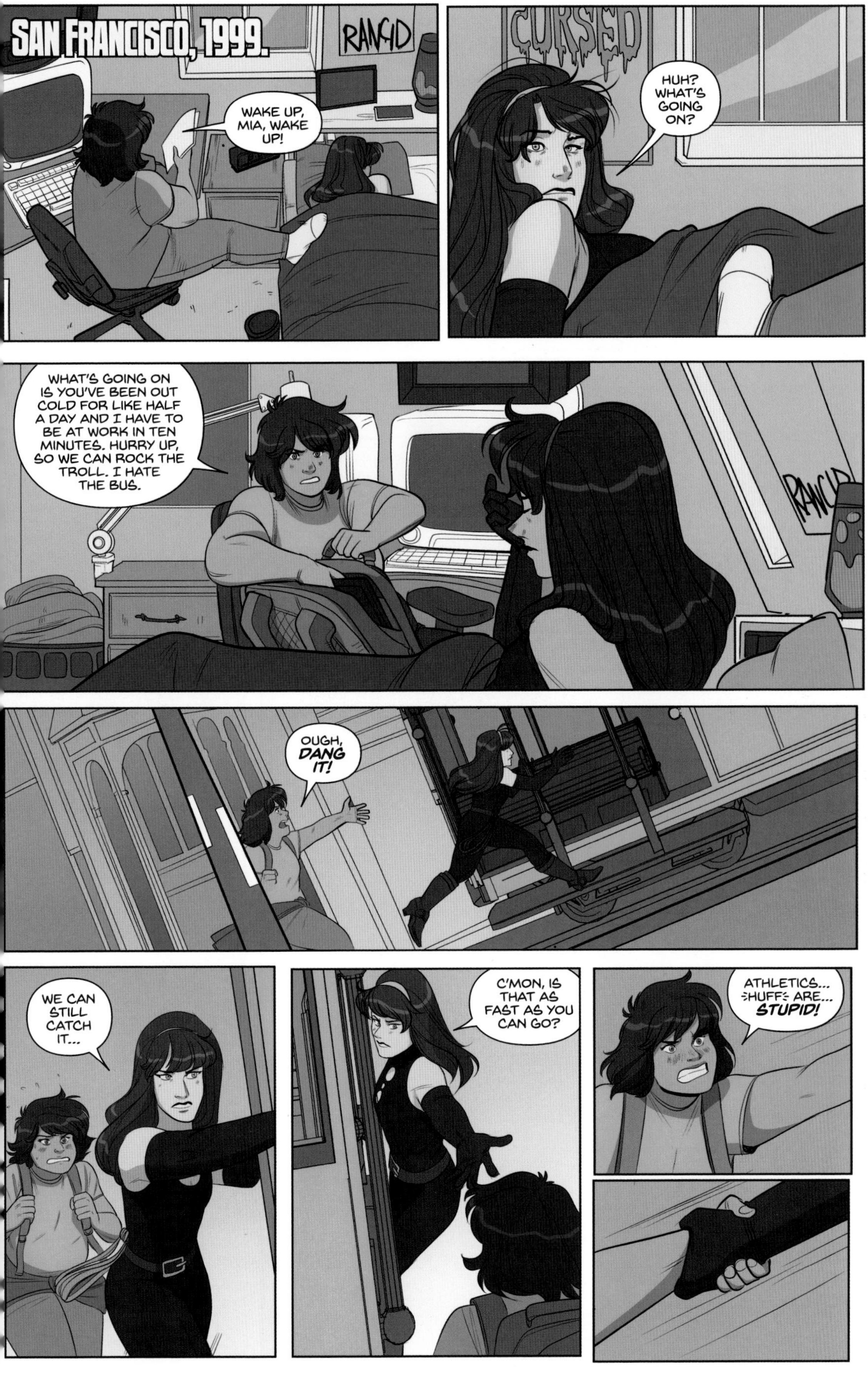
SAN FRANCISCO, 1999.
RANCID
WAKE UP, MIA, WAKE UP!
CURSED
HUH? WHAT'S GOING ON?
WHAT'S GOING ON IS YOU'VE BEEN OUT COLD FOR LIKE HALF A DAY AND I HAVE TO BE AT WORK IN TEN MINUTES. HURRY UP, SO WE CAN ROCK THE TROLL. I HATE THE BUS.
OUGH, DANG IT!
WE CAN STILL CATCH IT...
C'MON, IS THAT AS FAST AS YOU CAN GO?
ATHLETICS... HUFF ARE... STUPID!

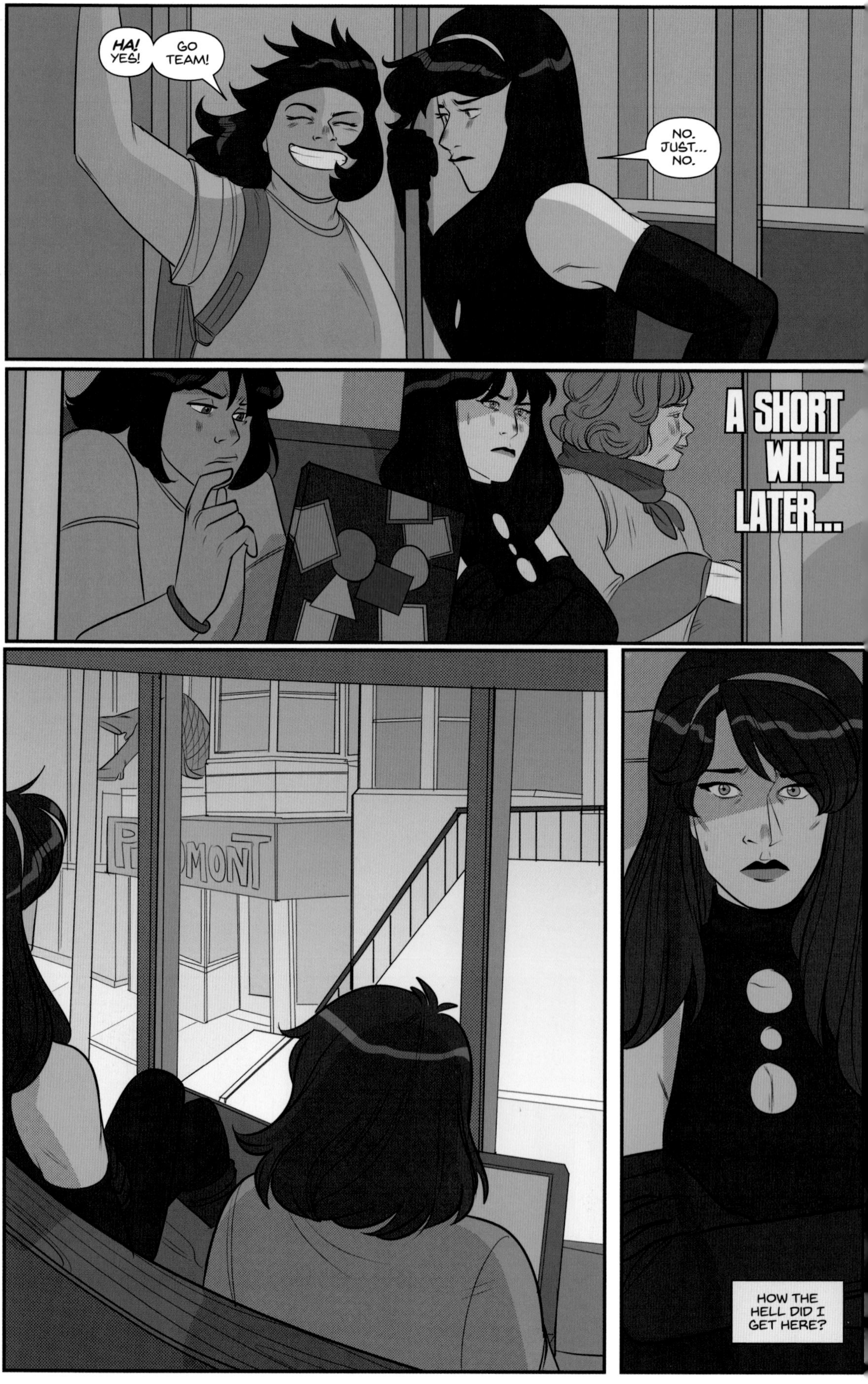

HA! YES!
GO TEAM!
NO. JUST... NO.
A SHORT WHILE LATER...
PIEDMONT
HOW THE HELL DID I GET HERE?

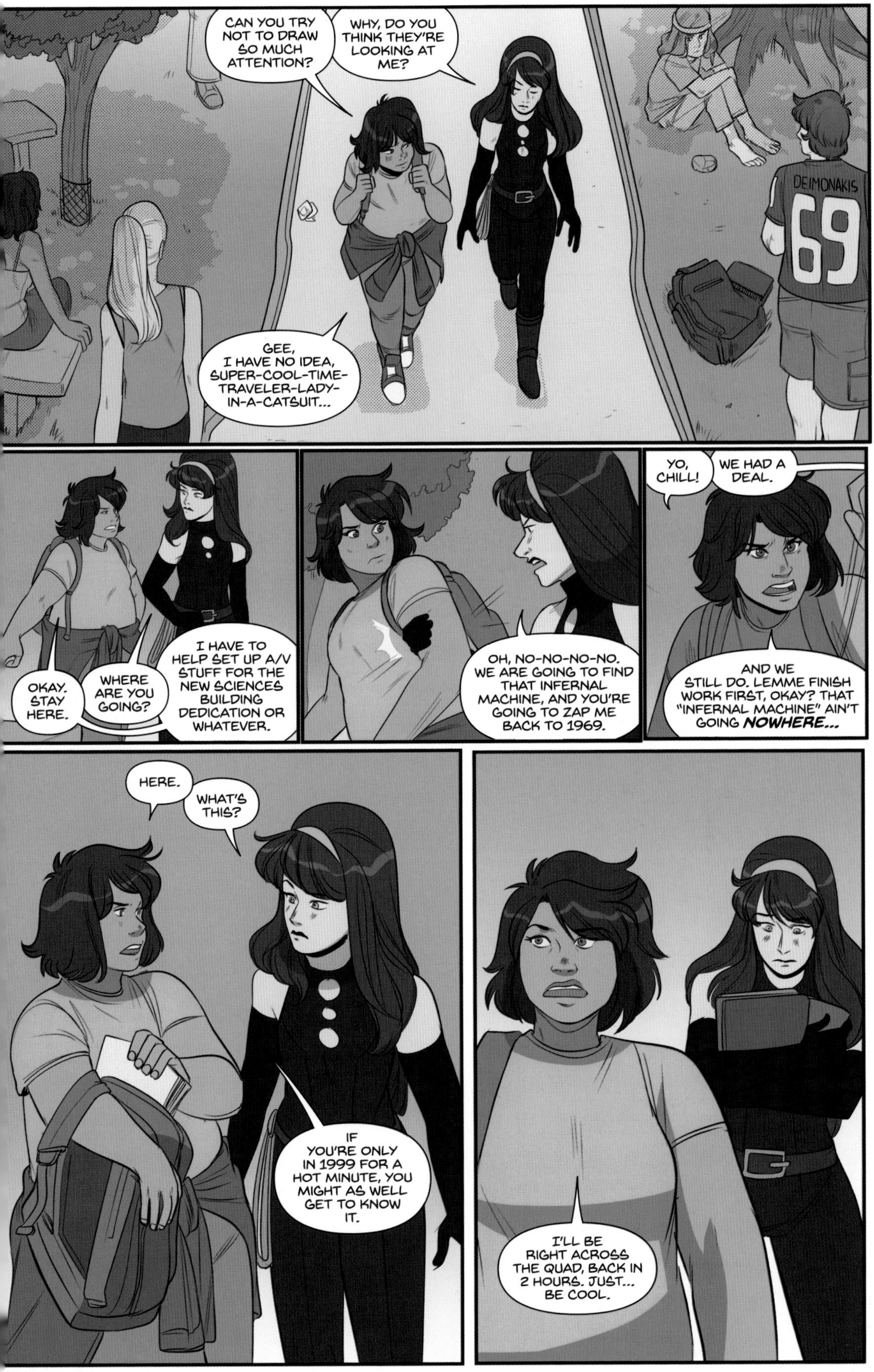
CAN YOU TRY NOT TO DRAW SO MUCH ATTENTION?
WHY, DO YOU THINK THEY'RE LOOKING AT ME?
GEE, I HAVE NO IDEA, SUPER-COOL-TIME-TRAVELER-LADY-IN-A-CATSUIT...
DEIMONAKIS
69
OKAY. STAY HERE.
WHERE ARE YOU GOING?
I HAVE TO HELP SET UP A/V STUFF FOR THE NEW SCIENCES BUILDING DEDICATION OR WHATEVER.
OH, NO-NO-NO-NO. WE ARE GOING TO FIND THAT INFERNAL MACHINE, AND YOU'RE GOING TO ZAP ME BACK TO 1969.
YO, CHILL!
WE HAD A DEAL.
AND WE STILL DO. LEMME FINISH WORK FIRST, OKAY? THAT "INFERNAL MACHINE" AIN'T GOING ***NOWHERE...***
HERE.
WHAT'S THIS?
IF YOU'RE ONLY IN 1999 FOR A HOT MINUTE, YOU MIGHT AS WELL GET TO KNOW IT.
I'LL BE RIGHT ACROSS THE QUAD, BACK IN 2 HOURS. JUST... BE COOL.

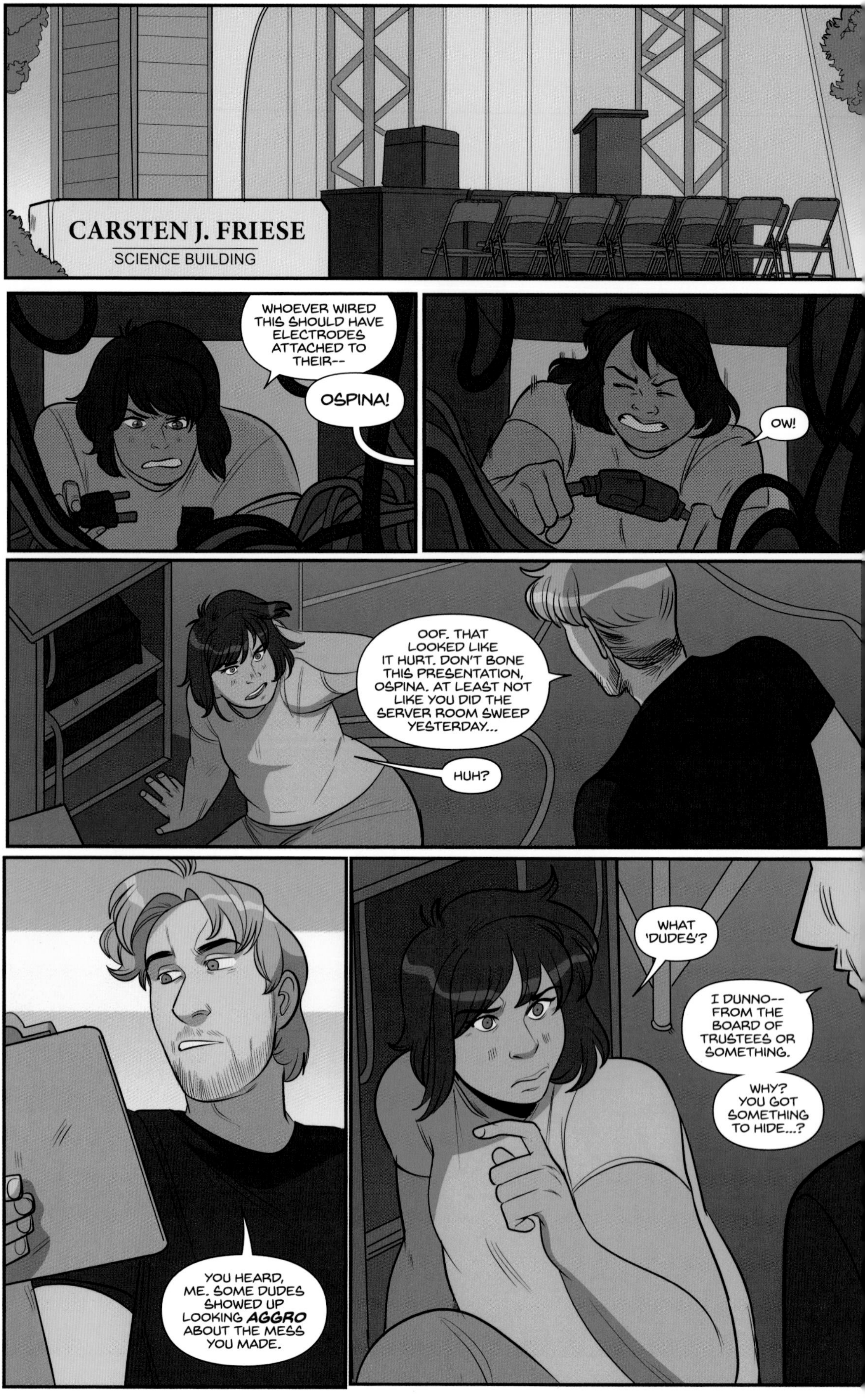
CARSTEN J. FRIESE
SCIENCE BUILDING
WHOEVER WIRED THIS SHOULD HAVE ELECTRODES ATTACHED TO THEIR--
OSPINA!
OW!
OOF. THAT LOOKED LIKE IT HURT. DON'T BONE THIS PRESENTATION, OSPINA. AT LEAST NOT LIKE YOU DID THE SERVER ROOM SWEEP YESTERDAY...
HUH?
YOU HEARD, ME. SOME DUDES SHOWED UP LOOKING AGGRO ABOUT THE MESS YOU MADE.
WHAT 'DUDES'?
I DUNNO-- FROM THE BOARD OF TRUSTEES OR SOMETHING.
WHY? YOU GOT SOMETHING TO HIDE...?

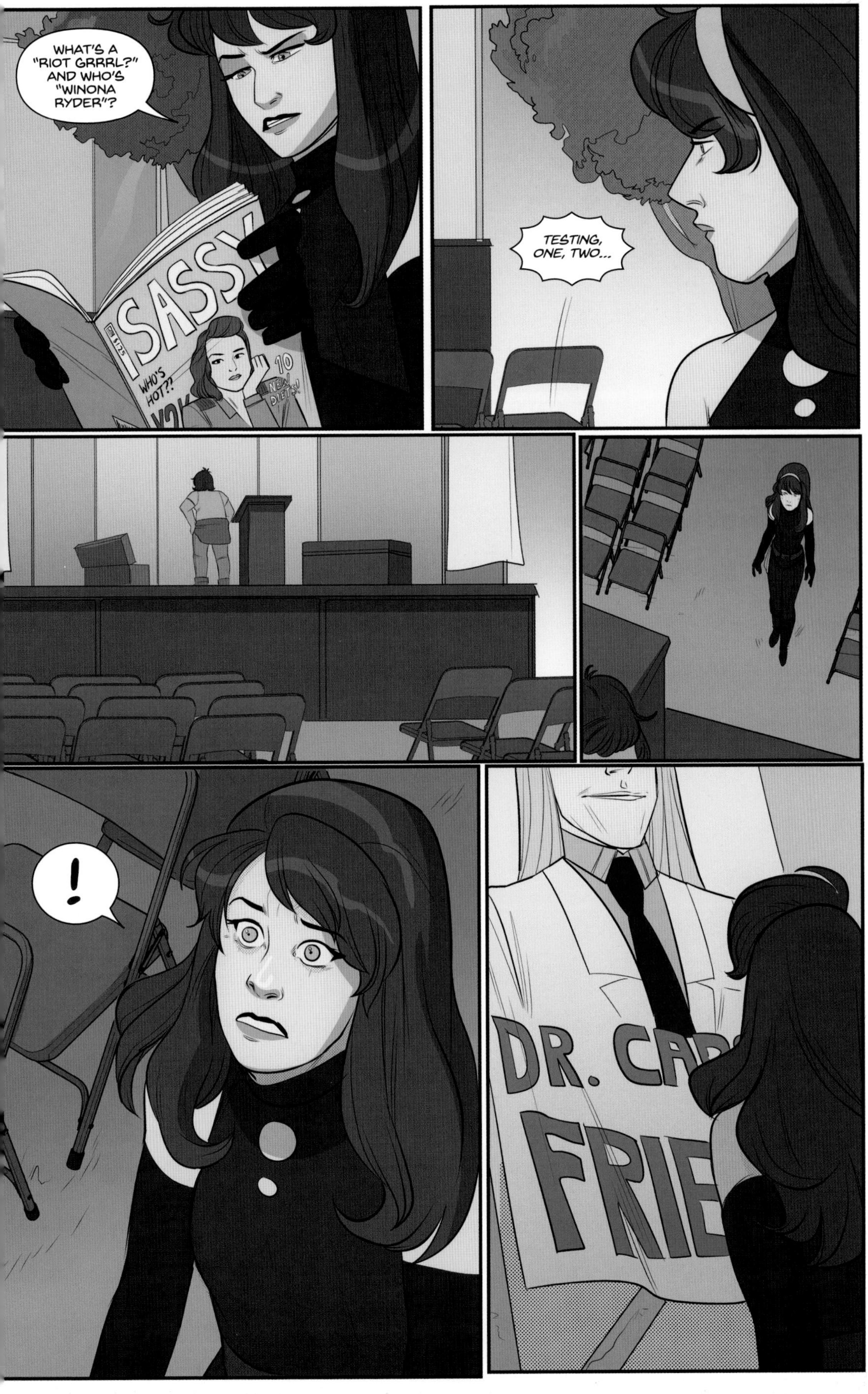

WHAT'S A "RIOT GRRRL?" AND WHO'S "WINONA RYDER"?
SASSY
WHO'S HOT??
10 NEW DIETS!
TESTING, ONE, TWO...
!
DR. CA
FRIE

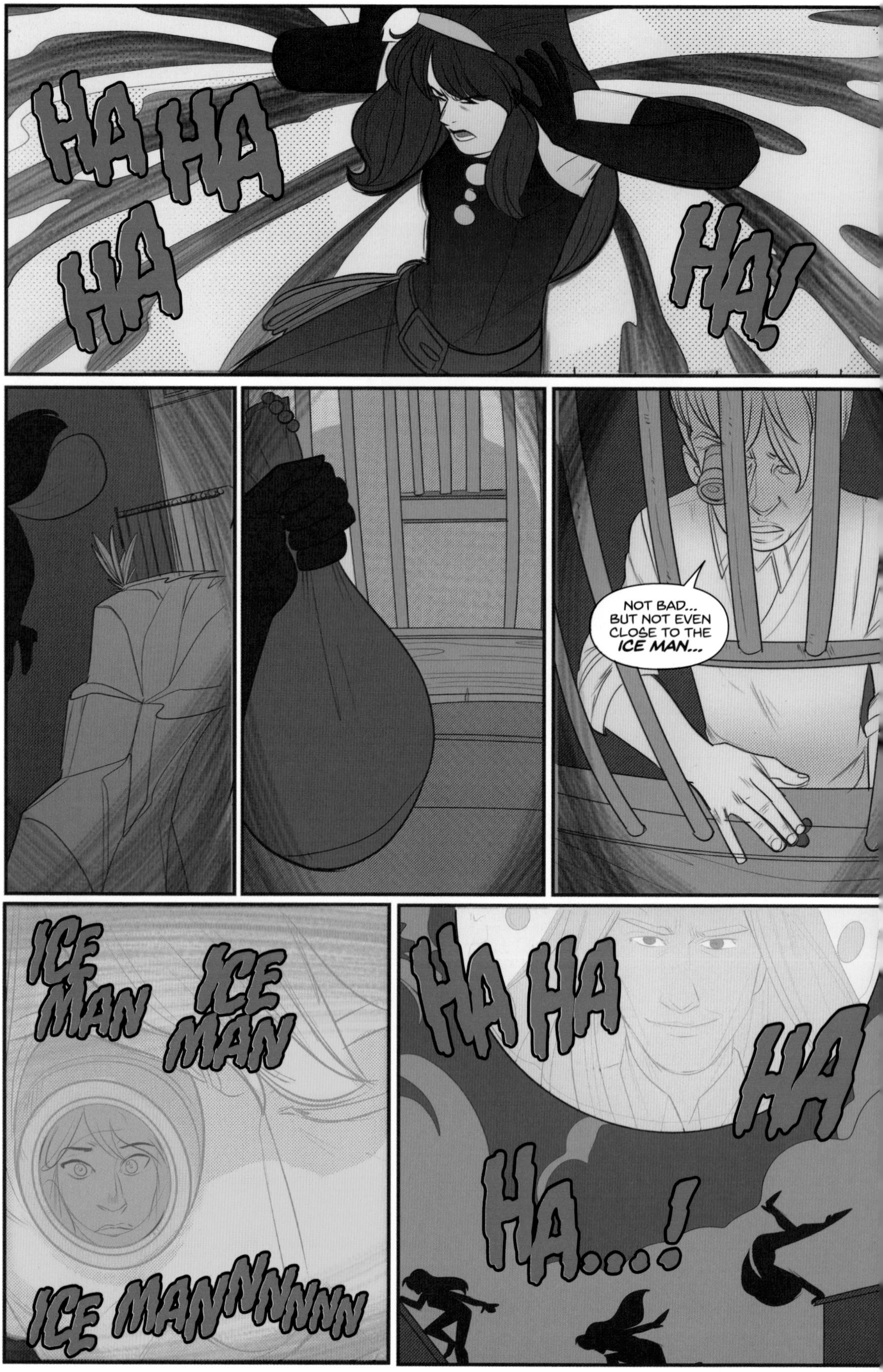
HA HA HA
HA
HA!
NOT BAD... BUT NOT EVEN CLOSE TO THE ICE MAN...
ICE MAN
ICE MAN
ICE MANNNNNN
HA HA
HA
HA...!

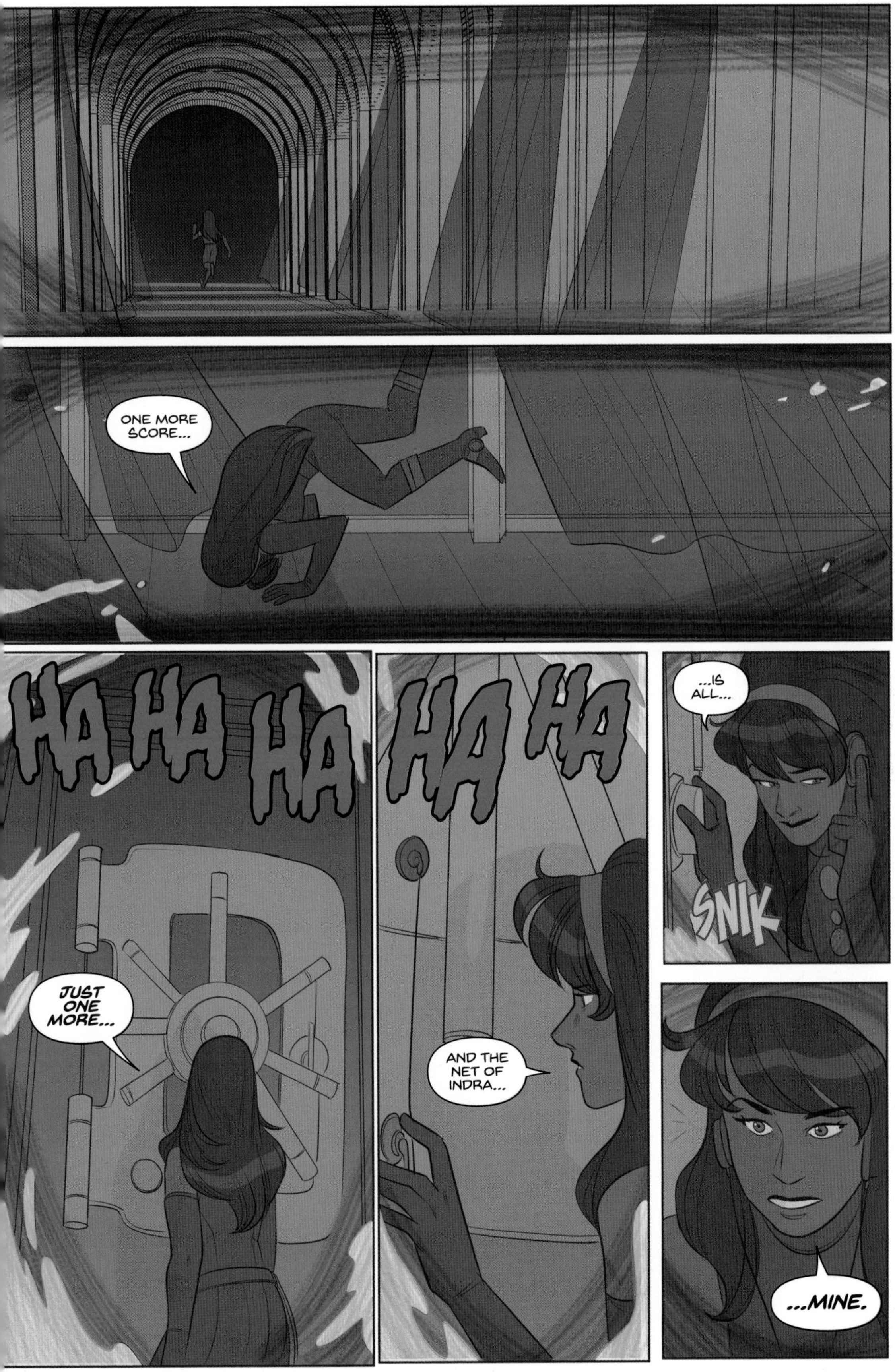
ONE MORE SCORE...
HA HA HA HA HA
JUST ONE MORE...
AND THE NET OF INDRA...
...IS ALL...
SNIK
...MINE.

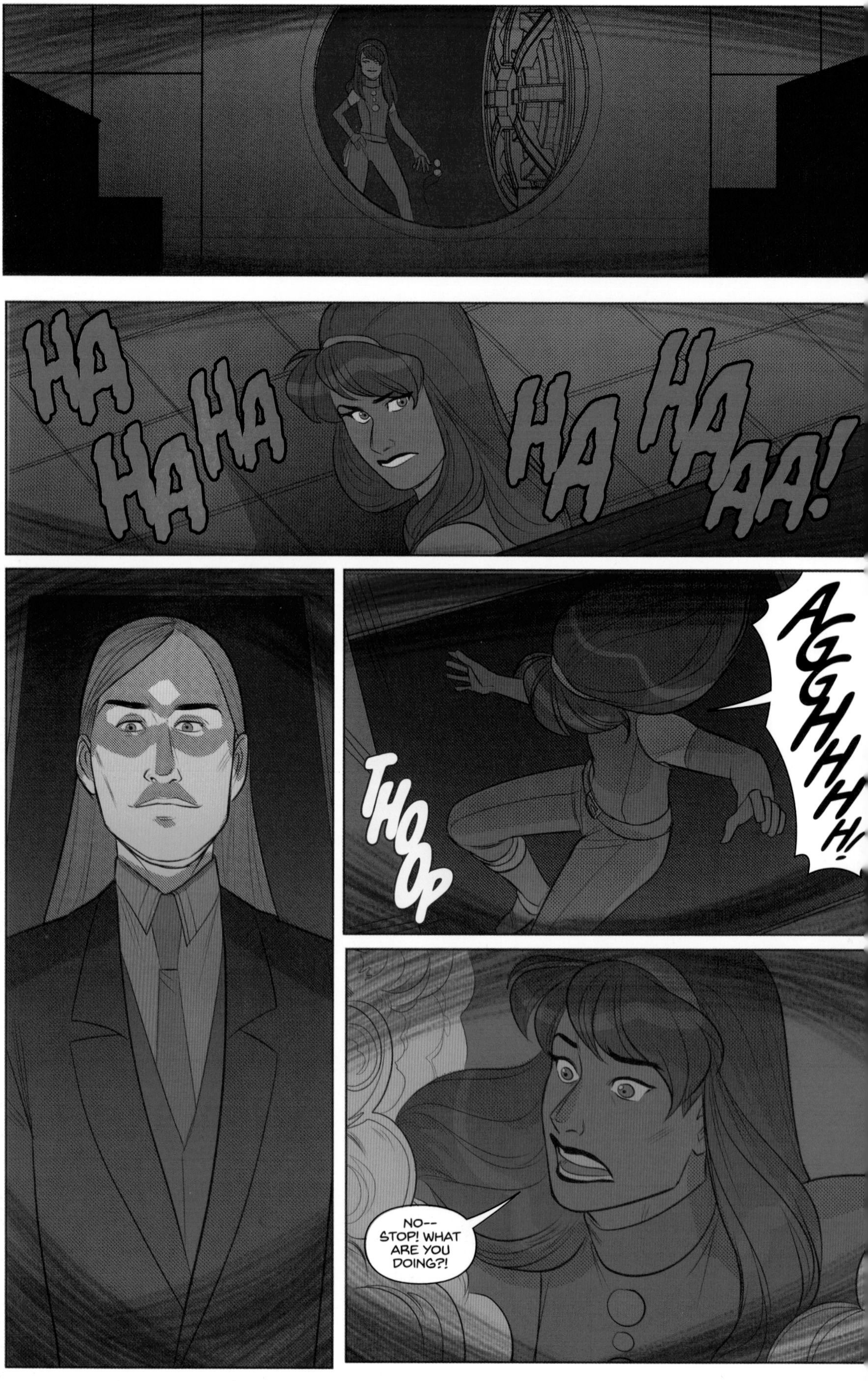
HA HAHA HA HA HAAA!
AGGHHHHH!
THOOP
NO-- STOP! WHAT ARE YOU DOING?!

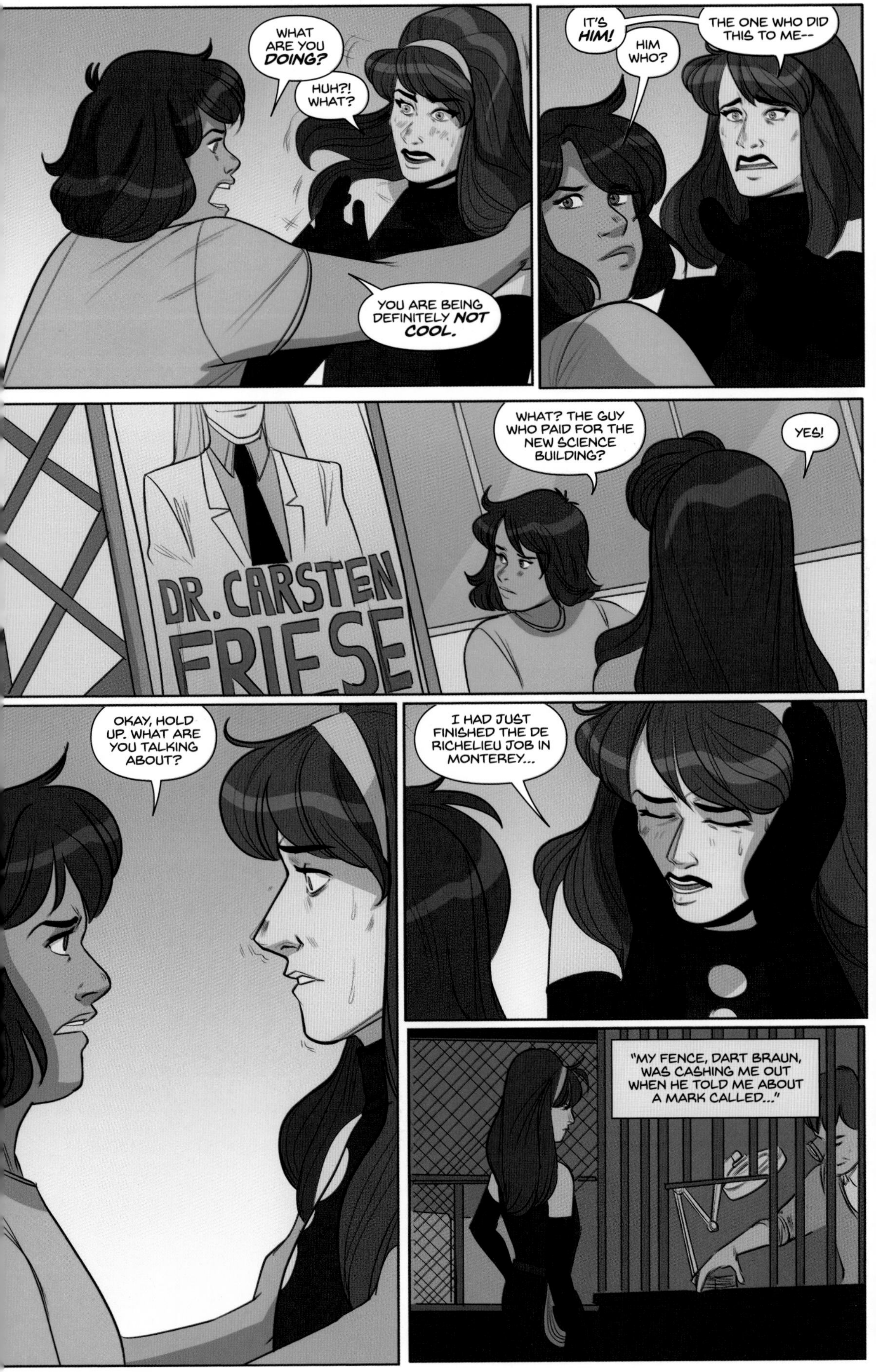
WHAT ARE YOU DOING?
HUH?! WHAT?
YOU ARE BEING DEFINITELY NOT COOL.
IT'S HIM!
HIM WHO?
THE ONE WHO DID THIS TO ME--
DR. CARSTEN FRIESE
WHAT? THE GUY WHO PAID FOR THE NEW SCIENCE BUILDING?
YES!
OKAY, HOLD UP. WHAT ARE YOU TALKING ABOUT?
I HAD JUST FINISHED THE DE RICHELIEU JOB IN MONTEREY...
"MY FENCE, DART BRAUN, WAS CASHING ME OUT WHEN HE TOLD ME ABOUT A MARK CALLED..."

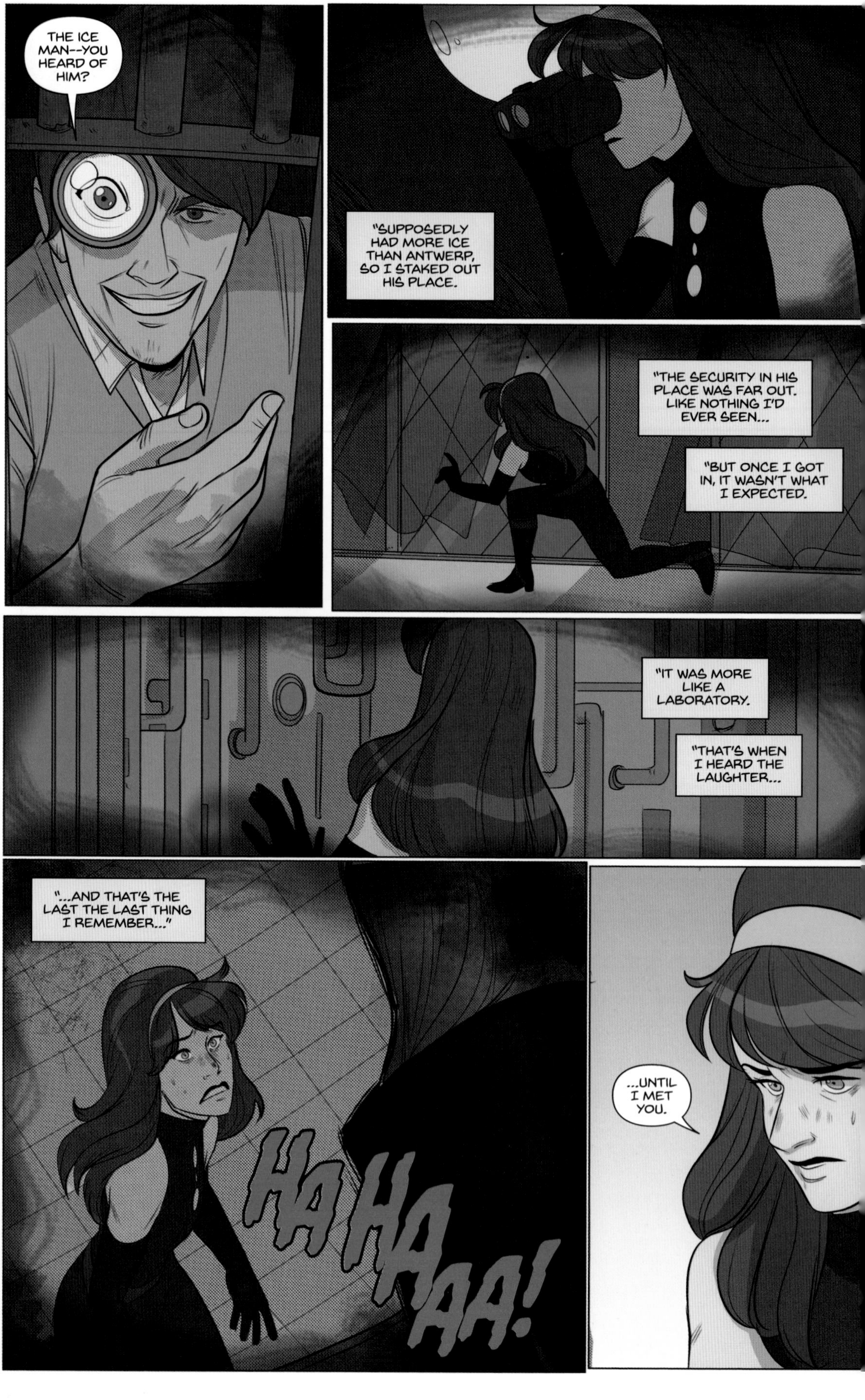
THE ICE MAN--YOU HEARD OF HIM?
"SUPPOSEDLY HAD MORE ICE THAN ANTWERP, SO I STAKED OUT HIS PLACE.
"THE SECURITY IN HIS PLACE WAS FAR OUT. LIKE NOTHING I'D EVER SEEN...
"BUT ONCE I GOT IN, IT WASN'T WHAT I EXPECTED.
"IT WAS MORE LIKE A LABORATORY.
"THAT'S WHEN I HEARD THE LAUGHTER...
"...AND THAT'S THE LAST THE LAST THING I REMEMBER..."
HA HA HA AA!
...UNTIL I MET YOU.

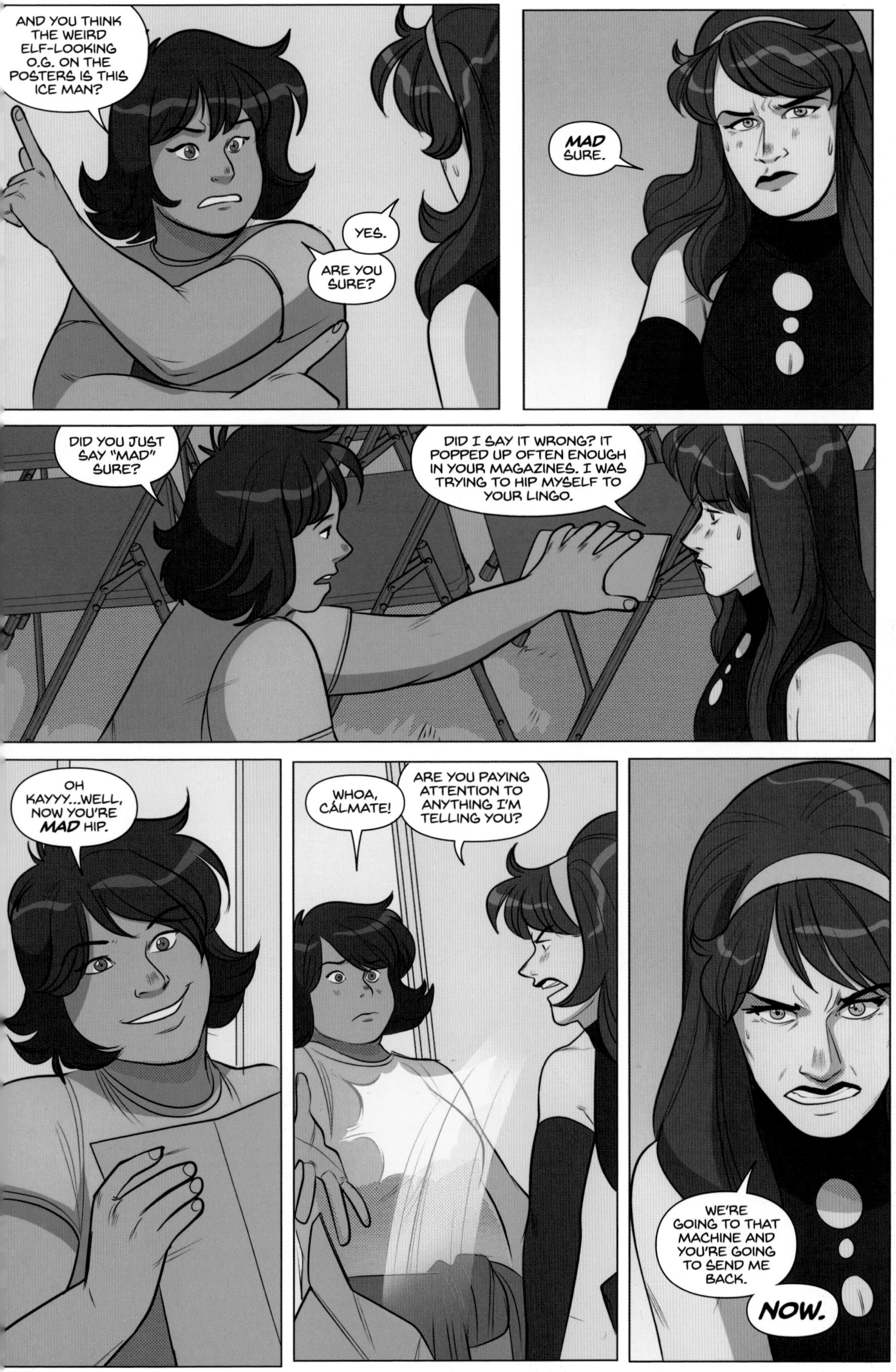
AND YOU THINK THE WEIRD ELF-LOOKING O.G. ON THE POSTERS IS THIS ICE MAN?
YES.
ARE YOU SURE?
MAD SURE.
DID YOU JUST SAY "MAD" SURE?
DID I SAY IT WRONG? IT POPPED UP OFTEN ENOUGH IN YOUR MAGAZINES. I WAS TRYING TO HIP MYSELF TO YOUR LINGO.
OH KAYYY...WELL, NOW YOU'RE MAD HIP.
WHOA, CÁLMATE!
ARE YOU PAYING ATTENTION TO ANYTHING I'M TELLING YOU?
WE'RE GOING TO THAT MACHINE AND YOU'RE GOING TO SEND ME BACK.
NOW.

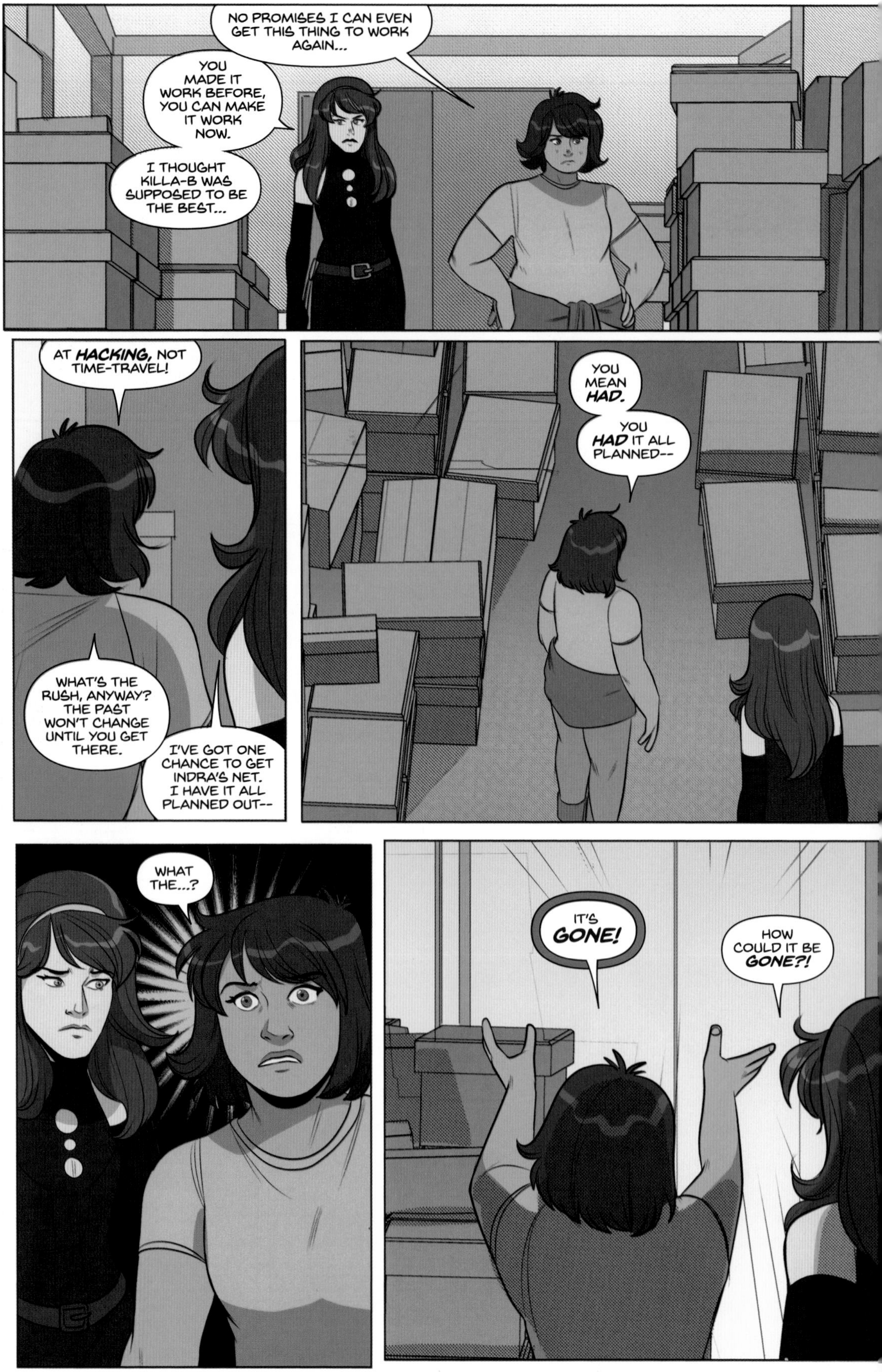
NO PROMISES I CAN EVEN GET THIS THING TO WORK AGAIN...
YOU MADE IT WORK BEFORE, YOU CAN MAKE IT WORK NOW.
I THOUGHT KILLA-B WAS SUPPOSED TO BE THE BEST...
AT HACKING, NOT TIME-TRAVEL!
WHAT'S THE RUSH, ANYWAY? THE PAST WON'T CHANGE UNTIL YOU GET THERE.
I'VE GOT ONE CHANCE TO GET INDRA'S NET. I HAVE IT ALL PLANNED OUT--
YOU MEAN HAD.
YOU HAD IT ALL PLANNED--
WHAT THE...?
IT'S GONE!
HOW COULD IT BE GONE?!

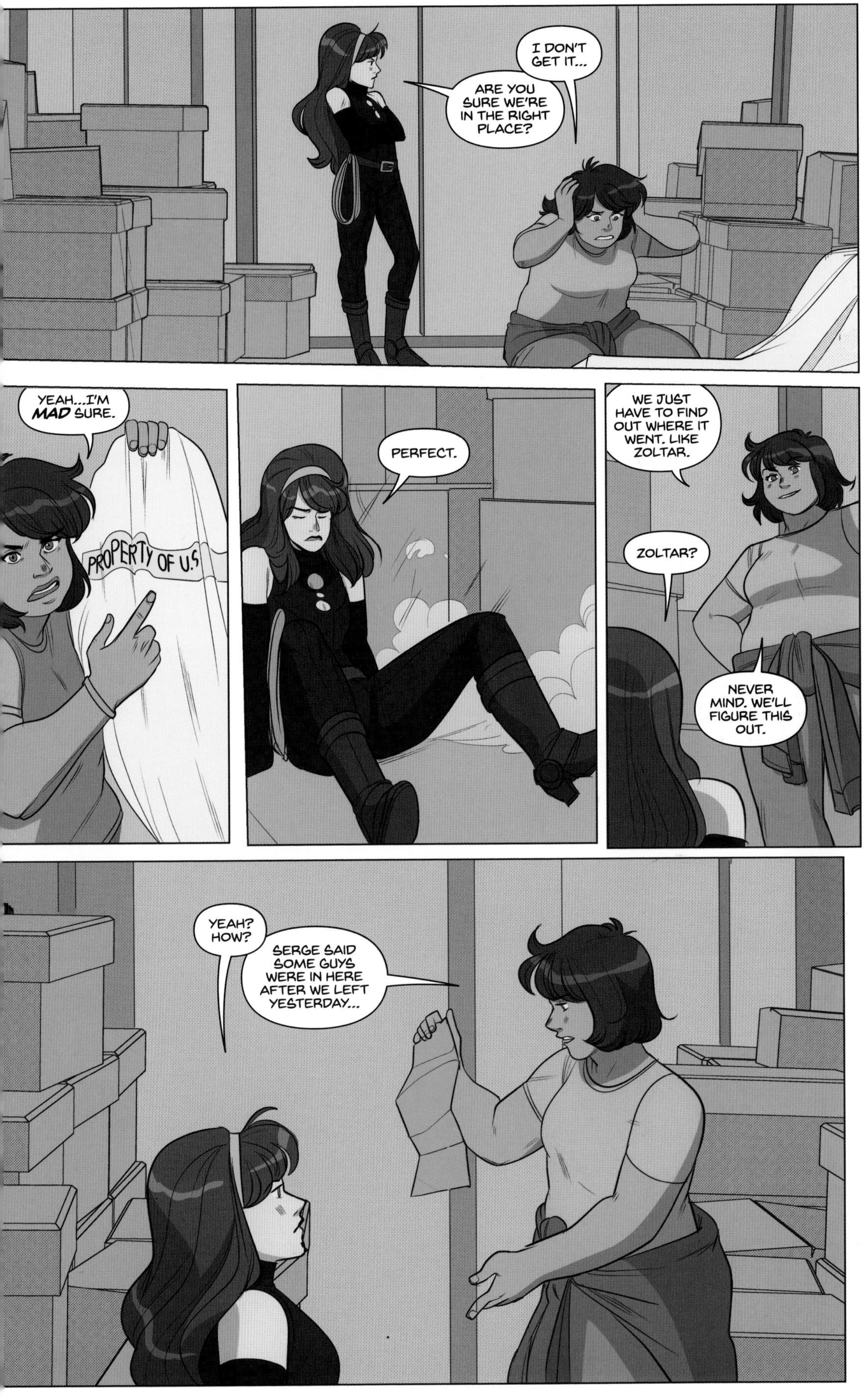
ARE YOU SURE WE'RE IN THE RIGHT PLACE?
I DON'T GET IT...
YEAH...I'M *MAD* SURE.
PROPERTY OF U.S
PERFECT.
WE JUST HAVE TO FIND OUT WHERE IT WENT. LIKE ZOLTAR.
ZOLTAR?
NEVER MIND. WE'LL FIGURE THIS OUT.
YEAH? HOW?
SERGE SAID SOME GUYS WERE IN HERE AFTER WE LEFT YESTERDAY...

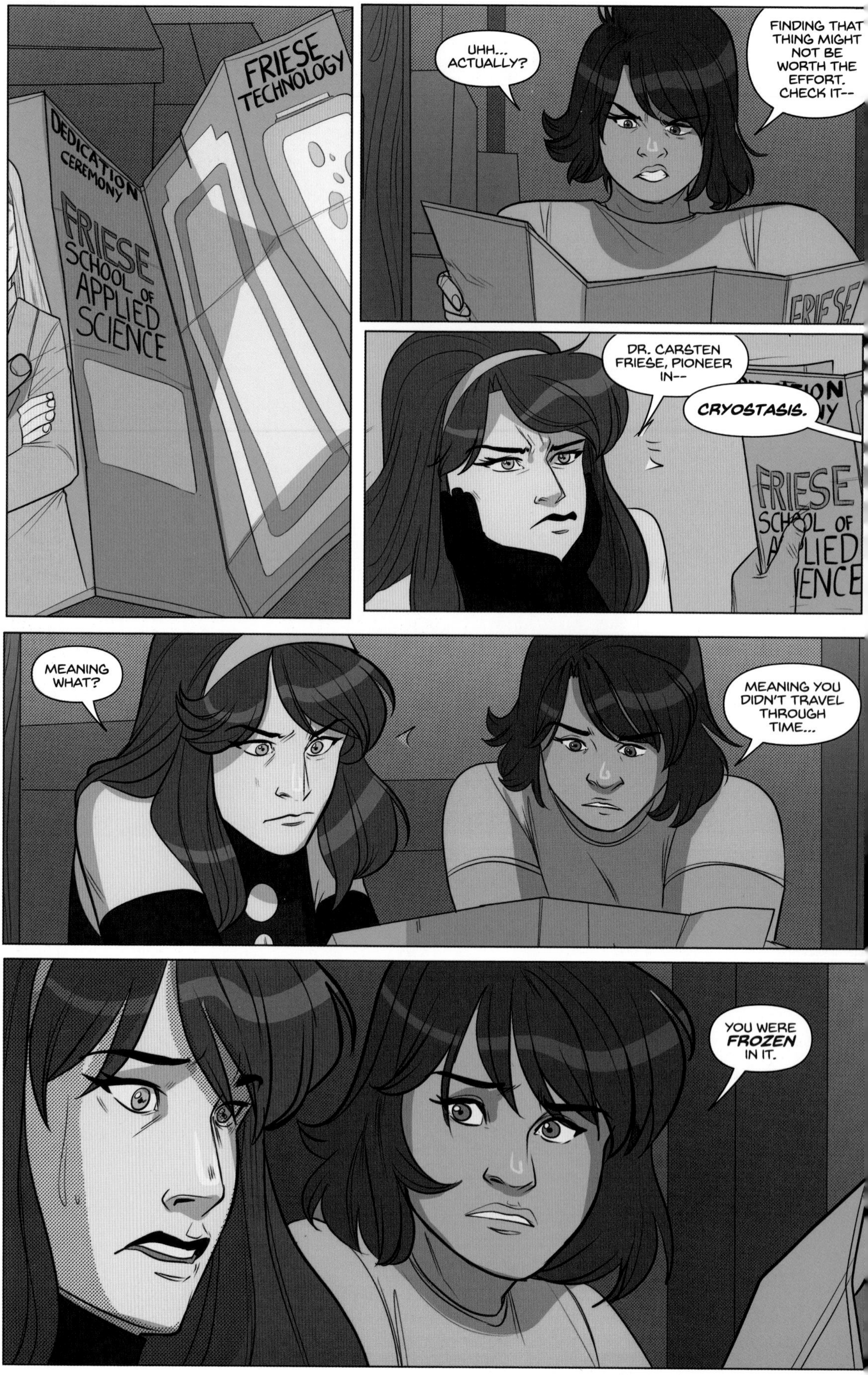
DEDICATION CEREMONY
FRIESE SCHOOL OF APPLIED SCIENCE
FRIESE TECHNOLOGY
UHH... ACTUALLY?
FINDING THAT THING MIGHT NOT BE WORTH THE EFFORT. CHECK IT--
DR. CARSTEN FRIESE, PIONEER IN--
CRYOSTASIS.
MEANING WHAT?
MEANING YOU DIDN'T TRAVEL THROUGH TIME...
YOU WERE FROZEN IN IT.

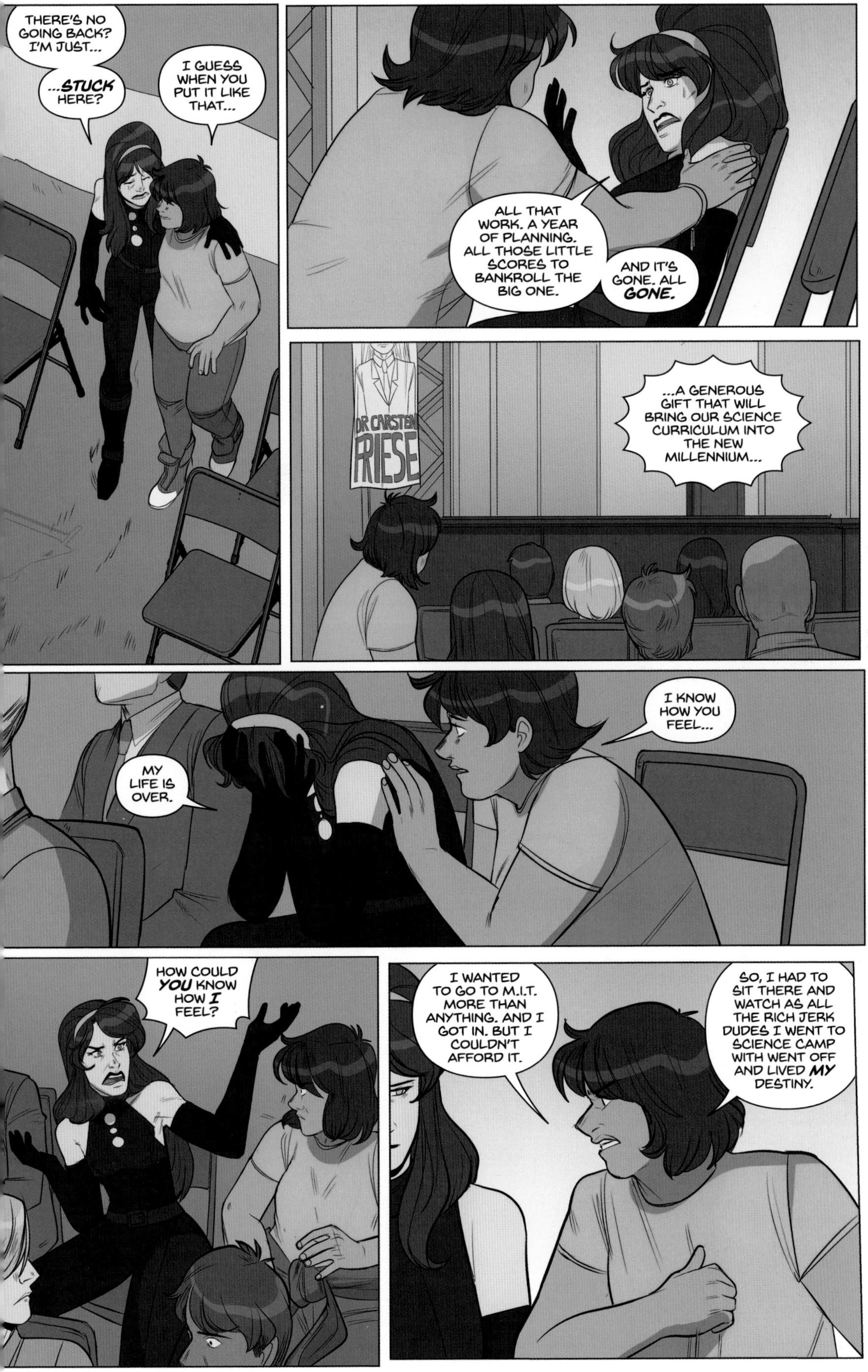
THERE'S NO GOING BACK? I'M JUST...
...STUCK HERE?
I GUESS WHEN YOU PUT IT LIKE THAT...
ALL THAT WORK. A YEAR OF PLANNING. ALL THOSE LITTLE SCORES TO BANKROLL THE BIG ONE.
AND IT'S GONE. ALL GONE.
DR CARSTEN FRIESE
...A GENEROUS GIFT THAT WILL BRING OUR SCIENCE CURRICULUM INTO THE NEW MILLENNIUM...
I KNOW HOW YOU FEEL...
MY LIFE IS OVER.
HOW COULD YOU KNOW HOW I FEEL?
I WANTED TO GO TO M.I.T. MORE THAN ANYTHING. AND I GOT IN. BUT I COULDN'T AFFORD IT.
SO, I HAD TO SIT THERE AND WATCH AS ALL THE RICH JERK DUDES I WENT TO SCIENCE CAMP WITH WENT OFF AND LIVED MY DESTINY.

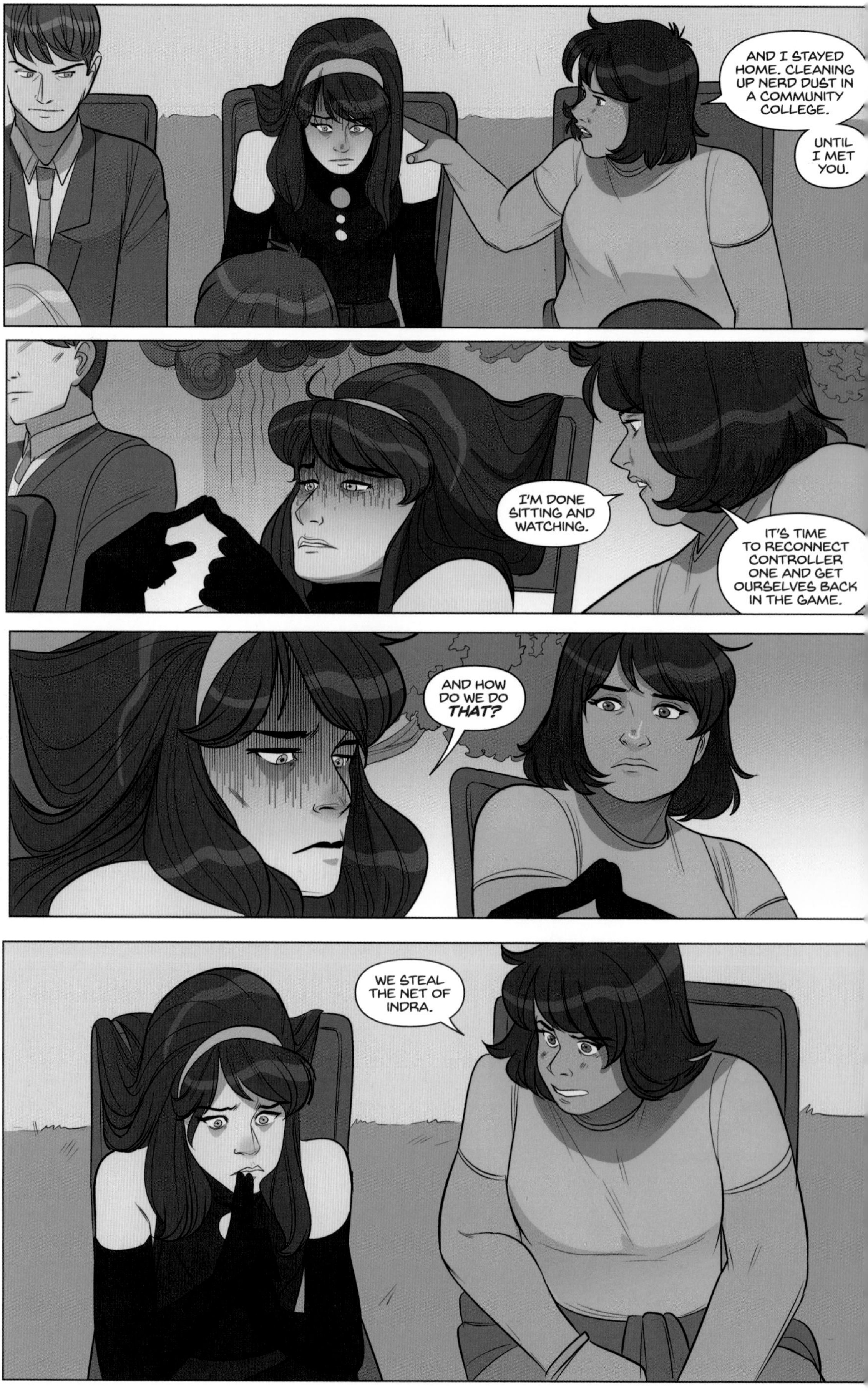
AND I STAYED HOME. CLEANING UP NERD DUST IN A COMMUNITY COLLEGE.
UNTIL I MET YOU.
I'M DONE SITTING AND WATCHING.
IT'S TIME TO RECONNECT CONTROLLER ONE AND GET OURSELVES BACK IN THE GAME.
AND HOW DO WE DO *THAT?*
WE STEAL THE NET OF INDRA.

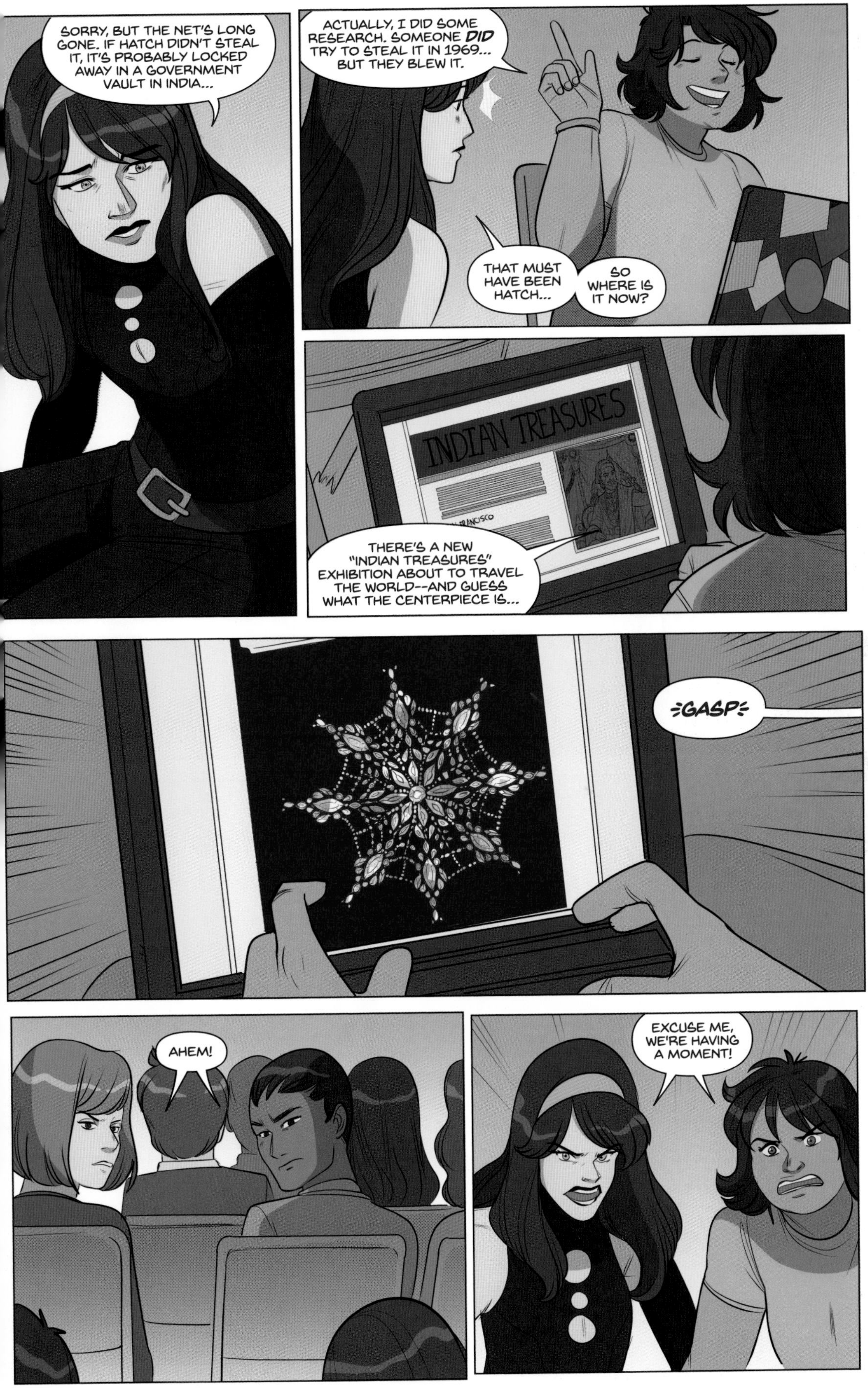
SORRY, BUT THE NET'S LONG GONE. IF HATCH DIDN'T STEAL IT, IT'S PROBABLY LOCKED AWAY IN A GOVERNMENT VAULT IN INDIA...
ACTUALLY, I DID SOME RESEARCH. SOMEONE *DID* TRY TO STEAL IT IN 1969... BUT THEY BLEW IT.
THAT MUST HAVE BEEN HATCH...
SO WHERE IS IT NOW?
INDIAN TREASURES
THERE'S A NEW "INDIAN TREASURES" EXHIBITION ABOUT TO TRAVEL THE WORLD--AND GUESS WHAT THE CENTERPIECE IS...
GASP
AHEM!
EXCUSE ME, WE'RE HAVING A MOMENT!

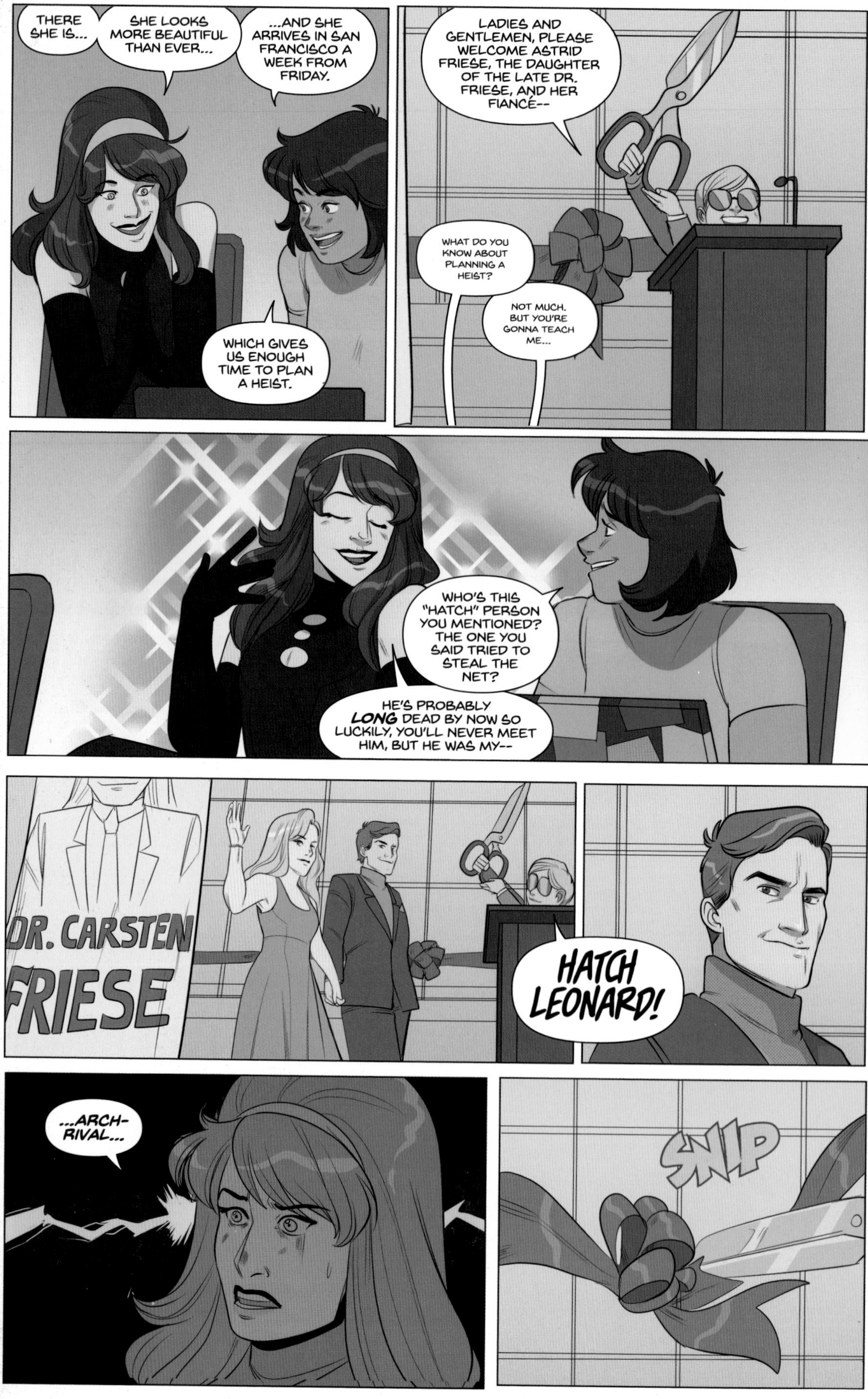
THERE SHE IS...
SHE LOOKS MORE BEAUTIFUL THAN EVER...
...AND SHE ARRIVES IN SAN FRANCISCO A WEEK FROM FRIDAY.
WHICH GIVES US ENOUGH TIME TO PLAN A HEIST.
LADIES AND GENTLEMEN, PLEASE WELCOME ASTRID FRIESE, THE DAUGHTER OF THE LATE DR. FRIESE, AND HER FIANCÉ--
WHAT DO YOU KNOW ABOUT PLANNING A HEIST?
NOT MUCH. BUT YOU'RE GONNA TEACH ME...
WHO'S THIS "HATCH" PERSON YOU MENTIONED? THE ONE YOU SAID TRIED TO STEAL THE NET?
HE'S PROBABLY LONG DEAD BY NOW SO LUCKILY, YOU'LL NEVER MEET HIM, BUT HE WAS MY--
DR. CARSTEN FRIESE
HATCH LEONARD!
...ARCH-RIVAL...
SNIP

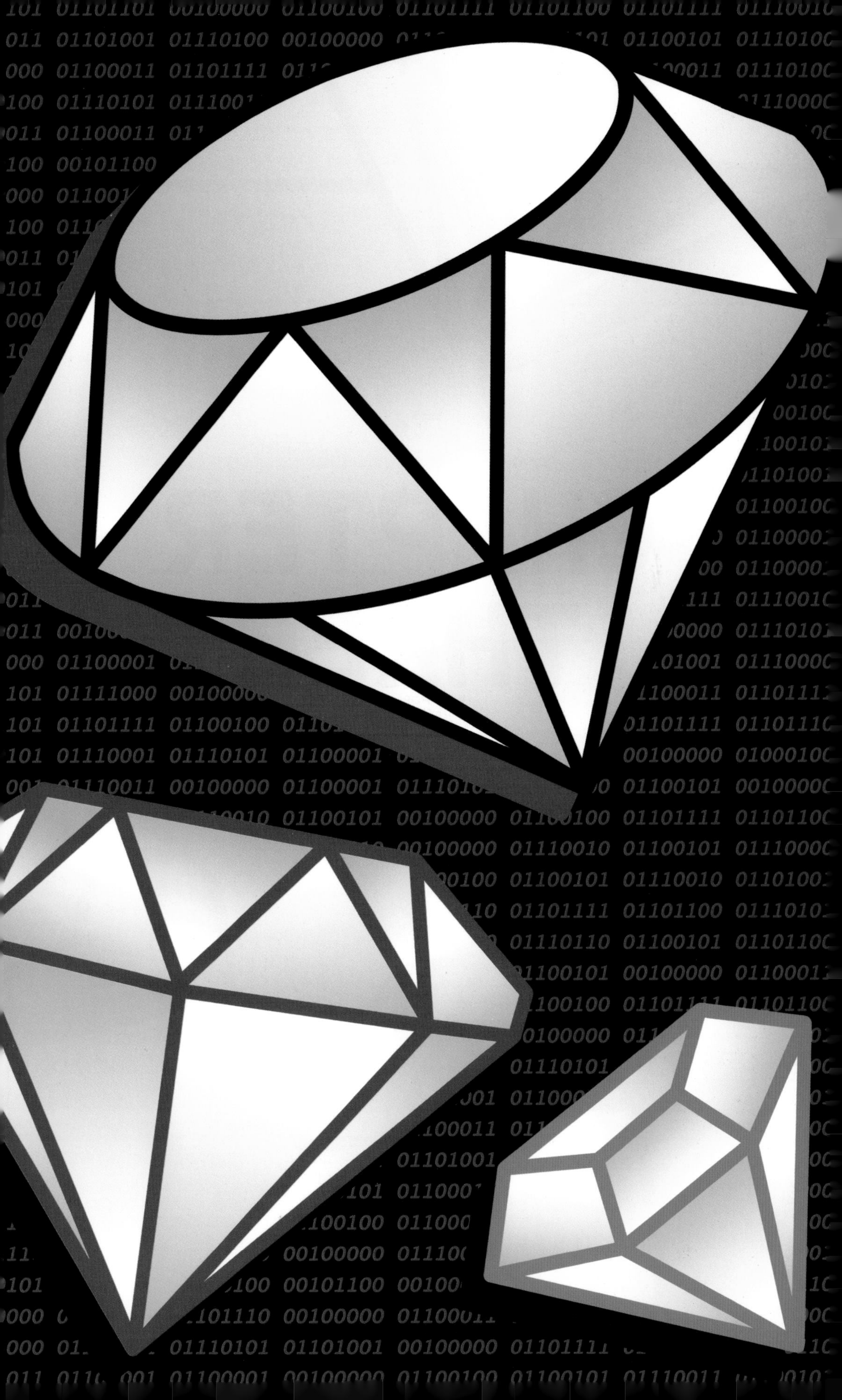

# CHAPTER THREE

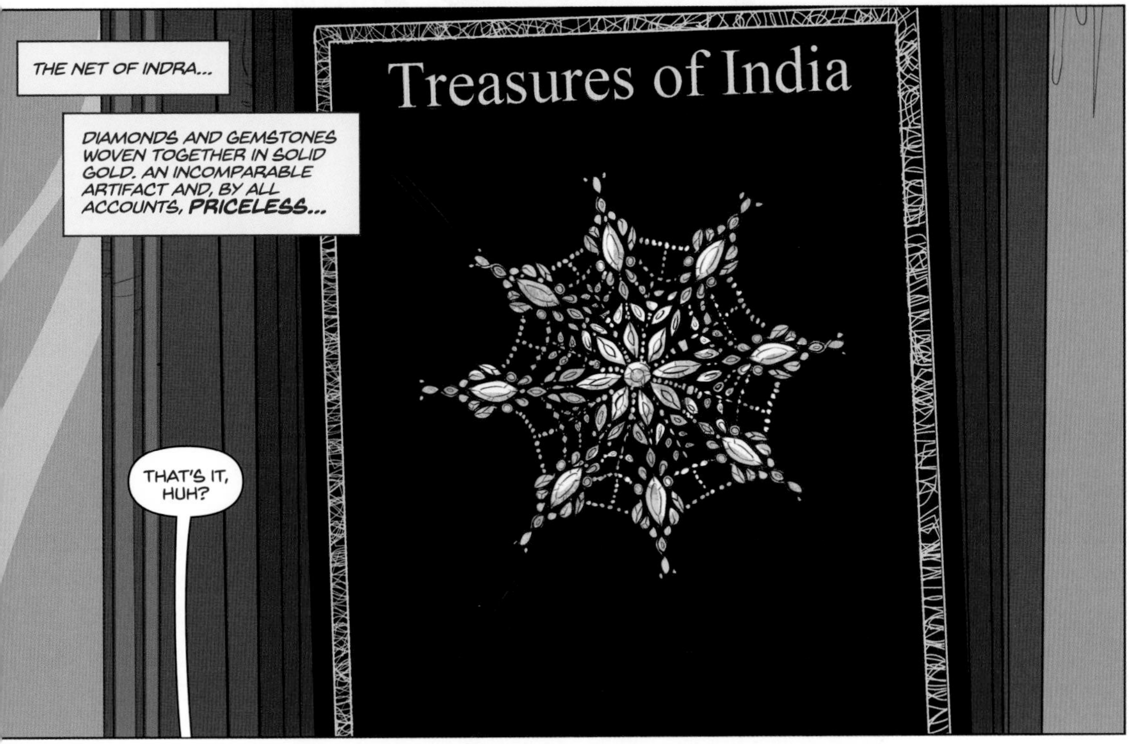

Treasures of India
THE NET OF INDRA...
DIAMONDS AND GEMSTONES WOVEN TOGETHER IN SOLID GOLD. AN INCOMPARABLE ARTIFACT AND, BY ALL ACCOUNTS, PRICELESS...
THAT'S IT, HUH?


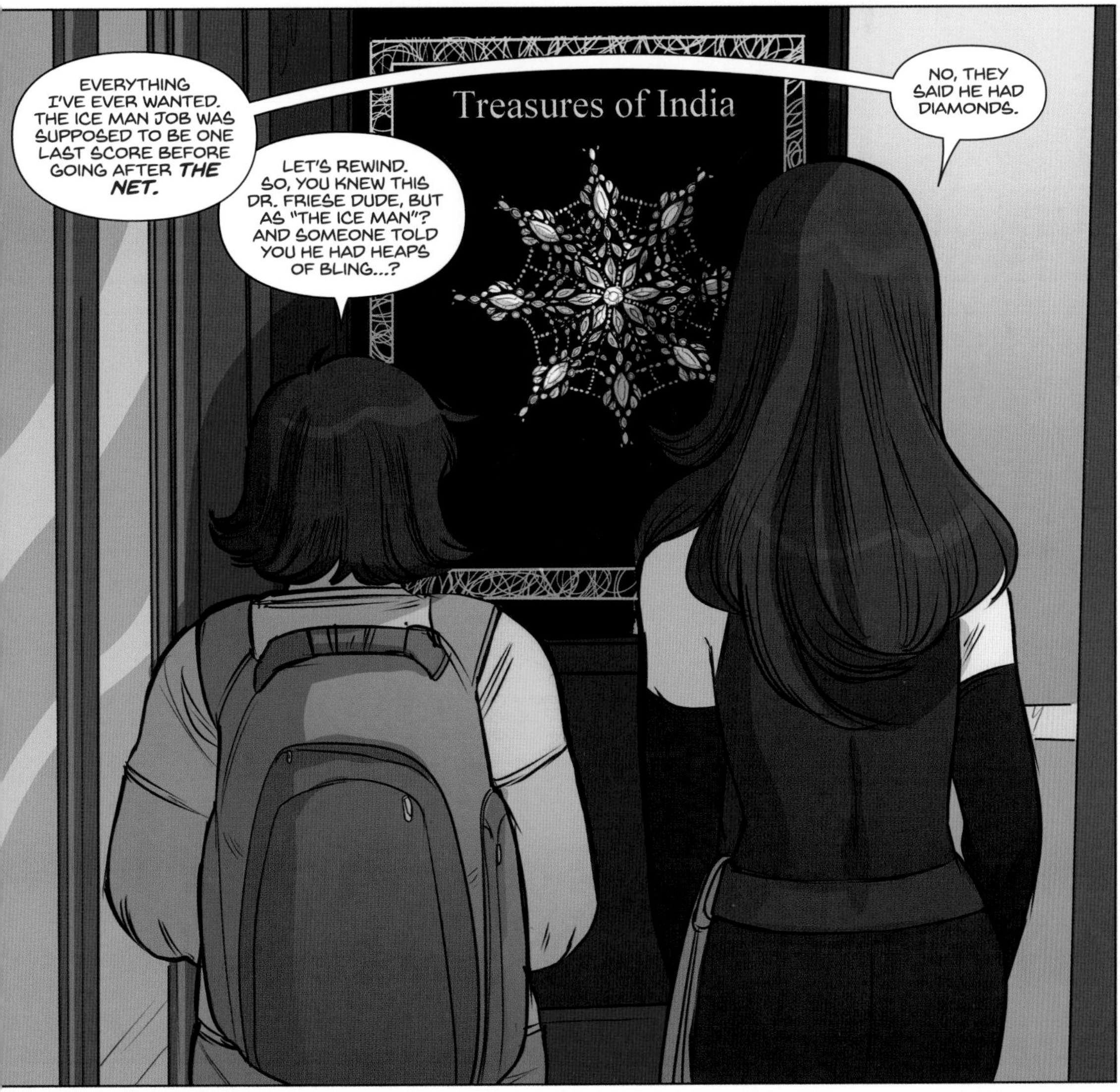

Treasures of India
EVERYTHING I'VE EVER WANTED. THE ICE MAN JOB WAS SUPPOSED TO BE ONE LAST SCORE BEFORE GOING AFTER THE NET.
LET'S REWIND. SO, YOU KNEW THIS DR. FRIESE DUDE, BUT AS "THE ICE MAN"? AND SOMEONE TOLD YOU HE HAD HEAPS OF BLING...?
NO, THEY SAID HE HAD DIAMONDS.

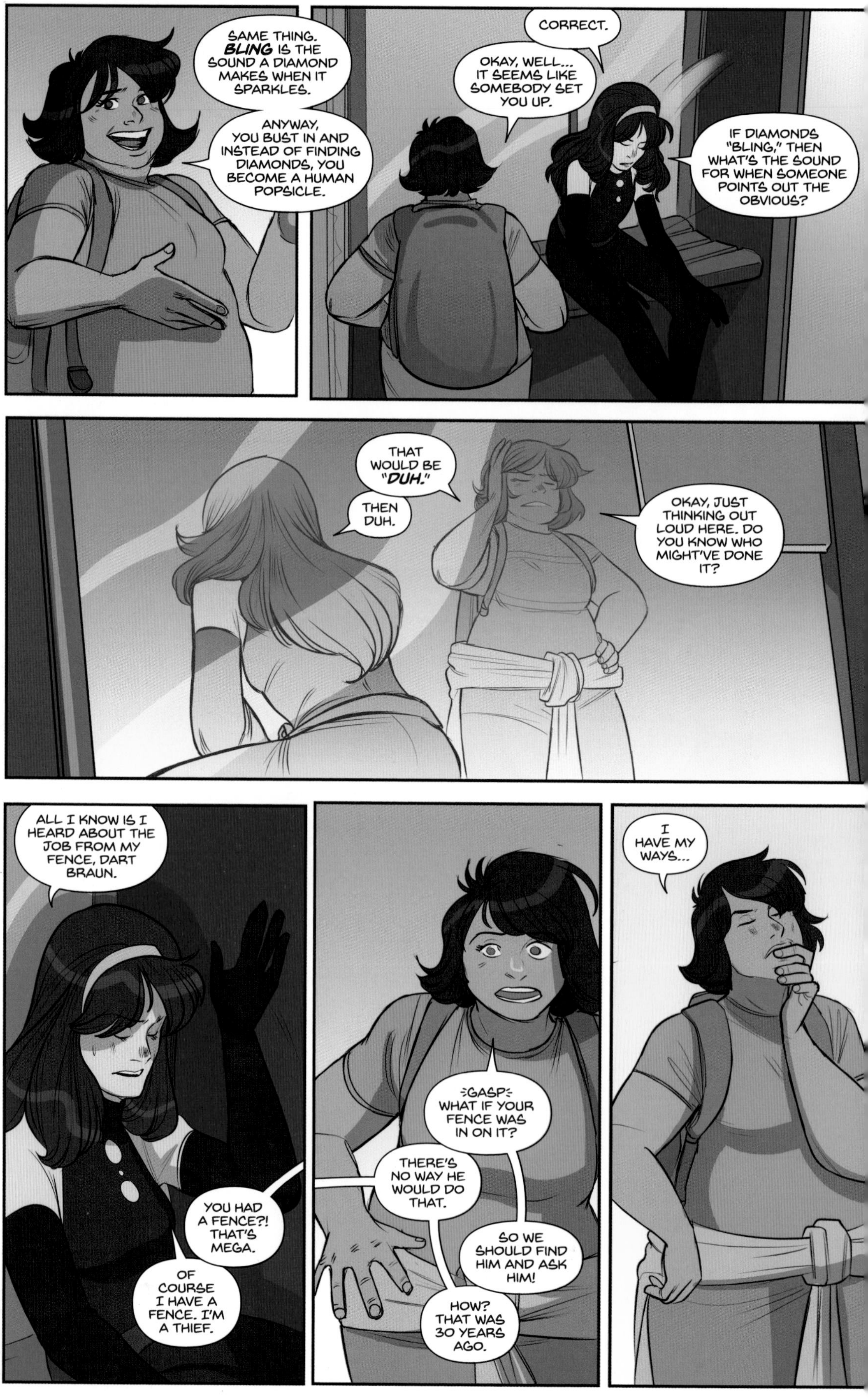
SAME THING. BLING IS THE SOUND A DIAMOND MAKES WHEN IT SPARKLES.
ANYWAY, YOU BUST IN AND INSTEAD OF FINDING DIAMONDS, YOU BECOME A HUMAN POPSICLE.
CORRECT.
OKAY, WELL... IT SEEMS LIKE SOMEBODY SET YOU UP.
IF DIAMONDS "BLING," THEN WHAT'S THE SOUND FOR WHEN SOMEONE POINTS OUT THE OBVIOUS?
THAT WOULD BE "DUH."
THEN DUH.
OKAY, JUST THINKING OUT LOUD HERE. DO YOU KNOW WHO MIGHT'VE DONE IT?
ALL I KNOW IS I HEARD ABOUT THE JOB FROM MY FENCE, DART BRAUN.
YOU HAD A FENCE?! THAT'S MEGA.
OF COURSE I HAVE A FENCE. I'M A THIEF.
GASP
WHAT IF YOUR FENCE WAS IN ON IT?
THERE'S NO WAY HE WOULD DO THAT.
SO WE SHOULD FIND HIM AND ASK HIM!
HOW? THAT WAS 30 YEARS AGO.
I HAVE MY WAYS...

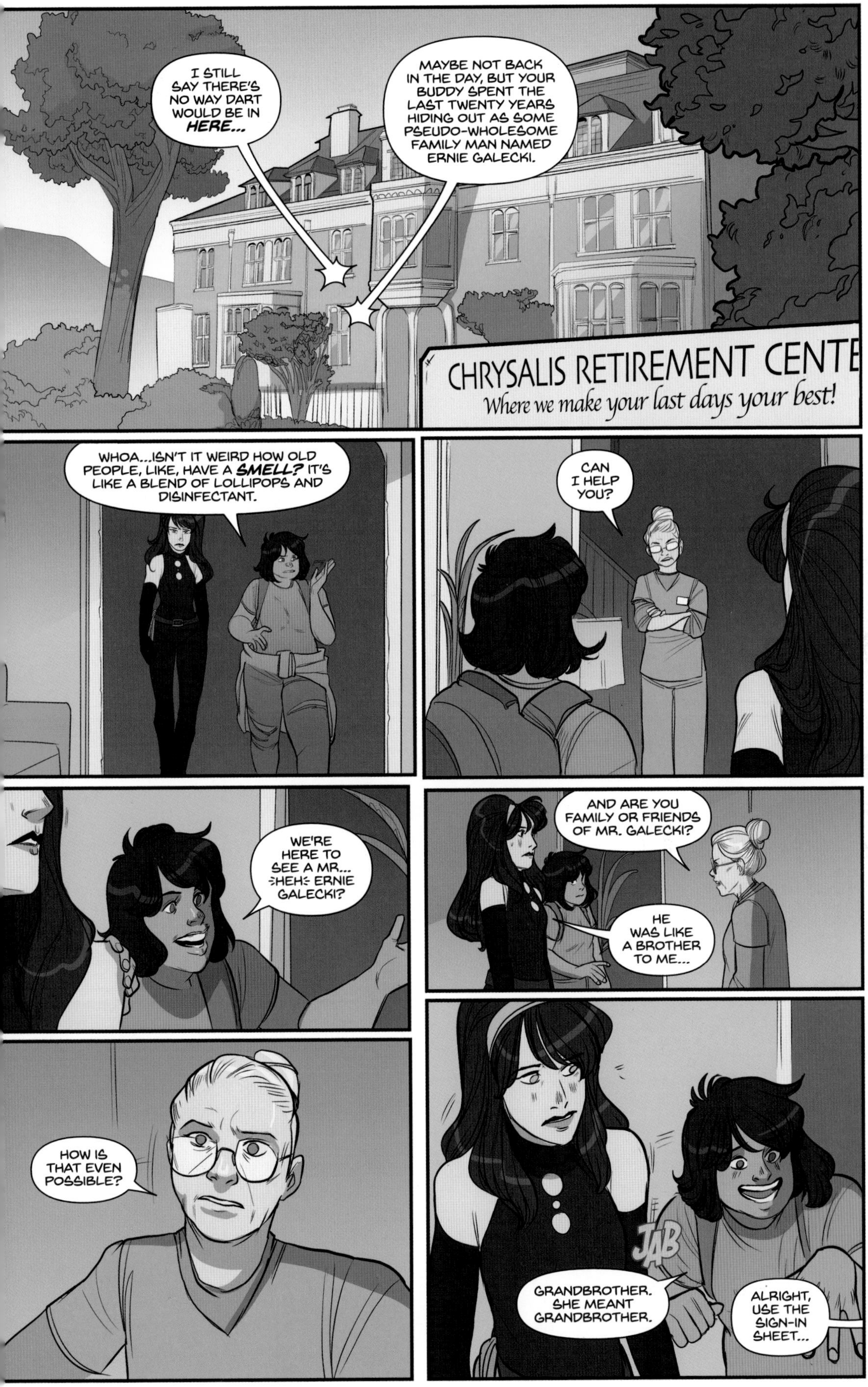

I STILL SAY THERE'S NO WAY DART WOULD BE IN HERE...
MAYBE NOT BACK IN THE DAY, BUT YOUR BUDDY SPENT THE LAST TWENTY YEARS HIDING OUT AS SOME PSEUDO-WHOLESOME FAMILY MAN NAMED ERNIE GALECKI.
CHRYSALIS RETIREMENT CENTE
Where we make your last days your best!
WHOA...ISN'T IT WEIRD HOW OLD PEOPLE, LIKE, HAVE A SMELL? IT'S LIKE A BLEND OF LOLLIPOPS AND DISINFECTANT.
CAN I HELP YOU?
WE'RE HERE TO SEE A MR... HEH ERNIE GALECKI?
AND ARE YOU FAMILY OR FRIENDS OF MR. GALECKI?
HE WAS LIKE A BROTHER TO ME...
HOW IS THAT EVEN POSSIBLE?
JAB
GRANDBROTHER. SHE MEANT GRANDBROTHER.
ALRIGHT, USE THE SIGN-IN SHEET...

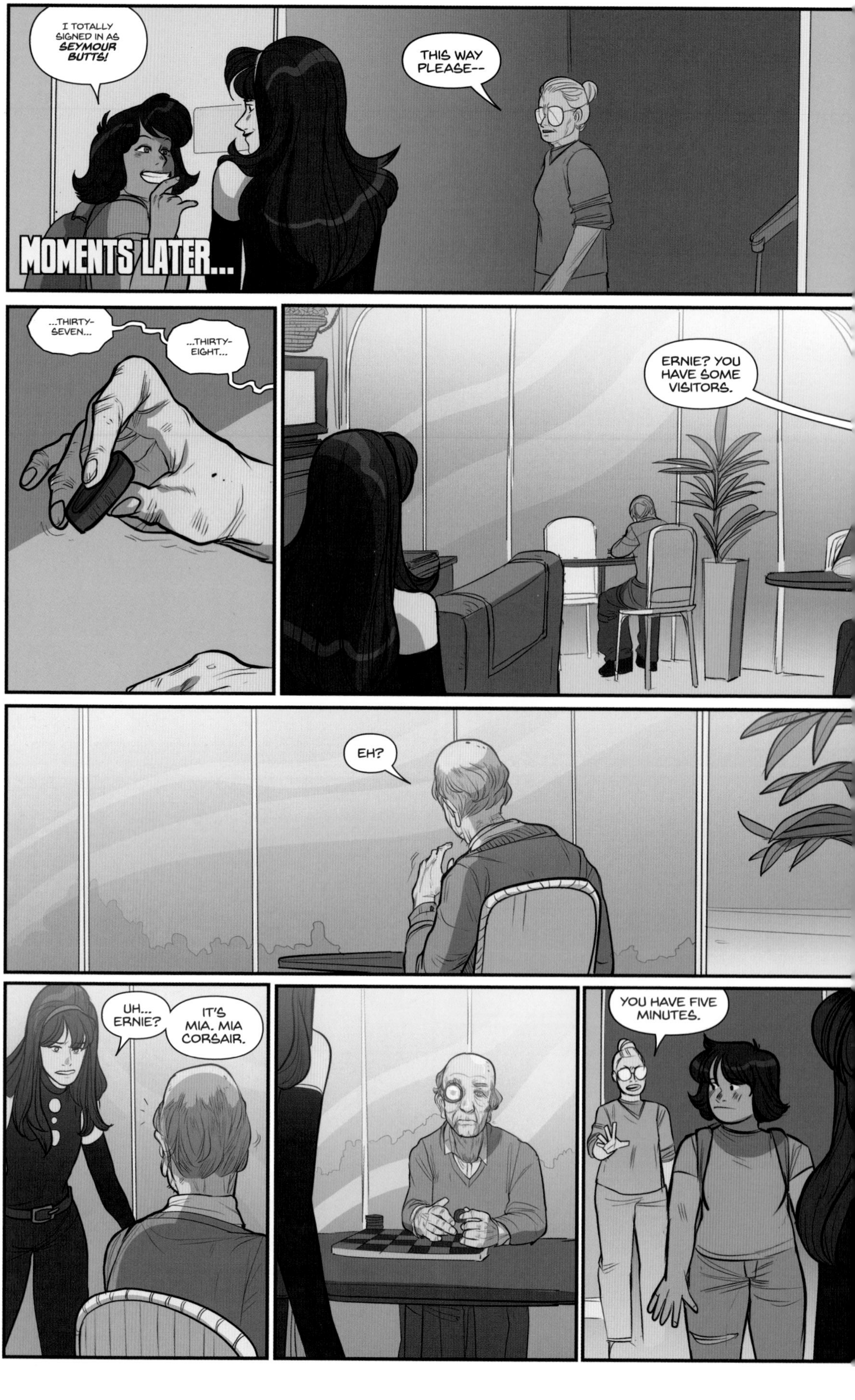
I TOTALLY SIGNED IN AS SEYMOUR BUTTS!
THIS WAY PLEASE--
MOMENTS LATER...
...THIRTY-SEVEN...
...THIRTY-EIGHT...
ERNIE? YOU HAVE SOME VISITORS.
EH?
UH... ERNIE?
IT'S MIA. MIA CORSAIR.
YOU HAVE FIVE MINUTES.

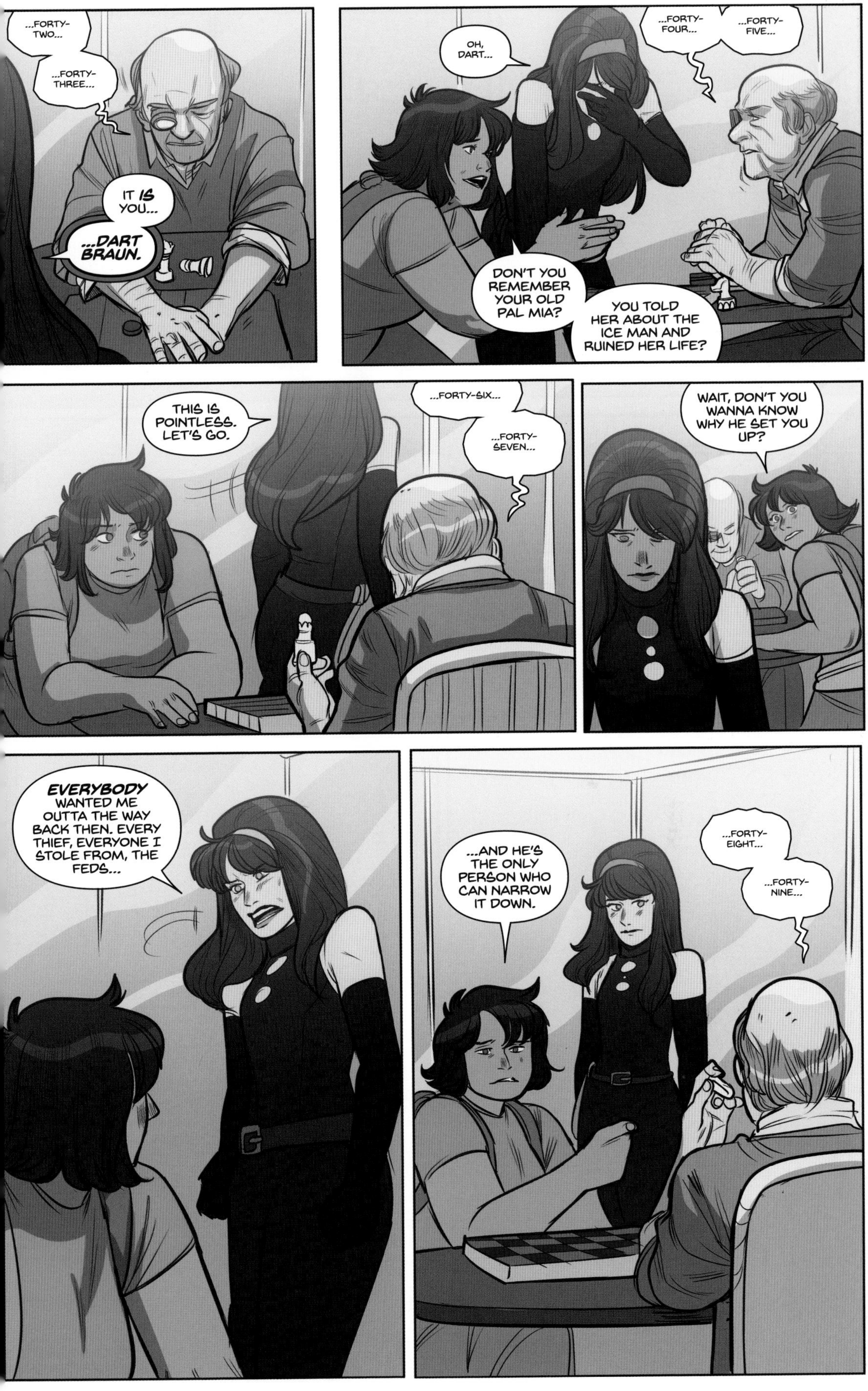

...FORTY-TWO...
...FORTY-THREE...
IT IS YOU...
...DART BRAUN.
OH, DART...
...FORTY-FOUR...
...FORTY-FIVE...
DON'T YOU REMEMBER YOUR OLD PAL MIA?
YOU TOLD HER ABOUT THE ICE MAN AND RUINED HER LIFE?
THIS IS POINTLESS. LET'S GO.
...FORTY-SIX...
...FORTY-SEVEN...
WAIT, DON'T YOU WANNA KNOW WHY HE SET YOU UP?
EVERYBODY WANTED ME OUTTA THE WAY BACK THEN. EVERY THIEF, EVERYONE I STOLE FROM, THE FEDS...
...AND HE'S THE ONLY PERSON WHO CAN NARROW IT DOWN.
...FORTY-EIGHT...
...FORTY-NINE...

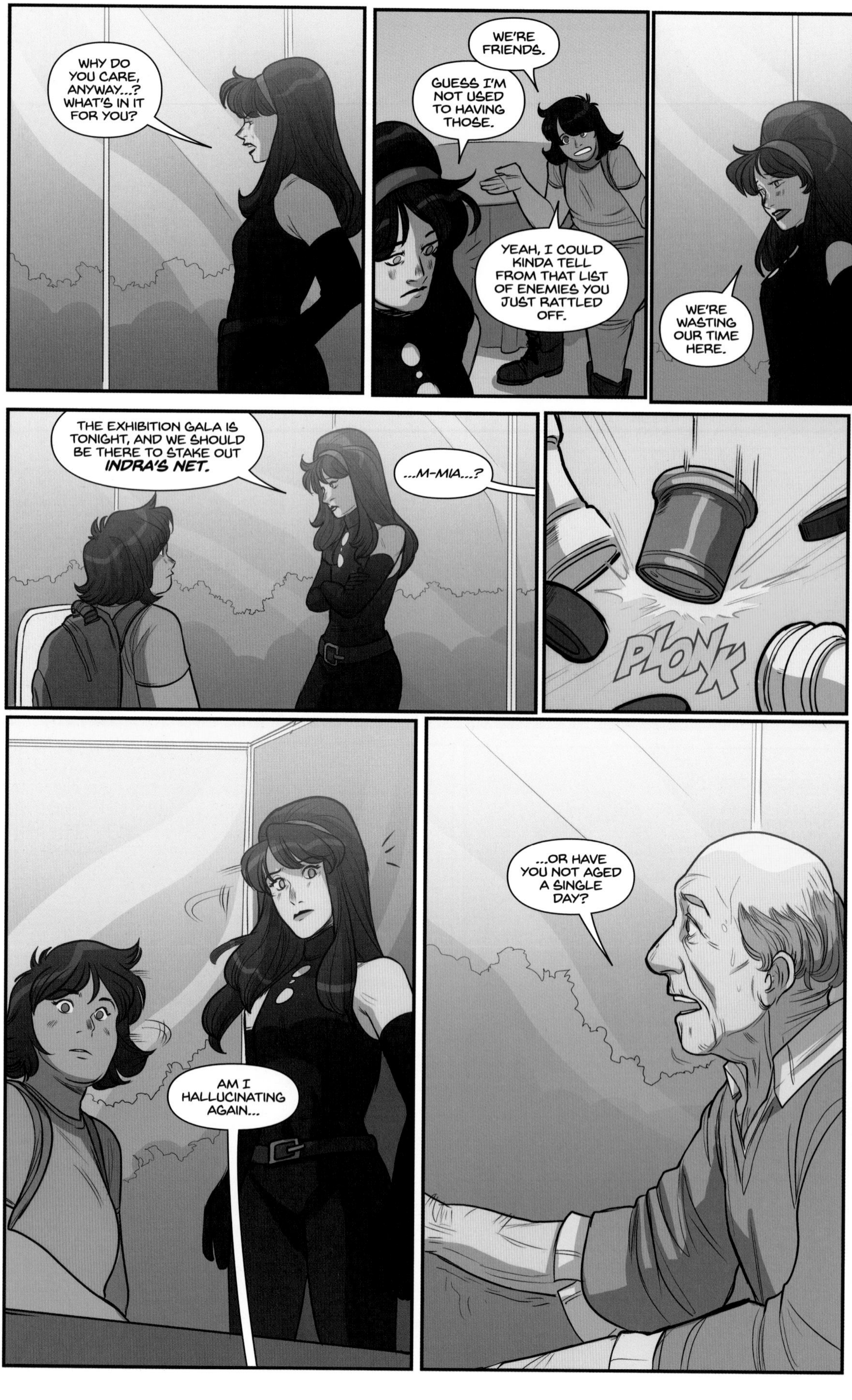
WHY DO YOU CARE, ANYWAY...? WHAT'S IN IT FOR YOU?
WE'RE FRIENDS.
GUESS I'M NOT USED TO HAVING THOSE.
YEAH, I COULD KINDA TELL FROM THAT LIST OF ENEMIES YOU JUST RATTLED OFF.
WE'RE WASTING OUR TIME HERE.
THE EXHIBITION GALA IS TONIGHT, AND WE SHOULD BE THERE TO STAKE OUT INDRA'S NET.
...M-MIA...?
PLONK
AM I HALLUCINATING AGAIN...
...OR HAVE YOU NOT AGED A SINGLE DAY?

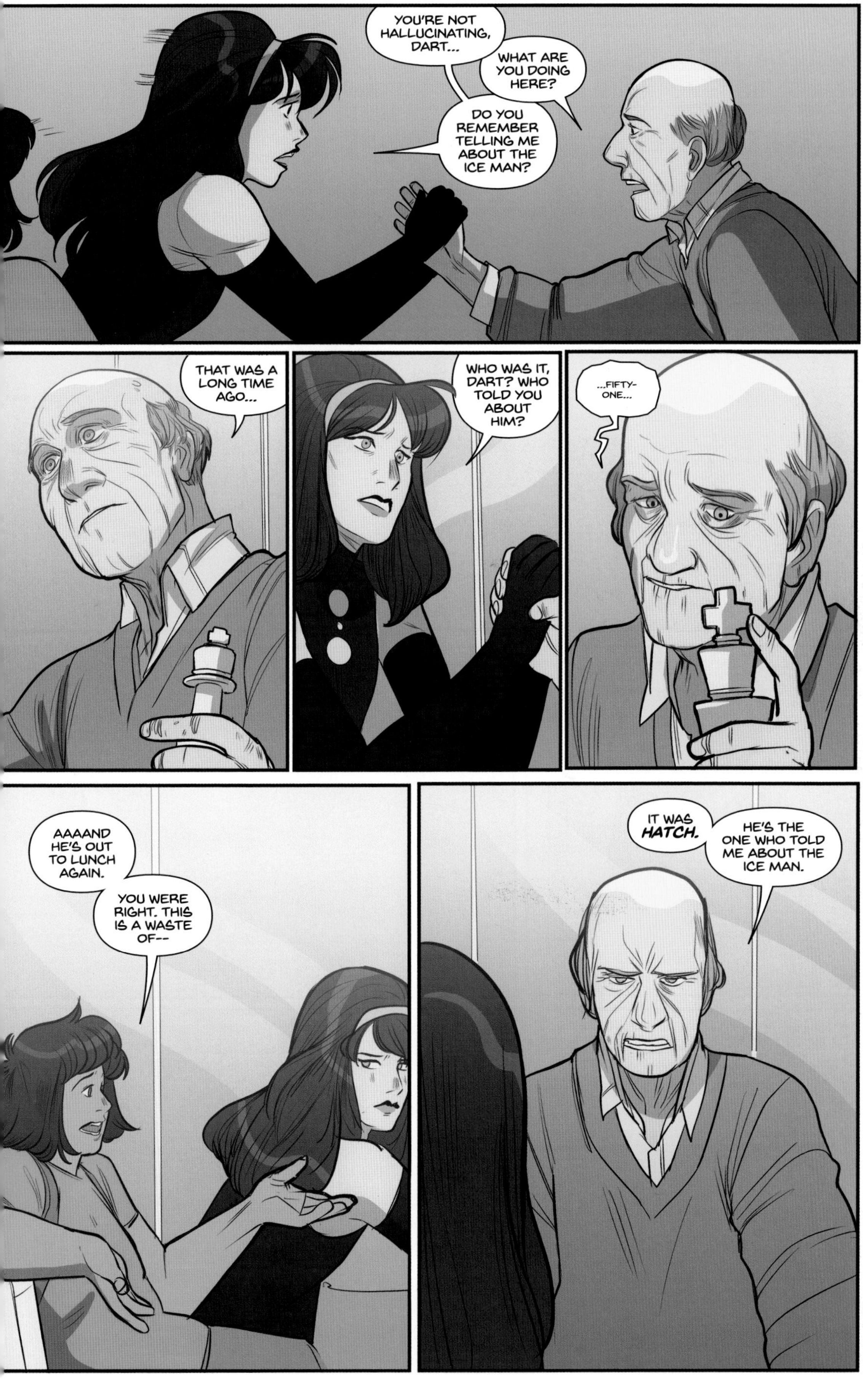
YOU'RE NOT HALLUCINATING, DART...
WHAT ARE YOU DOING HERE?
DO YOU REMEMBER TELLING ME ABOUT THE ICE MAN?
THAT WAS A LONG TIME AGO...
WHO WAS IT, DART? WHO TOLD YOU ABOUT HIM?
...FIFTY-ONE...
AAAAND HE'S OUT TO LUNCH AGAIN.
YOU WERE RIGHT. THIS IS A WASTE OF--
IT WAS *HATCH.*
HE'S THE ONE WHO TOLD ME ABOUT THE ICE MAN.

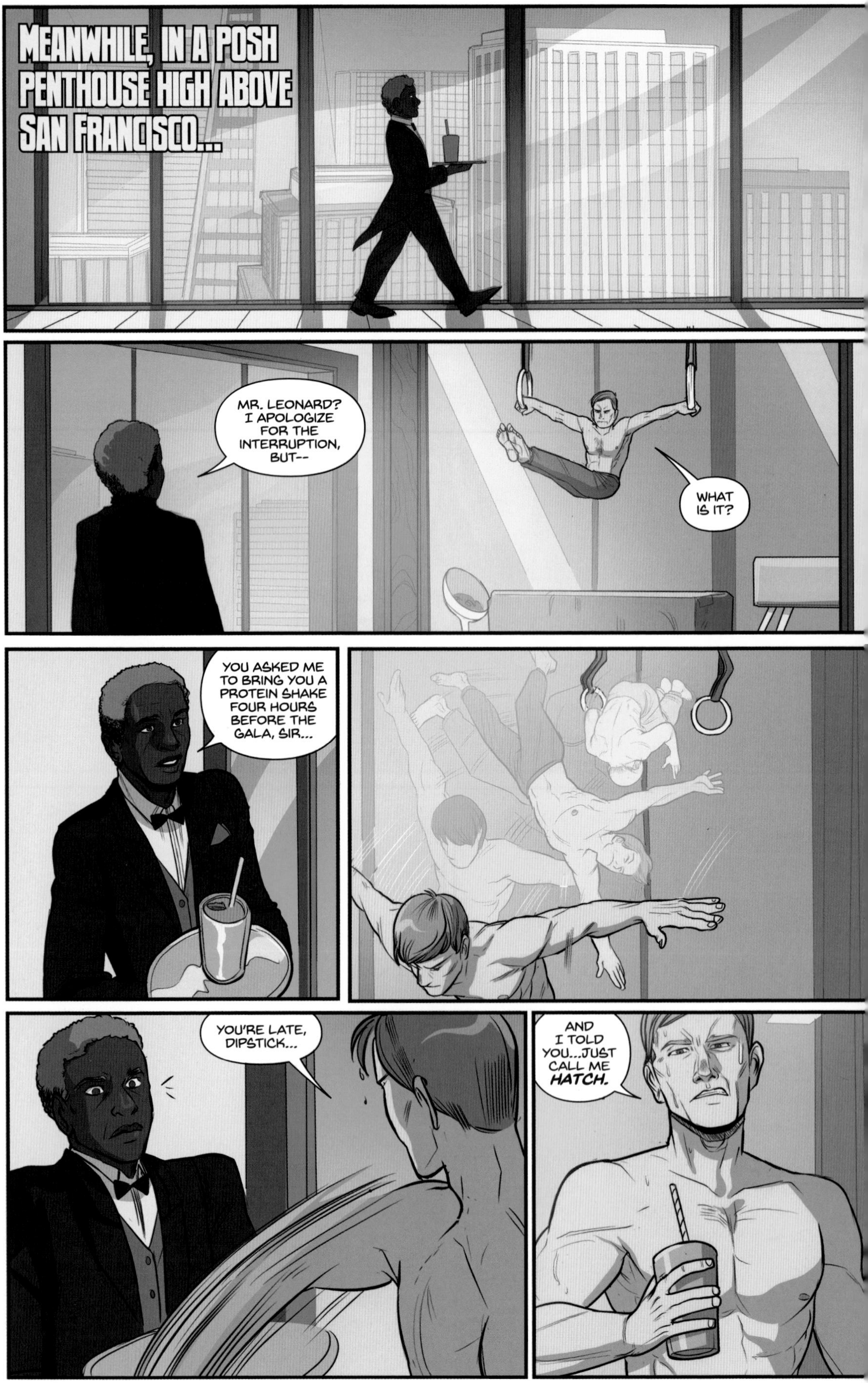
MEANWHILE, IN A POSH PENTHOUSE HIGH ABOVE SAN FRANCISCO...
MR. LEONARD? I APOLOGIZE FOR THE INTERRUPTION, BUT--
WHAT IS IT?
YOU ASKED ME TO BRING YOU A PROTEIN SHAKE FOUR HOURS BEFORE THE GALA, SIR...
YOU'RE LATE, DIPSTICK...
AND I TOLD YOU...JUST CALL ME HATCH.

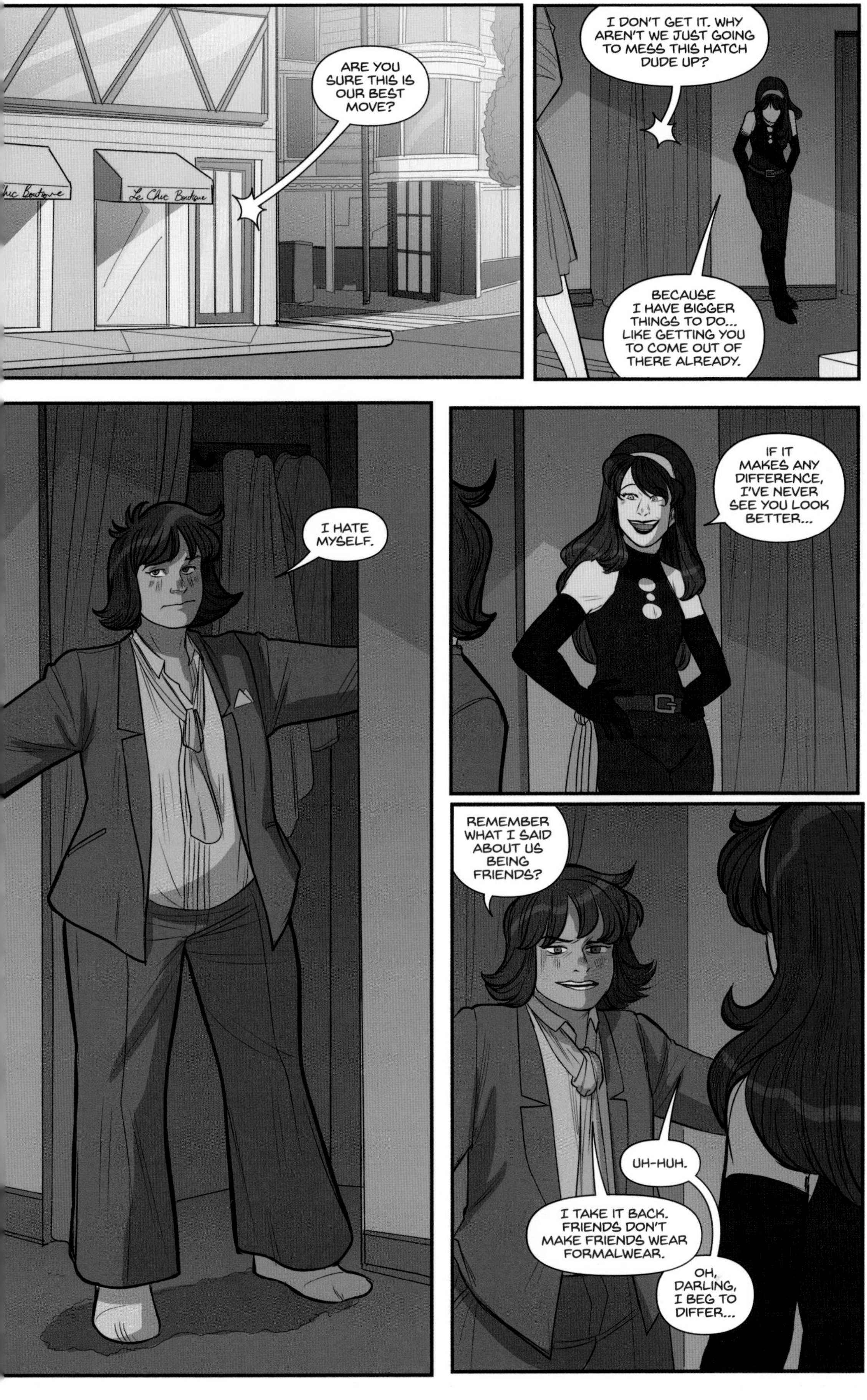
ARE YOU SURE THIS IS OUR BEST MOVE?
Le Chic Boutique
I DON'T GET IT. WHY AREN'T WE JUST GOING TO MESS THIS HATCH DUDE UP?
BECAUSE I HAVE BIGGER THINGS TO DO... LIKE GETTING YOU TO COME OUT OF THERE ALREADY.
I HATE MYSELF.
IF IT MAKES ANY DIFFERENCE, I'VE NEVER SEE YOU LOOK BETTER...
REMEMBER WHAT I SAID ABOUT US BEING FRIENDS?
UH-HUH.
I TAKE IT BACK. FRIENDS DON'T MAKE FRIENDS WEAR FORMALWEAR.
OH, DARLING, I BEG TO DIFFER...

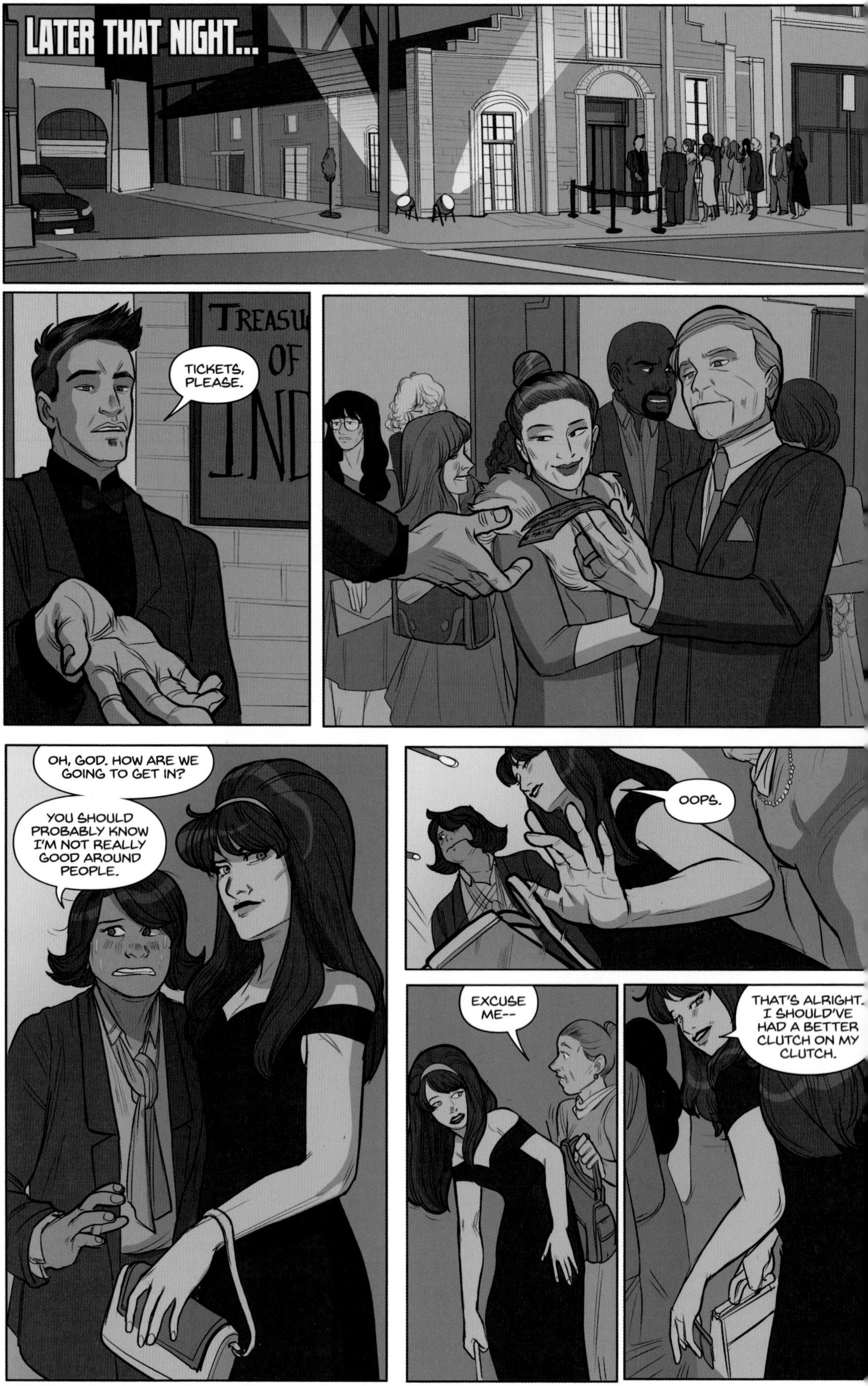
LATER THAT NIGHT...
TREASU
OF
IND
TICKETS, PLEASE.
OH, GOD. HOW ARE WE GOING TO GET IN?
YOU SHOULD PROBABLY KNOW I'M NOT REALLY GOOD AROUND PEOPLE.
OOPS.
EXCUSE ME--
THAT'S ALRIGHT. I SHOULD'VE HAD A BETTER CLUTCH ON MY CLUTCH.

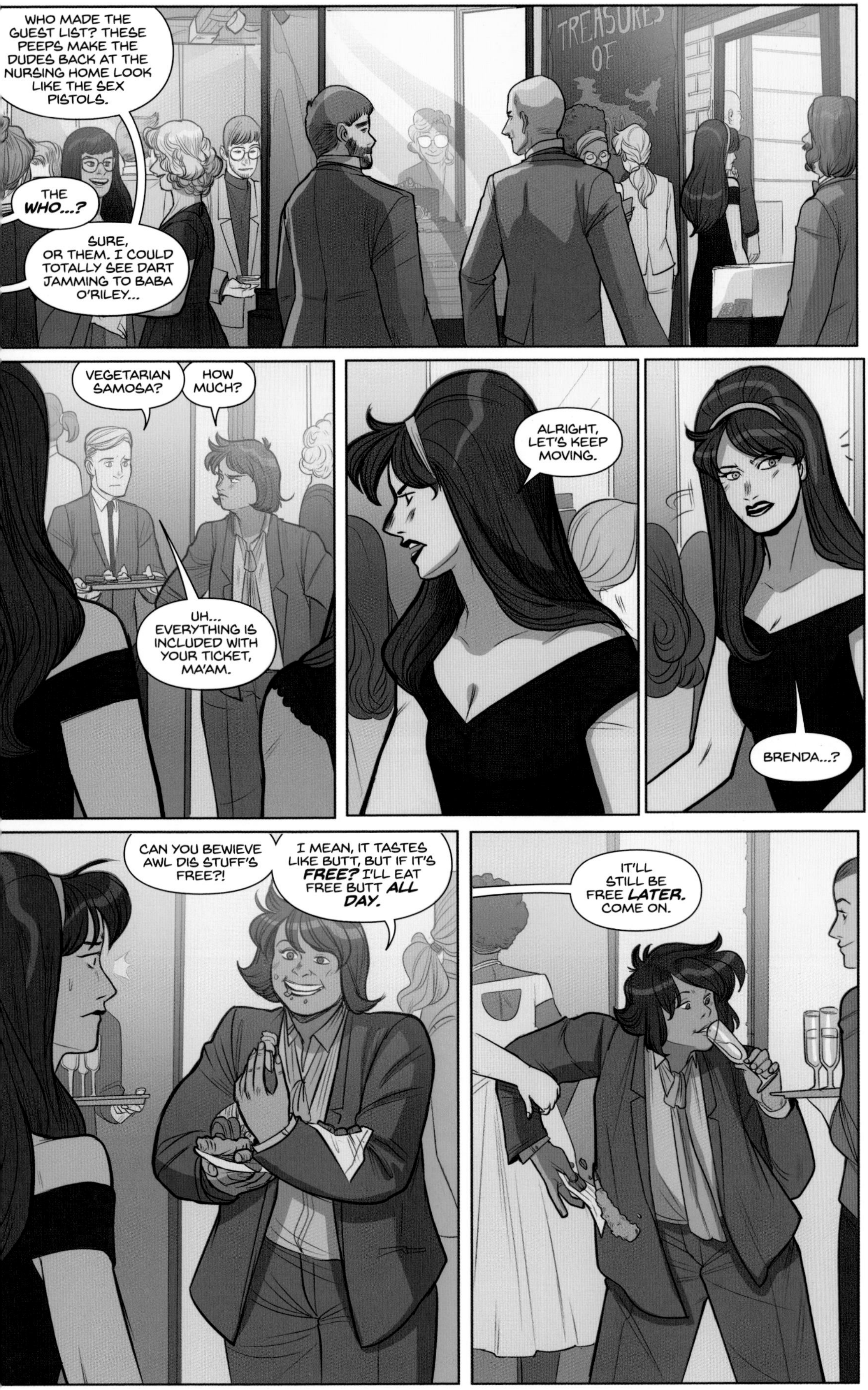

WHO MADE THE GUEST LIST? THESE PEEPS MAKE THE DUDES BACK AT THE NURSING HOME LOOK LIKE THE SEX PISTOLS.
THE WHO...?
SURE, OR THEM. I COULD TOTALLY SEE DART JAMMING TO BABA O'RILEY...
TREASURES OF
VEGETARIAN SAMOSA?
HOW MUCH?
UH... EVERYTHING IS INCLUDED WITH YOUR TICKET, MA'AM.
ALRIGHT, LET'S KEEP MOVING.
BRENDA...?
CAN YOU BEWIEVE AWL DIS STUFF'S FREE?!
I MEAN, IT TASTES LIKE BUTT, BUT IF IT'S FREE? I'LL EAT FREE BUTT ALL DAY.
IT'LL STILL BE FREE LATER. COME ON.

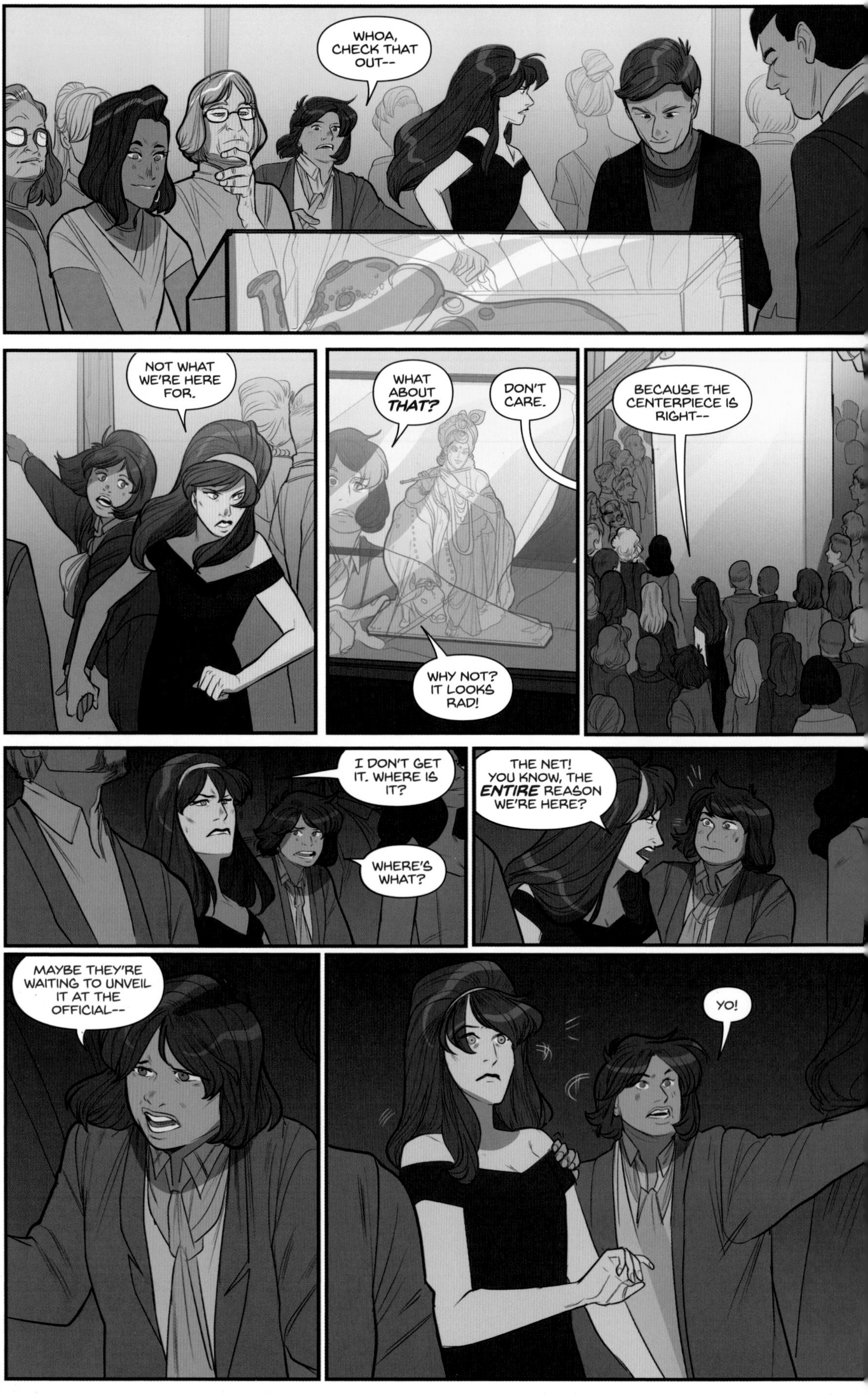
WHOA, CHECK THAT OUT--
NOT WHAT WE'RE HERE FOR.
WHAT ABOUT *THAT?*
DON'T CARE.
WHY NOT? IT LOOKS RAD!
BECAUSE THE CENTERPIECE IS RIGHT--
I DON'T GET IT. WHERE IS IT?
WHERE'S WHAT?
THE NET! YOU KNOW, THE *ENTIRE* REASON WE'RE HERE?
MAYBE THEY'RE WAITING TO UNVEIL IT AT THE OFFICIAL--
YO!

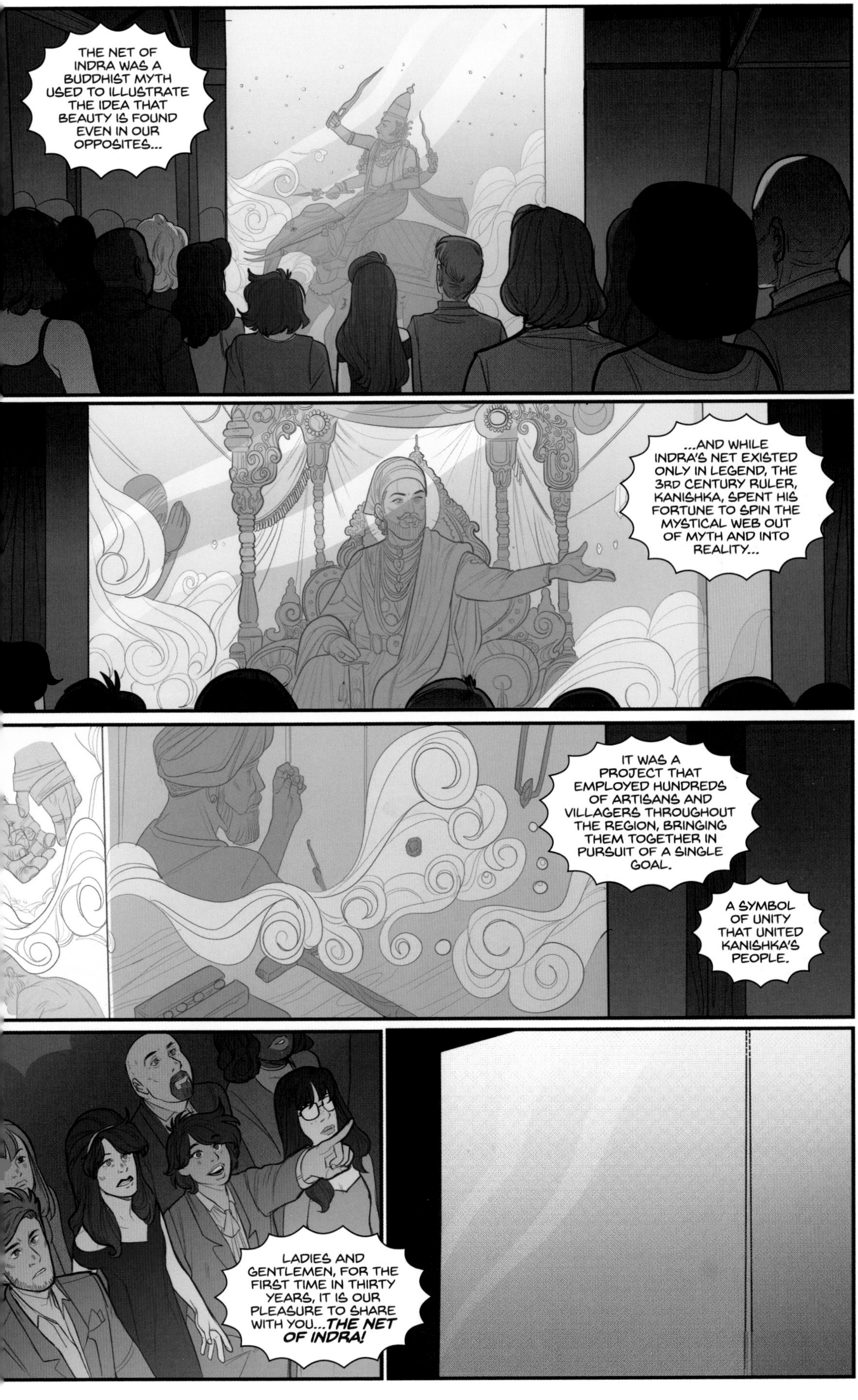
THE NET OF INDRA WAS A BUDDHIST MYTH USED TO ILLUSTRATE THE IDEA THAT BEAUTY IS FOUND EVEN IN OUR OPPOSITES...
...AND WHILE INDRA'S NET EXISTED ONLY IN LEGEND, THE 3RD CENTURY RULER, KANISHKA, SPENT HIS FORTUNE TO SPIN THE MYSTICAL WEB OUT OF MYTH AND INTO REALITY...
IT WAS A PROJECT THAT EMPLOYED HUNDREDS OF ARTISANS AND VILLAGERS THROUGHOUT THE REGION, BRINGING THEM TOGETHER IN PURSUIT OF A SINGLE GOAL.
A SYMBOL OF UNITY THAT UNITED KANISHKA'S PEOPLE.
LADIES AND GENTLEMEN, FOR THE FIRST TIME IN THIRTY YEARS, IT IS OUR PLEASURE TO SHARE WITH YOU...*THE NET OF INDRA!*

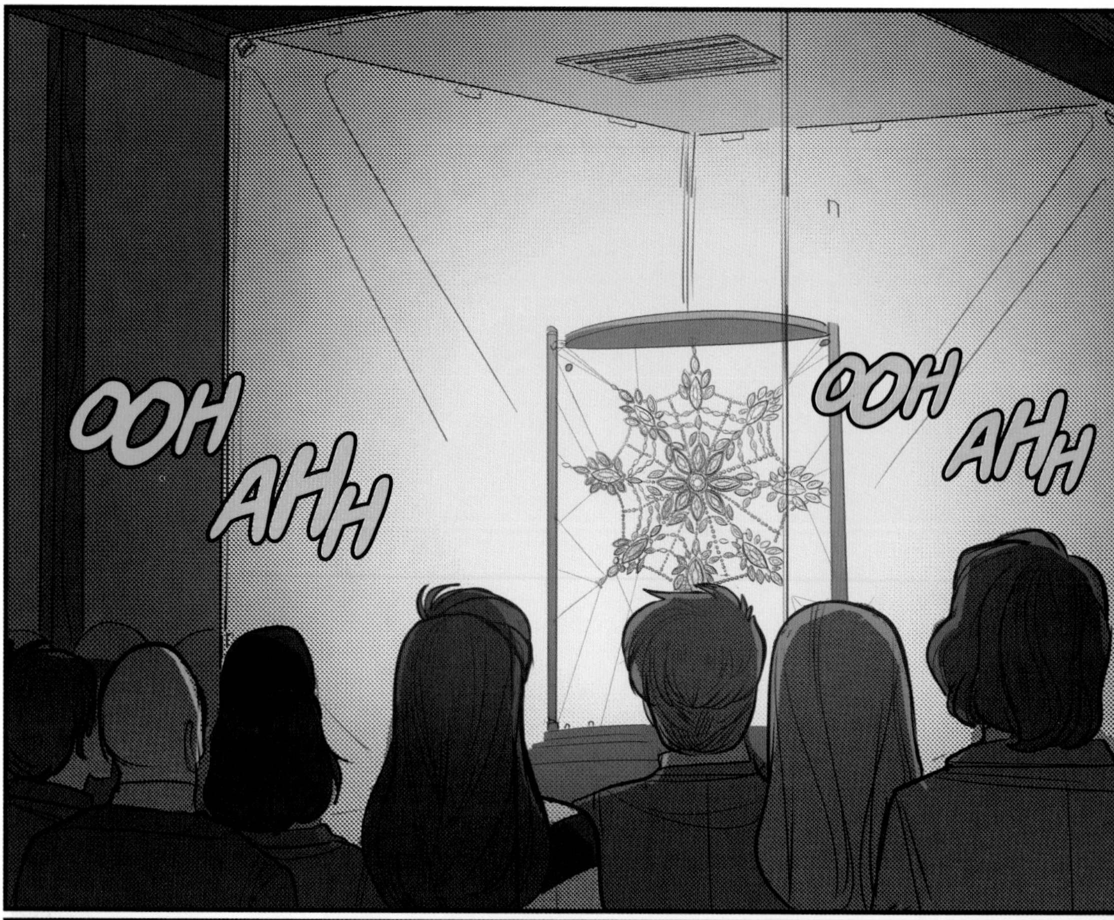
OOH
AHH
OOH
AHH

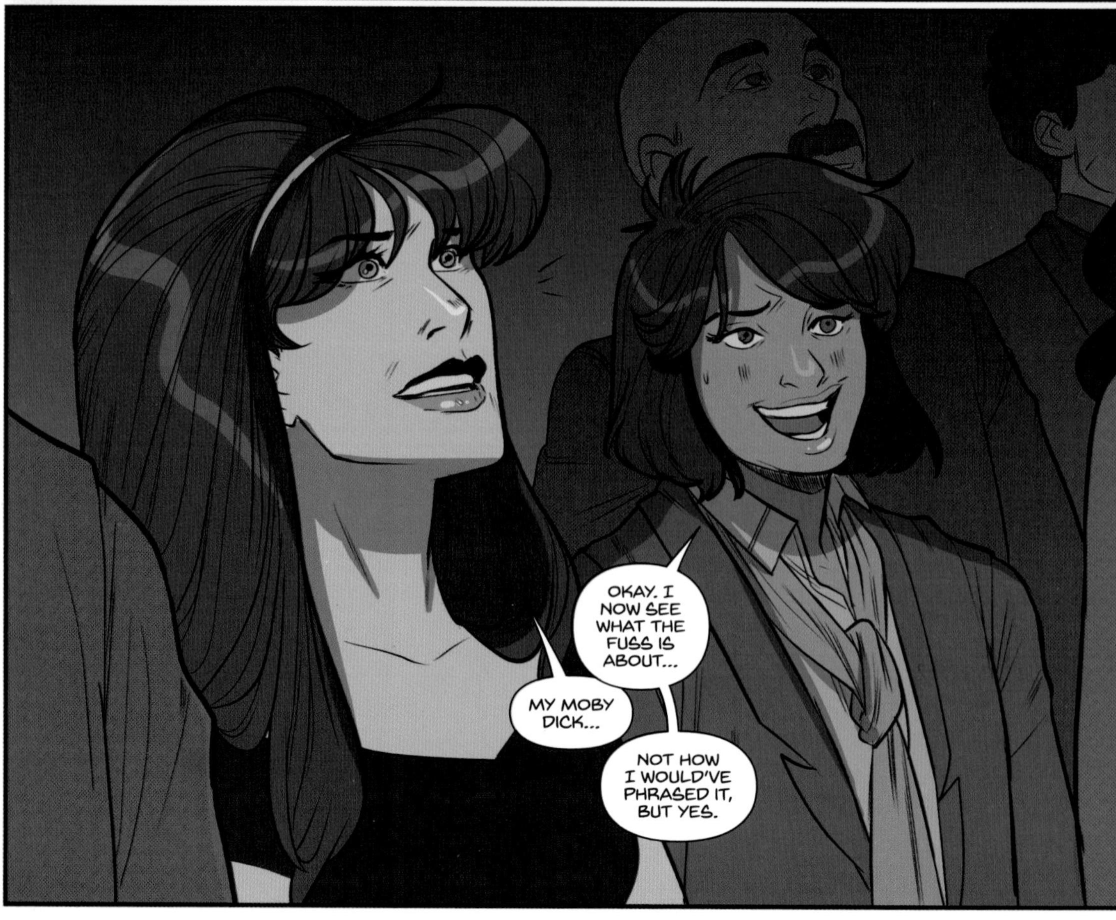
OKAY. I NOW SEE WHAT THE FUSS IS ABOUT...
MY MOBY DICK...
NOT HOW I WOULD'VE PHRASED IT, BUT YES.

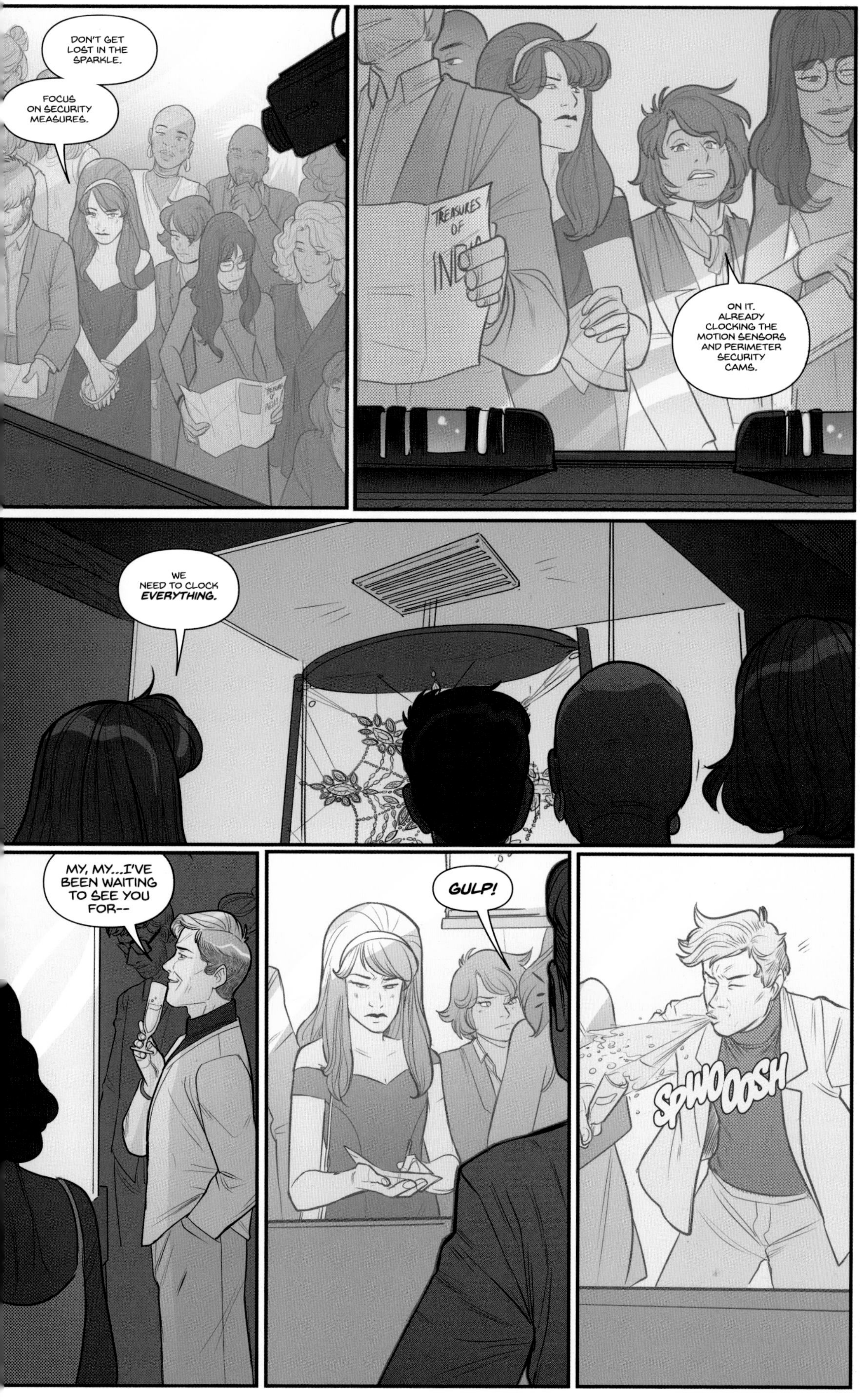
DON'T GET LOST IN THE SPARKLE.
FOCUS ON SECURITY MEASURES.
TREASURES OF INDIA
ON IT. ALREADY CLOCKING THE MOTION SENSORS AND PERIMETER SECURITY CAMS.
WE NEED TO CLOCK *EVERYTHING.*
MY, MY...I'VE BEEN WAITING TO SEE YOU FOR--
GULP!
SPWOOOSH

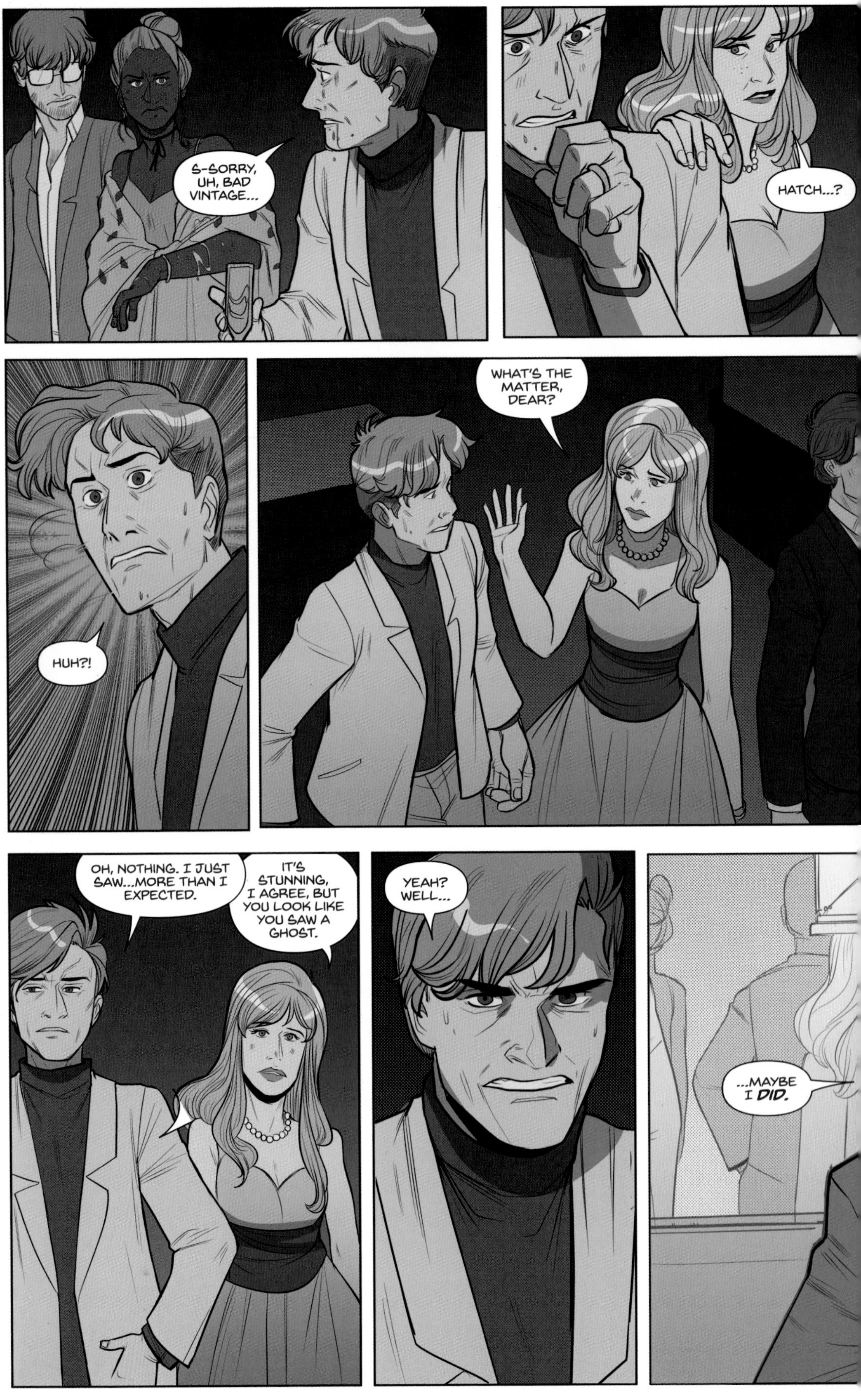
S-SORRY, UH, BAD VINTAGE...
HATCH...?
HUH?!
WHAT'S THE MATTER, DEAR?
OH, NOTHING. I JUST SAW...MORE THAN I EXPECTED.
IT'S STUNNING, I AGREE, BUT YOU LOOK LIKE YOU SAW A GHOST.
YEAH? WELL...
...MAYBE I **DID.**

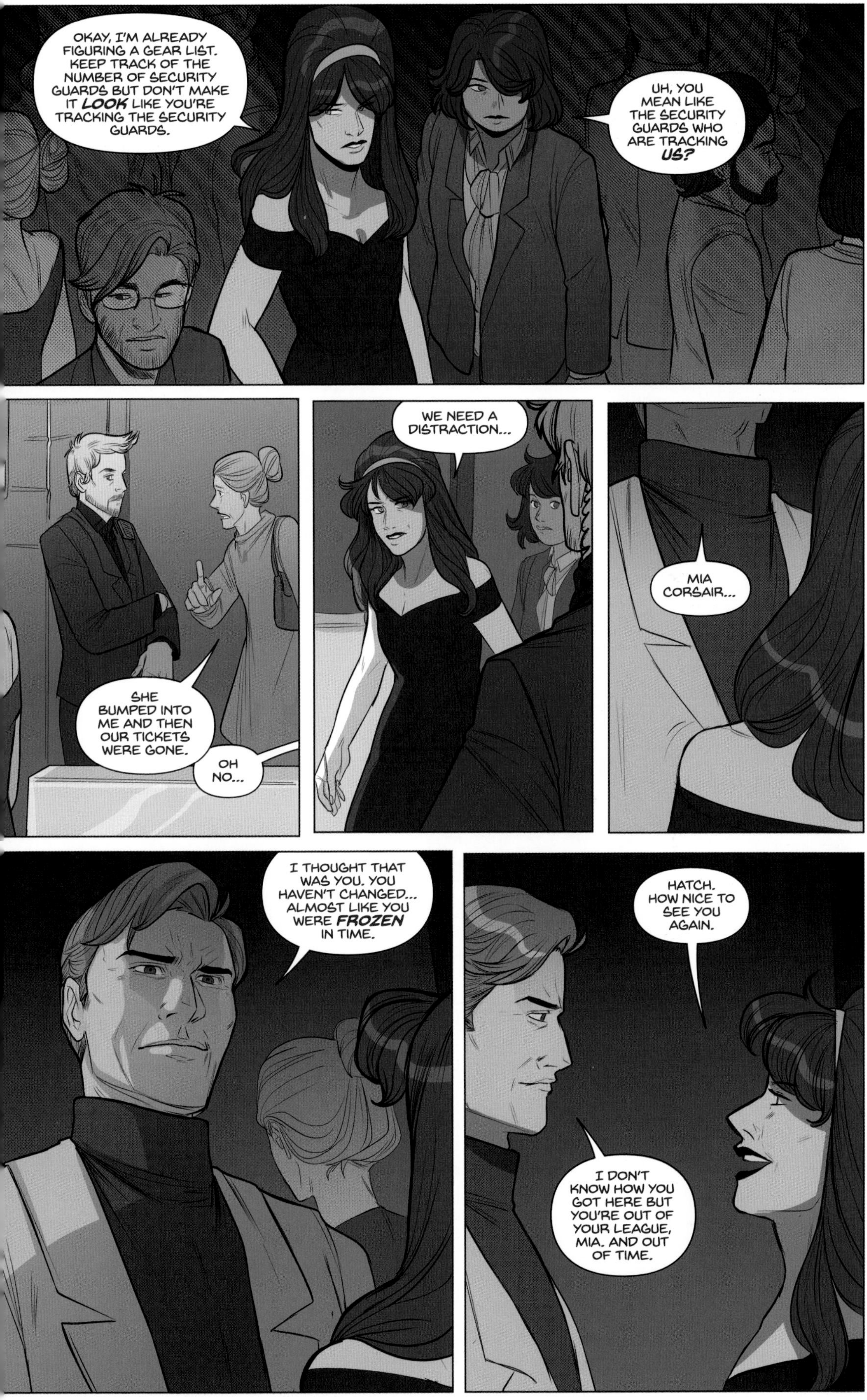
OKAY, I'M ALREADY FIGURING A GEAR LIST. KEEP TRACK OF THE NUMBER OF SECURITY GUARDS BUT DON'T MAKE IT LOOK LIKE YOU'RE TRACKING THE SECURITY GUARDS.
UH, YOU MEAN LIKE THE SECURITY GUARDS WHO ARE TRACKING US?
SHE BUMPED INTO ME AND THEN OUR TICKETS WERE GONE.
OH NO...
WE NEED A DISTRACTION...
MIA CORSAIR...
I THOUGHT THAT WAS YOU. YOU HAVEN'T CHANGED... ALMOST LIKE YOU WERE FROZEN IN TIME.
HATCH. HOW NICE TO SEE YOU AGAIN.
I DON'T KNOW HOW YOU GOT HERE BUT YOU'RE OUT OF YOUR LEAGUE, MIA. AND OUT OF TIME.

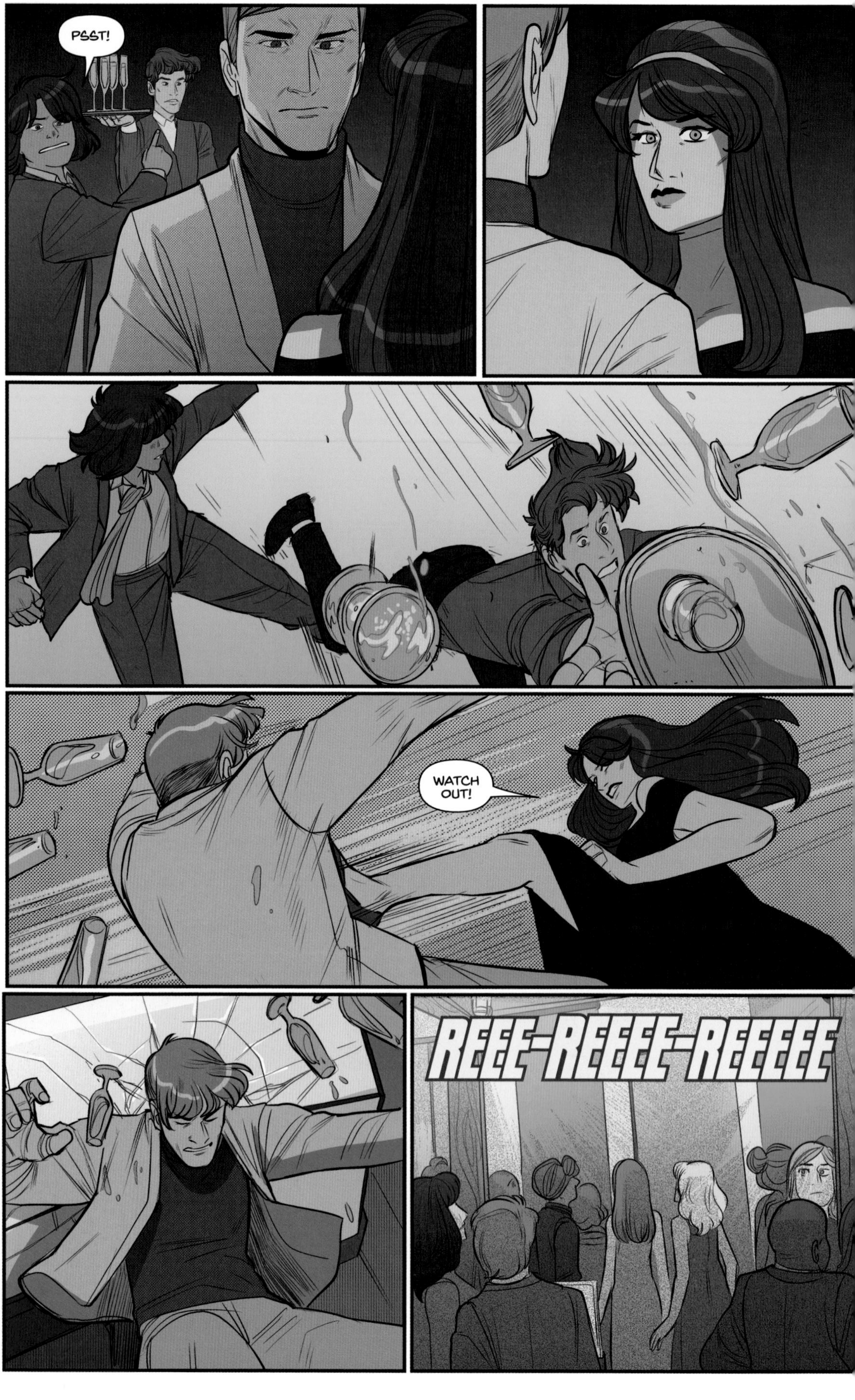
PSST!
WATCH OUT!
REEE-REEEE-REEEEE

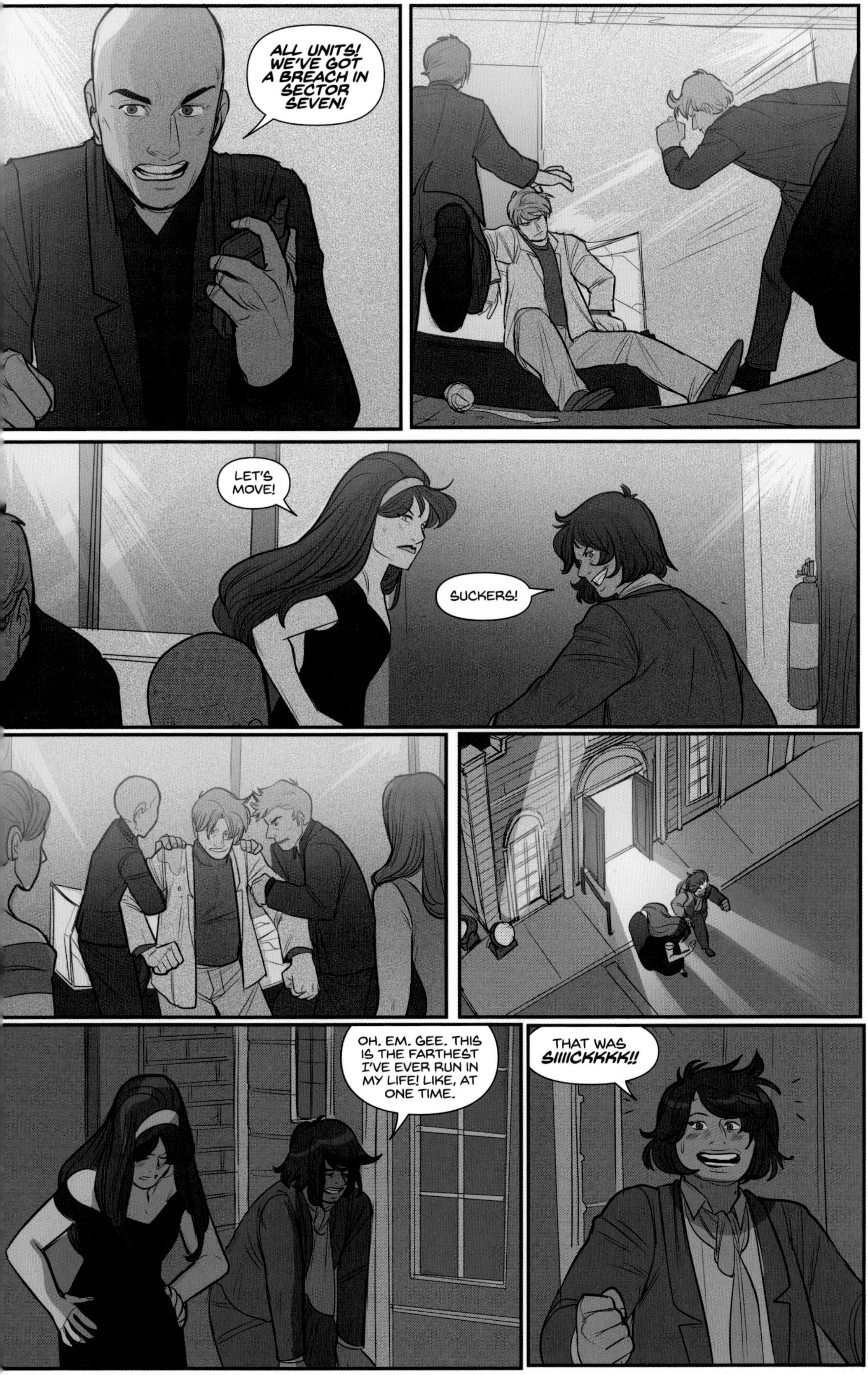
ALL UNITS! WE'VE GOT A BREACH IN SECTOR SEVEN!
LET'S MOVE!
SUCKERS!
OH. EM. GEE. THIS IS THE FARTHEST I'VE EVER RUN IN MY LIFE! LIKE, AT ONE TIME.
THAT WAS SIIIICKKKK!!

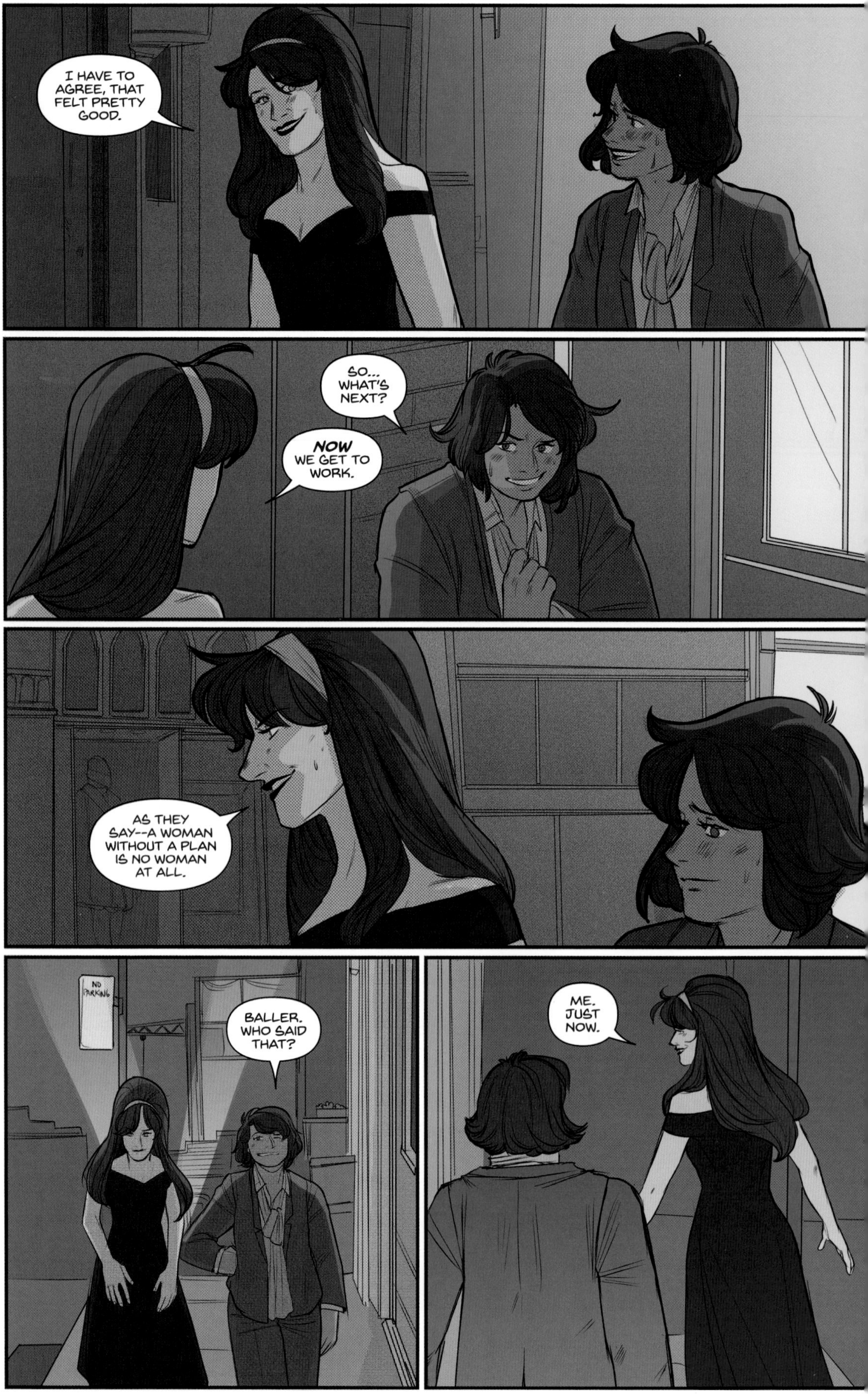
I HAVE TO AGREE, THAT FELT PRETTY GOOD.
SO... WHAT'S NEXT?
NOW WE GET TO WORK.
AS THEY SAY--A WOMAN WITHOUT A PLAN IS NO WOMAN AT ALL.
NO PARKING
BALLER. WHO SAID THAT?
ME. JUST NOW.

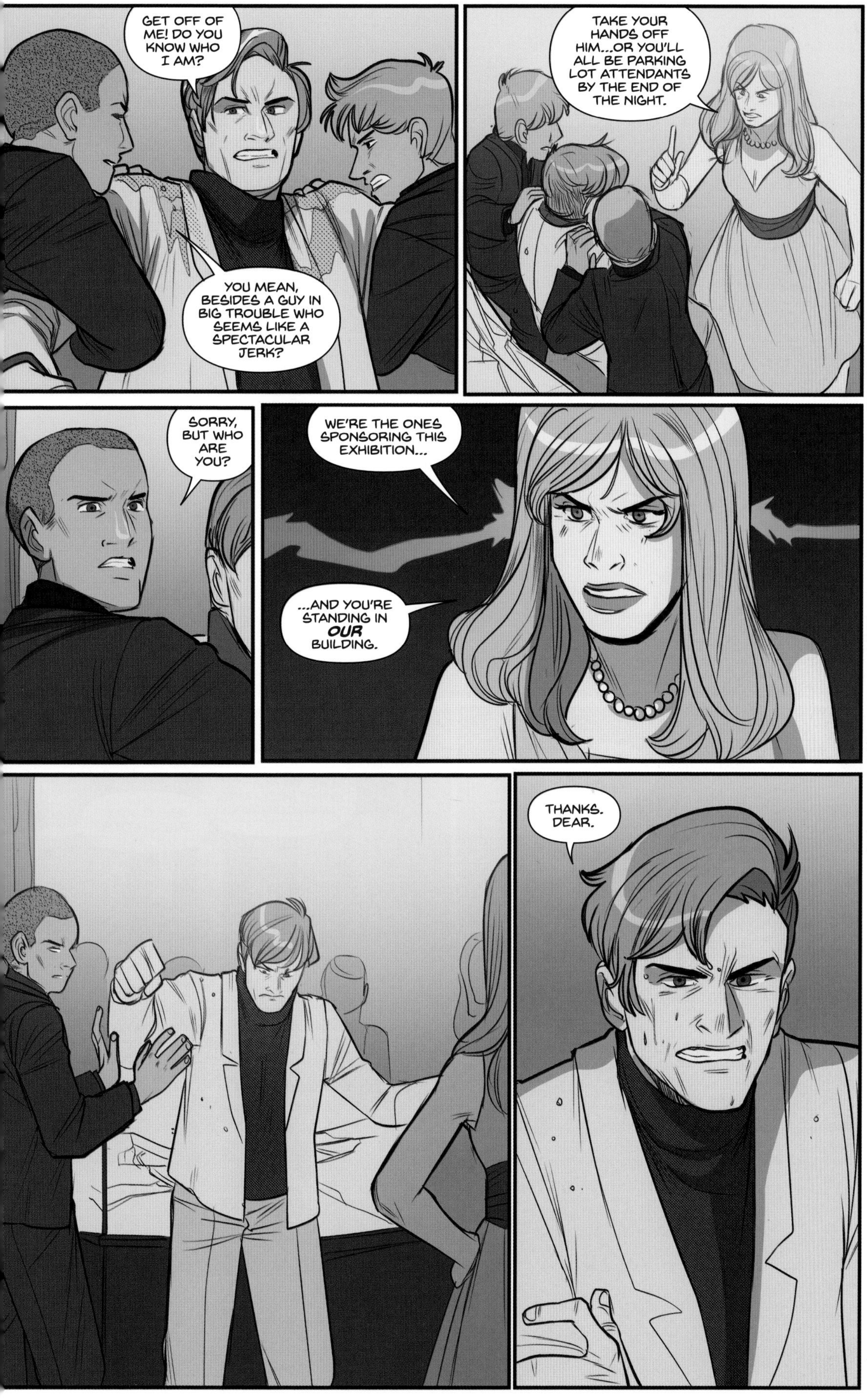
GET OFF OF ME! DO YOU KNOW WHO I AM?
YOU MEAN, BESIDES A GUY IN BIG TROUBLE WHO SEEMS LIKE A SPECTACULAR JERK?
TAKE YOUR HANDS OFF HIM...OR YOU'LL ALL BE PARKING LOT ATTENDANTS BY THE END OF THE NIGHT.
SORRY, BUT WHO ARE YOU?
WE'RE THE ONES SPONSORING THIS EXHIBITION...
...AND YOU'RE STANDING IN *OUR* BUILDING.
THANKS. DEAR.

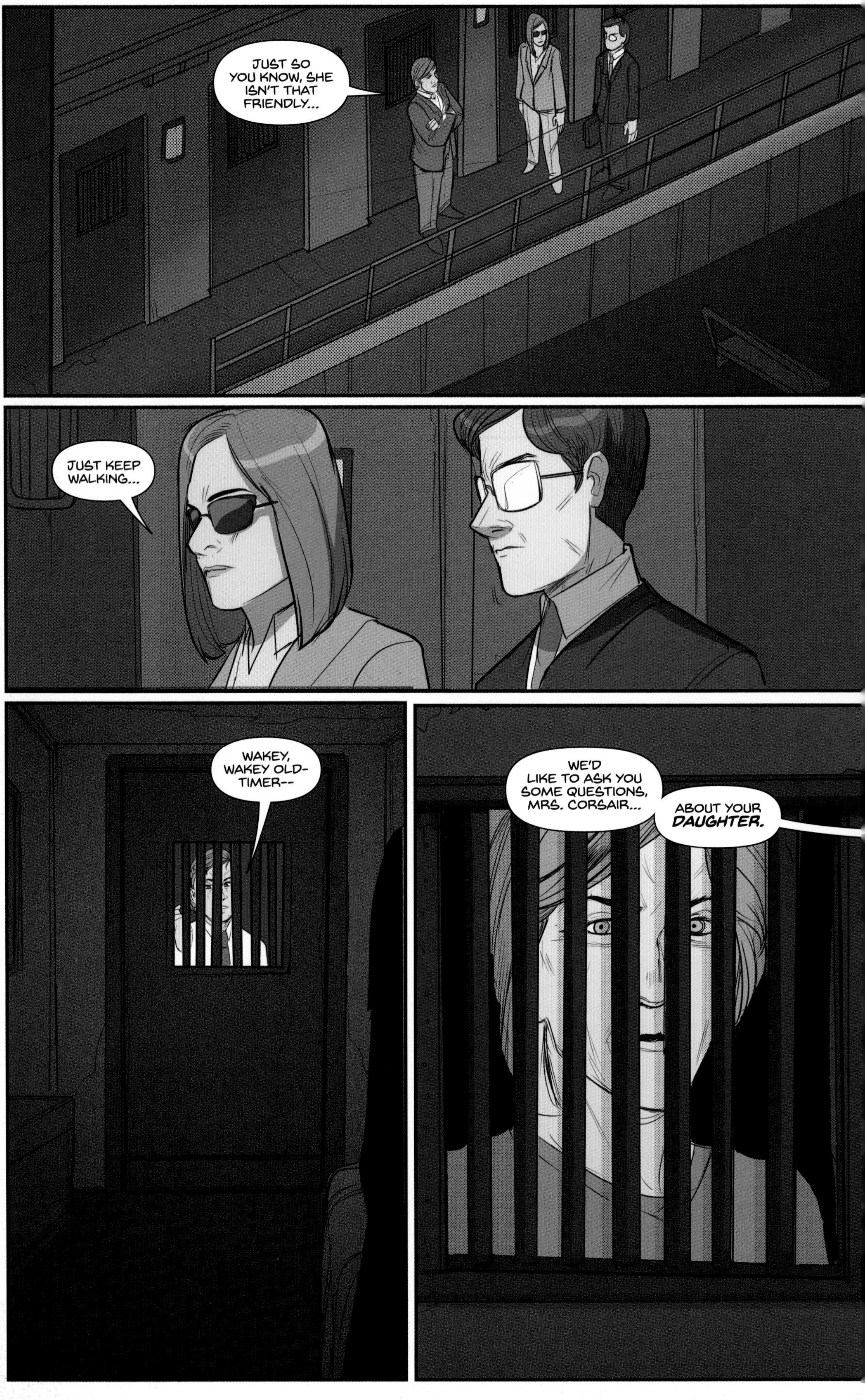
JUST SO YOU KNOW, SHE ISN'T THAT FRIENDLY...
JUST KEEP WALKING...
WAKEY, WAKEY OLD-TIMER--
WE'D LIKE TO ASK YOU SOME QUESTIONS, MRS. CORSAIR...
ABOUT YOUR DAUGHTER.

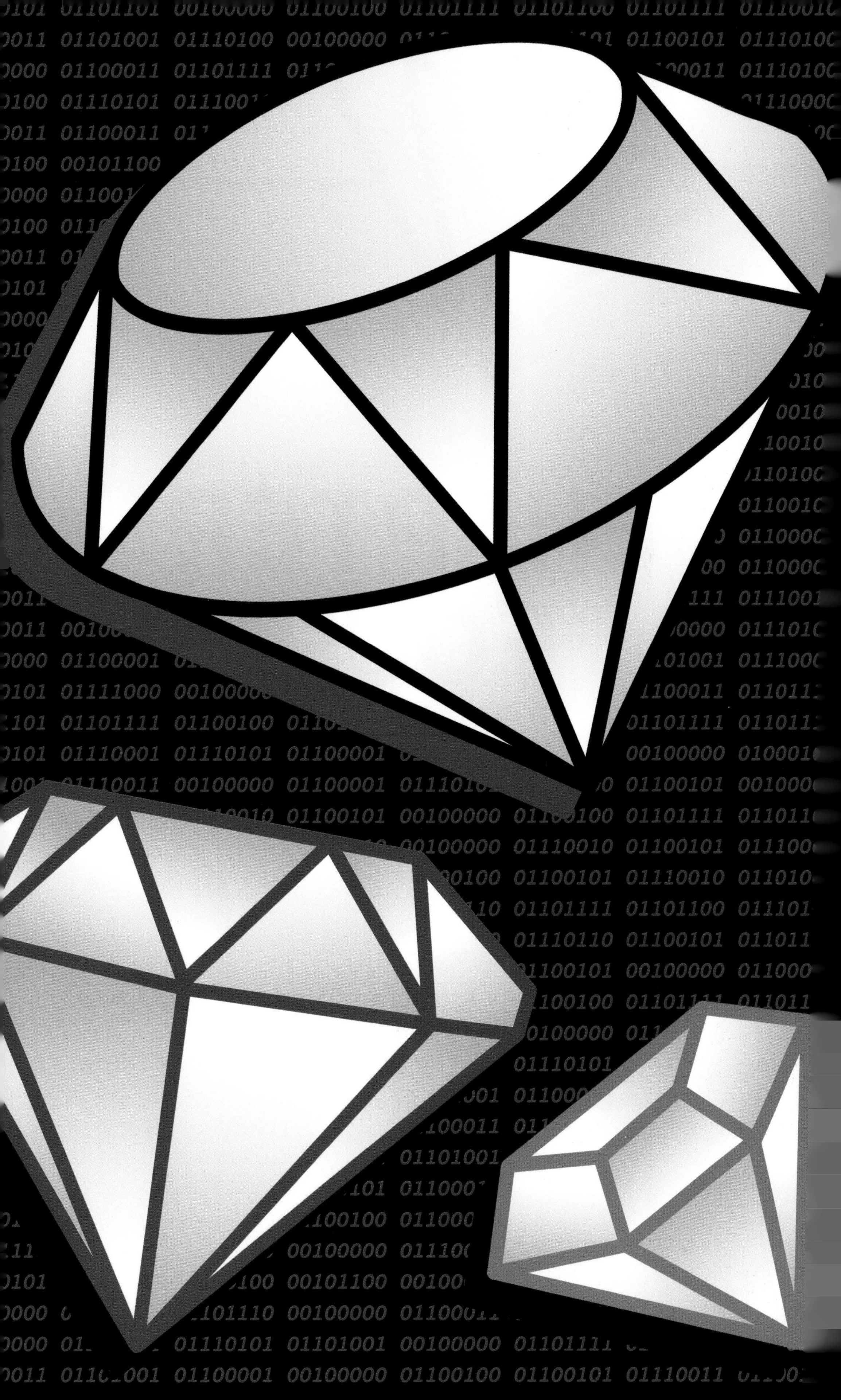

# CHAPTER FOUR

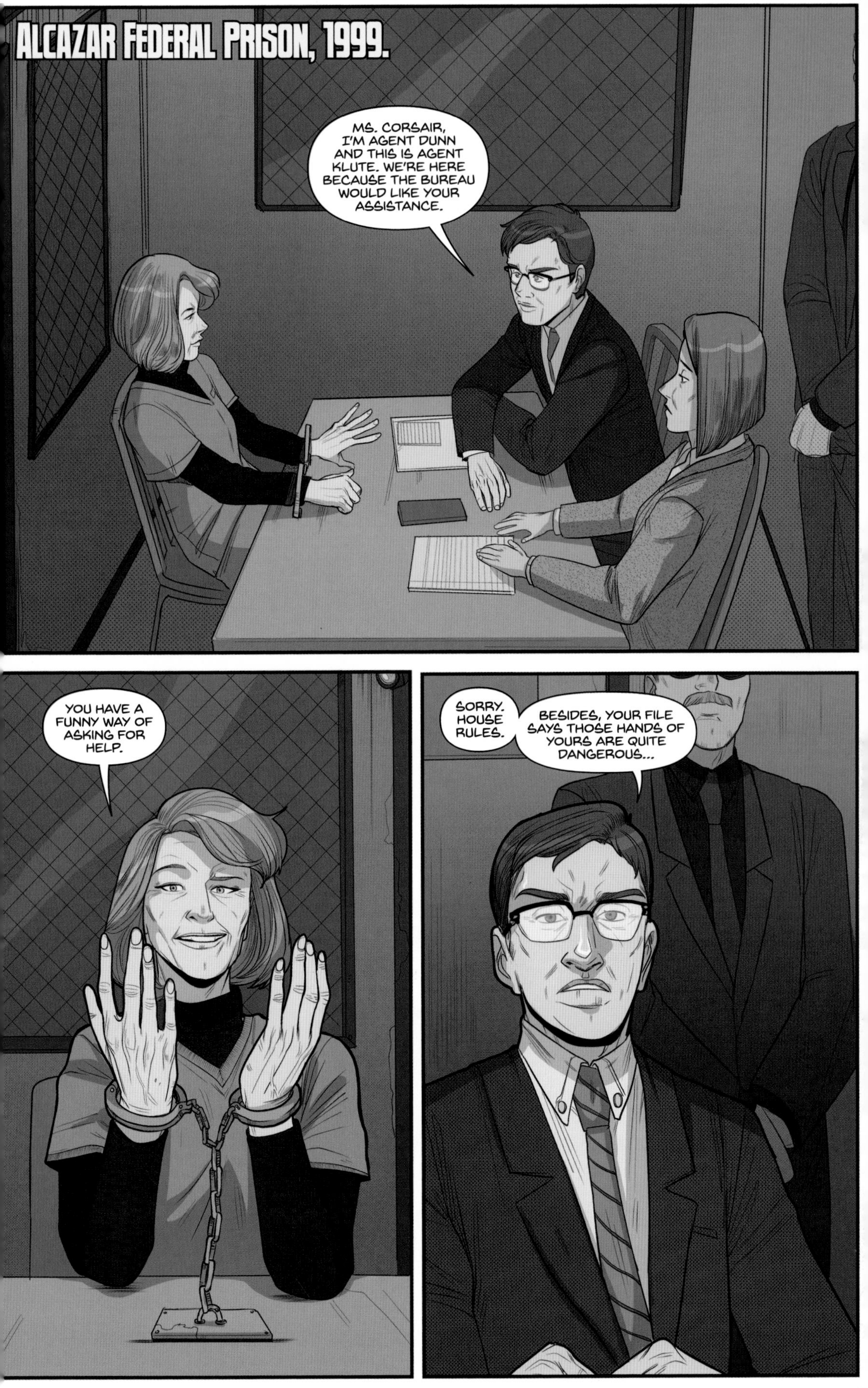
ALCAZAR FEDERAL PRISON, 1999.
MS. CORSAIR, I'M AGENT DUNN AND THIS IS AGENT KLUTE. WE'RE HERE BECAUSE THE BUREAU WOULD LIKE YOUR ASSISTANCE.
YOU HAVE A FUNNY WAY OF ASKING FOR HELP.
SORRY. HOUSE RULES.
BESIDES, YOUR FILE SAYS THOSE HANDS OF YOURS ARE QUITE DANGEROUS...

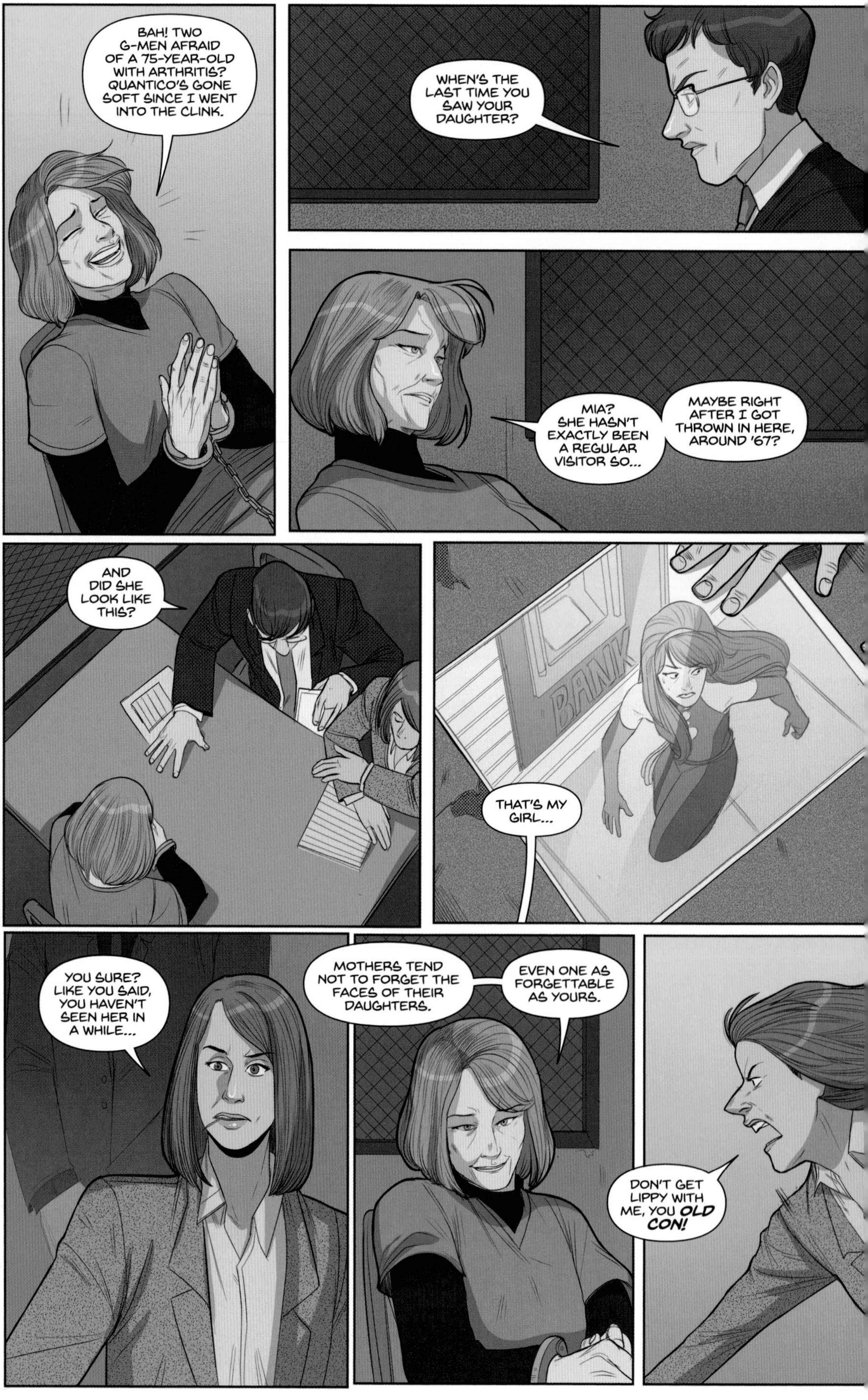
BAH! TWO G-MEN AFRAID OF A 75-YEAR-OLD WITH ARTHRITIS? QUANTICO'S GONE SOFT SINCE I WENT INTO THE CLINK.
WHEN'S THE LAST TIME YOU SAW YOUR DAUGHTER?
MIA? SHE HASN'T EXACTLY BEEN A REGULAR VISITOR SO...
MAYBE RIGHT AFTER I GOT THROWN IN HERE, AROUND '67?
AND DID SHE LOOK LIKE THIS?
BANK
THAT'S MY GIRL...
YOU SURE? LIKE YOU SAID, YOU HAVEN'T SEEN HER IN A WHILE...
MOTHERS TEND NOT TO FORGET THE FACES OF THEIR DAUGHTERS.
EVEN ONE AS FORGETTABLE AS YOURS.
DON'T GET LIPPY WITH ME, YOU ***OLD CON!***

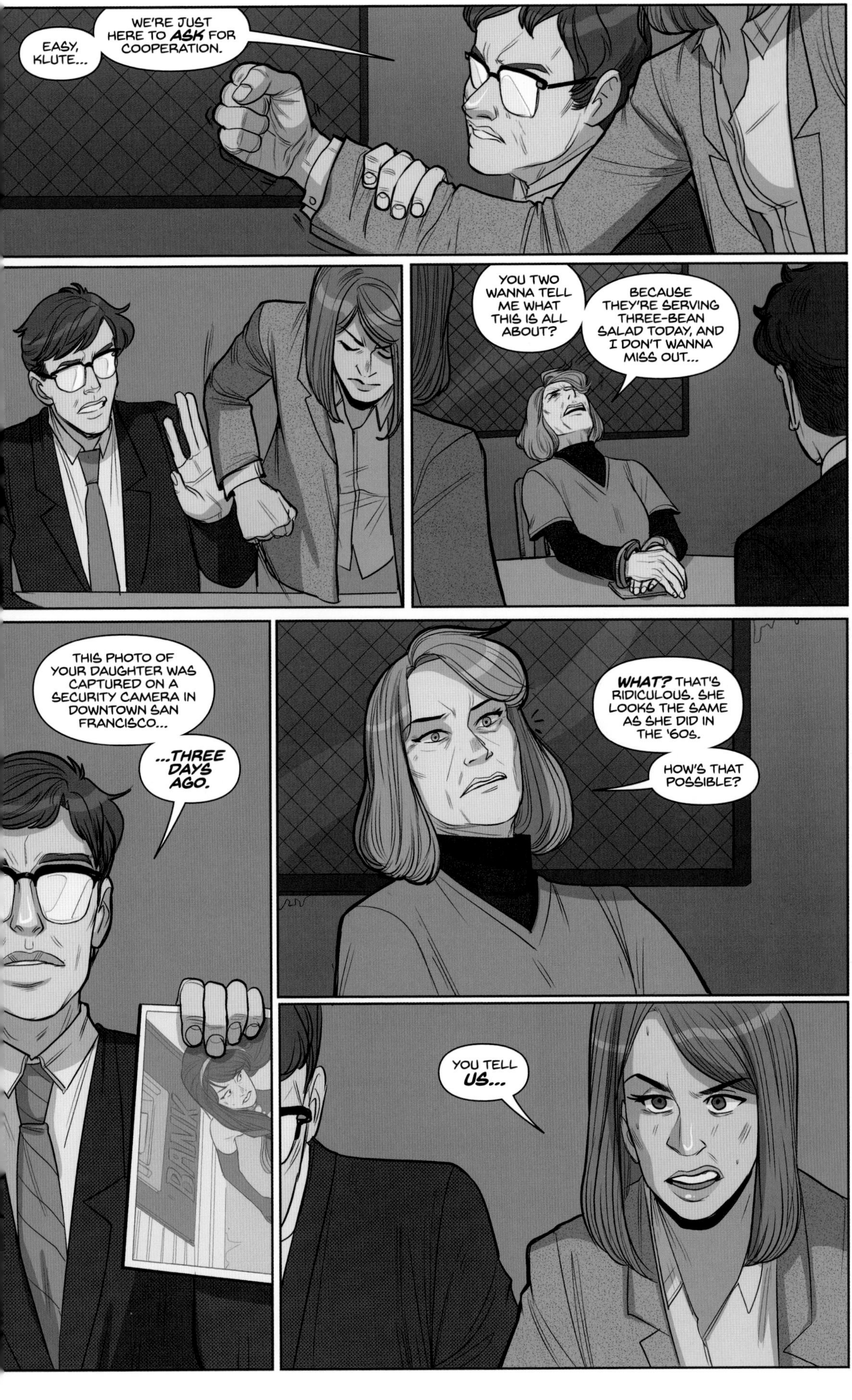
EASY, KLUTE...
WE'RE JUST HERE TO ASK FOR COOPERATION.
YOU TWO WANNA TELL ME WHAT THIS IS ALL ABOUT?
BECAUSE THEY'RE SERVING THREE-BEAN SALAD TODAY, AND I DON'T WANNA MISS OUT...
THIS PHOTO OF YOUR DAUGHTER WAS CAPTURED ON A SECURITY CAMERA IN DOWNTOWN SAN FRANCISCO...
...THREE DAYS AGO.
WHAT? THAT'S RIDICULOUS. SHE LOOKS THE SAME AS SHE DID IN THE '60s.
HOW'S THAT POSSIBLE?
YOU TELL US...

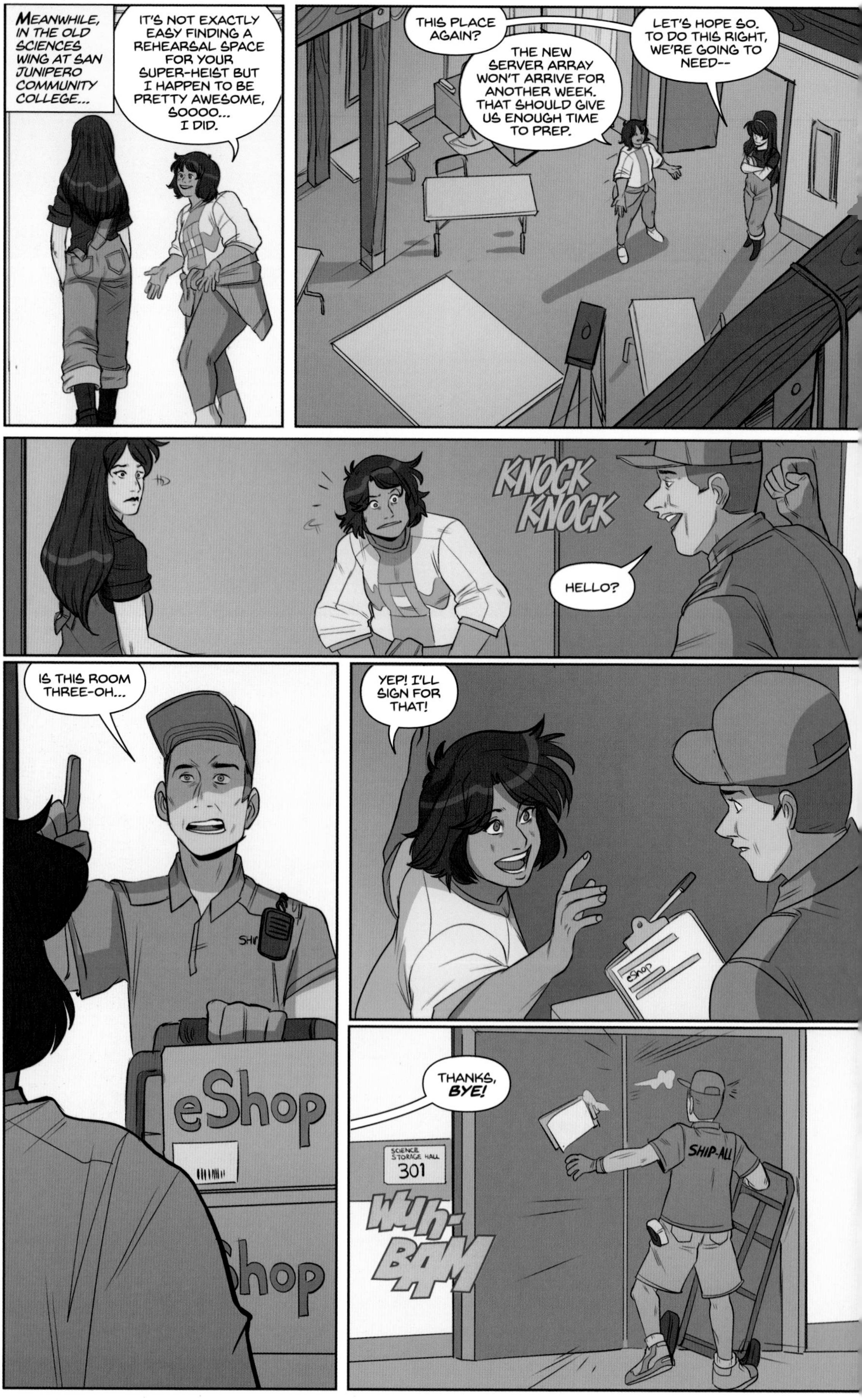
MEANWHILE, IN THE OLD SCIENCES WING AT SAN JUNIPERO COMMUNITY COLLEGE...
IT'S NOT EXACTLY EASY FINDING A REHEARSAL SPACE FOR YOUR SUPER-HEIST BUT I HAPPEN TO BE PRETTY AWESOME, SOOOO... I DID.
THIS PLACE AGAIN?
THE NEW SERVER ARRAY WON'T ARRIVE FOR ANOTHER WEEK. THAT SHOULD GIVE US ENOUGH TIME TO PREP.
LET'S HOPE SO. TO DO THIS RIGHT, WE'RE GOING TO NEED--
KNOCK KNOCK
HELLO?
IS THIS ROOM THREE-OH...
eShop
YEP! I'LL SIGN FOR THAT!
eShop
THANKS, BYE!
SCIENCE STORAGE HALL
301
SHIP-ALL
WUH-BAM

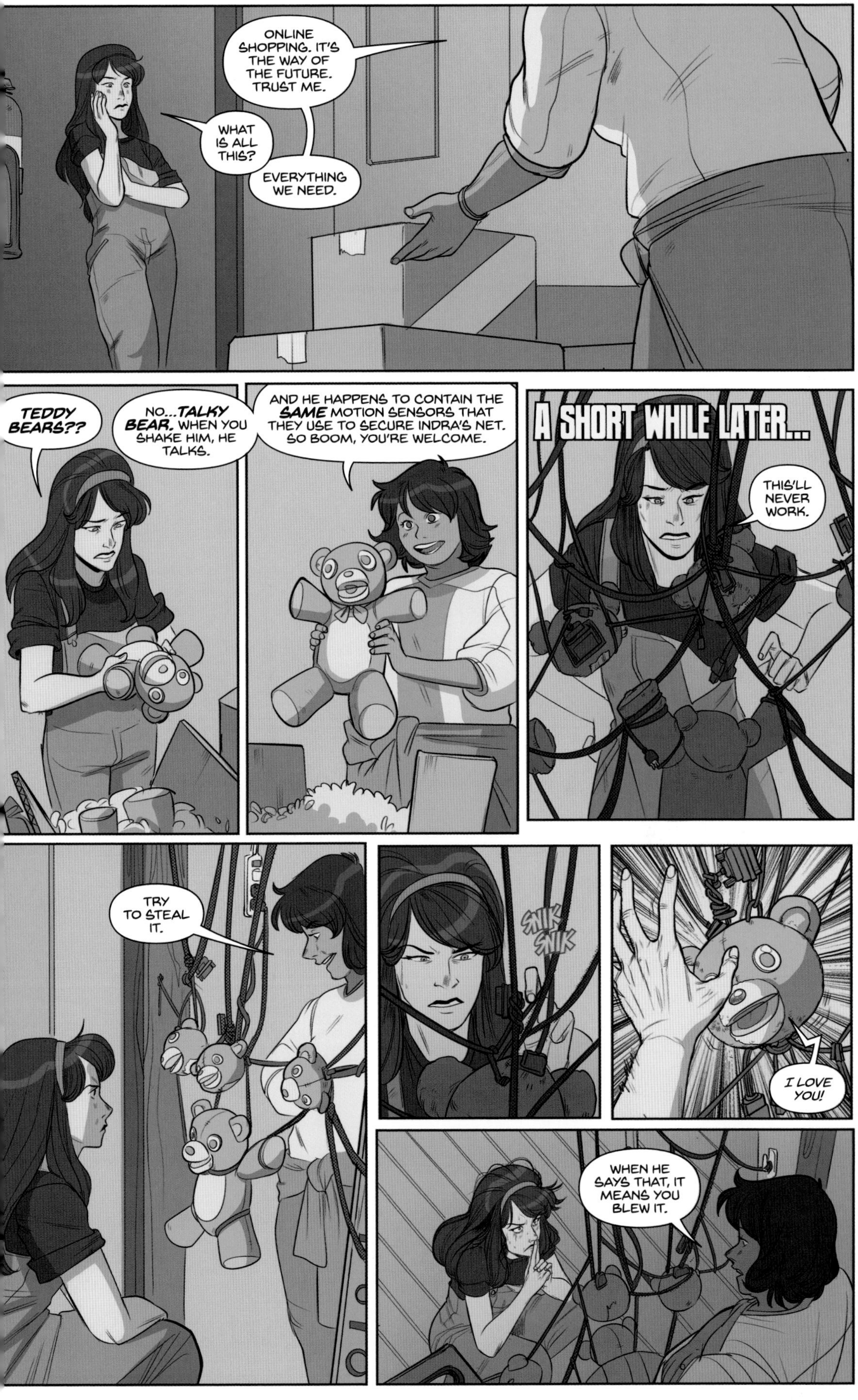

ONLINE SHOPPING. IT'S THE WAY OF THE FUTURE. TRUST ME.
WHAT IS ALL THIS?
EVERYTHING WE NEED.
TEDDY BEARS??
NO...TALKY BEAR. WHEN YOU SHAKE HIM, HE TALKS.
AND HE HAPPENS TO CONTAIN THE SAME MOTION SENSORS THAT THEY USE TO SECURE INDRA'S NET. SO BOOM, YOU'RE WELCOME.
A SHORT WHILE LATER...
THIS'LL NEVER WORK.
TRY TO STEAL IT.
SNIK SNIK
I LOVE YOU!
WHEN HE SAYS THAT, IT MEANS YOU BLEW IT.

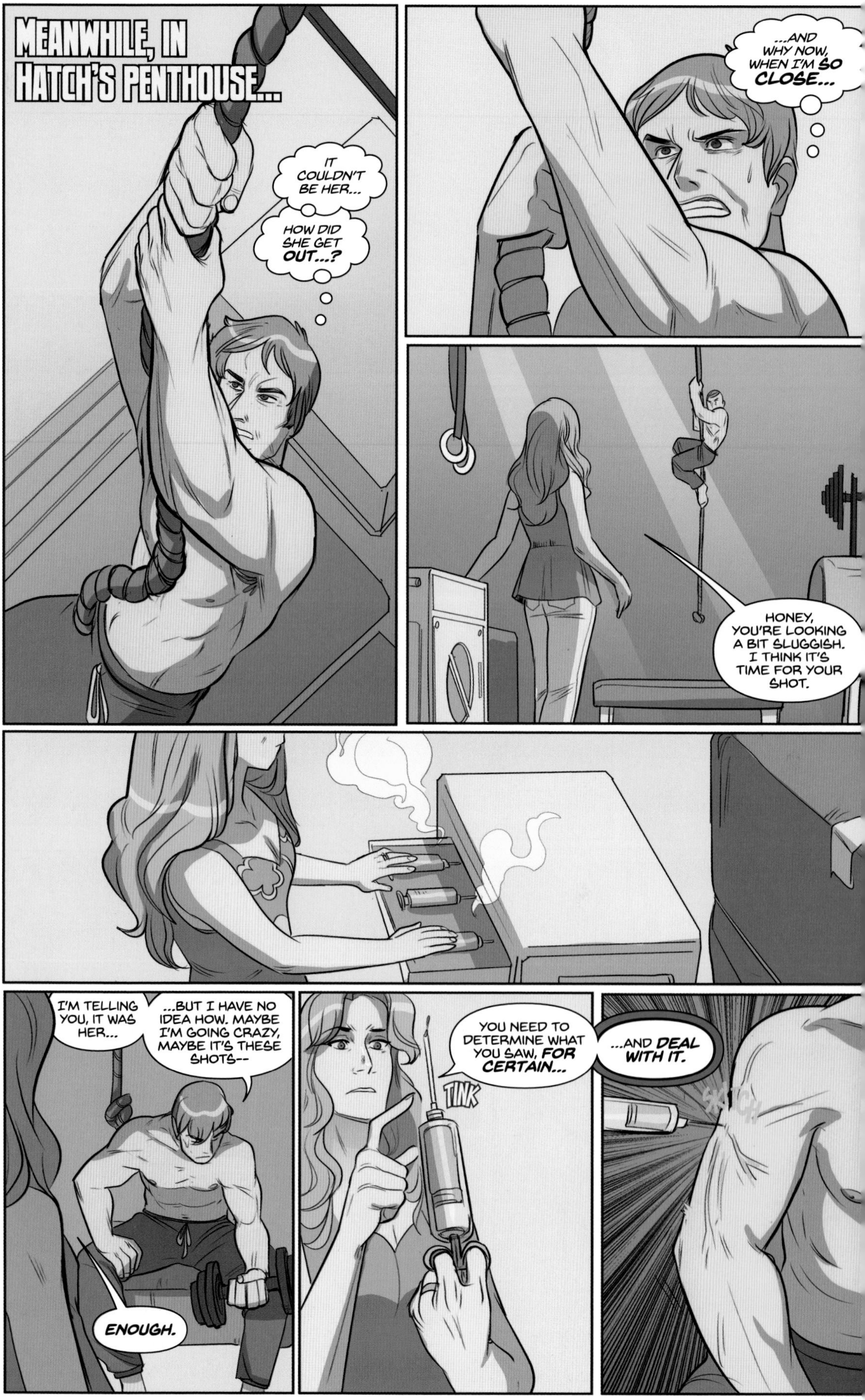

MEANWHILE, IN HATCH'S PENTHOUSE...
IT COULDN'T BE HER...
HOW DID SHE GET OUT...?
...AND WHY NOW, WHEN I'M SO CLOSE...
HONEY, YOU'RE LOOKING A BIT SLUGGISH. I THINK IT'S TIME FOR YOUR SHOT.
I'M TELLING YOU, IT WAS HER...
...BUT I HAVE NO IDEA HOW. MAYBE I'M GOING CRAZY, MAYBE IT'S THESE SHOTS--
ENOUGH.
YOU NEED TO DETERMINE WHAT YOU SAW, FOR CERTAIN...
TINK
...AND DEAL WITH IT.

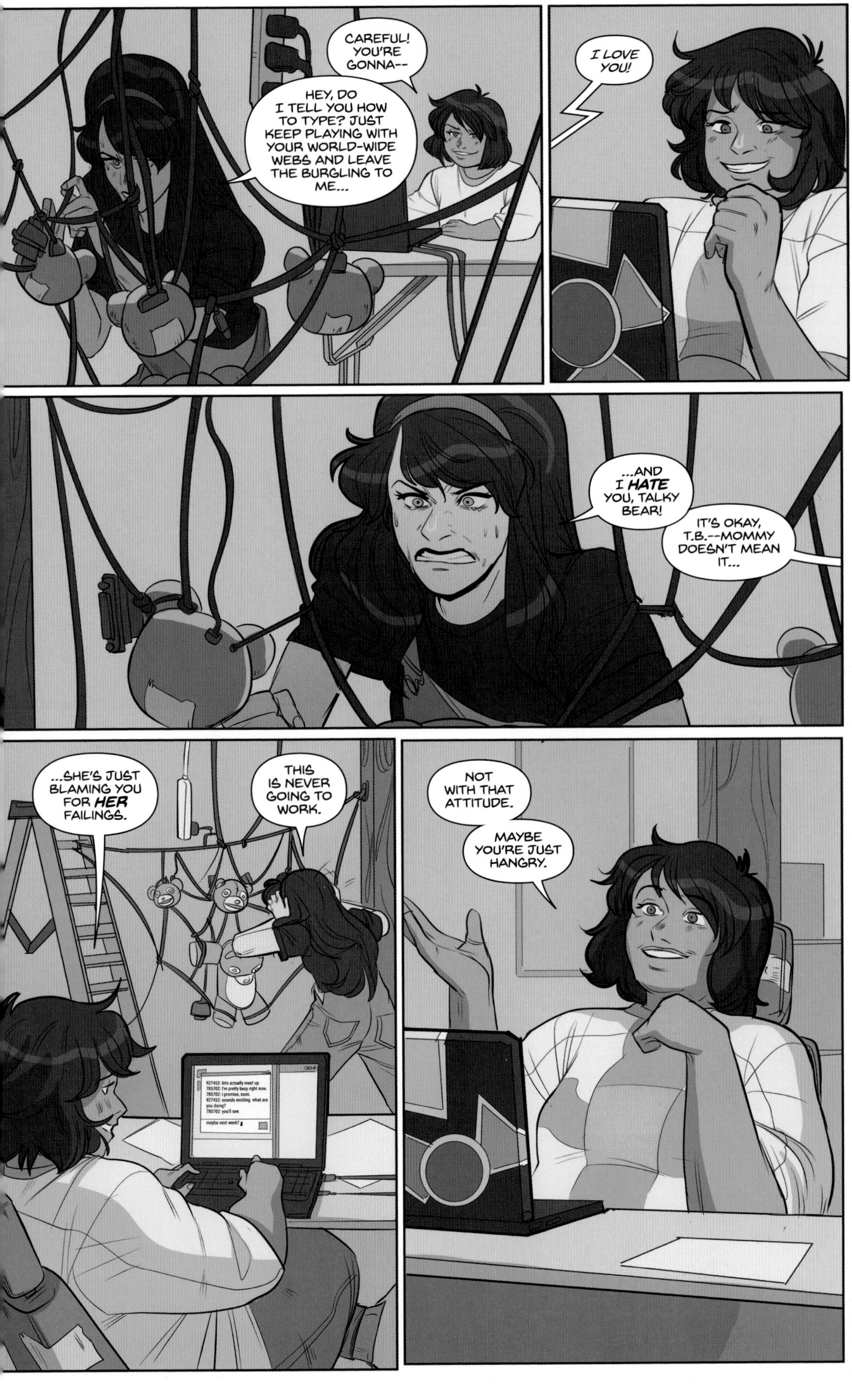

CAREFUL! YOU'RE GONNA--
HEY, DO I TELL YOU HOW TO TYPE? JUST KEEP PLAYING WITH YOUR WORLD-WIDE WEBS AND LEAVE THE BURGLING TO ME...
I LOVE YOU!
...AND I **HATE** YOU, TALKY BEAR!
IT'S OKAY, T.B.--MOMMY DOESN'T MEAN IT...
...SHE'S JUST BLAMING YOU FOR **HER** FAILINGS.
THIS IS NEVER GOING TO WORK.
927452: lets actually meet up
785702: I'm pretty busy right now.
785702: i promise, soon.
927452: sounds exciting. what are you doing?
785702: you'll see.
maybe next week?
NOT WITH THAT ATTITUDE.
MAYBE YOU'RE JUST HANGRY.

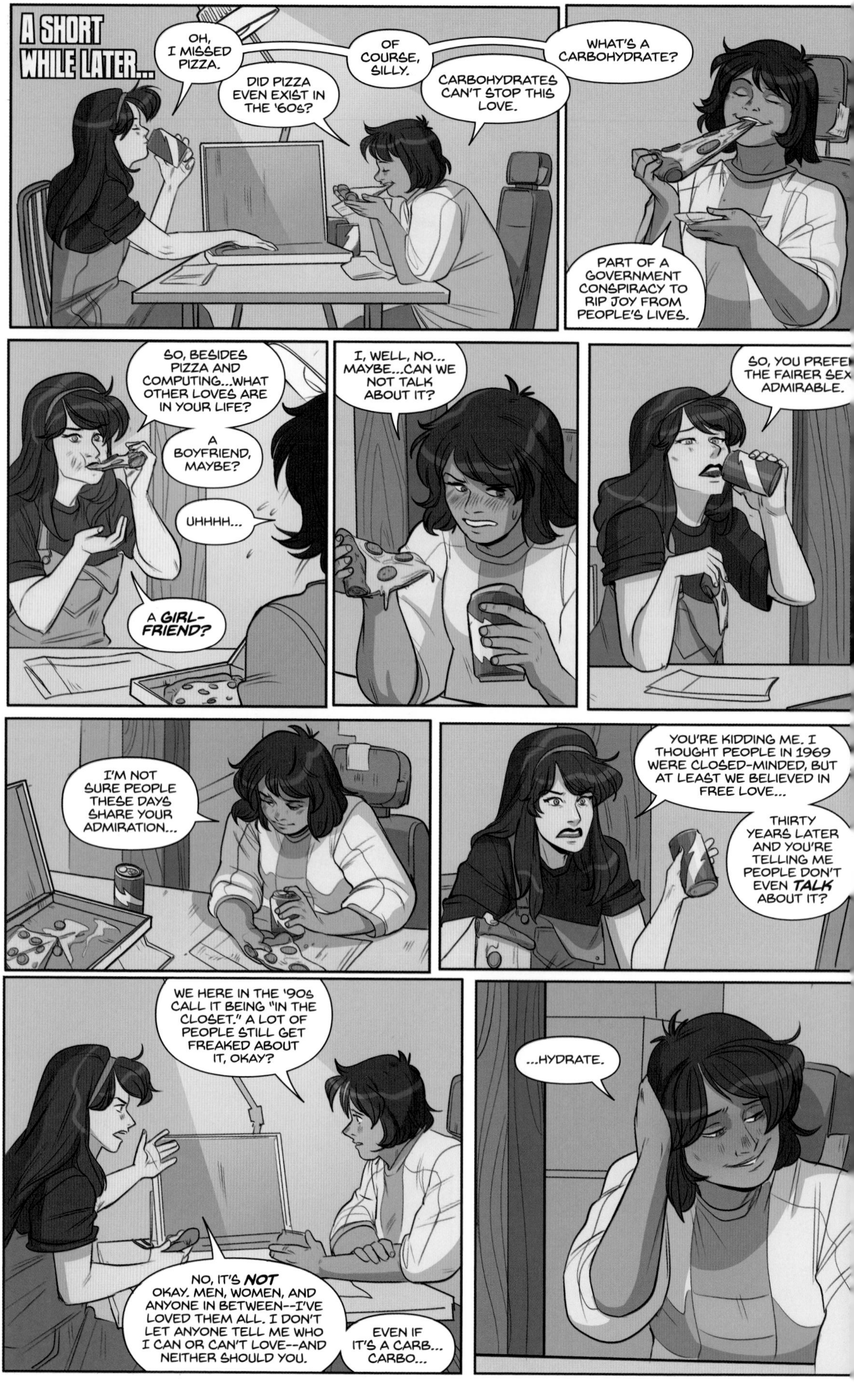
A SHORT WHILE LATER...
OH, I MISSED PIZZA.
DID PIZZA EVEN EXIST IN THE '60s?
OF COURSE, SILLY.
CARBOHYDRATES CAN'T STOP THIS LOVE.
WHAT'S A CARBOHYDRATE?
PART OF A GOVERNMENT CONSPIRACY TO RIP JOY FROM PEOPLE'S LIVES.
SO, BESIDES PIZZA AND COMPUTING...WHAT OTHER LOVES ARE IN YOUR LIFE?
A BOYFRIEND, MAYBE?
UHHHH...
A GIRL-FRIEND?
I, WELL, NO... MAYBE...CAN WE NOT TALK ABOUT IT?
SO, YOU PREFE THE FAIRER SEX ADMIRABLE.
I'M NOT SURE PEOPLE THESE DAYS SHARE YOUR ADMIRATION...
YOU'RE KIDDING ME. I THOUGHT PEOPLE IN 1969 WERE CLOSED-MINDED, BUT AT LEAST WE BELIEVED IN FREE LOVE...
THIRTY YEARS LATER AND YOU'RE TELLING ME PEOPLE DON'T EVEN TALK ABOUT IT?
WE HERE IN THE '90s CALL IT BEING "IN THE CLOSET." A LOT OF PEOPLE STILL GET FREAKED ABOUT IT, OKAY?
NO, IT'S NOT OKAY. MEN, WOMEN, AND ANYONE IN BETWEEN--I'VE LOVED THEM ALL. I DON'T LET ANYONE TELL ME WHO I CAN OR CAN'T LOVE--AND NEITHER SHOULD YOU.
EVEN IF IT'S A CARB... CARBO...
...HYDRATE.

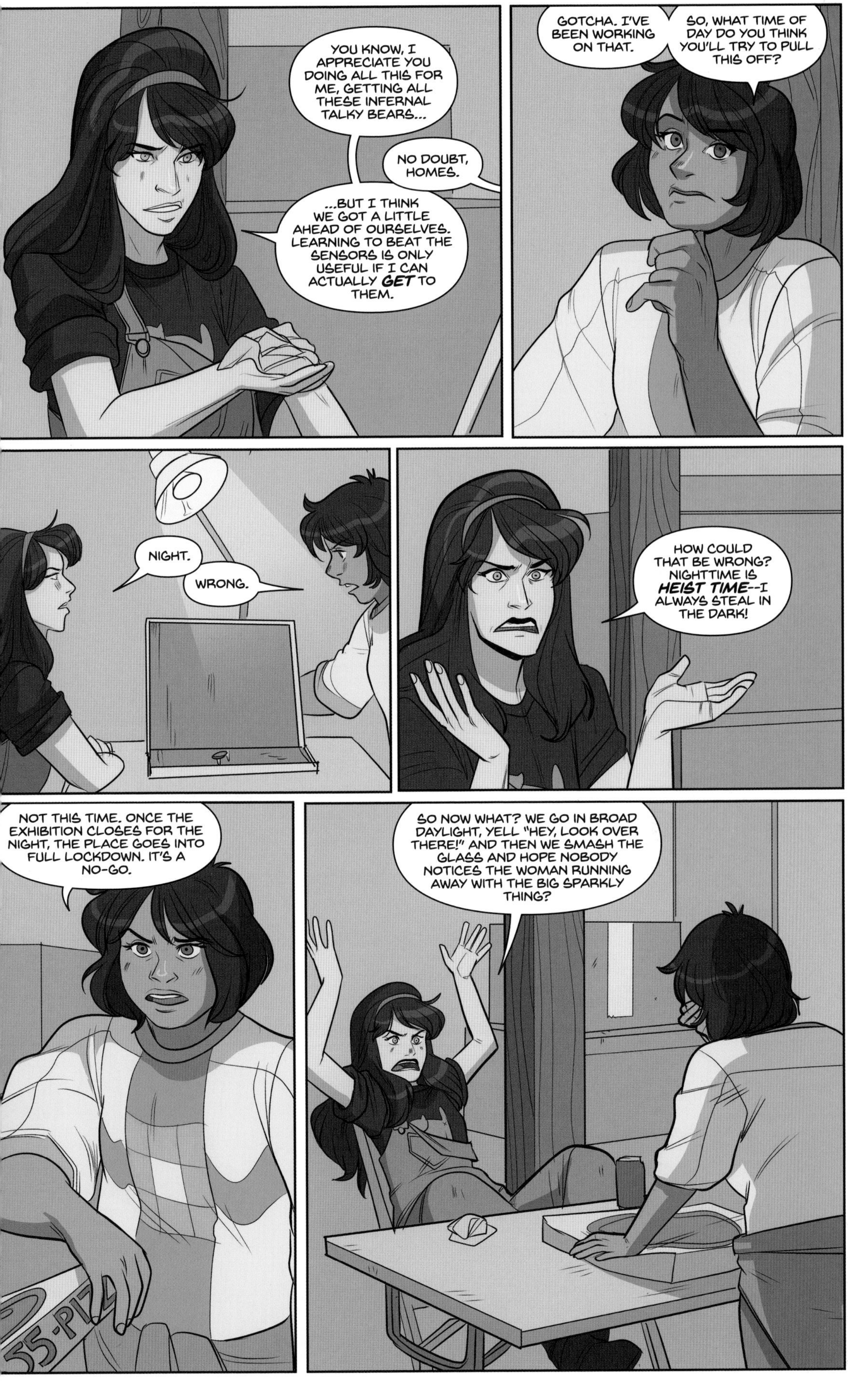

YOU KNOW, I APPRECIATE YOU DOING ALL THIS FOR ME, GETTING ALL THESE INFERNAL TALKY BEARS...
NO DOUBT, HOMES.
...BUT I THINK WE GOT A LITTLE AHEAD OF OURSELVES. LEARNING TO BEAT THE SENSORS IS ONLY USEFUL IF I CAN ACTUALLY **GET** TO THEM.
GOTCHA. I'VE BEEN WORKING ON THAT.
SO, WHAT TIME OF DAY DO YOU THINK YOU'LL TRY TO PULL THIS OFF?
NIGHT.
WRONG.
HOW COULD THAT BE WRONG? NIGHTTIME IS ***HEIST TIME***--I ALWAYS STEAL IN THE DARK!
NOT THIS TIME. ONCE THE EXHIBITION CLOSES FOR THE NIGHT, THE PLACE GOES INTO FULL LOCKDOWN. IT'S A NO-GO.
55-PIZ
SO NOW WHAT? WE GO IN BROAD DAYLIGHT, YELL "HEY, LOOK OVER THERE!" AND THEN WE SMASH THE GLASS AND HOPE NOBODY NOTICES THE WOMAN RUNNING AWAY WITH THE BIG SPARKLY THING?

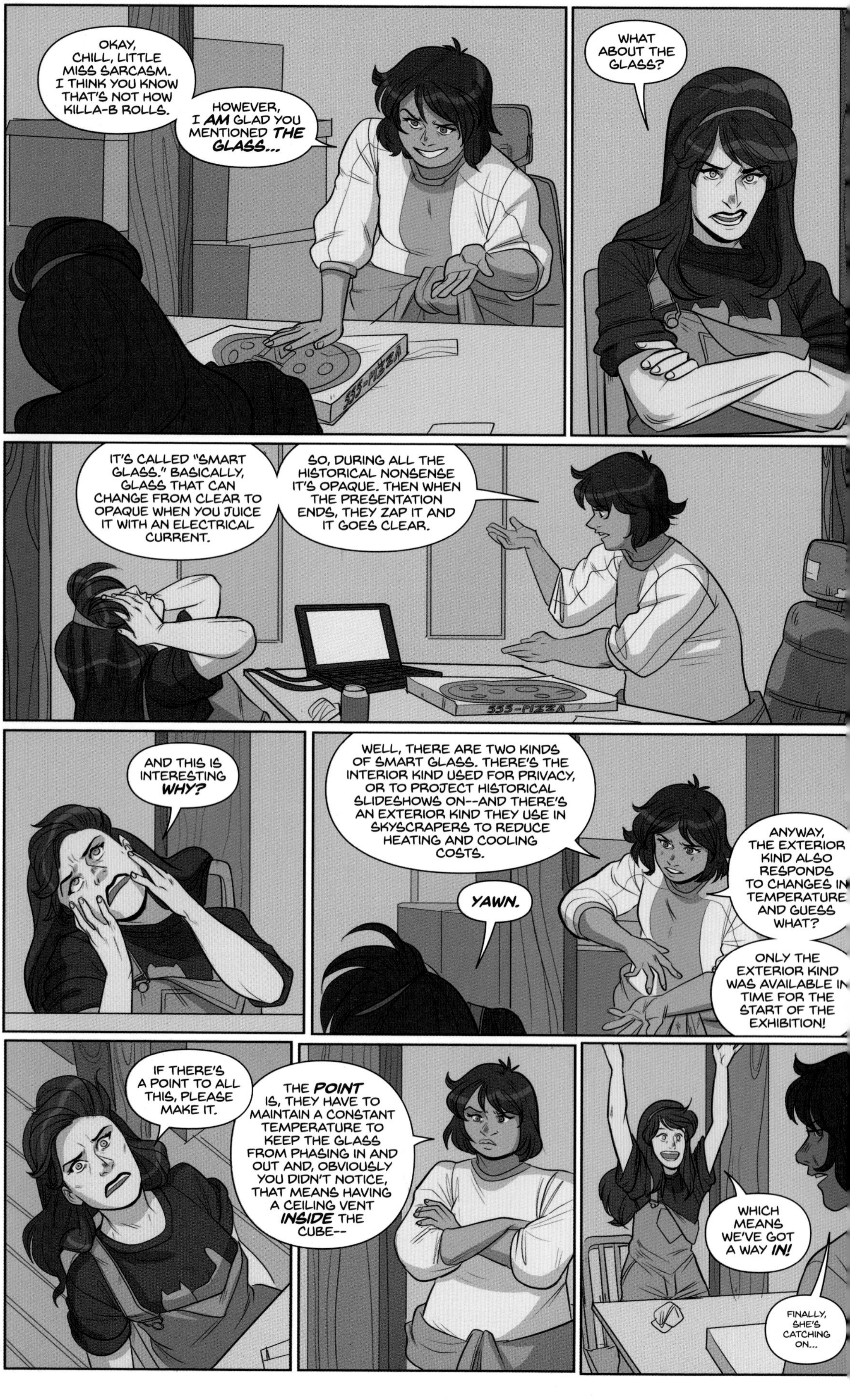

OKAY, CHILL, LITTLE MISS SARCASM. I THINK YOU KNOW THAT'S NOT HOW KILLA-B ROLLS.
HOWEVER, I AM GLAD YOU MENTIONED THE GLASS...
WHAT ABOUT THE GLASS?
555-PIZZA
IT'S CALLED "SMART GLASS." BASICALLY, GLASS THAT CAN CHANGE FROM CLEAR TO OPAQUE WHEN YOU JUICE IT WITH AN ELECTRICAL CURRENT.
SO, DURING ALL THE HISTORICAL NONSENSE IT'S OPAQUE. THEN WHEN THE PRESENTATION ENDS, THEY ZAP IT AND IT GOES CLEAR.
555-PIZZA
AND THIS IS INTERESTING WHY?
WELL, THERE ARE TWO KINDS OF SMART GLASS. THERE'S THE INTERIOR KIND USED FOR PRIVACY, OR TO PROJECT HISTORICAL SLIDESHOWS ON--AND THERE'S AN EXTERIOR KIND THEY USE IN SKYSCRAPERS TO REDUCE HEATING AND COOLING COSTS.
YAWN.
ANYWAY, THE EXTERIOR KIND ALSO RESPONDS TO CHANGES IN TEMPERATURE AND GUESS WHAT?
ONLY THE EXTERIOR KIND WAS AVAILABLE IN TIME FOR THE START OF THE EXHIBITION!
IF THERE'S A POINT TO ALL THIS, PLEASE MAKE IT.
THE POINT IS, THEY HAVE TO MAINTAIN A CONSTANT TEMPERATURE TO KEEP THE GLASS FROM PHASING IN AND OUT AND, OBVIOUSLY YOU DIDN'T NOTICE, THAT MEANS HAVING A CEILING VENT INSIDE THE CUBE--
WHICH MEANS WE'VE GOT A WAY IN!
FINALLY, SHE'S CATCHING ON...

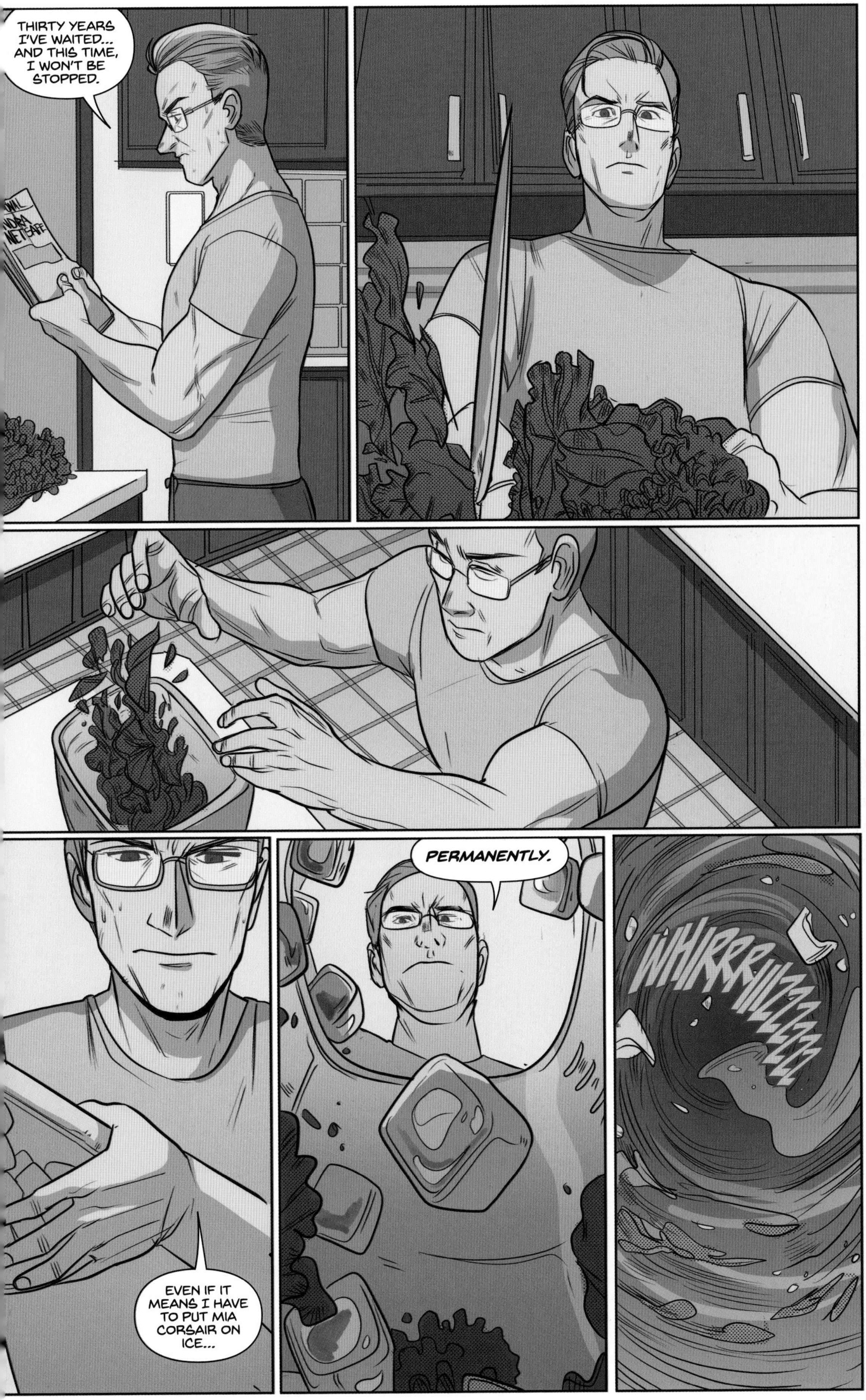
THIRTY YEARS I'VE WAITED... AND THIS TIME, I WON'T BE STOPPED.
EVEN IF IT MEANS I HAVE TO PUT MIA CORSAIR ON ICE...
PERMANENTLY.
WHIRRRMMZZZZ

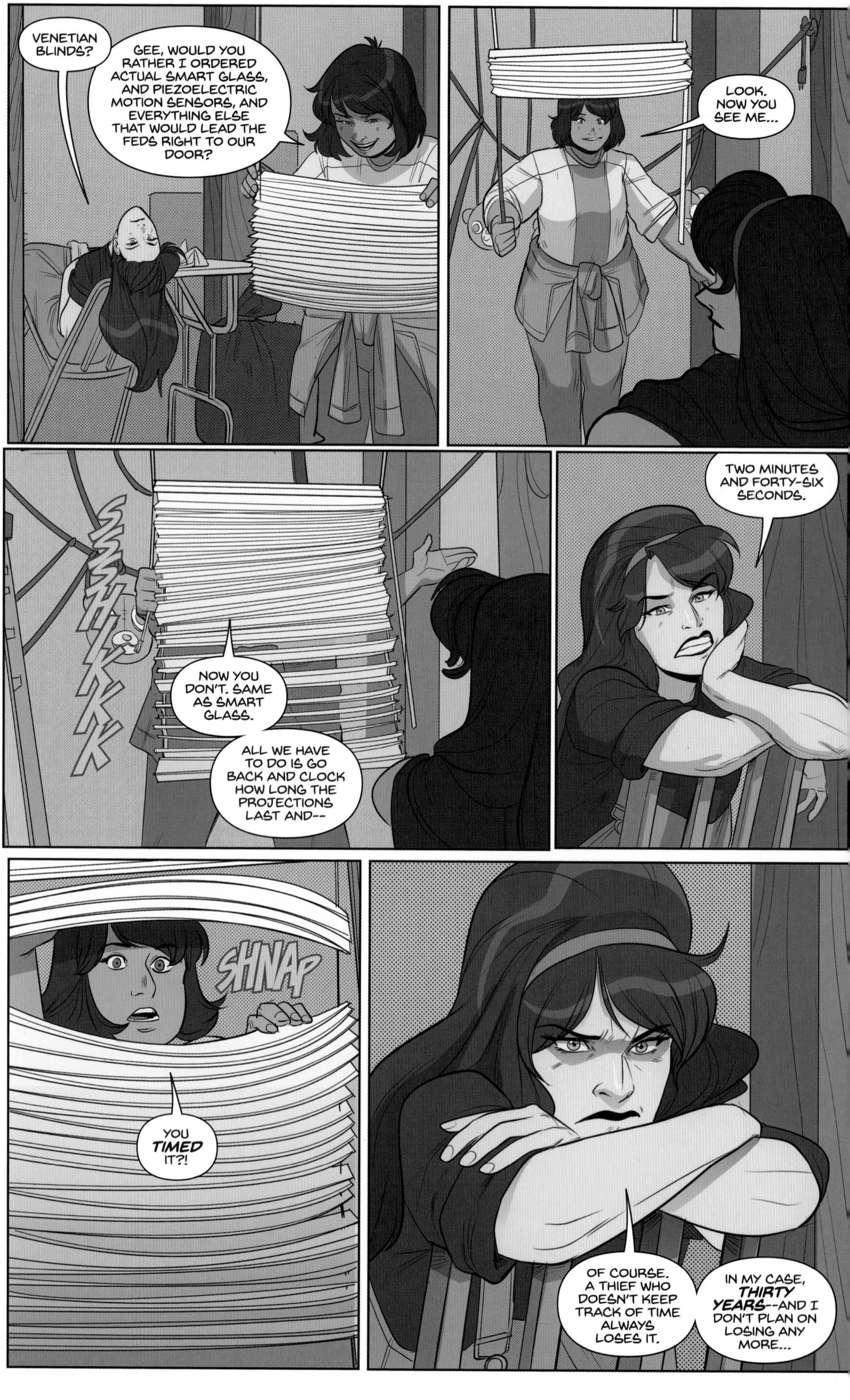
VENETIAN BLINDS?
GEE, WOULD YOU RATHER I ORDERED ACTUAL SMART GLASS, AND PIEZOELECTRIC MOTION SENSORS, AND EVERYTHING ELSE THAT WOULD LEAD THE FEDS RIGHT TO OUR DOOR?
LOOK. NOW YOU SEE ME...
SSHHKKKK
NOW YOU DON'T. SAME AS SMART GLASS.
ALL WE HAVE TO DO IS GO BACK AND CLOCK HOW LONG THE PROJECTIONS LAST AND--
TWO MINUTES AND FORTY-SIX SECONDS.
SHNAP
YOU **TIMED** IT?!
OF COURSE. A THIEF WHO DOESN'T KEEP TRACK OF TIME ALWAYS LOSES IT.
IN MY CASE, **THIRTY YEARS**--AND I DON'T PLAN ON LOSING ANY MORE...

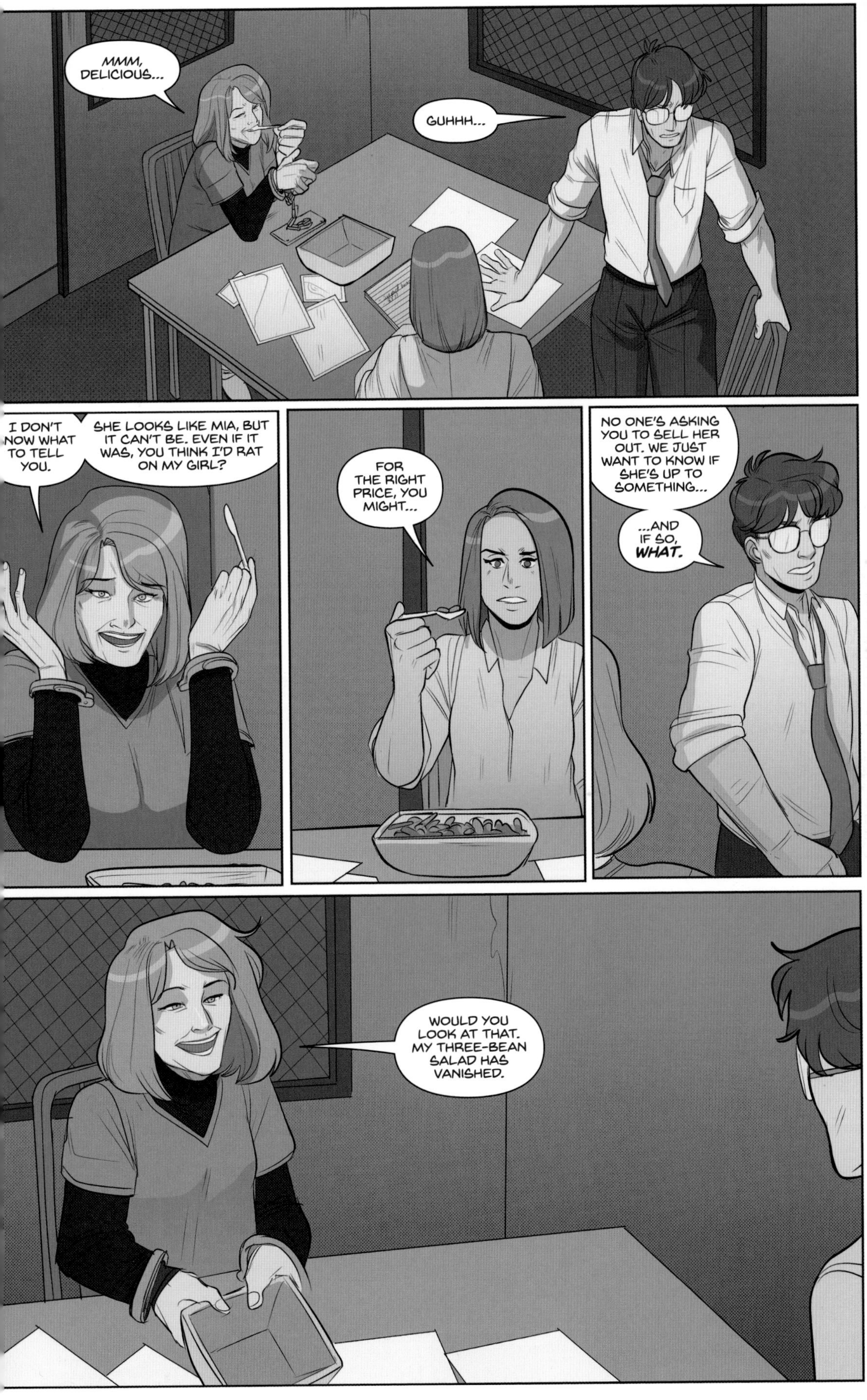
MMM, DELICIOUS...
GUHHH...
I DON'T NOW WHAT TO TELL YOU.
SHE LOOKS LIKE MIA, BUT IT CAN'T BE. EVEN IF IT WAS, YOU THINK I'D RAT ON MY GIRL?
FOR THE RIGHT PRICE, YOU MIGHT...
NO ONE'S ASKING YOU TO SELL HER OUT. WE JUST WANT TO KNOW IF SHE'S UP TO SOMETHING...
...AND IF SO, WHAT.
WOULD YOU LOOK AT THAT. MY THREE-BEAN SALAD HAS VANISHED.

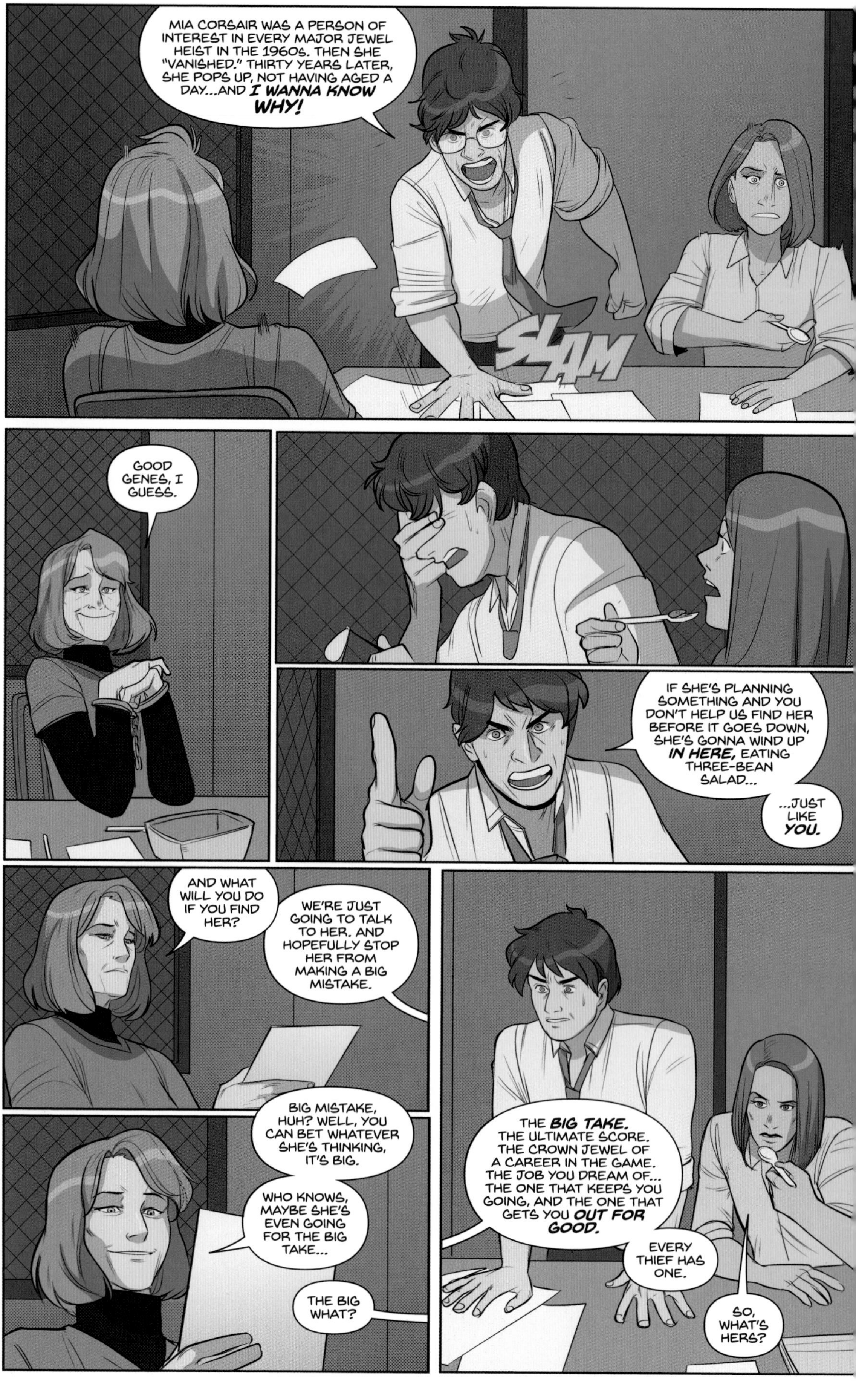
MIA CORSAIR WAS A PERSON OF INTEREST IN EVERY MAJOR JEWEL HEIST IN THE 1960s. THEN SHE "VANISHED." THIRTY YEARS LATER, SHE POPS UP, NOT HAVING AGED A DAY...AND ***I WANNA KNOW WHY!***
SLAM
GOOD GENES, I GUESS.
IF SHE'S PLANNING SOMETHING AND YOU DON'T HELP US FIND HER BEFORE IT GOES DOWN, SHE'S GONNA WIND UP ***IN HERE,*** EATING THREE-BEAN SALAD...
...JUST LIKE ***YOU.***
AND WHAT WILL YOU DO IF YOU FIND HER?
WE'RE JUST GOING TO TALK TO HER. AND HOPEFULLY STOP HER FROM MAKING A BIG MISTAKE.
BIG MISTAKE, HUH? WELL, YOU CAN BET WHATEVER SHE'S THINKING, IT'S BIG.
WHO KNOWS, MAYBE SHE'S EVEN GOING FOR THE BIG TAKE...
THE BIG WHAT?
THE ***BIG TAKE.*** THE ULTIMATE SCORE. THE CROWN JEWEL OF A CAREER IN THE GAME. THE JOB YOU DREAM OF... THE ONE THAT KEEPS YOU GOING, AND THE ONE THAT GETS YOU ***OUT FOR GOOD.***
EVERY THIEF HAS ONE.
SO, WHAT'S HERS?

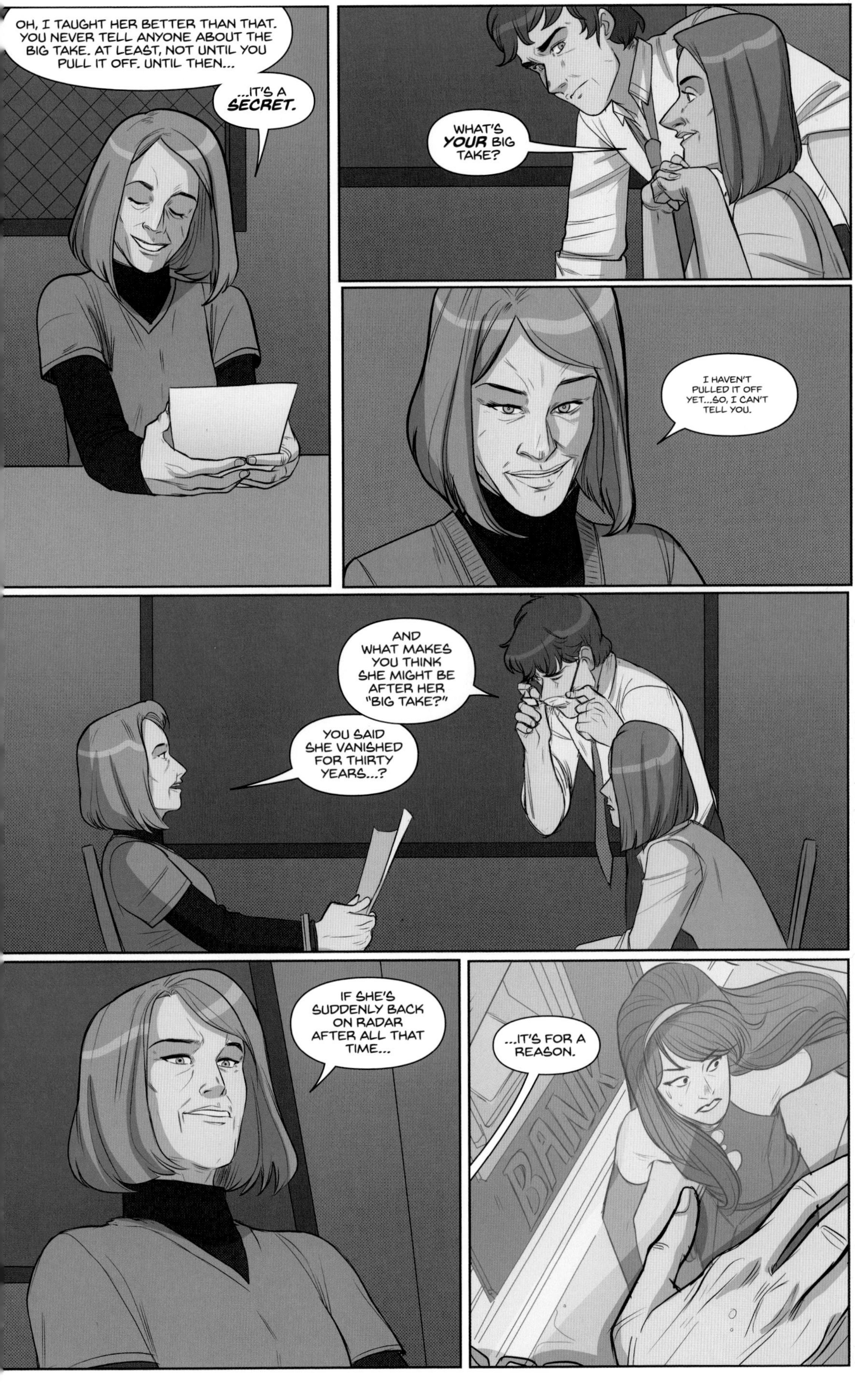
OH, I TAUGHT HER BETTER THAN THAT. YOU NEVER TELL ANYONE ABOUT THE BIG TAKE. AT LEAST, NOT UNTIL YOU PULL IT OFF. UNTIL THEN...
...IT'S A **SECRET.**
WHAT'S ***YOUR*** BIG TAKE?
I HAVEN'T PULLED IT OFF YET...SO, I CAN'T TELL YOU.
AND WHAT MAKES YOU THINK SHE MIGHT BE AFTER HER "BIG TAKE?"
YOU SAID SHE VANISHED FOR THIRTY YEARS...?
IF SHE'S SUDDENLY BACK ON RADAR AFTER ALL THAT TIME...
...IT'S FOR A REASON.

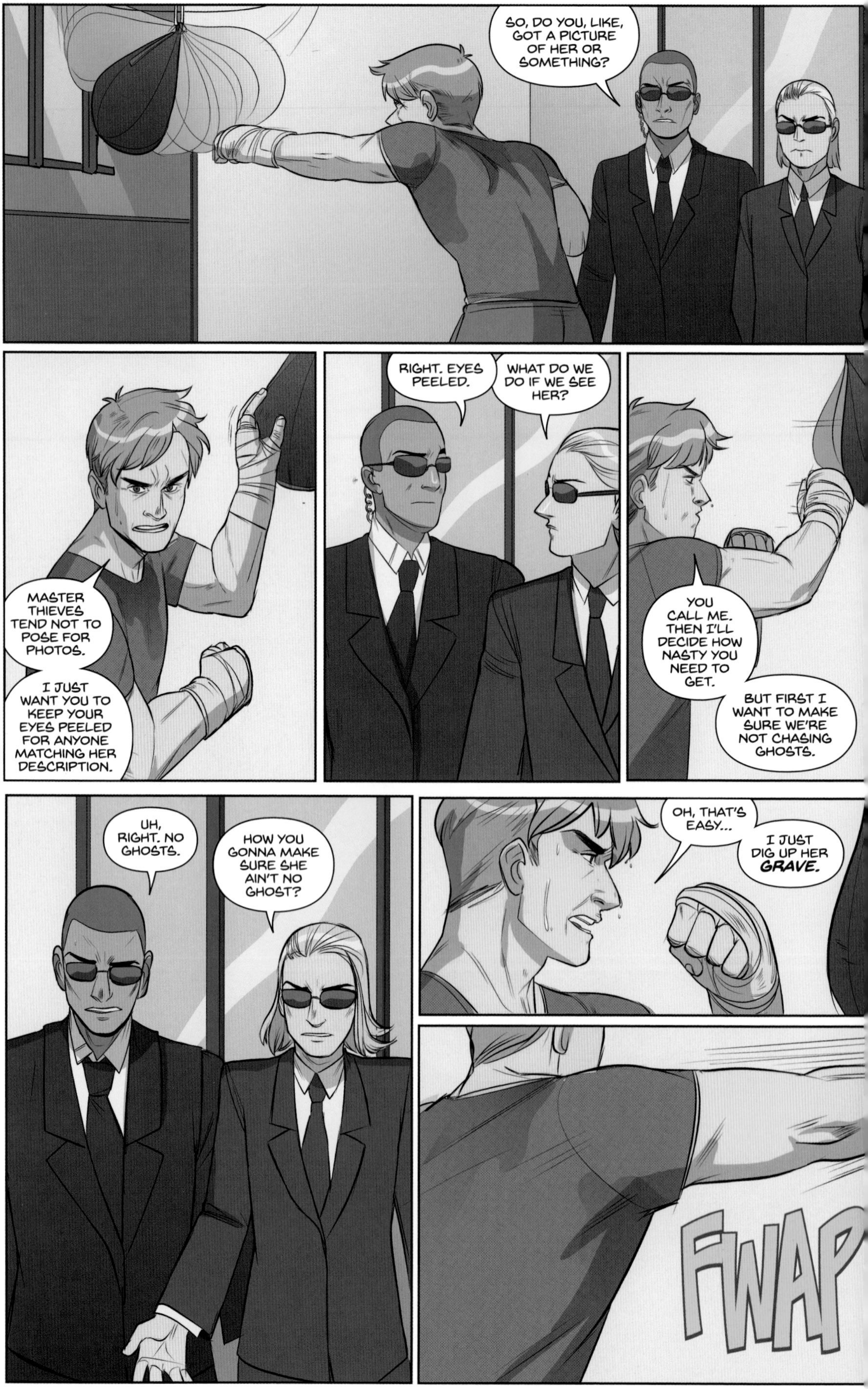
SO, DO YOU, LIKE, GOT A PICTURE OF HER OR SOMETHING?
MASTER THIEVES TEND NOT TO POSE FOR PHOTOS.
I JUST WANT YOU TO KEEP YOUR EYES PEELED FOR ANYONE MATCHING HER DESCRIPTION.
RIGHT. EYES PEELED.
WHAT DO WE DO IF WE SEE HER?
YOU CALL ME. THEN I'LL DECIDE HOW NASTY YOU NEED TO GET.
BUT FIRST I WANT TO MAKE SURE WE'RE NOT CHASING GHOSTS.
UH, RIGHT. NO GHOSTS.
HOW YOU GONNA MAKE SURE SHE AIN'T NO GHOST?
OH, THAT'S EASY...
I JUST DIG UP HER ***GRAVE.***
FWAP

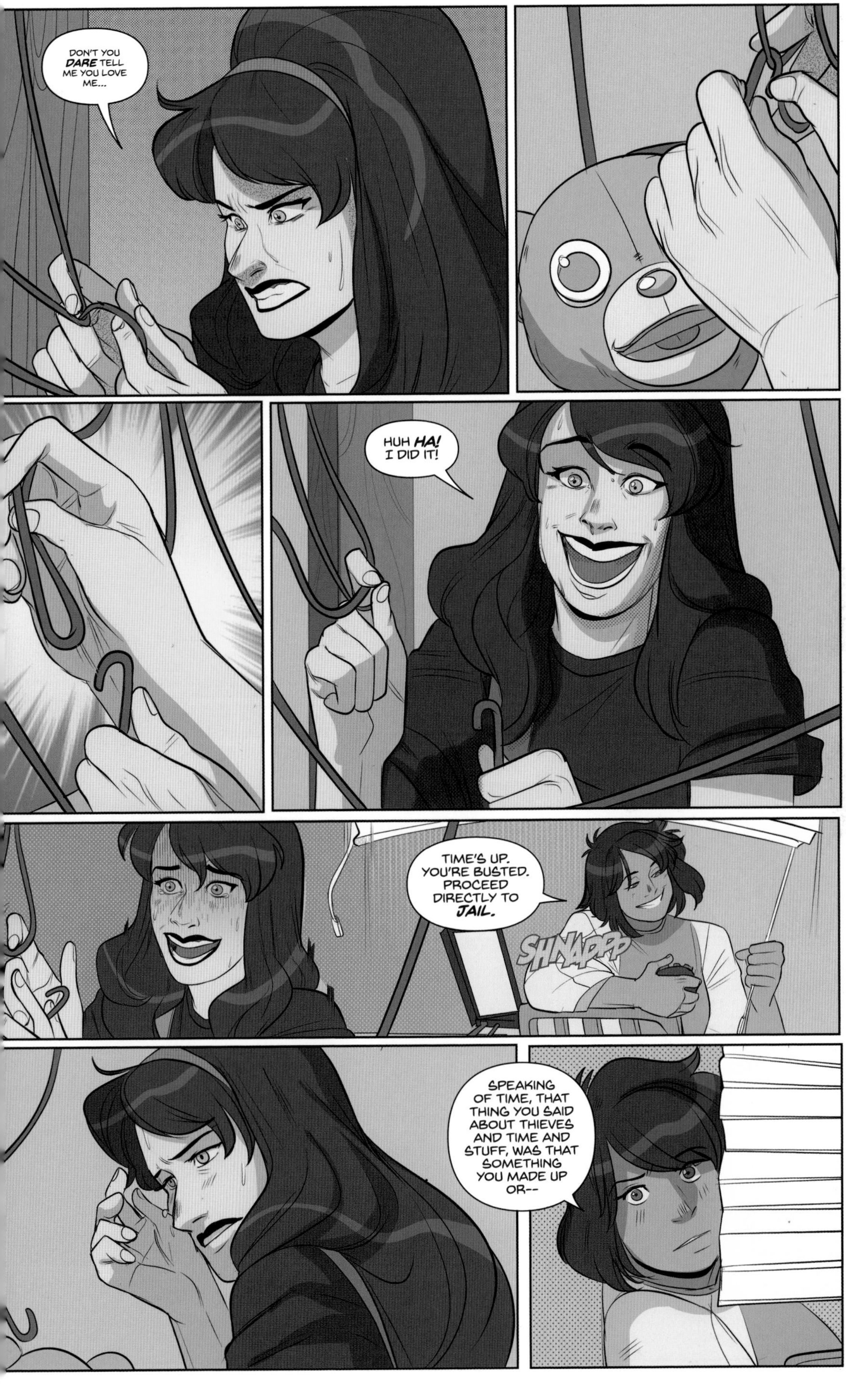
DON'T YOU DARE TELL ME YOU LOVE ME...
HUH HA! I DID IT!
TIME'S UP. YOU'RE BUSTED. PROCEED DIRECTLY TO JAIL.
SHNAPP
SPEAKING OF TIME, THAT THING YOU SAID ABOUT THIEVES AND TIME AND STUFF, WAS THAT SOMETHING YOU MADE UP OR--

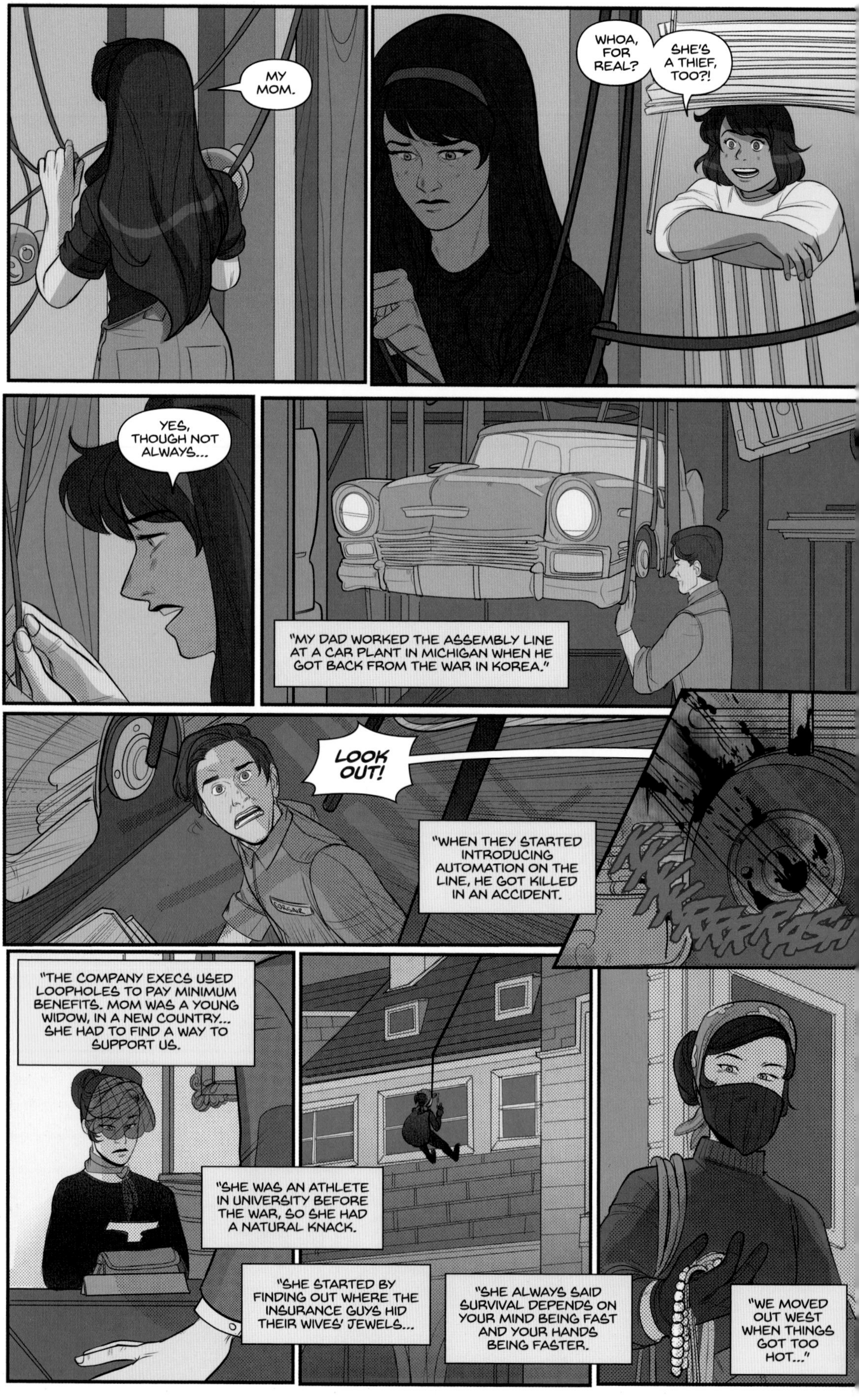
MY MOM.
WHOA, FOR REAL?
SHE'S A THIEF, TOO?!
YES, THOUGH NOT ALWAYS...
"MY DAD WORKED THE ASSEMBLY LINE AT A CAR PLANT IN MICHIGAN WHEN HE GOT BACK FROM THE WAR IN KOREA."
LOOK OUT!
"WHEN THEY STARTED INTRODUCING AUTOMATION ON THE LINE, HE GOT KILLED IN AN ACCIDENT.
CORSAIR
"THE COMPANY EXECS USED LOOPHOLES TO PAY MINIMUM BENEFITS. MOM WAS A YOUNG WIDOW, IN A NEW COUNTRY... SHE HAD TO FIND A WAY TO SUPPORT US.
"SHE WAS AN ATHLETE IN UNIVERSITY BEFORE THE WAR, SO SHE HAD A NATURAL KNACK.
"SHE STARTED BY FINDING OUT WHERE THE INSURANCE GUYS HID THEIR WIVES' JEWELS...
"SHE ALWAYS SAID SURVIVAL DEPENDS ON YOUR MIND BEING FAST AND YOUR HANDS BEING FASTER.
"WE MOVED OUT WEST WHEN THINGS GOT TOO HOT..."

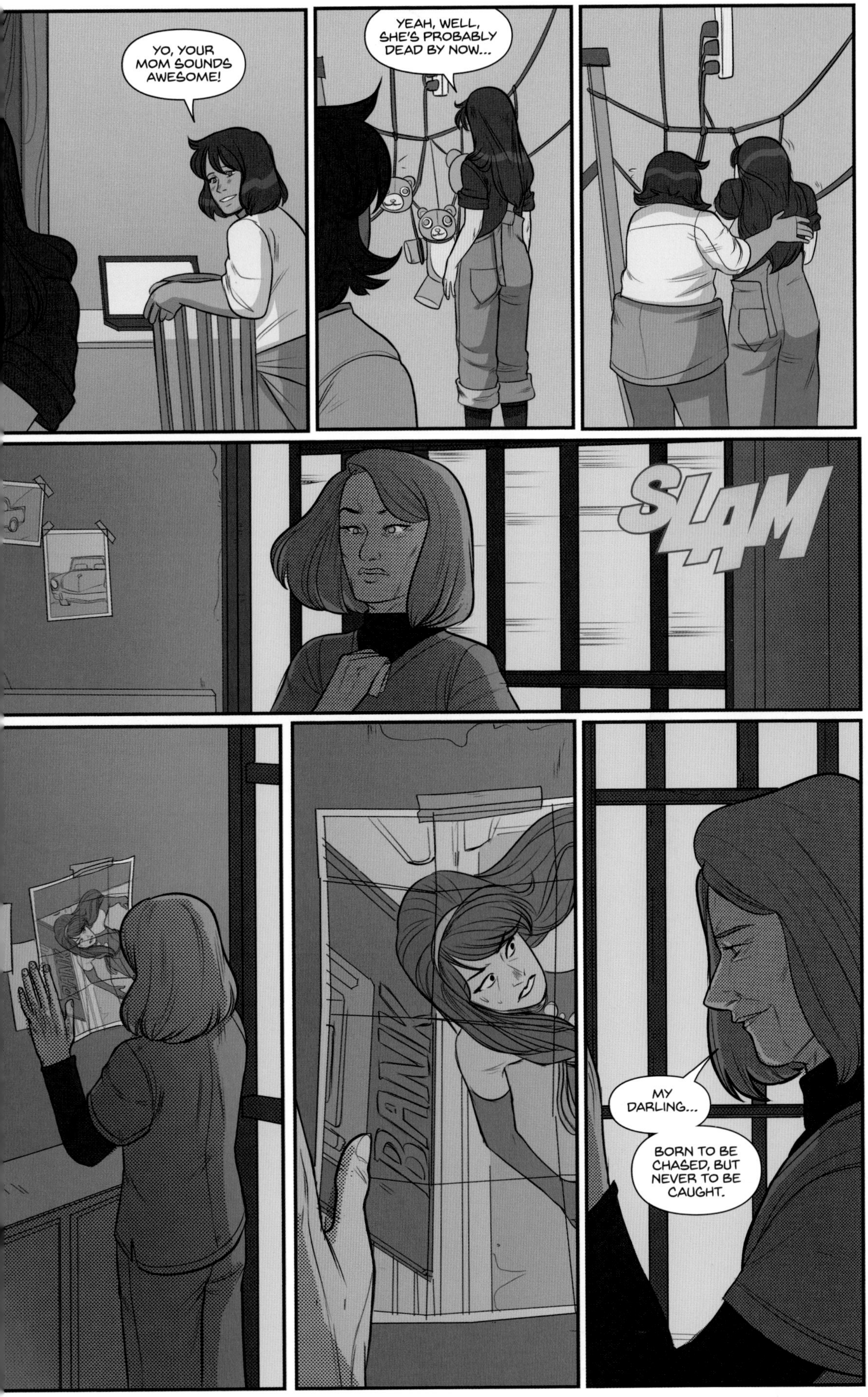
YO, YOUR MOM SOUNDS AWESOME!
YEAH, WELL, SHE'S PROBABLY DEAD BY NOW...
SLAM
BANK
MY DARLING...
BORN TO BE CHASED, BUT NEVER TO BE CAUGHT.

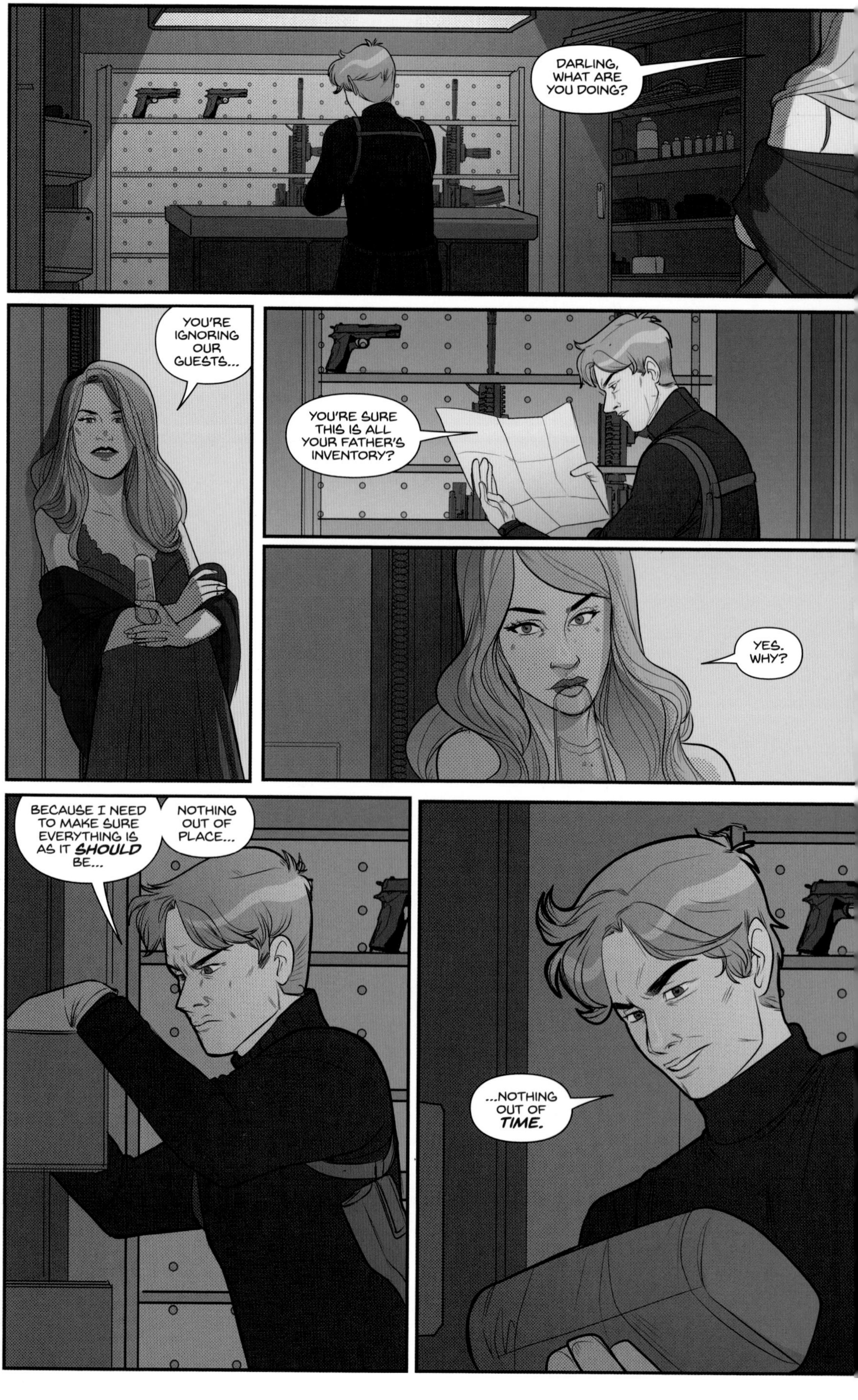
DARLING, WHAT ARE YOU DOING?
YOU'RE IGNORING OUR GUESTS...
YOU'RE SURE THIS IS ALL YOUR FATHER'S INVENTORY?
YES. WHY?
BECAUSE I NEED TO MAKE SURE EVERYTHING IS AS IT *SHOULD* BE...
NOTHING OUT OF PLACE...
...NOTHING OUT OF *TIME.*

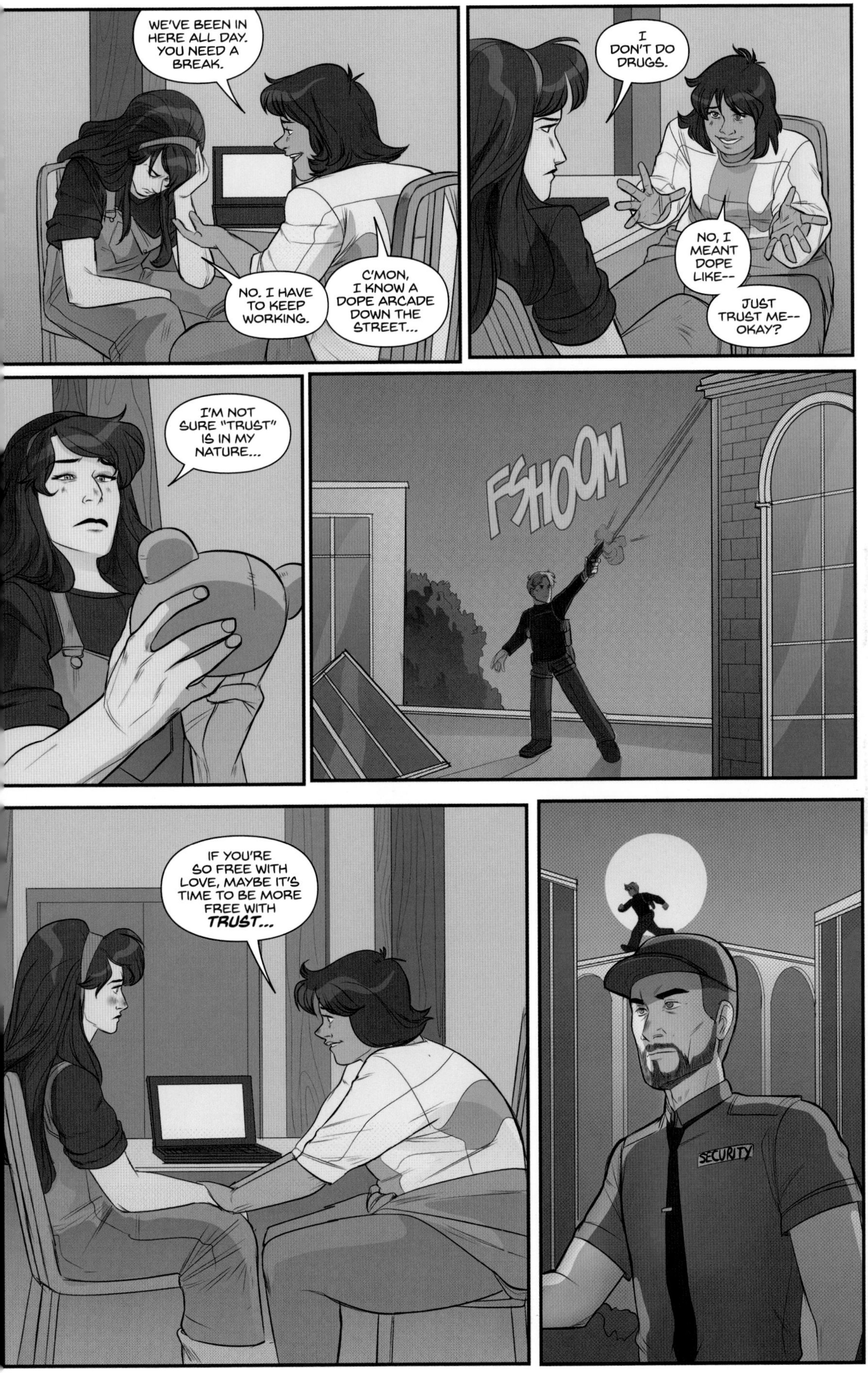
WE'VE BEEN IN HERE ALL DAY. YOU NEED A BREAK.
NO. I HAVE TO KEEP WORKING.
C'MON, I KNOW A DOPE ARCADE DOWN THE STREET...
I DON'T DO DRUGS.
NO, I MEANT DOPE LIKE--
JUST TRUST ME-- OKAY?
I'M NOT SURE "TRUST" IS IN MY NATURE...
FSHOOM
IF YOU'RE SO FREE WITH LOVE, MAYBE IT'S TIME TO BE MORE FREE WITH TRUST...
SECURITY

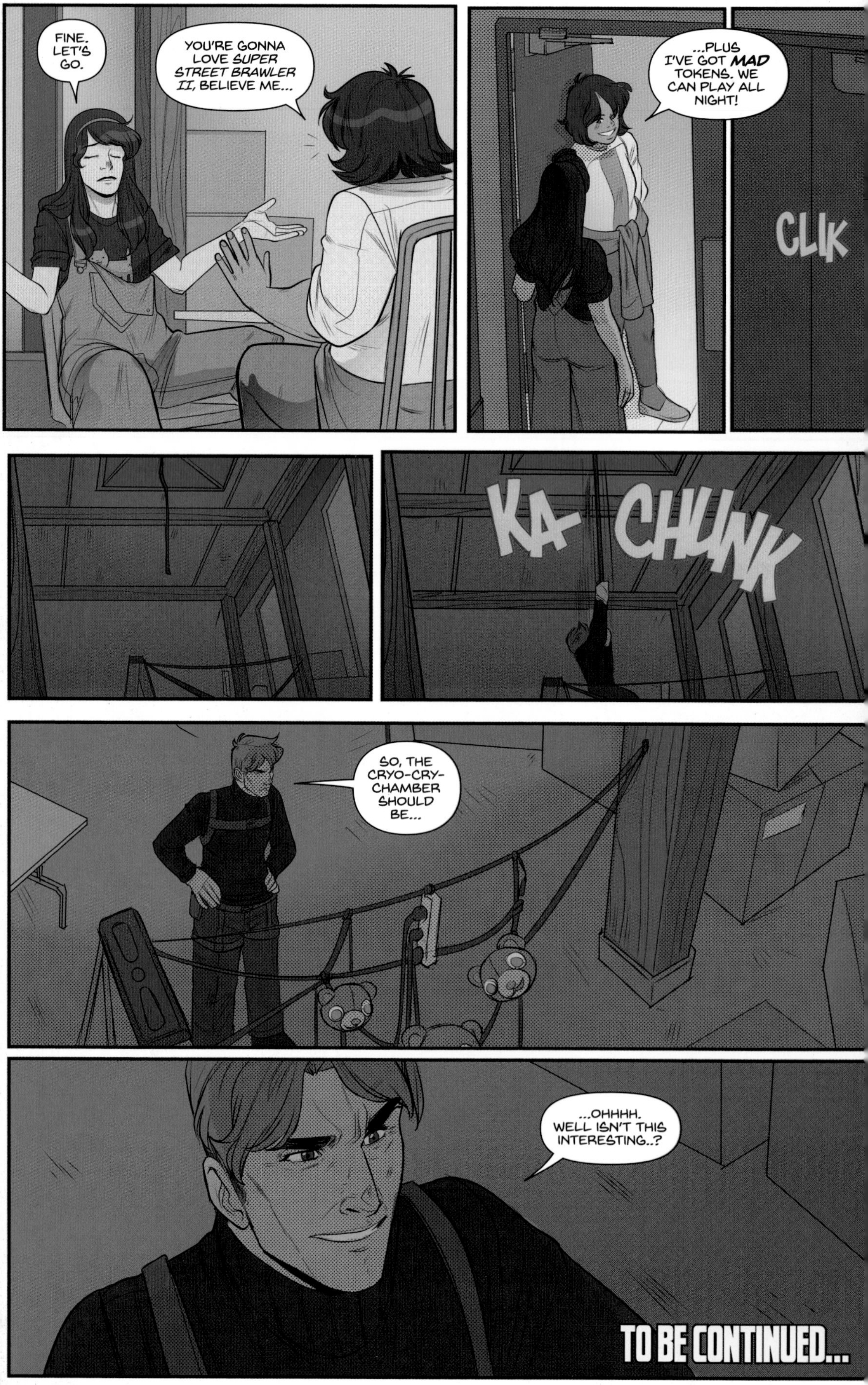
FINE. LET'S GO.
YOU'RE GONNA LOVE *SUPER STREET BRAWLER II*, BELIEVE ME...
...PLUS I'VE GOT **MAD** TOKENS. WE CAN PLAY ALL NIGHT!
CLIK
KA CHUNK
SO, THE CRYO-CRY-CHAMBER SHOULD BE...
...OHHHH. WELL ISN'T THIS INTERESTING..?
TO BE CONTINUED...

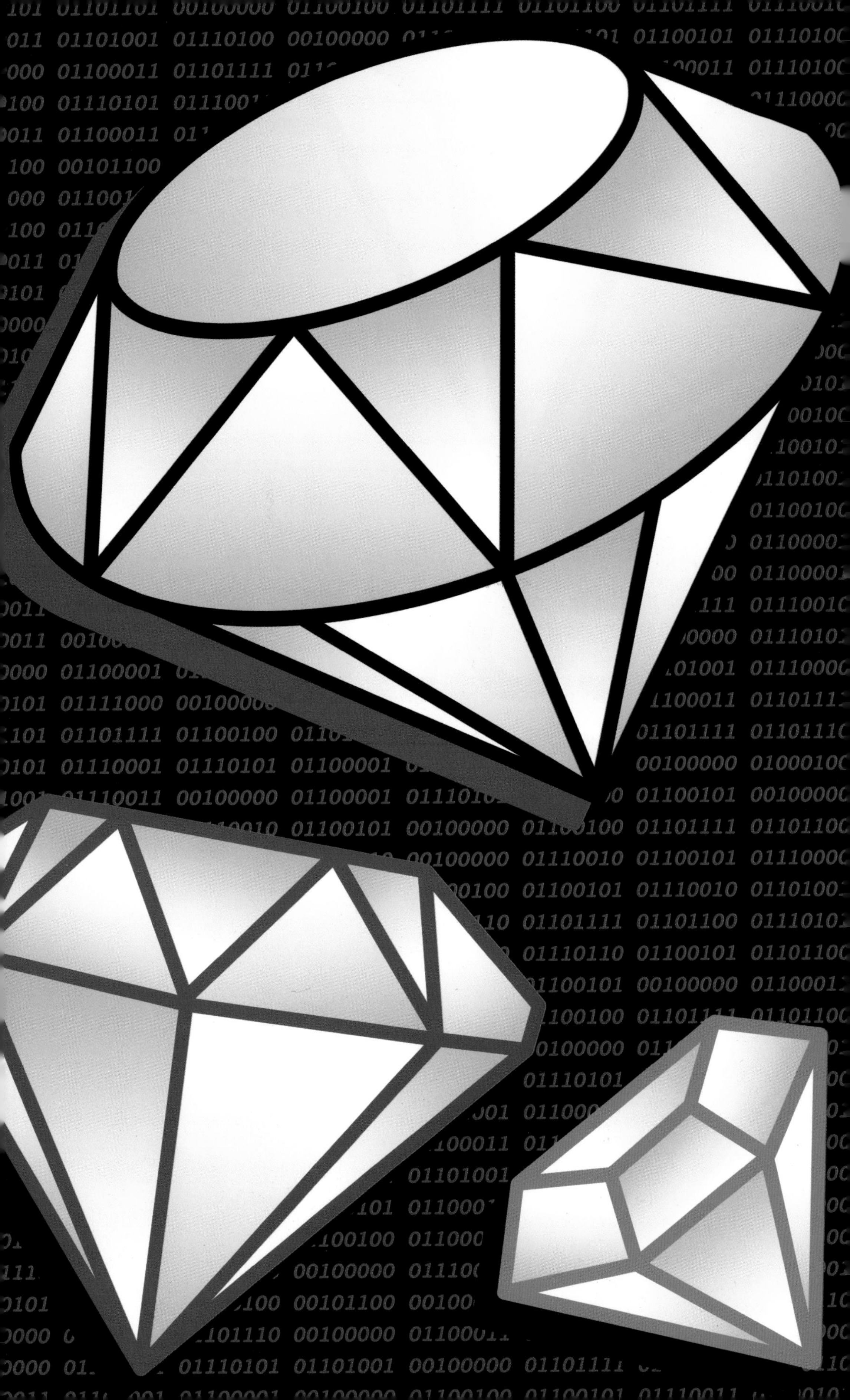

# COVER
# GALLERY

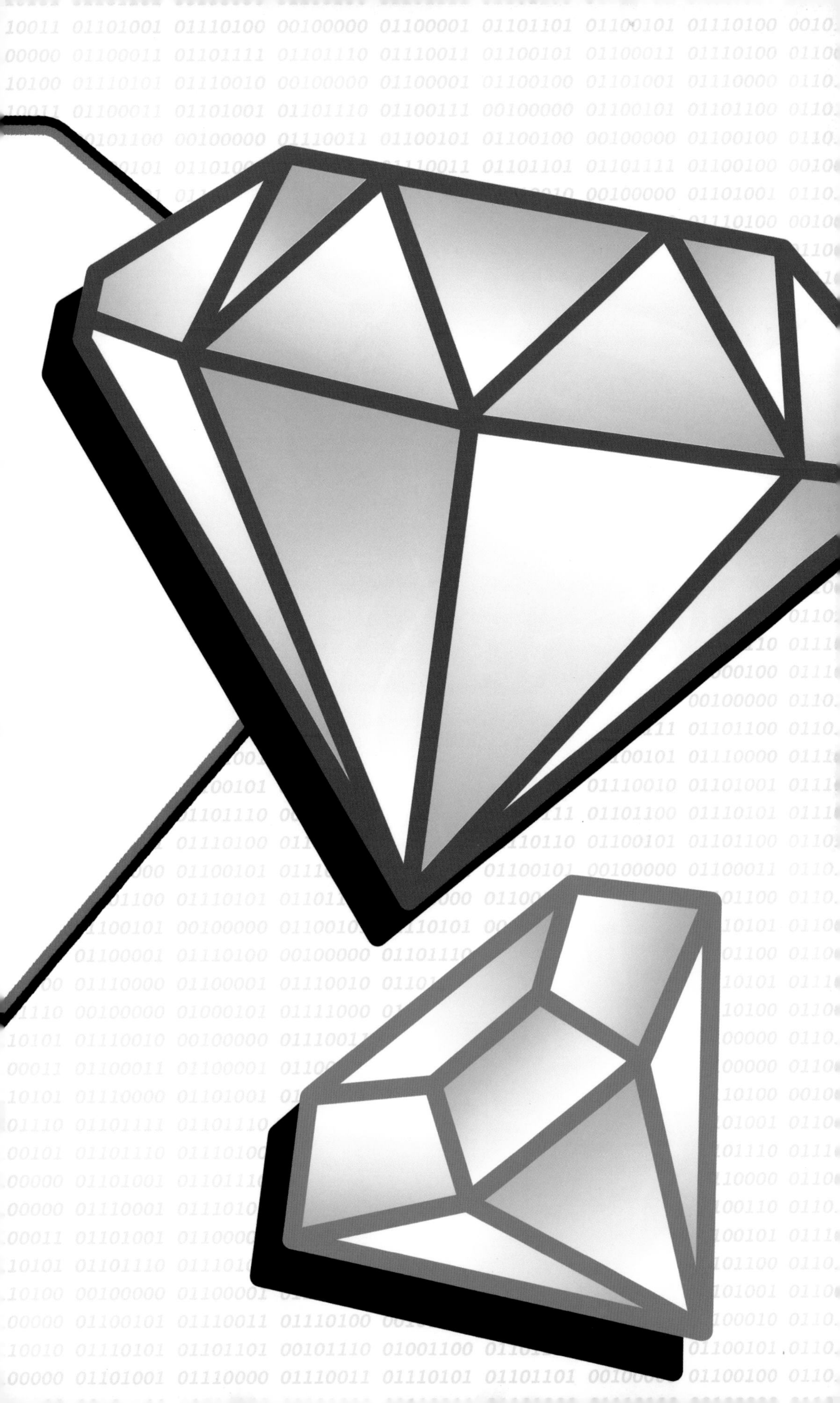

ISSUE 1 COVER
AUDREY MOK

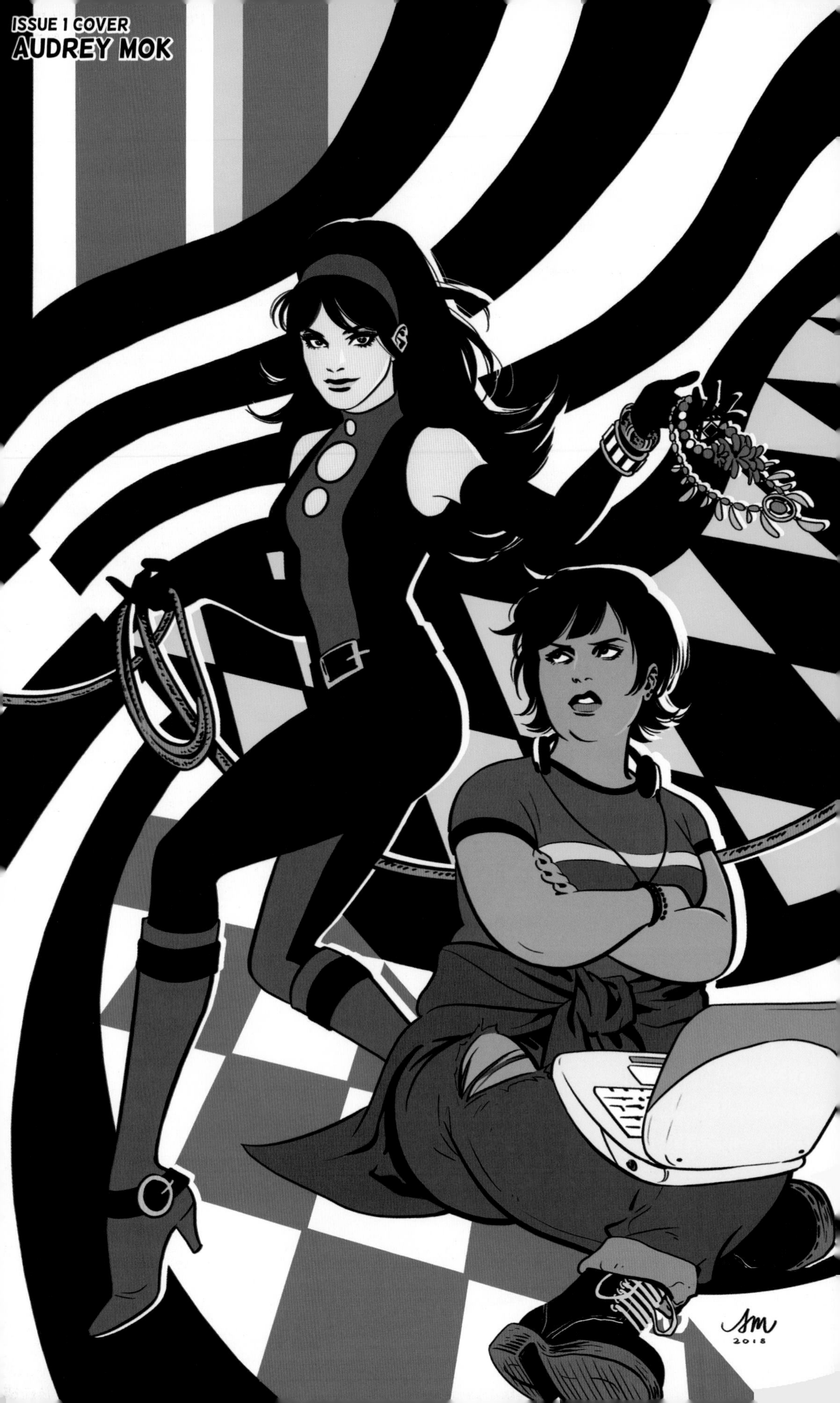
2018

ISSUE 1 VARIANT COVER
CHYNNA CLUGSTON FLORES

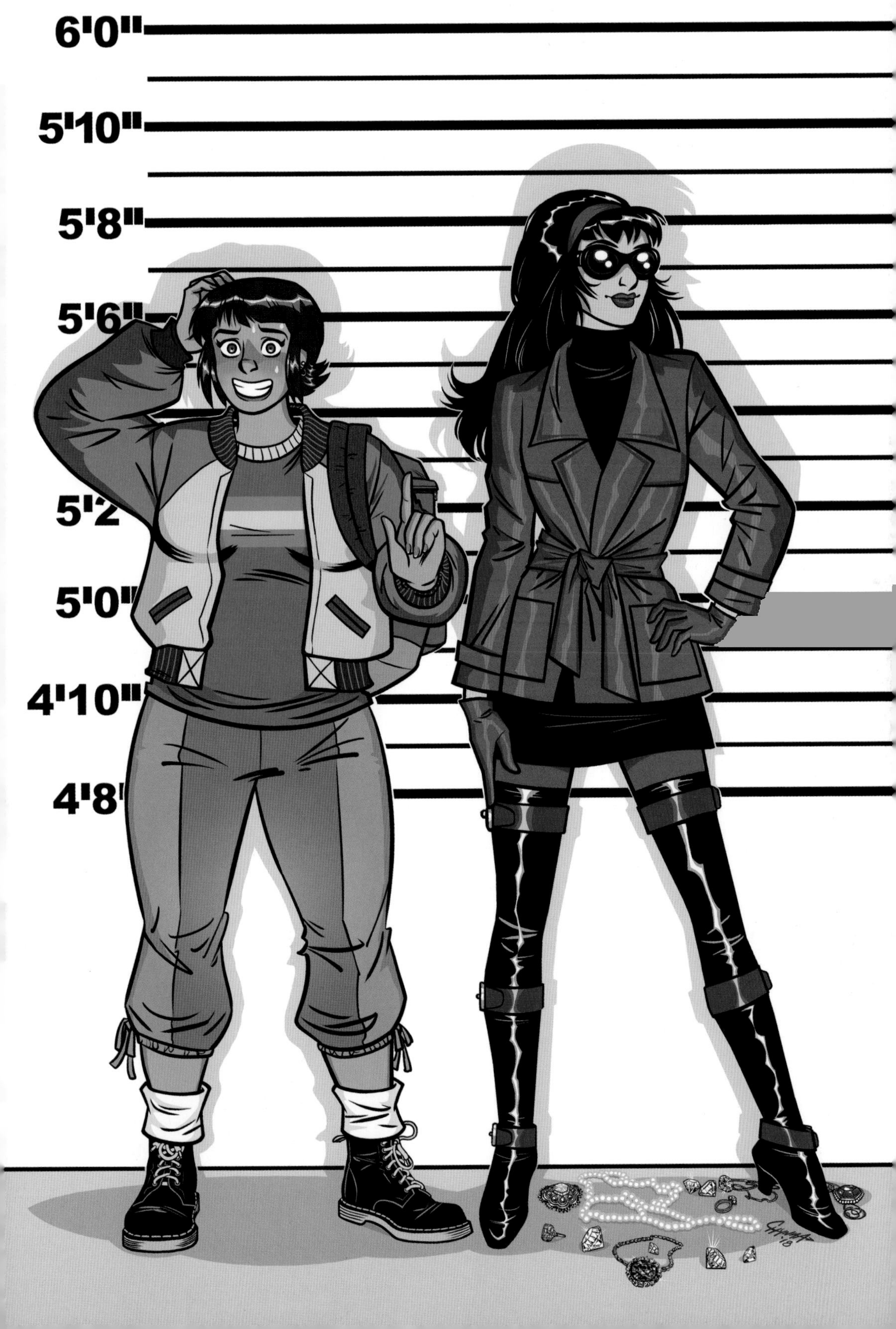
6'0"
5'10"
5'8"
5'6"
5'2
5'0"
4'10"
4'8"

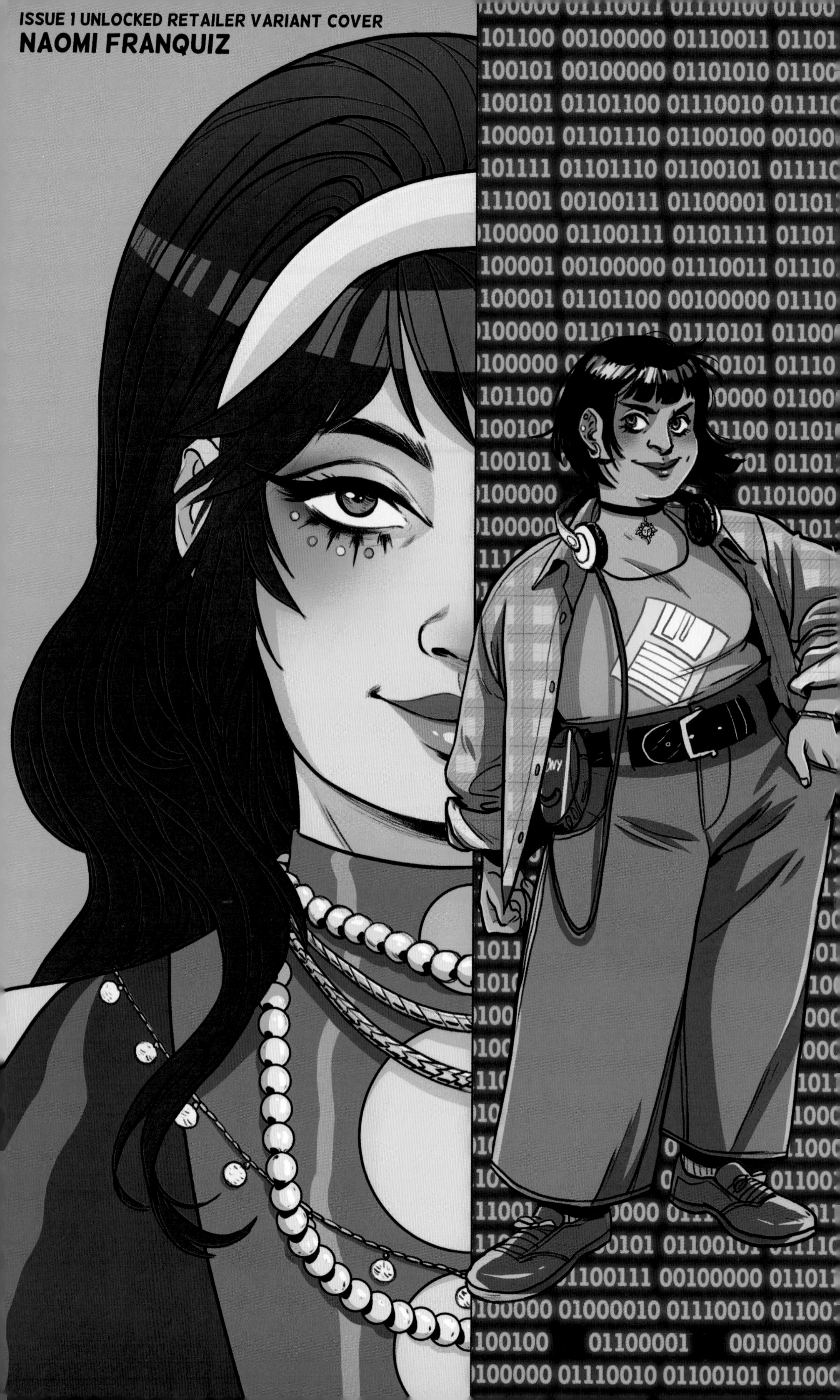

ISSUE 1 UNLOCKED RETAILER VARIANT COVER
**NAOMI FRANQUIZ**

ISSUE 2 COVER
**AUDREY MOK**

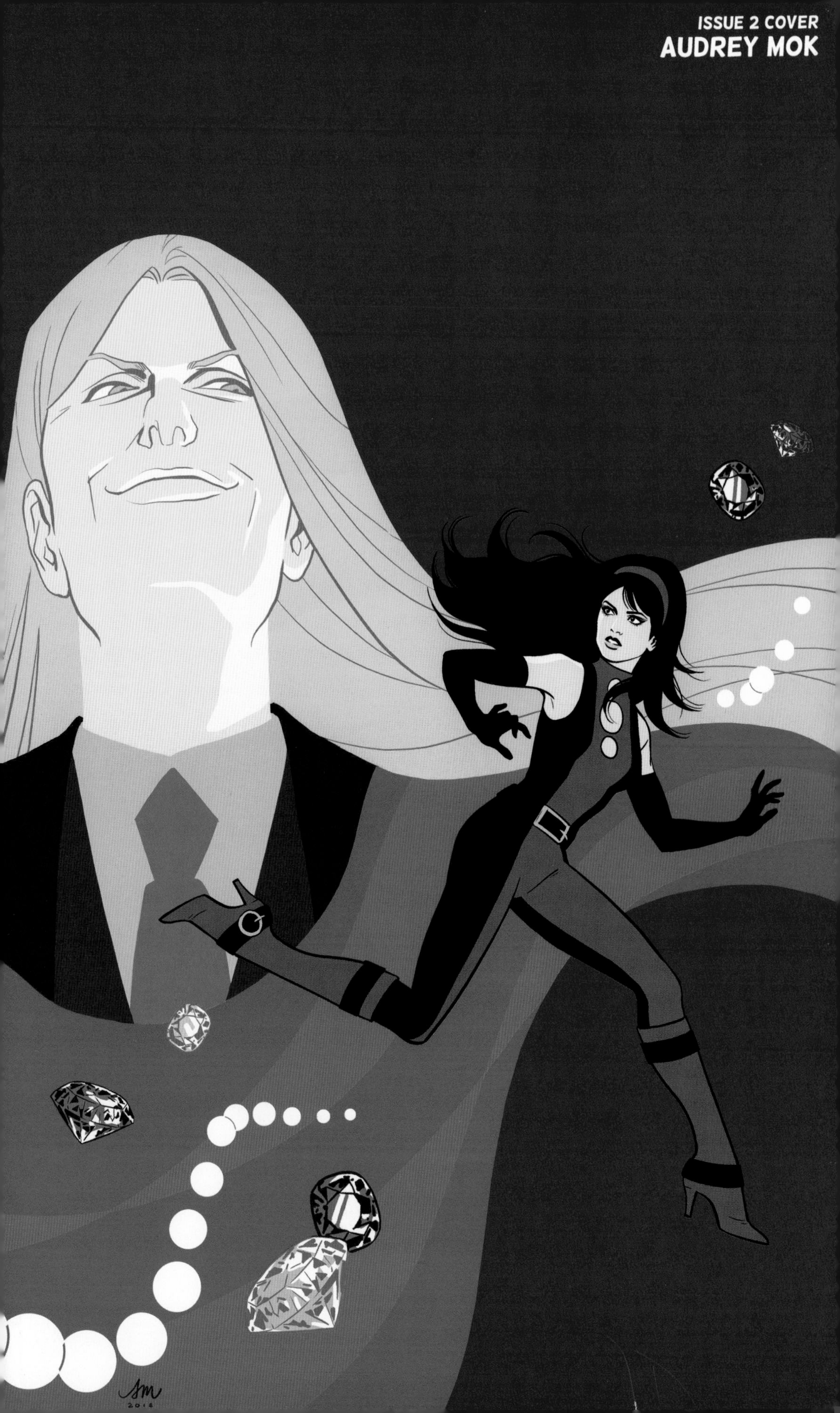

ISSUE 3 COVER
**AUDREY MOK**

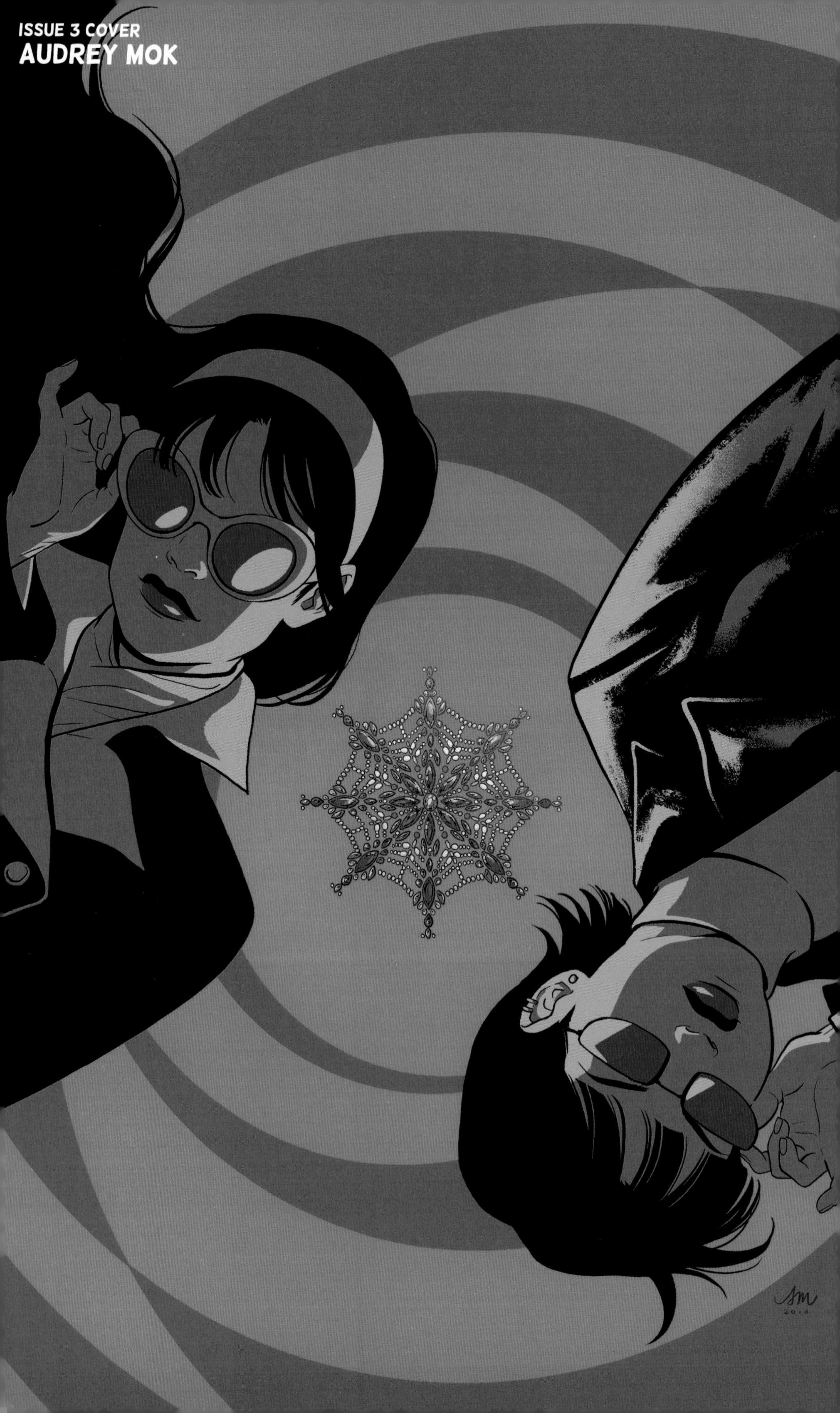

**ISSUE 4 COVER**
**AUDREY MOK**

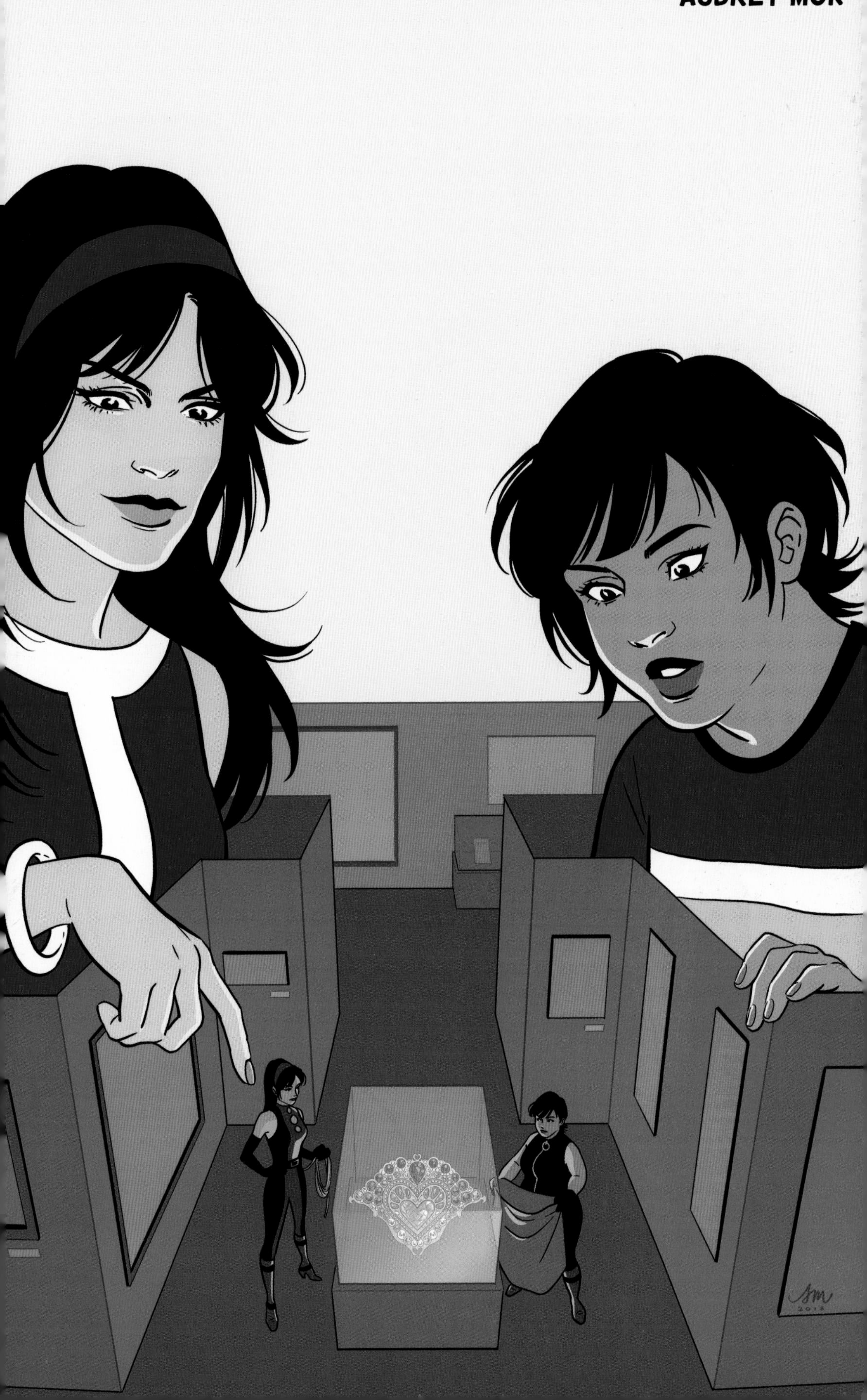

SKETCHES AND DESIGNS BY
## CHYNNA CLUGSTON FLORES

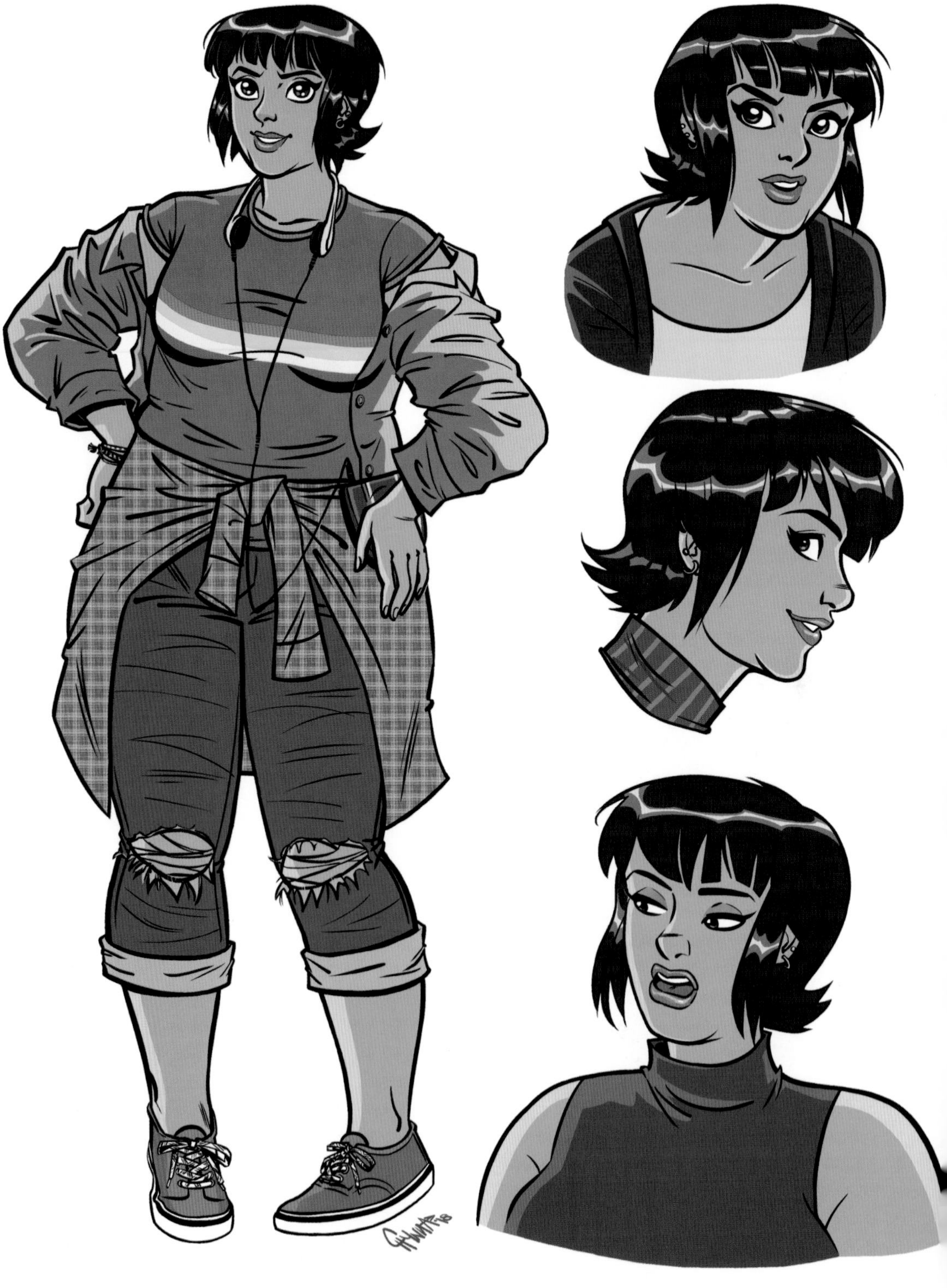

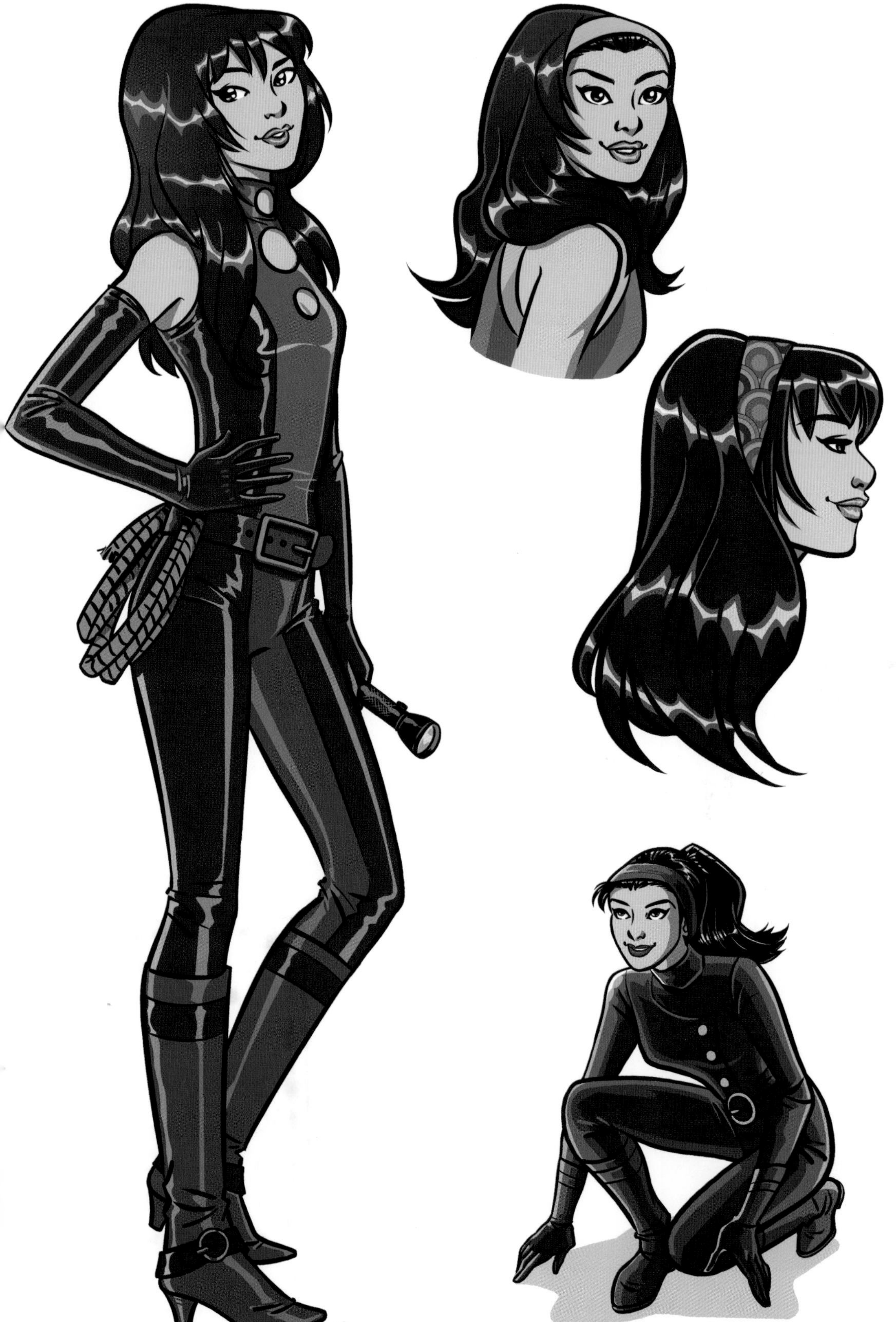

DISCOVER
# ALL THE HITS

STEVENSON · ELLIS · WATTERS · ALLEN
LUMBERJANES
BEWARE THE KITTEN HOLY
NEW YORK TIMES BESTSELLING SERIES

Allison + Treiman + Cogar
GIANT DAYS
VOLUME ONE

RIBON · FISH · PEER
SLAM!
VOLUME ONE

Hope Larson · Brittney Williams · Sarah Stern
GOLDIE VANCE
Volume One

JAMES TYNION IV · RIAN SYGH · WALTER BAIAMONTE
THE BACKSTAGERS

TYSON HESSE'S
DIESEL
IGNITION

BOOM! BOX

**AVAILABLE AT YOUR LOCAL COMICS SHOP AND BOOKSTORE**

To find a comics shop in your area, visit www.comicshoplocator.com

WWW.**BOOM-STUDIOS**.COM



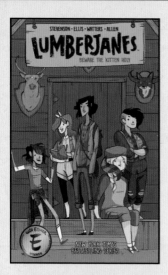

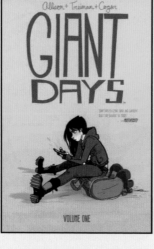

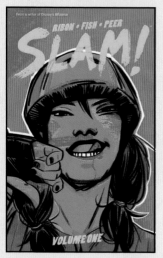

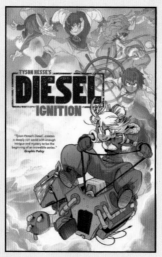

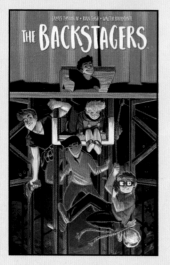

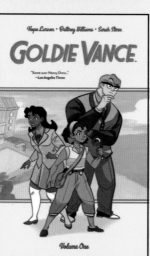

**Lumberjanes**
*Noelle Stevenson, Shannon Watters, Grace Ellis, Brooklyn Allen, and Others*
**Volume 1: Beware the Kitten Holy**
ISBN: 978-1-60886-687-8 | $14.99 US
**Volume 2: Friendship to the Max**
ISBN: 978-1-60886-737-0 | $14.99 US
**Volume 3: A Terrible Plan**
ISBN: 978-1-60886-803-2 | $14.99 US
**Volume 4: Out of Time**
ISBN: 978-1-60886-860-5 | $14.99 US
**Volume 5: Band Together**
ISBN: 978-1-60886-919-0 | $14.99 US

**Giant Days**
*John Allison, Lissa Treiman, Max Sarin*
**Volume 1**
ISBN: 978-1-60886-789-9 | $9.99 US
**Volume 2**
ISBN: 978-1-60886-804-9 | $14.99 US
**Volume 3**
ISBN: 978-1-60886-851-3 | $14.99 US

**Jonesy**
*Sam Humphries, Caitlin Rose Boyle*
**Volume 1**
ISBN: 978-1-60886-883-4 | $9.99 US
**Volume 2**
ISBN: 978-1-60886-999-2 | $14.99 US

**Slam!**
*Pamela Ribon, Veronica Fish, Brittany Peer*
**Volume 1**
ISBN: 978-1-68415-004-5 | $14.99 US

**Goldie Vance**
*Hope Larson, Brittney Williams*
**Volume 1**
ISBN: 978-1-60886-898-8 | $9.99 US
**Volume 2**
ISBN: 978-1-60886-974-9 | $14.99 US

**The Backstagers**
*James Tynion IV, Rian Sygh*
**Volume 1**
ISBN: 978-1-60886-993-0 | $14.99 US

**Tyson Hesse's Diesel: Ignition**
*Tyson Hesse*
ISBN: 978-1-60886-907-7 | $14.99 US

**Coady & The Creepies**
*Liz Prince, Amanda Kirk, Hannah Fisher*
ISBN: 978-1-68415-029-8 | $14.99 US